CHAPTERS AND CONTENTS

AGENTS & ANGELS II

THE WOLFPAW INITIATIVE

BY J.T. RATH

CHAPTER I

DARK CONCLUSIONS

FRIDAY | SEPTEMBER 14TH | 2018

The man's neck almost sounded like popping knuckles underneath the force of Rachel's grasp. She could feel his consciousness giving way as he desperately clawed, tossing and pulling at her hair. It was a futile attempt to save himself as Rachel applied a harder squeeze and felt the man go limp. He was out cold.

"Shit." An exasperated sigh accompanied the quiet curse. Even with all of the training over the past year, she still had a hard time taking a life, both physically and mentally. She often had to remind herself of what led her here and why she was doing what she was doing. Physically she had never been stronger, even during her early training days at N.E.T.S. before she had been assigned as the private assistant to David Harper. *That seems like eons ago…* she thought, quickly forgetting the fond memories she had of the organization as more recent…interactions…had proven less favorable.

Before long, Rachel realized she had been going through the motions of hiding the man's unconscious body in a nearby dark corner. Carefully, she sat him down and leaned his mass against the intersecting walls, pushing his legs out from view as best she could. Replaying the altercation in her head, she criticized her approach. *Way too loud, Rachel* came the mental scolding. *Remember: light on toes, no one knows.* The rhyme she had created months ago always made her smile, given that the subject matter was dealing pain. Her crazy life never ceased to amaze her; crazy, deadly rhymes and all.

In all seriousness, she counted herself lucky. The man, while short, was bulky and easily could have overpowered her with just a moment's more time to react. Or called in help. *Yeah, that would have been really bad.*

When she had finished hiding the body, Rachel continued to the server room. There was still a way to go and time was likely running short. It was very early morning, and soon a new batch of soldiers would be arriving for their guard shifts. It was always best to infiltrate at the end of a guard shift as that's when the mindset is most vulnerable with the sense of near completion. Infiltrating during a guard "switch" was foolish as there are often *double* the number of enemies in the same vicinity.

Rachel peeked carefully around the corner of a dark hallway and saw that the opposite wall was draped with the growing shadow of an approaching patrol. Without much contemplation, she silently ran down the hallway, took a great leap, shimmied up the wall a bit, and straddled the hallway's width. Now she just had to hope it was dark enough that the guard wouldn't see her, or that he wouldn't, by some random chance, look up.

Lactic acid began to build throughout her legs as the guard rounded the corner of the hall and started down the narrow path towards Rachel. *Breathe. Focus.* Rachel enjoyed the burn; it told her that she was pushing herself, but at the same time she wondered if she could hold the spread position much longer.

It was almost comedic; the guard seemed to be sauntering through his shift…slowly. *Of course he would be*

the world's slowest soldier right now. She silently drew her suppressed handgun and rolled her eyes as the man *finally* approached her, still completely oblivious to the woman overhead.

PCHEW!

PCHEW!

Two quiet shots rang out and Rachel dropped down on the man, covering his mouth, before the shells even hit the ground. Her shots had hit him in the shoulder and grazed his throat, leading to some minor blood loss. There was shock in the man's eyes, more so than pain, as he found himself staring up at an attractive female that had seemingly dropped from the sky and was now straddling his midsection. It wasn't until a few seconds later when he realized it wasn't *that* kind of situation and he'd been shot.

"Ugh…mmmph…MMMPH!" Rachel's hand clamped down across his nose and mouth harder.

"Shut up." She bossed. "I'm going to server room 75," his eyes widened again at this announcement. "And you're going to help me. When I remove my hand, you'll give me the key code to the door. If you say anything other than numbers, there will be consequences." Rachel slowly removed her hand, now moist from the frantic breathing of the injured man.

"I…UGH – don't know it."

Rachel pointed the gun at his thigh and pulled the trigger, pressing down against his mouth once more. The man let out a brief grunt of agony and began choking back tears beneath the cover of Rachel's hand. Their faces were now very close together as Rachel leaned in to whisper in his ear.

"I will shoot you in the other leg if you lie to me again. I know you're an officer. You've got clearance for the code. Tell me. Now." The smell of sweat and fear lingered in Rachel's nostrils as she pulled away, once more removing her hand.

"Seven, five, three, three, four, eight, pound, pound, asterisk, pound, one." He was visibly shaking as he recited the sequence of numbers and characters.

"Cute." Rachel wasn't surprised he had given her that code. "I already know that's the emergency security code." The man shook his head in disagreement as Rachel continued. "No? So you're saying, if I were…to go to the server room and enter that code I wouldn't be surrounded by guards within half a minute? Remember what happened last time you lied to me?"

The man looked desperate to give her an answer but was obviously also unwilling to give her the correct one. For what it was worth, he was good at his job. Rachel took her hand off his mouth and let out an audible sigh.

"Are you –" His words were cut short by the butt of her gun knocking him unconscious. Rachel reached into a pocket on his tactical vest and pulled out an encryption device. She placed the smooth end of the device on his thumb and the front lit up to display the code to server room 75.

"This was all I wanted." She waved the small electronic at his face. Her explanation fell on deaf ears as the man was clearly unconscious. He would eventually be found alive after she was long gone – probably with a limp and bruised ego. She stood up, recounting the layout of the complex, knowing that she was close to where she needed to be. Not to mention, there shouldn't be another guard coming this way for at least thirty-two minutes.

Before she could continue forward, a small burst of static filled her ear, followed by a male voice.

"Seventy-seven, this is Alpha Nine. What exactly are

you doing?" Rachel smirked. Of course Ian had been watching her feed. "Seventy-seven? Please respond."

"Hello, Alpha Nine. Good to know you're watching my every move." Over the course of the past year, Ian and her "relationship" had been full of many interesting…exchanges. "I was simply practicing my interrogation skills. Looks like I need some more work I suppose."

"Yeah, well…" Ian had never been good with banter. "You're wasting fucking time. Get a move on. We need those I.P. addresses."

"Aye aye, Captain!"

"It's *Alpha Nine*, Seventy-seven. Alpha. Nine."

"Aye aye, Alpha Nine!" Rachel smiled, but knew that Ian was right; she had wasted plenty of time with this little endeavor and needed to finish up the mission. *Maybe I'm getting too cocky. How does that even work?*

It was peculiar…having to deal death when necessary, even feeling *guilty* about it, but knowing that she was damn good at it. Rachel knew that most of the people she had killed in the last year – much unlike these innocent guards – deserved it, at least in the good versus evil sense of the judgment. Though she couldn't help but feel remorse. This remorse, coupled with her newfound confidence, was a mystery to her. Why was it so effortless for her to take a life, but at the same time, so painful? *Did Bryson or Elena ever feel this way?* She winced at the memory of her deceased friends, whom she still missed dearly. There was a hole there that would never be filled, particularly for Bryson who had been so absolutely selfless in his final act.

They were good people. A simple sentiment echoed in Rachel's mind as she made her way to the server room while remembering her friends and her heroes. *Am I a good person?* Her internal dialogue was attempting to reason and answer for her conflicting emotions.

It would have to wait.

Server room 75 was in the next hallway, along with all the security technology that surrounded it.

"Seventy-seven, you're approaching the server room. We're only going to have one shot at this." Silence. "You ready?"

"Copy that Alpha Nine. Let's do this."

"Give me ten seconds before you go into that hallway." She could hear him furiously typing at the other end of the line.

"Remind me again, Alpha Nine, why I'm the one doing this and not you?" There was a curt laugh in her ear, but she knew that they were both wondering the same thing. Ian was highly trained for this type of mission and had far more experience, although his resume was largely comprised of his time as a terrorist with the Dead Scorpions.

"Because you need the training," Rachel opened her mouth to protest the statement. "And because you insisted. Remember?" She ignored the fact that she had clearly forgotten that snippet.

"You ready yet, Nine?"

"Almost there…" There was a brief pause. "Ok. Once I trigger the EMP in your suit, the pressure-sensitive floor plates will be off for sixty seconds. You need to get in, find the right server, and get off the ground in that span of time. The floor plates can only be offline for ninety seconds in any 24 hour period. Once you have the info, let me know, I'll activate the EMP again, and you'll have thirty seconds to get out."

"Won't the EMP fry the servers too?" Rachel inquired.

"Different electronic frequency." She could almost

picture Ian waving his arm in semi-frustration. "Listen, don't worry about any details other than what I just told you. Get in. Get out. Now…I'm ready. On your mark."

Rachel took a deep breath, and one more glance at the encryption device, trying to memorize the first few digits. *Pound, eight, seven, four, nine, two…*

"Now." There was a small, but audible click from the left arm of her suit which she assumed was the EMP triggering silently.

Sixty…

Her feet turned the corner and she sprinted down the length of the barren, brown hallway until she came to the steel door with a red "75" painted off center on its cold surface. Once stopped, she slid an invisible panel on the door upwards, and began typing on the neon green keys staring back at her.

Pound…eight…seven…four…nine…two

Fifty…

Rachel glanced at the encryption device for the remaining integers.

One…one…one…asterisk…pound…seven…pound

A small beep coupled with a blue bar of light at the top of the keypad signaled that she was in. The door's handle was heavy, cold, and thick and the entire frame creaked as Rachel walked in, leaving the door open behind her.

Inside, the room was abuzz with the deafening hum of tens of large servers. The tall black monuments were sprinkled with flickering lights and ports – all a bit intimidating, even to the tech-savvy Rachel.

Forty…

"You're looking for a purple light, Seventy-seven." Ian explained. "It should be in the northeast corner of the room."

"Copy."

The dark room was larger than Rachel had expected and as she entered farther, it became increasingly eerie. Light from the door continued to dim and was replaced with the accumulation of all the smaller lights on the server surfaces. *It's like Christmas lights…with secrets*. She was about halfway to the room's corner.

Thirty…

"Rachel, get off the ground! Now!" There was a frantic tone to Ian's command. With a swift vertical leap, Rachel pulled herself up on top of the nearest server.

"What the hell, Alpha Nine?"

"Something in their system overrode the EMP frequency quicker than I anticipated. And I lied." Ian trailed off.

"Yeah and you called me by my real name."

"Sorry about that. 'Seventy-seven' is a lot of syllables. Might need to rethink your code name."

"What did you lie about, Alpha Nine?" Rachel was seated on top of a warm server, starting to get impatient.

"Their system is constantly changing. That ninety second open period every 24 hours that I mentioned earlier? Yeah well…it went down to sixty seconds."

"Wait so…" Rachel was approximating the math in her

head.

"Once I hit the EMP again, you'll have about twenty-three seconds. Twenty-three point six seconds, to be exact."

"Son of a bitch." Rachel quietly cursed to herself.

"You should still have plenty of time to get out of there; just make sure that you're running. Fast."

"Yep." Rachel knew it wasn't Ian's fault, but she wanted someone to blame for the inconvenience. *All part of the job I guess.*

It was a slow process but eventually she had made her way across the tops of the computer towers to the corner of the room. Slowly situating herself on her stomach on top of the server, she leaned downward and scanned its surface for the small purple light. *Where are you?* Blood began to rush to her head, and she soon found herself needing to take short breaks as she craned her neck to look for the damn purple light. After what felt like five minutes Rachel was beginning to get frustrated and there was no sign of anything remotely purple on the black server surfaces.

"Alpha Nine…this is Seventy-seven." She continued to scan the server lengths. "I'm not seeing any purple li–"

There it was. In the worst spot imaginable.

"Seventy-seven, it's definitely in that corner. Keep looking."

"No I…I found it. It's just going to complicate things somewhat."

"How so?"

Rachel sighed as she tried to piece together how she was going to do this.

"It's almost at the very bottom of the server, right above the floor."

"Hmmm." Ian's reply was short.

"'Hmmm' *what*, Alpha Nine?" Rachel persisted, clearly annoyed.

"Oh nothing. Just a good hiding spot, that's all."

Ass. Rachel thought it but didn't say it. *How do I get down there without touching the floor?* The tower she was on was sturdy, but she was pretty confident they would tip over if she placed all her weight to one side. It was a scenario she definitely didn't want to test out. At about eight feet in height, they were also far too high for her to reach down to access the port.

"You good, Seventy-seven?" Ian broke her concentration.

"Yeah…just give me some radio silence. I'm trying to figure this out. Wait for my signal to turn the floors off again."

There was an idea…maybe turn the floors off quickly, hop down, plug in the device, and hop back up while it downloaded the data? It was risky. *Only 23.6 seconds and I still have to get out and down the hall.* It was *too* risky. Even if she got down there and immediately knew where to plug in, she would waste at least five seconds.

Time was wasting and she had to make a decision soon. *How wide is the gap between the wall and the server?* Rachel was putting together an idea, one that would be very painful for her abdominal region. She figured the distance was no greater than four feet; easily a span she could plank across. *You've got this, Rachel.*

With her mind made up, she started to precariously edge her lower half towards the corner. She was going to walk down the wall in order to get to the port at the bottom. There was a push against her feet; she had reached the wall. She pressed the weight of her body through her legs and began to carefully make her way down towards the perilous floor. Switching hands down the server shelves proved to be the most difficult, quickly leading to a deep burn in Rachel's arms to accompany the strain in her abs.

Purple was fast becoming Rachel's least favorite color and she could have sworn that the static light was getting *farther* away. Pain was racing through her entire body and she was only halfway down, carefully taking each step and handhold with the utmost caution. The room seemed to have increased in temperature by at least ten degrees and Rachel could feel the sweat beginning to bead on her brow. Drops of the bodily fluid began to pool on her forehead and silently fell to the floor. Rachel held her breath, wondering whether or not the floor was sensitive enough to be triggered by the liquid form of her physical stress.

PLOP, PLOP

Nothing…

Thank God, Rachel internally sighed. She was nearly to the damn purple light now and only had a foot to go. Her hands were slippery and clammy – she missed her next hand hold and the front of her body started to fall.

All of her training kicked in and she disregarded the shock of slipping and pain of the exertion. The only thing that mattered now was not touching the floor. Her hands shot above her head and clamped onto the closest shelf they could reach while her core pushed back against the wall. There was a shake as the server column reacted against the force, but it remained in place and Rachel's fall froze, mere inches above the ground. Her racing mind cleared as she looked forward and saw the purple light staring directly back at her.

"Ok…" She was finally here and it would be ok. Ever so carefully she reached one hand across to the opposite wrist and found the USB device hidden in her shirt sleeve, removing it and slowly lowering it towards the port near the light. *I swear to God if I have to flip this USB over*…Rachel mused about the hilariousness of the seemingly 50/50 chance USB devices had of being plugged in correctly on the first try. To her surprise, the miniature device slid in with a click. There was a brief pause and the purple light cycled through a plethora of colors – orange, green, yellow, red, and finally settling on blue.

"Alpha Nine this is Seventy-seven. You're a go for the download."

"Copy that Seventy-seven. Good work. Download is starting now. Approximately ninety seconds until completion."

"Christ!" Rachel exclaimed, the lactic acid still swirling in her muscles.

"Sorry."

Rachel closed her eyes and tried to focus for the remaining seconds. *It's just like doing normal planks, Rachel. Just focus.* That was the more confident side of her psyche. The more cynical side was screaming. *Yeah a plank that if you fail will send twenty something guards headed this way.* She shook both of the thoughts away and practiced deep breaths. She would make it, no problem.

"About twenty five percent downloaded Seventy-seven. Sixty seconds out." There was a silent nod from her in acknowledgment. "As soon as this download hits one-hundred percent and flushes the data to the device I'm triggering the floor sensors. Remember, 23.6 seconds. I'll give you the cue. Hang in there."

Ian's voice trailed off and Rachel tried to return to her

focus but was disturbed by a shuffling sound coming from the door of the room. *Shit…*

"Who's in there? Where did you go?" The voice was demanding but weakened by a noticeable whimper: pain. "What are you here –" The man was interrupted by an ugly cough, "What are you here for? I know you're here!" Rachel knew, without question, that this was the man she had interrogated and knocked out. Somehow he had already woken up.

Rachel whispered slowly to Ian, "Alpha Nine, there's a tango in the room with me. Does that mean the floor sensors are off?" The answer was immediate.

"Negative. I repeat, negative. Guards are outfitted with a paired sensor to indicate they are friendly. Your weight *will* set off the alarm."

"Fuck. What's the status on the download?"

"Fifty-seven percent. Forty seconds out."

"Any way we can speed that up?"

"No."

The silver lining to the guard coming into the room was that Rachel's adrenaline was soaring, erasing most of the burning in her extremities.

"I know you're in here! I've already called back-up!"

Double shit.

"That's a negative Seventy-seven. He's bluffing. I'm not reading any radio signals coming in or out. You most likely damaged his radio earlier." Rachel let out a brief sigh but otherwise remained completely silent. This guard was tough; Rachel had shot him three times, including a point-blank to the thigh. He had to be losing a lot of blood by now. His steps were clearly uneven and it was obvious that he was struggling moving around, most likely barely escaping the shores of unconsciousness. Despite that, he was getting closer to her corner by the second. This down-load needed to be done, *now*.

"Almost there. Hold tight."

"Come on…" Rachel murmured through grit teeth.

"Show yourself!" Hums from the servers barely covered the man's exclamation and Rachel knew he was only one or two server blocks away. She was a sitting duck, or rather a planking duck, and was nearly defenseless in this position; especially considering he probably still had his firearm. Her eyes darted to where the man was approaching and there was a light outline of a shadow on the dark floor. It was growing, but clearly impeded by the bloody, dragging limp from the bullet in his thigh. Shadows stopped moving as the guard checked the server lane in front of Rachel, and continued their course towards her, only a few steps away.

"Seventy-seven, download is at ninety-five…ninety-six…ninety-seven…ninety-eight…ninety-nine…flushing data…one hundred-percent!"

At that moment the guard turned the corner, shocked to see the spy stretched between the wall and the server, but with gun ready nonetheless. The dark barrel of the weapon was pointed at Rachel. She released her grasp of the shelves and reached for the gun on her hip, falling to the floor.

In her ear she heard, "Floor sensors off!" and fired her shot. The thud of her body on the floor was drowned out by the silenced gunfire and she saw the blood exit the back of the man's head. His pained expression went blank and his legs gave out, dropping him to the floor, dead.

"Twenty seconds! Get moving!" Screamed the voice in her ear.

"Shit!" Rachel reached over to the icy blue light and

removed the USB drive, switching the color back to damn-purple. Without hesitation she was on her feet, running towards the exit. As she passed the deceased man, one whom she had intended to let live, she glanced at his eyes: blank and barren, staring off into nothingness. There was a chill up her back as she turned the corner of servers.

It was going to have to be a full out sprint to make it back out the door and down the hallway to neutral floor territory again. A voice in the back of Rachel's head told her she wouldn't make it. Deep down, her body was still incredibly sore from the painful plank, but again, the adrenaline of killing the man and the potential of having two shifts of guards headed her way was keeping her going. Placed leg after placed leg shot her towards the open door where light was flooding into the dank, dark server room now smelling like a gunshot.

Rachel put on the brakes and slid on her heels, hoping to stop herself and turn out the doorway on her right. The blood trail on the floor from the man's injured leg had different ideas. Her own legs went out from underneath as her shoes forgot their traction on the crimson fluid and she slammed hard into the floor, blood smearing thick and wet across her cheek. Her body continued sliding for a few feet after the impact while a small sigh of pain escaped.

There was no time to be disoriented and Rachel tried to fight said natural response. *Focus...you...have to get out...to the floor.* Her eyes were readjusting and she attempted to wipe most of the blood off her face, its metallic smell pungent in her nostrils. The sight of it all over her palm sent a ripple of fear through her and she reminded herself it wasn't hers.

"What the fuck are you doing? Six seconds! Get the hell out of there Seventy-seven!"

The ferocity in her ear had her scrambling. Disorientation be damned, Rachel was not tripping that alarm. She was on her feet again and left the room, counting the seconds down in her head. The hallway was much longer than she remembered and she pumped her arms for all they were worth, working her entire core in the sprint. *You're not going to make it…no way.* She was only halfway there and had three seconds. *Just a few more steps…*

Rachel had counted down to one and leapt into the air, placing her foot on the hallway wall and propelling towards the corner where the sensors ended. A loud thud followed her hard landing into the next hallway and she held her breath, waiting to hear the sound of blaring alarms.

"Jesus, Seventy-seven! Cutting it a little close, yeah?"

Rachel ignored the question. "Am I clear Alpha Nine?"

"Yeah, you made it. But barely. You okay?"

"That fall hurt like a bitch, but I'm good now. Let's get out of here before the patrols find this mess."

"Copy that. Move to the extraction point. Meet you there."

She nodded to herself in agreement and got back on her feet again, retracing the path she had used to infiltrate the compound. Aches and pains were dominating most of her muscles; she would need a damn good nap after all of this. *And maybe a massage.* Her core was especially tender, with even small movements needed for walking causing a considerable, pulsing pain.

The hallways were eerily quiet, as if they were about to explode into chaos at any moment. Eventually, Rachel made her way to the darkened hallway where she had first encountered the now-deceased guard. She hadn't noticed his blood trail until now. There lie a small pool of the liquid, brown and drying underneath the darkened light, where they'd met during their earlier altercation. She slowed her pace, coming to a stop, and lost herself in thought over the journey of the man she had intended to let live.

It was complicated – she felt like many of her previous kills had been unavoidable, thus making them justifiable. She had made a *decision* to kill them. But this man…this man's death could have been avoided. She *intended* for him to live. There was a deep pang of guilt that accompanied the thought. *He could have survived. I wanted him to survive. I decided he could live.*

These thoughts returned Rachel to her earlier wonderings about Bryson and Elena. *Who am I to decide life and death?* She knew that both of them had been able to make that decision effortlessly. *They were good people.*

Rachel's mind raced back to the bullet she had put between the man's eyes. The man whom she had shot three times, knocked out, and then killed. It was vicious. A wild conclusion swept over her that almost forced her to tears. The thoughts swirled around in her head and she was afraid to put them together. It had been a notion that had followed her for the better part of the recent year, but she had suppressed it, until now, until the borderline torture and killing of that fateful guard. She didn't want to accept it, although she knew it to be true. She knew that after thinking it that everything would be different: the field work, her decision making, her relationships (the few of them that she had left) – everything. Slowly, the thought materialized and there was no turning back. Rachel continued on towards the extraction point with a single sentence plastered in her mind, now driving her:

I am a bad person.

CHAPTER II

27,598

Denver was not the only city attacked in the United States on July 5th, 2017.

Bryson Cooper's mission in Pakistan days before had been the discovery of a single cell of the terrorist group, Aqarab Mayta, also known as the Dead Scorpions. This cell had been designated to attack only the city of Denver as human projectile missiles packed to the brim with explosive vests and C4.

In a heroic show of bravery, N.E.T.S. Agent Cooper, had foiled the Denver attack completely, but gave his life in the process. His body was never recovered, but in the days subsequent to the attack, rumors of explosions detonating over the city were widespread. Soon after, it was revealed that an unnamed hero, claimed as an agent of the C.I.A., had discovered information about the attack and acted alone to stop the terrorists. In all, Bryson had saved at least 3,066.44 lives.

3,066.44 represents the average number of lives lost in each of the other nine cities across the United States that were attacked on that historic date which shall survive through the generations known simply as: "The Will". New York, Los Angeles, Chicago, Boston, Houston, Washington D.C., San Diego, San Francisco, and Seattle were also all attacked in the exact same fashion.

The final death toll for The Will stands at 27,598 innocent men, women, and children, most of whom were United States citizens.

It was the single greatest terrorist attack in the history of mankind.

The attack was coordinated by the Dead Scorpions, acting from ten separate cells scattered across the Middle East, Eastern Europe, and Africa. Documents indicate that plans for it had begun over two decades ago, even before 9/11. Nearly every detail had been taken into consideration, including racial profiling, leading the Aqarab Mayta to expand their highly secretive recruiting tactics in the years preceding The Will.

Each target city had been assigned a designated number of suicide missiles years before, proportionate to its projected population. Denver had twenty "jumpers" (as they were referred to in the months after the attack), one of the fewer counts, and equal to the number in Seattle and Washington D.C.

New York and Los Angeles, however? They had 259 and 120 jumpers assigned, respectively, resulting in enormous death tolls that fateful morning. Many New Yorkers had reported seeing several large planes in the air that day, some sightings narrating that there had been jumpers evacuating from them. The Aqarab Mayta believed that there were too many planes in New York, Los Angeles, and Chicago (which had 84 jumpers), and rather than leaving further evidence, the pilots of these city's attacks flew the aircrafts into various buildings and, in some cases, into the ground.

In total that day, there were 677 jumpers across the ten cities, and eleven planes that crashed in New York, L.A., and Chicago. The number of fatalities in these three cities were responsible for seventy percent of the death toll, with New York alone reporting over 10,500 deaths, or nearly forty percent of the number of lives lost. Each city was devastated and heavily damaged. Some jumpers had targeted buildings, exploding on impact with copious amounts of C4 on top of their explosive vests, and others had targeted high-population areas. Smoking rubble remained for months after the attacks, in some cities longer than others, and in many instances there were no remains to gather of a loved one.

All around the United States, many people had lost hope and feared that The Will might be the beginning of the end for the once-great nation. Their President had been assassinated before the attacks, to be replaced quickly by Vice President Greyson who, luckily, had survived The Will, and their economy had taken several blows, crashing hard in the wake of the destruction and chaos. Internationally, United States allies tried to help out as best they could, but most were heavily intimidated by the Aqarab Mayta and their seemingly far-reaching arm of terror.

It was clear that there was a new world power, one that wasn't constrained by governmental processes or a duty to its citizens: the terrorist group known as the Dead Scorpions. Through fear, death, and destruction, not to mention a complete aura of mystery, they had crippled a nation and left many other opposing countries shaking in their dark recesses of the globe. Officials from the U.S., Great Britain, Germany, Australia, and Canada, among others, agreed that something needed to be done to control terrorism of this scale, but they were left mostly spinning their wheels due to a combination of a lack of information about their enemy, fear of retaliation, and bureaucratic red tape. This meant that there had been no invasion of a terrorist-harboring nation, no single terrorist leader plastered across the mainstream media for the public to hate, no real smaller players captured and tried; in fact, what had followed The Will was a complete lack of retaliation from the world's strongest countries.

It was this fact that truly destroyed the hope of Americans across the nation. Their fellow countrymen had been savagely murdered and no one was answering for it.

Truthfully, the only glimmer of hope that many Americans could see *was* that unknown hero in Denver. The single man, the single C.I.A. operative they were being told, who had not only discovered the enemy, but thwarted one of their ten attacks, and given his life in the process. He was known as the "Angel of Denver" and some even called him God's Will, in direct comparison to the terrorist-given name for the attack. The public cried out for the identity of the Angel.

Who was he?

How did he find out about the attack?

How could they provide support, gratitude, and condolences to his family?

Obviously, given that the C.I.A. agent was actually N.E.T.S. agent, Bryson Cooper, his identity would never be revealed. N.E.T.S., who had been publicly outed in Abd Al Aziz's threat days before the attack, had been lucky to escape any reveal. There were murmurings of an investigation into just who the "N.E.T.S." agency was, but it was quickly forgotten by the media after the unprecedented attacks, and over the course of the past year, no one had really ever thought to look back into it.

A few conspiracy theorists had their stories that the assassination of the President and the attacks had been planned by the U.S. government, and that the Angel had been a staged event, in order to once again put faith back in the Central Intelligence Agency. They too, often failed to mention N.E.T.S. and many of their opinions were quickly washed to the side when they couldn't explain the reasoning for the significant loss of life or any politically positive outcome that came from the event.

Despite the nation banding together behind the Angel, they were still distraught with grief, confusion, and fear. Many citizens couldn't focus on their jobs, especially those who had witnessed the horrors that day. The death toll had been high enough that most people were connected to it in some way, some by a few degrees of separation less than others. Purchasing habits became radically different across the board, resulting in many companies seeing decreased profits. People, particularly in downtown regions, were moving either farther out into rural areas, or leaving the country entirely. Tourism was greatly decreased around the globe, further ensuring the international community that its economic woes would continue.

Now, even a year past the fateful, history-altering day, the world was still reeling in a thousand different ways. Emotions ranged from deep grief and guilt, resulting in a spike in suicide rates across the U.S. which remained high for several months, to violent anger, with many nations seeing increased crime rates. Before the attacks, a website known as EOD.com (which stood for End of Days), had seen large amounts of traffic, but had since been pulled by the U.S. government for causing mass panic both in the days preceding The Will and subsequent to it. Many believed it was too little too late however; the "end" was already nigh. Religious extremists across the world were claiming that this was the beginning of the end, and even those who often argued against them had neither the reasoning nor the energy to disagree.

Despite the outside world's appearance of crumbling, N.E.T.S. was fairly unscathed. There had been time to grieve Bryson's passing, but sadness for his loss was quickly turned to pride for what N.E.T.S. stood for and the greater good of the nation. Mysteriously, Rachel had only remained with the organization for a couple of weeks after the attacks and had not been seen or heard from since. Many believed it was because she had now replaced Bryson as top agent, and was deep undercover, trying to unearth the Aqarab Mayta.

Every member of the organization had a new-found respect for their work, thanks to Bryson. Unbeknownst to the American public, N.E.T.S. was making steady progress digging up information on the Dead Scorpions. Names, locations, communications – all had been discovered and led to a slowly growing, but impressive spider web of players, motives, and plans. There had even been a few very basic field operations conducted, most of which were information retrieval or surveillance in nature. It was safe to say that spirits were up and everyone knew that no one else was going to put an end to the Aqarab Mayta except for them. N.E.T.S. was the last line of defense in both preventing another attack and avenging the horrible loss from the original.

Of course, this is how David Harper had planned it all out. There had been a short while where he had been sweating, fearing that his plan wouldn't come to fruition. But then came July 5th, 2017 and David couldn't believe what he was seeing. It had been three decades in the making.

Incredible amounts of planning, tedious organizing of details, and too many secrets and lies to count had finally surmounted in something very, very tangible. And this was just the beginning.

As the leader of N.E.T.S. and the provost of the Dead Scorpions, David had become the most powerful man in the world overnight and not a single soul knew about it. Except for Rachel Monroe.

Somehow she had intelligence linking him to Bryson's death and even had the audacity to threaten him at the funeral. Whether it had been serious, he couldn't tell. He knew that Rachel had been very good friends with both Bryson and his wife, Elena, and there were signs that there might have been a deeper, romantic connection with Bryson. It could have simply been anger towards him for sending him on that mission, or sadness needing to be projected somewhere. Either way, David didn't lose sleep over it. In fact, he slept incredibly well these days and his "double agent" lifestyle was getting easier to manage every day.

Once in a while he would feed information into a pipeline that would eventually make it back to the N.E.T.S. analysts and agents, exciting them that they had found another piece of the puzzle. On the surface, David had been encouraging them with constant praise, and patriotic speeches almost daily, many of which recalled Bryson's heroic sacrifice. Underneath his hardened red, white, and blue resolve however, David was hard at work monitoring the next leg, the one that truly mattered. It was a balance of power and sanity that he was addicted to; he reveled in its complexities, and he found that he was accomplishing more in a single day than most do in an entire month.

Yes, being the leader of two opposing factions had now secured him a following in both lanes. The Dead Scorpions' plan, The Will, had gone perfectly, and he was now on the precipice of changing history further.

To David though, The Will ended up being better than perfect.

It had killed the only man he ever feared and the paramount agent at N.E.T.S.: Bryson Cooper.

CHAPTER III

MIXED INTENTIONS

FRIDAY | SEPTEMBER 14TH | 2018

Ian's back bounced against the wall, hard. He set his feet on the floor, their slight perspiration sticking to the dark hardwood. The throw had disoriented him a bit and his head was swimming with anticipation over his next move – he would only have a few seconds to make up his mind.

Control was something that eluded him at the moment. Normally this would have angered and frustrated him. Ian always sought to be in charge of each situation, and if he wasn't he did his best to find a way to change that. But this situation…it was different. Ian didn't feel the urge to be leading right now as he was enjoying the sensation of being on the other side.

Of course, it probably had to do with the fact that Rachel had been the one who pushed him into the wall and was now removing her shirt.

She looked at him with hunger, the same way she had numerous times before over the course of the last few months. *I am a bad person…time to be bad.* The thought was a subconscious and primal one as she threw her shirt to the cold floor and briskly walked to Ian. He began to come off the wall and Rachel pushed his shoulder and closed the space between them, pinning him against the beige-painted surface. Without much thought or technique, she pressed her lips against his with force and he accepted. Their mouths opened despite the pressure and their tongues intertwined again and again. Ian tried to push Rachel off, whether it was to say something or get air, she didn't care. Her hands were on his chest and she slammed him back into the wall, eliciting a loud thud from the contact and a quick groan from the man.

Her skin was burning up, even with her shirt off. She could feel the adrenaline coursing through her, although it was a very different adrenaline than the kind she was used to experiencing in the field. This one was more toxic; it clouded her judgement, made time a fuzzy concept, and flushed blood to other areas of her body. Rachel was loving it. She continued to kiss Ian with her tan, warm stomach pressing against the soft cotton of his t-shirt as it tickled her and sent shivers down her spine.

Finally, Ian pushed off the wall enough to frantically and somewhat clumsily pull his shirt off, trying to avoid interrupting the lustful kissing as much as possible. Rachel instantly began to run her hands everywhere: his defined back, broad shoulders, strong chest, and rippled core. Her soft hands felt amazing on his skin and his skin began to heat up too as it pressed once more against her defined stomach.

The kissing hadn't stopped for more than a few short moments as the intense encounter continued. Ian tried to take control, mostly out of curiosity to see what would happen, by attempting to grab Rachel's arms. She quickly maneuvered them out of his grasp and grabbed his wrists, bringing his arms above his head and pinning him to the wall for what seemed like the hundredth time that evening.

This was her game and she would be calling the plays.

Time was a loose construct, and certainly one that neither of them were keeping track of. Seconds turned to minutes, and they went onward with their ravenous desires for the taste of each other's lips. Ian overpowered Rachel's intense grasp and reached behind her. Once she was aware that he was going for her bra clasp, she allowed the motion and Ian pinched the contraption inward. The bra loosened off Rachel's shoulders and fell to the ground, revealing her small, but full breasts. As the newly exposed skin came in contact with Ian's chest, Rachel let out a slight moan. *God this feels good.* Ian could feel her hard nipples against his skin and he desperately wanted to move to the bed. His mind was a flood of thoughts, none of which were sticking for very long.

Rachel reached for Ian's wrists again and placed his hands onto her breasts. Palms full, he began urgently squeezing them. The sensation felt amazing and Rachel had to turn her head away from his mouth to even concentrate. Ian took advantage and began to kiss her neck – tasting her salty, warm perspiration with his tongue. Her skin was so smooth and she smelled sweet, naturally so, not from any perfume. He was feeling her with his fingers, his tongue, and other parts of his anatomy and she felt miraculous.

Rachel was truly an incredible specimen and as he had learned, quite a handful in the bedroom. But tonight was different. There was some other type of passion present within her. Anger. Power. Confidence. Cockiness? Ian couldn't tell what it was, but it was exciting.

Despite the sensations cascading from her breasts and neck, Rachel gained enough focus to grab Ian's hair with a yank, pulling his mouth from its current task, and sink her tongue deep into it. She rubbed up against him, pressing her hips and legs against his, feeling his excitement in a very physical form. *He's going to have to wait.*

The thought had barely crossed her mind when Ian had maneuvered from against the wall, spun on his heels, and pressed her against the spot where he had just been. *No!* She was losing control of the situation. She needed to get it ba –

A wet, warm, and firm touch threw her mind back to its pleasure centers as Ian had moved his kissing down to her breasts. He caressed them with his mouth and moved his hands down the back of her pants, grabbing her buttocks with an indecent grip. *This is MY show* Rachel told herself through the moans and dips in and out of concentration. She was determined to take back this sexual encounter, despite how phenomenal he was making her feel at the moment. *You're about to make me feel even better.*

Intending to interrupt whatever Ian's plans consisted of, she began to undo the button from her pants; they were the same tight, combat oriented ones she'd been wearing on the mission. There hadn't been much time to change after the plane ride back. Slowly she pulled down the tab on the zipper and put her thumbs between her skin and underwear, pulling both bottom layers off in one motion. *Trying to save time here…*

Whether Ian had noticed her naked sex or not didn't concern Rachel. The air of the room was cold now that it was breezing against her. It felt like relief. With force, she placed her hands on top of Ian's head, intertwining her fingers through his soft hair, and pushed downward. For a half second there was resistance, but Ian soon figured out what she wanted and followed her lead. His kisses caressed her stomach, crossing her abdomen, and arrived near her hip. He was teasing her by holding out and she wouldn't have any of it.

With a second push downward, she forced his face into her wetness and let out a deep, uncontrollable moan. His tongue played around inside and outside of her, causing her legs to tremble and her eyesight to grow blurry. There was intensity with Ian's actions and it was getting her close. Within minutes she was shaking, barely standing, screaming out, and then trying to catch her breath as she hunched over Ian, coated in sweat. The climax had been incredible – sending her vision to explode in colors and her toes to curl against the floor

Once she came down from her excitement, Ian threw her on the bed and they continued their pleasures into the night.

————————————  ————————————

Rachel awoke sometime later in the bed, separated by a small tangle of white sheets from Ian, who remained sound asleep in the quiet, dark room. A ceiling fan spun above them, providing a comforting hum and a cooling airflow. Her gaze caught the fan and the ceiling beyond its rotating blades and she lost herself deep in thought. There was never any cuddling after her and Ian's sexual encounters…how could there be? *Less than a year ago, this man was a terrorist. I AM a bad person.* Usually Rachel didn't even fall asleep in his bed, but rather would return to her room of the house. She shot a glance at the nude man lying next to her, feeling almost angry that he had allowed all of their relations to happen. *I am not in love with him. Then why am I addicted to this?* The question had been troubling her for a few weeks now – after each mission she seemed to feel incredibly aroused.

She wanted to take control…

In order to feel out of control.

But every time after they finished, once all of the passion and excitement had subsided, she felt hollow. Not because of the sex or because she felt dirty for giving herself up to him. No, she knew that sex was a necessary primal act at times. This was a different feeling, one that left her at odds with herself and struggling to know what path she was on. She slowly began to realize that the sex was taking her mind off everything else happening in her life, but the second her head would clear from its pleasures, the whole world was back to being shit.

Bryson and Elena were dead.

David was incredibly powerful with hardly anyone to stand in his way.

She was having sex with a man she barely knew other than the fact he was a terrorist at some point.

And their leader still went by the guise of "Someone".

The sex seemed like the only time that Rachel really felt any control over her life and its fate these days. The sex, and out in the field performing missions. *What the fuck is wrong with you Rachel? Addicted to near-death*

She had had enough of this room, and slowly sat up in bed, sliding her feet off the edge. Out from under the covers, the room was a bit colder, and goosebumps began to form over her naked body. Rachel decided that she would come back for her clothes in the morning; it's not like they were going anywhere. *Someone* slept on the other end of the house, so waking him was the least of her worries and she walked casually back to her room, stepping lightly on the hardwood. Despite having already slept soundly for half the night, she realized that she was both exhausted and feeling a bit dehydrated.

The pale light in the bathroom attached to her room flickered on and she turned on the faucet, bending over to slurp some cold water. After a few substantial gulps she stood up and studied her reflection in the mirror. She knew that she had always been a good looking woman but her body had made some drastic changes in the last twelve months. Her arms, chest, and abs were toned with their constant use and she had converted a significant amount of the small percentage of body fat she had left into muscle. She thought her breasts looked smaller than normal, but she was still proud of the specimen reflected. She turned her back to the mirror and saw a similar phenomenon; her shoulders, upper, and lower back were all very toned, without even having to flex.

Bruises covered parts of her sides, back, and abdominals – they were from a combination of her missions and weekly training with Ian. There was a particularly nasty one forming on the outside of her hip where she had slipped in the guard's blood while trying to run out of the server room. It was a dark grey on the outer edges, but became yellow and blue towards the center. She poked the center of it gently and found that it didn't hurt nearly as bad as it looked like it should. Additionally, there was a long scratch on her shoulder, from a previous reconnaissance mission, that was finally beginning to heal. It had hurt like a son of a bitch at first, and bled a decent amount too.

Despite the ugly appearance of her wounds, Rachel didn't really mind them and even appreciated their vicious reminder that she was in fact, human. She knew that she was no Bryson, or Elena, or even Ian, but still, she was proud of what she had accomplished. *I just hope I'm still on the right side...* She shook the troubling thought from her mind, turned the faucet on again, and took a few more gulps of cold water. The clear liquid filled her palms as she cupped them underneath its stream and splashed her face, relishing in the coolness. A few droplets dripped down the length of her hair as she straightened, took a final look at herself in the mirror, and flipped the light off.

The sheets on her bed were unmade from the last time she had slept in it, but she didn't exactly have anyone to impress. Still nude, she slipped under the covers, situated her pillows to her liking – two under her head and one between her legs – and let her thoughts send her to dream.

Golden sunlight softly draped the room's entirety and its warm rays eventually woke Ian from his slumber. The smell of sex still hung in the air from last night and made the room feel hotter than it really was, despite the ceiling fan's continued rotation. Ian was used to Rachel being a handful in the bedroom, ever since they had started this escapade, but last night had been different. She seemed more aggressive than usual. *I wonder if something is going on. Is she ok?* His thoughts stopped right there and he reminded himself that this was not a romantic relationship. They had both agreed and established that from the beginning, and realistically, there was no way it could be any different. She was the equivalent to an upstanding American citizen who served her country (unbeknownst to it) and he was a terrorist…or ex-terrorist…or…*Hell I don't even know what I am anymore.*

Lines and sides of this war had become blurred, and Someone still hadn't revealed too many chunks of information other than mission objectives and brief reasoning for "why" they were carrying out the actions they were. Someone had seemed off lately – a bit distracted, irritable at times, and his ability to make eye contact with Ian was almost non-existent. All clear signs of a person who was expecting impending doom, or trying to find some sort of retribution for past sins. *Or both…*

Worry wasn't the plague that bothered Ian. If anything, he was frustrated. The Dead Scorpions, most likely David Harper, had tried to have him killed, and he had no form of control in this situation. Ian didn't mind taking orders, but he enjoyed a certain level of autonomy in this line of work. Autonomy that wasn't present here. Several times in recent months he'd entertained the idea of leaving; simply vanishing in the middle of the night and heading down to South America, most likely disappearing forever. But something kept him here. Whether it was the job security, an odd premonition he had of Someone, Rachel herself, or the sex with Rachel, he could not decide. Whatever the reason, every time he got close to leaving, he talked himself out of it.

And with that, his thoughts all circled back to Rachel, which is what truly worried him. He had grown attached to and protective of her, much to his own shock, and he was fearful it would eventually be a problem, in some form or another. Unsurprisingly, it was yet one more thing that he didn't have control over: Rachel's heart. Ian knew that he himself could resist the distractions of attraction and distance himself if need be, but he wasn't sure if she could. Of course, Ian was worrying about all of this without having actually had a conversation about it with Rachel. *Having the conversation will make it known.*

Having had enough of his own thoughts for the time being, Ian sat up and enjoyed the sunlight-coated room's warmth. Per his routine, he slid out from under the covers, stretched upwards, hands high above his head and back arched, then placed his palms on the floor in front of him, slowly counting to ten and remembering to breathe. Outside his door he could smell some type of delicious breakfast, but he needed to take a shower to wash the sex off first. Both for his own comfort and to avoid any awkwardness at the dining table.

Cloth crumpled to the floor as he slid his compression shorts off and adjusted the shower to a high temperature. Underneath the falling streams, Ian travelled back to Washington D.C. and reminisced. It had been an intense firefight, not to mention that had been the day he almost died from a suicidal human missile, but damn had it been fun. He had taken a shower that morning, much like this one except scalding hot, and taken two Pentagon teams out soon after…all with a bath towel around his waist. The highway chase had followed soon after (which he vaguely remembered almost dying from too). There hadn't been too many, if any, violent, *fun* days like that since being "rescued" by Someone. He missed it. The adrenaline, the quick thinking, the ultimate testing of himself. It wasn't necessarily the killing he enjoyed, although he often didn't find moral reason to be upset with that, but it was the challenge that accompanied it.

Heated water continued to cascade over his head and shoulders, and before long his pruning fingertips told him that he had been in the shower for too long. A short screech echoed from the piping as he turned off the shower, dried off, and wrapped a towel around his waist. As he brushed his teeth and shaved, he smirked from a memory the towel had activated. He had tricked the Pentagon agent by throwing his towel in the air and shot him while he was naked. *Whatever it takes I suppose…one of his last sights was my package.* Ian found it both funny and a bit sad.

Back in his bedroom, he put on jeans and a v-neck, made his bed, and picked up both his and Rachel's clothes from yesterday off the floor. He neatly folded his and put them back in the closet and dresser, and did the same for hers, but placed them on a chair in the corner of the room instead. He wasn't quite sure how one folds thong underwear, so he took the purple garment and hid it somewhere in the middle of her stack of clothes, along with the matching bra. Despite holding her unmentionables, he willed his thoughts to avoid recalling last night. It was sex. That was it. Time to move on with his day.

Sizzles and pops echoed from the kitchen as he left his room, entered a hallway, and proceeded to the bar-style counter. Someone was making bacon and a full plate of eggs was already out. It didn't seem like Rachel was up yet, so Ian started to dish up, also grabbing an apple and a banana from the nearby fruit basket.

"Bacon will be ready in a sec." Someone mentioned without turning. Ian offered no reply and instead began to cut his fruit into small bites, separating the two distinct flavors. It was still one of his favorite, yet odd and slightly obsessive, pastimes to combine fruit flavors. A few moments and bites passed, "How did you sleep?" Someone asked, with little real interest implied into the inquiry.

"Why don't you stop pretending to give a shit, and I'll just go back to enjoying my fruit?" Ian snipped.

"Fair enough." A few more sizzles and pops broke the silence between them and Someone plated the brown strips of glorious meat and brought them over to the bar counter, placing them in front of Ian. Once his fruit was finished, Ian snagged a couple pieces and ate them with some eggs. "I've always loved bacon." Someone mentioned, seeming to be talking to himself.

Ian grunted, "Yeah. Me too."

Quietly, the two men continued with their breakfasts, Ian sitting at the counter and Someone standing, both drinking their coffee, black, and both absorbed in their own thoughts. Morning sunlight reflected off every surface and signified that it was a pleasant day outside in the coastal town.

There was a slow pitter-patter of bare feet against hardwood, and Rachel emerged from the hallway that led to her room, already showered and dressed as well.

"Morning." She said lightly. Both men gave a small grunt, nodded, and sipped their coffee, unknowingly doing so in awkward unison. "Well aren't you just two peas in a pod?" They glanced at each other, now conscious of their mimicry, and tried to focus on separating their actions.

Rachel made her way into the kitchen, her brown hair instantly lightened by the yellow light. Ian noticed that she smelled marvelous and between that and bacon, he lost himself for a moment. Grabbing a plate, she dished herself some breakfast, and sat down at the table next to the counter.

"Thanks for making breakfast, *Ralph*. It looks delicious." Someone let out a small smile. For months, Rachel had been playing a game by calling him a different name whenever she thought of one, trying to see if she could guess it correctly or get him to show a reaction to one of them.

"You've already guessed 'Ralph' before, Rachel. It's not Ralph."

"You sure? Because I'm pretty sure you look exactly like a 'Ralph'." She teased back.

"Do I now? Should I be offended?" The rhetorical question lingered barely a second before Ian interjected coldly.

"You're going to have to tell us your real name sooner or later. This 'Someone' nonsense is getting ridiculous." The old man's eyebrows raised, as if in agreement, even for the smallest of seconds. He smiled.

"Alright then. Don't like calling me Someone? Call me Ralph. Apparently it suits me."

"I wasn't joking." Ian commented – a tinge of anger in his tone. A darker spirit took over the room and there was now an awkward silence among them.

Separately, they all continued to eat their breakfast until finally Rachel broke the silence.

"So what did we find out from the server room? You

take a look at it yet?" Someone, still chewing a bite of egg, hurried to swallow and answer.

"Yeah I ran through the data as it downloaded directly from the server. Good work on that mission by the way, Rachel." She smiled. "Over the past year, I think it's become clearly obvious to all of us that, while David is the top of the food chain, there is no way he could have done all of this alone. The complexity and size of The Will proves that easily, not to mention the incredibly varied ethnic groups and races that were recruited for that day. No amount of social profiling would have ever seen that coming and that means he has to have cells all over the world...cells that we've been slowly taking out one by one.

"Before we make any type of play on David, I want to decrease his support network. And that includes anyone he may have turned within N.E.T.S. He needs to sweat, slip up. Hopefully make a mistake. On top of that, I still have no solid plan on how to kill him directly."

"So we're settled on killing him then?" Rachel inquired sincerely.

"Yes, and for three reasons. First, a public trial would ruin N.E.T.S. by bringing them out into the open. Just because David is its leader, doesn't mean the ship has to go down too. Next, David has access to a lot of money. That means buying people off at any point during the trial. Everyone is corruptible. Some just have a higher price than others. Lastly, we don't know the timeline of any future attacks. The Will could have been the Aqarab Mayta's Mona Lisa, or it could have just been their first attempt. If it ends up being two to four years before David is in prison, who knows what could happen in that timeframe? Likewise, if we put a bullet in his head tomorrow, his followers would scatter, but eventually still regroup, hence my strategy."

Ian interjected. "We've been doing a lot of killing lately, and all without a whole lot of intelligence behind it. Clearly I'm no moral figurehead, but the last time I was part of a chain of command with a lack of transparency, I was almost blown to shit by a suicidal skydiver. I think I speak for both Rachel and myself when I say that we'd like to start having some more extensive debriefs before and after each mission." Rachel stared at the ground, not disagreeing with Ian's opinion. "There are a lot of blurred lines in this…thing…right now. We just want to make sure we're on the right side of them."

"I can assure you that you're on the right side of them but –"

"Sometimes it's hard to believe that coming from a guy who still asks us to call him Someone." Ian retorted, then quickly added, "Sorry, *Ralph* now." Someone blinked slowly, letting the tense moment pass.

"What I was going to say was that I can assure you that you're on the right side of these so-called 'blurred lines' *but* that I agree with you. I've kept both of you in the dark on a lot of things for a while and it's time that I begin bringing you up to speed. I'm sure you understand. I needed to know that I could trust both of you."

"Who says you can?"

"You can never really trust someone." He began, "All you can ever do is hope that person is just as suspicious of *your* intentions and that neither of you fuck it up until the day the relationship ends." The words hung on cold silence. "That's what trust really is."

Ian and Rachel glanced at each other while Someone

seemed lost in memories staring at something on the countertop. Snapping out of his digression, he continued once more.

"The point is, I agree with you. To answer Rachel's earlier question, we infiltrated that server room because during my time monitoring David's emails on the hidden cloud network, I noticed a strange phenomenon. Most of his emails bounced around in data oblivion until I'd lose track of them or the list of possible transmission points would grow too long. I'd have no way of knowing where the email ended.

"One day I pulled all that data and lo and behold, for a couple hundred emails, the twentieth IP address was identical. The first nineteen? Not one of them was the same. Not even one. But the twentieth address of each one? Identical. And *that* IP address belonged to the specific server that you plugged into on the mission.

"As I looked at the data as it was downloading, the same pattern appeared, this time on the fiftieth IP address from the same digital footprints of the emails. That IP address? It belongs to a single computer located deep within a Russian forest. My guess is it's the personal computer of David's Eastern European cell contact…recruiter…whatever the hell you want to call him."

"How can we be certain that the owner of this address is someone deserving to die?" Rachel inquired and Someone answered her question simply.

"The content of their emails contains references to The Will and this contact is one of the most frequently emailed, at least before the attacks. That's a lot of evidence going against him."

Ian was less concerned about the man's guilt or innocence – he likely deserved to die – but more so about his value. He spoke.

"Why don't we capture him this time? If he is one of David's main associates, maybe he has some information that would be valuable to us in the long run." Someone appeared slightly frustrated with Ian's response, like a father disappointed in a son's obvious mistake.

"He wouldn't talk, even if we captured him and tortured him to within an inch of his life. And why interrogate him? We already know who the head of this snake is. What critical info would he provide? And there is no *long-term* here. This is all going to come to a head rather soon." Rachel, slightly tired of the men's bickering, didn't want to waste time arguing.

"So when do we leave for Russia?" She inquired.

"That's probably one of the things I should tell you…" Someone left the words hanging, as if he knew he would be in trouble. "We have a fourth player in this game."

"What do you mean a 'fourth player'?" Ian asked harshly.

"In our group I mean. There aren't just three of us, there are four of us. And there has been for some time. In fact, I've already sent him to Russia. He should be there now."

Rachel was surprised that another member of this "team" had remained hidden for this long, and she was also a little offended that Someone had kept him from them. Lord knows there were a few instances where they could have used an extra set of hands or eyes…or guns. *What else is he hiding from us?*

"Well, who is he then?" She tried to sound nice when she said it, but it came out demanding. Someone looked her straight in the eye.

"He's my assassin."

CHAPTER IV

UNEXPECTED REVENGE

WEDNESDAY | JULY 5TH | 2017

THE DAY OF THE WILL IN THE SKIES ABOVE DENVER…

There was a vacuum of air for a split second as Bryson dove out of the small plane, off to interfere with the Dead Scorpion suicide missiles below. Henry, still at the controls of the craft, frantically pushed the autopilot button and unbuckled from the pilot's seat. He envied Bryson's bravery, but still couldn't believe he had actually jumped, despite all the stories he had heard about the man's actions in the field.

Air was still rushing into the cabin, a deafening roar that made it hard to concentrate. Henry made his way back to the sliding hatch and looked outside and down, careful to make sure that he was holding on for dear life. Below him he could see a few dots and then a magnificent explosion, no…*multiple* explosions encapsulated inside of each other, as one of the planes was torn apart at the seams in a burst of searing yellow, orange, and red flame.

Henry was mesmerized by the sight, but remembered Bryson's instructions to not lose the planes. One of the planes was still out there and Henry was not about to fail Bryson now. His eyes earnestly scanned the cloudless Denver horizon but there was no sight of another plane.

Had it been that far ahead of us? Henry predicted where the plane should have been had it kept on course and again searched for it as a black dot against the blue sky. Seconds continued to pass as the battle raged beneath him and his searching was becoming frantic.

"Shit…*shiiiiit*. Where are you?" Henry asked himself aloud. He reasoned that the other plane couldn't have gone too much farther than he had, but the time was still ticking away. "Where the hell are you, you bastard?"

A glint of sun caught his eye from below and to the left. There, several thousand feet lower than Henry's current altitude, was the other plane. Relief filled Henry's chest and he quickly slid the hull door shut and got back into the pilot seat. After disengaging the autopilot, he found the plane a second time in the sky and adjusted his heading to follow it. Without knowing how long he would be following the plane, Henry wanted the element of surprise and decided to maintain his altitude above his prey at all times.

The cabin was quiet other than the humming of the propellers until a soft screech followed by a voice,

"Agent Stines, this is Sam Georges with the U.S. Air Force again. Just what the hell is going on out there? We've scrambled jets, but – "

"No need." Henry cut him off, maintaining his CIA identity as Peter Stines with the Air Force General. "We have an agent on it. The threat is using human suicide missiles to attack the city. I'm in pursuit of the second plane. Get down to the ground to make sure everyone is okay."

"Agent Stines, I'm not sure if you're aware, but…" There was a hesitation in the man's voice. It came across as fear, which sent a cold shiver up Henry's spine. He guessed that this was not a man who exhibited that emotion often.

"What is it Georges?"

"Denver isn't the only city under attack. We've gotten reports that at least five other cities, all across the U.S., are under similar situations. This was a coordinated effort. Please tell me that you have agents in the other cities?"

Henry felt his gut react, as if a 2x4 had been swung against it. He wanted to vomit. He wanted to cry. The answer to the General was no. *No* they did *not* have agents in other cities. They thought Denver was it. *We thought Denver was the big play. How could we have been so stupid?*

"Agent Stine? Are you there?" Henry swallowed what felt like a golf ball before he replied.

"I'm here. Georges, the country is under attack, obviously. You need to follow your protocols for this type of thing and if there aren't any protocols, then I want you to use your best judgement. Defend this country."

"Roger that, Agent. Do you need assistance with pursuit of the other plane?" Henry's fear turned into a boiling anger as he remembered that he was tailing one of the bastards.

"Absolutely not. I'm going to follow this piece of shit to the ends of the earth."

"Roger. Make sure to tell him hello from the United States Air Force for us."

"Will do." Henry ended the communication and settled his sights on the plane in front of him. He was going to take this man alive and turn him in to N.E.T.S. From there, he would undergo questioning and hopefully, by the grace of God, they would be able to squeeze some intelligence out of him. But before that, Henry was going to make sure that he would feel pain.

Time passed excruciatingly slowly in the cockpit. Both planes had been crossing the Rocky Mountains for some time and Henry wondered what the world was like down below. Up in the air, he was disconnected, except for his radio and his cell phone, both of which he had turned off for the time being. A strange and saddening thought entered his mind and he truly couldn't shake it: the world that he had left when this plane took off would not be the world that he would return to. America, having suffered a recent Presidential assassination and now a highly coordinated terrorist attack (just how deadly, he didn't yet know), was on its knees. Nations rise and fall all the time, but Henry wasn't so confident that the United States would make it back from this. The thought alone made him tear up, not only out of sadness for his country, but out of fear for the future. *Once the dust is settled, what will the world look like?*

High in the sky the sun hung, over this dreadful day in history, as if to remind Henry that humans were insignificant. Even if they were to all die right here, right now, the sun would rise again. It was another sobering thought. *Why are we so violent when none of it really matters? Why do we ridicule, hate, and kill when it gets us nowhere?* Quickly realizing he was going down an existential rabbit-hole, Henry cleared his mind and focused again on the plane below. He wasn't quite sure, but he believed they were almost in Utah, if not already there.

Craving some contact with the outside world, despite its current condition, Henry turned on his cell phone and began scouring news sites on the internet. The pages on his screen bled red with "Breaking News" banners or "Emergency Update" notifications. Images of highly damaged buildings, mostly skyscrapers, public areas that had turned into deep craters, civilians with cuts and scrapes running in terror, and emergency responders trying to save lives littered the pages as he scrolled, endlessly it seemed, through the photos. Little actual information was being posted other than pictures as he guessed that many of the news companies were frantically trying to create their stories and get field reporters on-site.

It was worse than he had even imagined. Georges had told him five cities other than Denver, and from what he could tell the total was up to ten. Seattle, L.A., San Francisco, San Diego, Houston, Chicago, D.C., Boston, and New York were all being listed. Death tolls had not yet started to be predicted but Henry could tell it was going to be bad. *Historically* bad. Tears welled in his eyes once more and he put his phone away, unable to look at the terror and destruction any further. That man on that plane, whoever he was, Henry didn't care. He just knew, without a shadow of a doubt, that he was going to make him hurt.

Agent Henry Cobble wondered to himself what N.E.T.S. was encountering. He didn't quite know where Rachel was – she had been extremely preoccupied the last few days with tracking down the person who had shot him in the alleyway. He just hoped she was safe; he had always liked her and enjoyed her company.

David was surely infuriated, mostly at himself, for N.E.T.S. missing the clues that led up to today. *Were there any clues that we missed? We know nothing about this organization…*Henry admired David to a vast degree and looked to him as a mentor. His only faults were accepting too much blame and being overly patriotic, but otherwise he was as strong a leader as Henry had ever encountered.

Pondering David's current status begged the question: what will N.E.T.S.' next move be? A full scale attack like this would mean United States (and most likely allied nations) military action. Would N.E.T.S. continue covert operations? Would they work with the other U.S. intelligence agencies now? Several logical, hypothetical, and procedural questions rattled through Henry's mind, none of them really begging to be analyzed or answered at that moment. It seemed to be his way of coping and getting his mind away from the terrors befalling the nation several thousand feet below him.

> *Do I even want to land?*
> *I could just fly this plane away and escape.*
> *I could be done with this world, this life.*
> *Start somewhere new…*

Henry knew it wasn't the answer, he just felt as if the idea pleaded to be entertained. Even still, he felt ashamed of it. Here he was, perfectly safe up in the air, with thousands of people injured and dying all over the nation, and an agent whom he looked up to had just willingly thrown himself out of the plane to stop an attack.

"Shit, Bryson!" The exclamation surprised even Henry but given everything he had just learned he had almost completely forgotten about him. He definitely should have landed by now, hopefully after taking out several of the targets. Admittedly the man had just skydived out of a plane with the intent to kill but Henry genuinely questioned whether or not he still had his cell phone. Was Bryson okay? Were people hurt on the ground? Should he circle back and help or pick him up?

Henry reached for his phone that he had placed on the dash after looking at the gruesome news. A few quick finger swipes later and the call was being placed to Bryson. It rang several times before disconnecting which didn't surprise Henry. Bryson probably had better things to do right now than assuage Henry's fears. Eager to find out what had happened in Denver since Bryson's jump, Henry sought the internet once more for answers.

Many of the other cities were drastically damaged – there was no doubt that they had fallen victim to the catastrophic attack. Denver however seemed to be unscathed. Among the main reports covering the attacks there were small blurbs here and there, mere sentences in the paragraphs detailing the other cities' destruction, about reported explosions above the Denver skyline. Henry couldn't find any evidence of possible damage.

Bryson had been successful then! Or at least it seemed that way for the time being. It certainly wasn't the first time in his life, but Henry felt a swell of pride and an intense admiration for Bryson. Before all of this – this chaos – had started happening, the two had rarely interacted, but Henry truly looked up to the man, similar to the way he did David, but for different reasons. Bryson and Elena's track record among N.E.T.S. was unparalleled and as a rather new agent, he couldn't think of anyone better to look up to than them. Even after the recent loss of Elena, Bryson was as dangerous as he was before, perhaps even more so. This day would go down as a hellish one in the United States, but the glimmer of hope would be the saving of Denver, as small as it was. It would give the country something to cling to.

Denver's avoidance of the havoc reinvigorated Henry and quelled his doubts. Bryson killed twenty of them, in a very small window of time, and saved who-knew-how-many lives on the ground. *The least I can do is follow this little shit back to his hole.*

Rocky peaks turned into steep hills that eventually turned into red and tan desert. Several thousand feet away, the other plane began to shrink and get smaller than the dot in the sky that it already was. Beneath the two aircrafts was a rare, mostly untouched portion of the American west. A couple paved streets, watering holes, and various, singular shacks littered the ground amongst the desert valleys and rock formations. Henry dropped the plane's altitude, wondering if he had been spotted. *Either that or he's getting ready to land.* Moments passed as his height decreased, but the plane below wasn't getting much closer. It was descending at a fast clip, as if it needed to make an emergency landing. Henry mimicked the descent, his stomach dropping as the plane did.

In the distance there was a strip of ground that seemed lighter in orange tint than the surrounding environment. Henry knew what was going on – the pilot of the other plane was going to land. He had guessed this would be the endgame at the start, but it occurred to Henry that he had no actual plan on how to *end* the pursuit. Without backup, he figured his options were limited to four:

1) Reference the location of the airstrip and return later or circle back.
2) Continue pursuit from the air.
3) Land his plane right after and continue the pursuit on foot or in a vehicle.
4) Crash into the plane as it lands.

It was obvious that his options had holes. Coming back to the airstrip at a later time would most likely mean the culprit would escape. Tracking his next vehicle from above was viable, but there were too many variables. *Where would I land? How long would my gas last? He would almost certainly notice me above.* Landing the plane afterwards was equally as useless; again, there were too many variables. *He could take off in a car immediately and leave me stranded, or have a weapon and gun me down as soon as I land.* Henry's fourth option was mostly just for his own amusement. Crashing his plane into theirs was almost surefire suicide and required a level of aviating skill that Henry wasn't confident he possessed.

But the more he thought about it…

Option four was steadily growing on him. Crashing their planes as they landed, if he could survive, would provide the strategic advantage of being a total surprise. Part of him wanted to entertain the idea of requesting backup, but N.E.T.S. would never get there in time and neither would local police. No. This capture needed to happen silently and swiftly. Which led to the biggest gap in Henry's plan. *How will I escape with him with two crashed planes?*

On the far edge of the airstrip stood a large rectangular building, dark brown against the lighter horizon. It seemed to be an abandoned air hangar for this equally as abandoned air strip. Henry figured if the man was landing in the middle of nowhere, he had to have arranged for a pickup or some form of transportation. *That means there could be others...* Henry slid his hand to the waistband of his pants and felt for his weapon. The handgun was still there and the cold steel against his fingers reassured him that he wasn't entirely alone either.

There was no use arguing with himself any further and time was running out; he would crash into the other plane as they landed and deal with the fallout. Without a moment's hesitation, Henry increased the airspeed of the aircraft to close the pursuit gap. Simultaneously he slowed the descent as he became collinear with his enemy. It would be about a minute and a half before wheels down and there was still a considerable distance between the two aircrafts. Not insurmountable by any means, but Henry knew that this was going to be a crash at an alarming velocity. His caution during pursuit had paid off, as the other pilot clearly had no notion of a pursuer, but he was paying for it now as he rushed to catch up.

A troubling thought entered Agent Cobble's mind as he remembered that he may not necessarily walk away from this. He was creating a *plane crash*...not an event that many people get to survive once it occurs. Granted it would be a low elevation and somewhat slower velocity crash, but a collision nonetheless. Oddly, Henry felt at ease with the possibility. A lot of people had lost their lives today. A lot of innocent people. As long as he was taking the terrorist to death's doorstep with him, that would be good enough for him.

Within moments Henry was nearly on top of the other aircraft and the other pilot was very much aware of her pursuer now, cursing at herself for being such a fool and not checking for a tail over the course of the past few hours. As irksome as the tailing aircraft was, they were still in the sky – a fact that limited their options to get rid of one another. Knowing that a car was waiting for her in the hangar, the terrorist pilot figured her best bet was to land as normal, ditch the plane as swiftly as possible, and escape in the car, leaving whoever was in the other plane stranded.

She did think it was curious that there didn't seem to be any backup at the hangar, at least not from what she could see in the distance. No flashing lights or black, hulking SUVs, just barren, clay colored desert. Although she wasn't exactly sure what that meant, she leaned towards the assumption that the pursuer was an agent of one of America's several intelligence agencies. There was the possibility that this could complicate things, but as long as she could shut down the plane and get to the car, they would be screwed and she would be alive.

The dirt runway was approaching quickly and she prepared her landing gear and adjusted her speed. From here on out she would ignore her chaser and focus on getting to the ground as safely and quickly as possible.

Henry saw the landing gear drop from the bottom of the plane and knew that it was coming to that moment.

He didn't bother to drop his wheels and instead increased his speed while dropping his altitude. He wanted to be right on top of the other plane, literally.

Shades of oranges and reds were replaced by shades of tan and brown as the landscape below became the airstrip. The nose of Henry's aircraft was halfway across the other plane's body and he once more adjusted the speed of the aircraft, slowing it down to match speeds. Space between the crafts and ground continued to decrease as their altitudes dropped and Henry estimated that the other plane's wheels were mere feet from touchdown.

A swift plunge of the controls had a similar consequence on Henry's plane. *Hope for the best.* The hull shook with a loud boom as the tail of the bottom plane crashed into the other's belly. The effect on the landing was immediate and the landing gear hit the ground with impact, snapping off in a shower of bent metal and glowing sparks. The nose of Henry's aircraft slammed into the roof of the one below, shattering the cockpit's glass and sending shards scattering outwards, inwards, and sideways.

Below, the other plane was bouncing violently off the dirt tarmac, crunching its oval frame each time with a fury of loud bangs and crisp cracks of breaking parts. One final bounce provided enough friction with the ground to slow the plane down and keep it sliding, turning sideways as it did so. Henry's plane continued its momentum as it slid off the top of the other's hull and slammed into the ground itself.

Both planes, now grounded permanently, continued their slide on the runway with dust pluming into the sky from all sides creating a hazy brown mist that hung in the air. Friction eventually won over motion as the planes came to a stop with one final, fleeting roar followed by the sound of dust raining back down onto the ground whence it came.

For a few moments there was silence, one which might have signaled that both parties were dead if there were others around to observe it. Henry sat in his cockpit, adrenaline pumping, but dazed. In his left arm there was a glass shard protruding outward. His other arm was fine and it gently wiggled the glass, signaling that it wasn't very deep. It came out with a quick tug and a warm trickle of crimson followed. By his measurements, that was the worst of his injuries and even if it wasn't he didn't really have time to sit around tending to them. He undid the latch of his seatbelt and threw his shoulder into the somewhat crumpled pilot-side door. An inch was all it opened.

Something was horribly wrong. *What happened?* She wondered to herself. The memory of landing the plane came to her, and then suddenly there were loud thuds, violent vibrations, and her memory stopped. Had that lunatic actually crashed into her during landing? It didn't matter now because she was in a decidedly precarious situation. The SUV, her only means of escape, was several hundred yards away in the hangar. She had yet to actually look down at her right leg but she had a sneaking suspicion that it was broken. There was a substantial amount of pain, which she was trying desperately to mentally subdue. Against her better judgement, she looked at the source of pain and found her tibia, white and shiny, had broken through the skin. Even with all the pain management training she had been through with the Aqarab Mayta, she could feel herself growing faint at the sight of her own bone. It looked to be a very clean break meaning that she would heal fine and it would grow back stronger, but that didn't really help her now.

Not wanting to suffer much more from the grisly image, she focused her attention elsewhere – to unbuckling her seatbelt and getting the hell out of this plane.

The third thud of his shoulder against the door had hurt the worst. It had impacted the area where the glass had stuck and a new stream of blood leaked out.

"Son of a bitch." Henry muttered. "This…" a fourth shoulder rammed the door panel and it gave way slightly more. "Fucking…" A fifth. "Door…" A sixth. "Better…" The seventh thrust sprung the door from its crinkled, metallic prison and it swung open with fervor, tossing Henry and his forward momentum out onto the ground.

"Open." Henry frustratingly finished his sentence and spat the sand out of his mouth, coming first to his knees, then standing cautiously, in case there were any unknown injuries. All felt fine, except for the minor wounds to his arm and his ego. He coughed, wiped the dirt from his eyes, and started towards the other plane several yards behind him.

With great effort, the seatbelt had come off and she was working on getting the door open. During this time she realized her vision was blurred, most likely some level of concussion, but even still she could see a figure making its way toward her in the distance. She expected that fear would have taken over but rather she felt at peace. If this man was going to kill her, at least she would be labeled among the many martyrs who had died today, including the brethren who had very recently jumped from her plane. Even still, she fought to open the door. *I want to go down with a fight.*

Despite her efforts, the door was significantly jammed and she couldn't get any worthwhile leverage on it. Instead she decided to let her oncoming assailant open it for her while she readied a surprise.

Henry could see the man with the shaved head struggling in the cockpit and not really making eye contact with him as he approached, as if he was looking at something behind Henry. Handgun at the ready, he rounded the plane's front to the pilot door and yanked on the handle. Much like his own door it had been crumpled and would require some effort. A second tug, with nearly his whole bodyweight behind it, proved successful and the door came completely off, its hinges damaged in the crash.

The door's weight was significant; Henry dropped it almost immediately. A foot shot out from the cockpit, connecting hard with the back of Henry's neck.

As he ripped the door off, she brought her foot round, with her heel landing square at the base of his neck. The move forced her off balance and she began to slide outside of the tilted plane. *This is going to hurt. Very badly.* The man fell face first into the earth, seeing spots most likely, as her broken leg attempted to support her fall out of the plane. Knowing that it couldn't take *any* weight, its contact with the ground was short lived; it buckled, forcing her to also go face first into the orange dirt. Pain ripped through her leg and up her core, quickly replaced by the pounding of her head on the ground.

"Agrh!" The brief scream was natural and loud.

He's a she? Henry realized as he heard the scream after what sounded like a hard fall. The world was black, she had thrown her whole weight into that kick, and he knew it would bruise. Badly. As his vision cleared he saw the other person, *her,* lying on the ground, same as him, struggling to get up as well. Their eyes locked. She was darker skinned, but still Caucasian, had a shaved head, but her eyes…they were startlingly gorgeous. *How is she a terrorist?* Henry was literally dazed and confused.

She could feel him looking at her in bewilderment. *Is it because I'm good looking or because I'm not a typical terrorist?* Although her pain was excruciating, she scrambled but failed to stand as the man got to his feet first and pointed his gun at her.

"Stay on the ground!" He shouted with a little too much vigor. His hand was dealt – she knew he was a "green" agent, rather new to this whole game. Even with that fact this would be a hard fight though. She was probably better trained than he, but the bottom half of one of her legs was a grotesque scene, and he had a gun. But if she could jus –

————————  ————————

Henry didn't want to risk anything and knocked her out with a kick to the side of the head. She had looked like she was planning something and he didn't want to take his chances against an unknown enemy. Even with a broken leg she could have been some sort of ninja, and despite his "better than average" hand-to-hand skills, he didn't want to risk it. *Ok...she's probably not a ninja. But who knows with the Dead Scorpions?*

Wind blew across the debris-strewn landing strip and a swirl of dust cascaded upwards in the distance. *What's my game plan here?* Henry figured it was probably time to call in N.E.T.S. support. His best bet was to restrain her, wait it out in the hangar a couple hundred yards from here, and she would be interrogated back at N.E.T.S. headquarters. She lay there unconscious, brown dust collecting on her clothes and hair as Henry rummaged through her plane's cockpit, eventually emerging with several seatbelt straps. The gun went in his waistline, the seatbelts went over his shoulders, and she went in his arms.

The walk was unfortunately long, but Henry was more fit and strong than many of his peers gave him credit for. Even still, his arm was bleeding and still hurt like a bitch, making the trip a lumbering one. Under different circumstances he imagined that this would be a somewhat romantic scene and laughed to himself. It couldn't have been further from the truth. She was a terrorist, despite her looks, and he had just crashed his plane into hers, resulting in a grisly broken appendage, and was now going to tie her up in an abandoned hangar until she could be taken away for interrogation. *Yeah. Real romantic, Cobble.*

A prickling feeling residing somewhere in her consciousness stirred her awake. Moments passed and she couldn't quite grasp the position that her body was in. The pulling on her shoulders told her that her arms were bound behind her back, and now she could feel the cold, steel pole, tall and narrow across her spine. There was a dull, numbing ache coming from one of her lower extremities and she saw that her broken leg had been elevated and the heel of her foot rested on the seat of an old rusted chair. Her head hurt something awful and it was then that the pieces of the puzzle began to fall into place.

Clearly I have underestimated my opponent. She let out an audible sigh, hoping that the man would come back now that she was awake. At this point, she had no Plan B...hell, she hadn't even really had a Plan A for this scenario. The agent had some skills and practiced caution above all else, while she was maimed to the point where escape would be nigh impossible. *Could I woo him? Or should I try to anger him…maybe he'll make a mistake that I can take advantage of?*

The hangar was dark and echoic. The ceilings were high, as in all hangars, and tinted rust could be seen on many of the beams above and pillars beside. It was completely deserted, just as she had planned for it to be.

A shadow emerged from behind her, as did a voice. The escape plot would have to be temporarily put on hold. His voice was nearing and she tried to listen in to the conversation he was having over the phone.

"Yeah I don't really care what's going on out there. This is urgent and he will want to hear this." A few moments passed as she watched his shadow pace slowly. "Angela, honestly, just shut the fuck up. I don't care how busy David is. Get him on the line. This is *directly related* to what's going on today." More silence and pacing. Suddenly she saw the shadow pause. "ANGELA! Holy hell, I swear that if you don't – " He stopped and listened. "Ok, okay. Sorry. Thank you. I'll wait for him."

The shadow remained behind her, gently rocking back and forth on its feet. She smiled, knowing that whatever agency this man was tied to was clearly in disarray. It wasn't much evidence to go off of, but it sounded like The Will had been successful. A pulse of relief washed over her. So many months of planning, training, practicing, and learning for so many people had finally paid off. *We have brought America to her knees.* It was a dark thought, pleasing to her, that trickled slowly through her mind like tree sap.

Time drew itself slowly against their environment, five minutes seeming to stretch on for a half hour. Henry had the phone pressed to his ear in anticipation and he could feel the oils and moisture from his skin beginning to transfer to the touchscreen. There wasn't really any timeline per say, and he knew David had to be in over his head today…*Maybe I should have just called an extract team instead?* Agent Cobble shook the idea from his mind, knowing that he was most likely the only N.E.T.S. operative to have an actual Dead Scorpions member in custody. It might have been too late to prevent today's attacks, but she could also be the key to revealing more secrets about the ghostly organization. Finally a voice came to the phone. It was David Harper's.

"Henry, sorry for the delay. Angela told me this was urgent. What's your status?"

"I'm fine sir, all injuries are minor. Thank you for speaking with me." Henry hesitated, not quite sure how to phrase what he wanted to divulge. "I've got one sir."

"Agent Cobble, please clarify. You've got one…one *what*?"

"One of the Dead Scorpions. It's the pilot of one of the planes in the Denver attack. I followed her and crashed my plane into hers as she landed."

"You said *she*? And you *crashed* your plane…into hers?" Henry smiled as surprise was not an emotion that he knew David Harper to express often.

"It was really the only way sir. I weighed the options and it was the best bet to prevent her escape. She's fine, has a nasty compound fracture, but she'll live."

"Where are you now?"

"My best guess would be Nevada or New Mexico. We flew for a while over the Rockies. It's some out-of-commission airstrip and I've got her tied up in the hangar. I just sent you my coordinates."

"Agent Cobble, great work. I don't need to tell you how important this is. As one of our wise Presidents once stated, today is a date which will live in infamy." An eerie silence came through the phone and Henry could almost feel the anger radiating from David through the phone. "They *fucked* us today, Henry. Badly. It's going to be a long road to recovery and this nation may never be herself again. I'm not going to pussyfoot around the possible truths. But if we can gather any information on them, it's a step in the right direction."

"Understood sir. I checked the news while I followed her. It…uh…" Tears began to well up as he remembered the horrors that he had read and the sheer size of the attack. "It's been a very hard day. *This*, this, has been a tough pill to swallow."

"Agreed, Agent." David stoically concurred. "Hang tight Cobble. Extract is coming to you via road and then we will interrogate the hell out of her. ETA four hours."

"Copy that. Thank you, sir." Henry was about to hang up and then remembered a question that had been burning through his thoughts for hours. "Wait! Sir?" Luckily, David had remained on the line long enough.

"What is it Cobble?"

"How's Bryson? Where is he? I saw reports that Denver was undamaged…" Nothing. The only sound was the virtual dead space between telephones; a quiet hum of nothingness that filled Henry's eardrum.

"Henry, I…" David struggled on the other end, finally deciding to go with the brutal truth. It was the only way on a day such as this one. "Henry, Bryson was successful in defending Denver completely, but he gave his life in the process. He's gone." There was little sympathy in David's voice, Henry guessed that it too was hard for him to accept. David finalized the call with a growling command, his voice raspy with hatred, "This is a war Henry. Do your fucking job and survive." A click and dial tone followed, as did a wave of pain.

Before he knew it, Henry's hands were on his knees, phone still in hand, and he was lurching. A mix of nausea and tears was choking him from inside and it was all he could do to gasp for air, saliva flying freely as he did so. *Bryson…Bryson is…dead?* The phrase seemed foreign to Henry, as if it was a math problem with no calculable solution. *I just saw him. He was just in the plane with me. I thought Denver was saved…how did he save Denver, but still die?* There was the short realization that he and Bryson had never been close, but Henry had always looked up to the man and their recent interactions had been so *recent*…he just sincerely couldn't believe it. Bryson Cooper was dead, in the midst of this shit storm, when N.E.T.S. was likely to need him most. He had died to protect the innocent people below.

Tears rolled from Henry's eyes, without him even realizing they were streaming. There was a deep pang in his stomach; one of guilt, sadness, and anger.

"FUGHHHHHCK!" The lengthy scream echoed through the ceilings of the hangar and Henry shattered his phone against a nearby wall, though the sound was hidden by his outburst. He wiped the sweat off his brow and the tears off his cheeks and took the gun out from his waistband.

The silhouette of his shadow trembled against the walls. Whoever had been on the phone had given him very bad news. Soon after, he had let out a frantic, cursing scream of emotional pain. The sound was enormous against the silence, and almost startled her leg off the chair. Looking at the reaching shadow on the floor, she saw now what his hand held: a gun. And the shadow grew larger. He was coming for her.

"Who the hell are you?" The question came as he came round in front of her, looking directly into her eyes. His own were puffy and red and wild, bulging in their sockets, signifying that he wasn't in his right mind.

"I am no one." She replied quietly. "Why don't you untie me and we can talk like civilized people?" Henry laughed at that.

"That's not going to happen. And you're about the furthest thing from civilized." There was a hint of disgust in his voice and his gaze had yet to break, even by blinking.

"Look, what am I going to do? My leg is basically severed in two." She nodded towards the blood. "I don't know what you think I am, but I can assure you that I had nothing to do with what happened today."

"Bullshit! You're with them. You're with the *Aqarab Mayta*." She was surprised that he knew their Arabic name but she played her game all the same.

"The *who*?"

Henry gave her a look that could have killed and raised the gun as well as his voice.

"I swear if you keep lying I'll shoot your damn leg off, bullet hole by bullet hole."

"Hey, I was just a pilot! I got paid a lot of cash to fly that group. I assumed they were just some illegal skydivers trying to pull off a stunt. I never thought…that…"

"LIAR! What? You never thought that they were going to dive bomb the city? You just thought all that extra C4 was for shits and grins?" She knew he had a point. *It might be time for something new: seduction.*

"I'm sorry! Ok? I knew they were planning something but they forced me to do it. They said they would kill me and my family if I didn't pilot the plane. Please…" The fake tears began as she broke his gaze and looked down.

"I didn't know the Dead Scorpions trained Oscar worthy actresses."

"I don't know what you want me to say? That I'm part of some crazy organization? I'm an American citizen!" She paused, getting her most sultry face ready. "Please believe me. Untie me and…and…I'll make it worth your while."

"What the fuck is that supposed to mean?"

"I'm a woman. You're a man. You do the math." She replied softly. Henry laughed, abruptly at first, but then a full-fledged chuckle.

"You picked the wrong spy to flirt with lady. I'm gay." She hid her shock from the declaration well, but studied him all the more. *I can't get caught. Time to piss him off and try to escape.*

"Good because I didn't feel like suppressing vomit anyway. Having sex with an American swine who's as much of a pussy as you are?"

Henry smiled, clearly aware of what she was trying to do.

"I've been called everything, although I admit 'swine' is a bit new. Either way, if you don't tell me who you are, your *real*, *legal* name, I'm going to knock you out, hard enough to leave a permanent scar, until my ride arrives. And I can promise you that once my peers get a hold of you, well, you'll wish this 'swine' had stayed true to his amputation-by-bullets threat." He turned away from her, straddling the decision between actually knocking her out or ignoring her for the remaining few hours they had together.

She had underestimated him once before and did not want to again, though she knew something had to be done. Once his colleagues arrived she knew what came next. *It's time for him to make a mistake*. His back was still turned to her but her face was dark, filled with hatred, as she uttered her next.

"We killed your man didn't we?" There was a gleeful pitch to the inquiry. "You all failed, fucking *miserably*, and we killed your friend." She smiled. "Or maybe he was your lover."

Heat swelled up behind the skin on his face and he turned to her.

"Shut your mouth. Or I'll put a bullet in your head."

"Will you? You need me alive." Henry pursed his lips in reluctant agreement as the female terrorist continued. "You know…it's interesting. That I'm here. Alive. And your friend, isn't. Because he's dead." Her eyes locked on his with a deep evil. "As he should be."

At that moment one might have actually been able to see the heat rising from Henry's pores. His stance was steadfast, if only for a few moments, before he snapped. With a kick, he sent the chair sliding. Her scream pierced the air before her foot hit the ground, jostling the bone even farther. She opened her eyes from the pain and Henry was already crouched down over her, silent but panting, the deadly muzzle only inches from her head. Sweat covered his brow and his eyes were glazed with wetness.

Out of her peripherals, she could see his trigger finger moving, ever so close to applying the weight needed to fire the bullet.

"Do it." She egged. "You won't." *I hope.*

"ARGH!" Henry grit his teeth through the yelp, and pressed the muzzle even farther against her head.

"You won't do it. And neither could he. It's why you'll soon be dead. And he already is."

Red cascaded over Henry's vision and he felt himself apply sufficient pressure to the trigger. Somewhere, deep in the back of his mind, he knew this was wrong. A faint *"We need her"* echoed out from the recesses of his thoughts. But it was too late.

The gun erupted with a booming clap that filled the hangar to its rafters and farther echoed out into the silent desert. Her body jolted suddenly as the bullet passed through her head, taking parts of her skull, brain matter, and life with it. There was absolute silence as her body slowly bled out over the concrete floor. Henry straightened and stood up, knowing he had just made a severe mistake. Strangely though, he didn't care. Bryson had died today, most likely a horrible death. He was simply returning the favor in kind.

Several hours later, David sat at his extravagant desk in the New York City Headquarters of N.E.T.S. It had been an incredibly stressful day and exhaustion was beginning to overtake him. For what seemed like the hundredth time, his desk phone rang, playing its cute chime over and over. Reluctantly, David pressed the answer button on the touchscreen and the headset he'd been wearing for the better part of the day connected the call.

"Yes?" He started robotically.

"Sir, we're here at the extraction point for Agent Cobble. Terrorist suspect is dead. Agent Cobble killed her."

Usual protocol dictated that Cobble be put under arrest, or at least investigation, for disobeying orders. In extreme cases where it was believed the agent had gone rogue, David had the power to suggest immediate execution.

"What would you like us to do, sir? Take him into custody?"

"No. No…no. It's been a long day for all of us, including Agent Cobble. Seems to me that he was just evening the score."

"Copy that, sir."

"Secure the scene, remove any and all evidence, and make sure Cobble gets back to New York City within the remaining hours of the day."

"Copy, sir. Gamma Squad out."

There was a quiet click and David leaned back in his chair with a subtle smirk. Agent Henry Cobble had just tied up one more loose end for him without even knowing it.

CHAPTER V

A BLOODY CRESCENDO
MONDAY | SEPT 17TH | 2018

Snow covered nearly all his exposed skin, which wasn't much at this point, but it was important as the contrast would give away his position immediately. With skin as black as night, snowy landscapes were often his least favorite places to carry out missions.

Dynadin was his name, Scottish for "knight", although he hadn't an ounce of Scottish blood in him. His life had begun in Africa, and after experiencing enough horrors on that continent, he had taken it upon himself to make something of his life, eventually meeting the man who would put his skills to work. During times of great boredom such as this, he would recall the tale of his life, but now was not the time for memories.

It was the time for focus.

Dynadin was deep within the northeastern territory of Russia, hiding among a thick constellation of trees, scattered like thin pencils stuck intermittently into the white and hard ground. Large, wet snowflakes danced peacefully as they made their way to the earth, never really accumulating to more than a couple of inches. Strange, but lucky weather for this time of year. It had been three days and Dynadin was growing anxious.

His partner had gotten new information in the form of an IP address location from a team that had recently infiltrated a server room of importance. The IP address was linked to a very wealthy Russian businessman who kept to himself and his large complex deep in the veins of the forest. Dynadin was here to kill him, as he had killed several people of importance in the last year. They had all been tied to the Dead Scorpions, some more tightly than others, but each had their own fairly extensive rap sheet beyond that sin.

This man for example, of whom Dynadin only knew his picture, had helped to recruit a decent bundle of young minds for The Will, not to mention discreetly funded the terrorist group, but was also known to partake in both the production and viewing of child pornography in his "free" time. Dynadin needn't know any more about the tall, burly Russian man with the thick mustache. He had his mission and it was just.

There hadn't been a clear shot for three days and he was contemplating assaulting the building alone. The ground was cold and hard, pressing against his hip bones as he lay flat in the snow, eyeball pressed constantly up against the scope of his AS50, which had been painted in his own personal style of artic camouflage to hide it against the elements. The gun had a range of 1,500 meters, but he was only 1,000 out. Plenty of distance to make a shot and retreat to his hiding spot, quickly followed by his extraction point.

When a body lies in the same position for an extended period of time, the extremities begin to forget to receive the blood they need (or rather, the heart cannot pump as effectively). Dynadin had been steadily injecting himself with a potent concoction, again, his own blend, in the last

72 hours, but his number of doses was waning. It contained a blood thinner with a small dose of adrenaline and the injections happened every six hours. Not to risk being seen, everything he did was done lying down. His injections were done one handed and slowly, the arm reaching for the pack on his waist, pulling out a filled syringe, and injecting through his pant legs. Food was ingested similarly, with a slow reach back to his pack for his nutrition bars, and then bringing them to his mouth to eat, his eye never leaving the scope of the rifle. Officially, he had peed himself five times thus far, drinking from the backpack hose that hung in front of his mouth. The lining of his pants were designed to allow the urine to freeze, while transferring it's warmth throughout the material. It was an awkward sensation, to say the least, and he'd be glad when he could take a piss in an actual toilet again.

Stranger things had happened, but he found it odd that an opportunity to take a shot hadn't presented itself over the course of 72 hours. His sights were set on the expansive foyer of the main house, glistening with all of its gaudy Russian decorations. Mr. Mustache had appeared only a handful of times, surrounded by a herd of men, most likely loyal as wolves but dumb as worms, at his side. One of them would likely stroll into the line of fire and end up botching the shot. This stakeout would go down as one of the longest (and coldest) he'd ever been on. The decision was made in his mind. 60 more minutes of waiting and if *that* shot didn't come, he was going to infiltrate and light their world on fire.

Time creeps slowly in the cold and the final 60 minutes was no different. Dynadin found his mind wandering, but he strained to keep it focused, even just a little while longer. *I wonder what it will feel like to stand up again?* The thought entertained him enough that he could feel his legs tingling with the anticipation of being used. *Not yet…not yet.* He pressed a small button near the trigger of the rifle and a HUD appeared on the inside of the scope. It contained a small compass direction icon, wind speed value, and a digital clock. Constant grey blanketed the skies so it was often hard to discern between morning and afternoon, but the clock revealed that it was slightly after 2:00 P.M. *Ten more minutes* Dynadin encouraged himself. Ten more minutes was all he needed to wait until he would allow himself to unleash.

CRRRACK!

Echoes of a twig being snapped in two reached his ears, tensing his muscles, but not moving them. Best case scenario was that the damage to nature was caused by a small mammal, possibly a rabbit, just trying to get back home from the cold. Worst case scenario (and the more likely one) was that a perimeter guard had finally made his way over towards the assassin's position. Over the last couple of days, Dynadin had kept mental tabs on the guards, mapping out their usual routes and gauging how close they came to him. The closest had been about 400 meters. Until now.

Crunch, crunch, crunch…

Muted footfalls were circling around toward his position and he began to hold his breath. The entirety of his body was covered by arctic camouflage, tree branches, snow, and dirt. Spotting him, especially against the softly falling snow would be nigh impossible. It was clear that whoever was behind him had no intention of sneaking…either that or they were very bad at being stealthy.

Crunch, crunch, crunch…

Every new step on the white surface was getting closer and Dynadin's disciplined relaxation on the matter was now turning to anticipation and slight anxiousness. With his eye still to the rifle's scope he checked the time once more. Seven minutes had passed and it was becoming increasingly obvious that the newly introduced tango would probably end up either stepping on him or tripping over the barrel of his gun.

The time was now.

Crunch, crunch, crunch…

It was the person's rhythm. One that would eventually betray them and result in their death at the hands of a hidden African sniper hiding in the snow at their feet.

CRUNCH!

One footstep landed very near to Dynadin's right ear. His next actions would have been a blur to anyone watching, but that was his signature. With a great gust of upward strength he threw the tarp and snow and dirt and branches off his body. His hands acted both in unison and completely separate from one another, one grabbing a silenced pistol and the other grabbing a small, curved blade.

He brought the blade across the man's stomach as he stood up and lunged to his opposite side.

Swinging around behind him was his other arm, already pulling the trigger, which released a bullet from the chamber into the side of the man's head.

A gentle thud came from the dead body as it fell in the snow, followed by the slightly louder shower of the debris that had been on top of him. The patrol guard hadn't even had a chance to let out a yap, much less compute what was happening to him.

Dynadin had heard that his technique was "stylized" -- it was fast, poetic, fluid, and lethal – but he took pride in also knowing that it was merciful. The man, like so many of the victims before him, had only felt a few milliseconds of pain, if that. The assassin's methods might have been considered over the top to some, but to him? *This is how I work best. It's efficient.*

As he hid the body and dispersed the crimson-splattered snow he recalled one of his favorite lessons he had learned while becoming a young warrior:

"Battles are a musical symphony, young one. Each with its own distinct beats, rhythms, crescendos, and measures. Make sure that you are the conductor."

The lesson was simple, yes, but one that he took to heart every instance where his life or wellbeing was on the line.

Now, he was getting ready to conduct a masterpiece.

Dynadin folded the sniper's tripod, placed it flat in a small trench in the ground, and covered it with the tarp. Within a few hours he would be far from this place, but covering his tracks was a force of habit. When he looked down all he saw was *white* snow which meant he had done a good job scattering the bloodied snow around. The guard's body was now buried under the stuff, not to be found again until warmer months.

There was a golden hue to the bullet that resided in the pistol's chamber as he double checked its existence (another force of habit). Stuck in the snow was the curved blade, its metallic and polished edge now deathly cold to the touch. Traces of red remained at its point. The blade had an extended handle that was hollowed out to keep it light. There was a small button near Dynadin's middle finger and he pressed it as he brought the knife closer to one of the magazines he had strapped to his upper thigh.

A high-intensity, low-range magnet switched on and pulled the magazine closer to it, eventually conjoining the magazine and knife hilt. With a simple press of the button once more the magnet would turn off, releasing the collection of bullets, allowing for Dynadin to reload the gun 10x faster than normal, often without even losing a beat in battle. He knew this because he had timed it during the extensive, self-created and self-taught training he had undergone to perfect this technique.

Be the conductor.

After double checking the straps and laces on his shoes he started toward the complex, running at a decent clip. Time was minimal; the guard he had killed would likely be required to check in any minute now. Dynadin worked best when he had an element of surprise and he was going to ensure that the men in the complex wouldn't know what hit them.

Fresh white snow seemed to fall a little slower as it bounced of this assassin's face like sheets of paper hitting a wall. He couldn't help that part of his dark skin was exposed at this point and as he ran, he did his best to make his footfalls light. Breakings of twigs and crunching of snow was how his last foe had revealed himself; he would not share the same fate.

Ahead of him was the start of the complex, or rather the "back" of it. In the nicer months of the year he imagined that this was a very large yard, somewhat barren of plant life, but outfitted with a glorious, multi-tiered pool. Now however, with the snowfall and bitter cold, the backyard had become a display for death. The scarce trees and bushes were barren, a few inches of snow covered the lawn, and the pool, which strangely had water left in it, was frozen over.

And there were four guards patrolling the area.

Without missing a step, Dynadin kept running head-first into the yard, sights set on the completely unaware guard that was taking a piss on the lawn. The leap he took was powerful, both propelling him upward and forward into the back of the guard.

He wrapped a knee across the man's chest and rolled forward, bringing the guard with him. The poor man hadn't even had a chance to stop urinating and an arc of gold and steam followed as he fell to the ground against his will.

One of the nearby guards was beginning to turn toward the commotion. A bullet entered his head and then the peeing man's head which was now behind him as the assassin's roll completed.

One.

Two.

Secrecy was depleting from the scene, even with the silenced weapon, but Dynadin was not only conducting this battle, he was *writing* it. A third guard stood across the bottom tier of the frozen pool and decided that it would be wiser to call for back-up on his radio first rather than shoot at the assailant.

The exit from his roll had set Dynadin up straight toward the pool and he took a few steps closer to its edge then dropped and slid across the icy, slick surface. Knowing he had made the incorrect decision, the guard dropped his radio in attempt to bring his gun up in time.

A shot entered and exited through his leg before the radio was even halfway to the ground.

Thrown off balance, the man teetered and fell forward, just in time for Dynadin to catch him, stand up, whip around, and slice his throat as the fourth guard riddled his co-worker with friendly fire from the top-most tier of the pool.

Shock plastered his face and he nearly dropped his gun. Had he just killed his comrade, Vlad? Hadn't he had *just* seen him falling into the pool? *How had he gotten up so quickly?*

It was his last thought ever as a dark man emerged from the shoulder of the bloodied body and released a single shot that pulsed through his head.

The backyard was now scattered with streams and streaks of red, and one spot of yellow, amongst the white. Violence littered what was supposed to be a peaceful domain, but Dynadin couldn't pause to feel. *Those men died quickly. I've done my service to them.* This had been the opening bars…it was time to write the music's climax.

He continued up the stairs on the side of the pool, trying not to slip on their wet sections. The loud shots from the guard's assault rifle would have tipped off whomever was left in the complex. That, combined with the fact that he was almost certainly on a camera feed at the moment, assured him that the element of surprise had been lost, at least to some degree. Onward he pressed, truly unconcerned that he could handle whatever resistance he found within the home. Lord knows he had taken on worse before and lived to see the other side.

Atop the stairs he came to the main building, split into several sections. The complex was massive, especially considering that it was someone's home, and was a clear symbol of the occupant's illegal wealth. Its look was square and modern, with sharp angles on nearly every edge, but the base structure was built with planks of wood, or at least that's what showed on the outside. Evil actions didn't have a thing to do with the fact that Mr. Mustache had damn good taste in architecture.

Decisions had to be made at a moment's notice, thus Dynadin chose to enter the door and section of the building to his right. The middle would most likely allow for him to get easily trapped so it had come down to the left or right and he was farther from the former by a wide margin. The door was unlocked and he found it had been a lucky choice as the room seemed to be some kind of laundry or washroom, not exactly the first place one would expect an assassin to look. From what he could tell, all other entrances to the room were closed doors for now and in the spirit of constant-motion, he made his way to the door at the very back, opposite from the one he had come in.

Slowing only for a moment, he placed an ear to the door's frame, listening for commotion on the other side. It seemed distant, but there were men mobilizing. A voice rang louder than the rest.

"Reports of shots in the yard. Cut through the laundry!"

Dynadin backed away from the door, flipped the room's lights off and hid to the hinged side of the frame. With a vehement burst, the door flung open toward the hidden assassin. Knowing the height of the average Russian male, he aimed his weapon at the door.

The bullet travelled through the wood, retaining enough of its speed to enter the man's skull, killing him immediately.

The body slid forward into the room and Dynadin rotated from behind the splintered wood, greeted by another handful of guards who had been following their fallen comrade. The next room, unsurprisingly, was a grand indoor pool, glistening under the natural light provided by its glass ceiling. Caramel-colored marble lined the pool's bottom and sides, with pillars of the stone arching high above to support the few metal beams on the ceiling.

Counting quickly, he tallied eight guards, though he assumed more were in the wings of other rooms connected to this one. Mere milliseconds had passed since he revealed himself and he fired off two more shots at two close enemies.

Each one a deadly head shot.

Blood leapt onto the stone and the remaining men took cover in other rooms or behind the pillars.

Dynadin released a couple cover shots, trying to direct the men where he wanted them to go and ran for a pillar himself, soon crashing into it with his shoulder and bearing down to avoid the gunfire that would be coming soon.

And it did come soon.

Bullets began to shred the marble pillar and litter the floor with dust and chunks of the graham-cracker-colored stone. For a brief moment he felt as if this symphony was no longer in his control. The conductor had changed to this collective of men. With determination he grit his teeth and focused, listening for a very particular sound.

Several seconds passed and he heard it…that indiscernible click among the gunfire that signaled one of them had run out of ammo and had to reload.

Dynadin raised his arm and released several rounds along the length of the glass ceiling.

Glass and snow showered down upon the men and the pool in shimmering unison, proving more than an ample distraction.

Turning the corner, he took back the emblematic baton and planned his next few measures as he bolted to the nearest enemy. There was snow packed around the guard's shirt collar which transformed to red as Dynadin ran past him, slicing his throat, aiming back and putting a bullet through his head.

Dynadin leapt, placed his foot on the wall, and pressed off, gaining more altitude. He soared back toward the pool at the center of the room and came down straddling a guard's shoulders as he fell, rolled, and used the leverage to toss the man into the pool.

A bullet connected with the guard's head as he fell, staining the water an alarming red.

Already up, Dynadin ran, cornering around the side of the pool outfitted with four men trying to aim at their assailant. Some deadly projectile pounded a pillar to the assassin's side, spraying him with debris. He ducked, releasing a rebuttal that connected with a man's cranium and was already upon the next one, once again bringing his knife against a throat and releasing him from the pain with a bullet through the brain.

Without having to be told, Dynadin knew he had spent his last bullet in that mag. Hours upon hours of specific training took over and muscle memory began by releasing the empty mag from the chamber. A bullet buzzed by on his left and he twitched his head to the right, feet still in motion towards the next enemy.

His knife hand came up, pressing the button that released the magnet, and the new collection of bullets began to fall.

The silenced weapon's black, empty butt swallowed the new magazine whole and the gun roared back to life, spitting two violent bullets at the next two guards.

During this, he brought the knife down towards his beltline and pressed the magnet back on; the hollow handle quickly absorbing the next mag and holding onto it. Red painted the walls as the previous two bullets passed through the men's heads.

From eight there were now two.

Water forming on the pool's smooth deck magnified the natural marble patterns underneath, playing tricks on one's eyes. Dynadin continued his lap around the pool, coming around to its long edge. Both of the remaining men had retreated to the room within the side wall and a passage that he guessed led to the middle of the house. The space in the wall drew closer, the door visibly open. Both men stood on the other side of the void, ready to kill the dark-skinned man that had taken out their brethren.

His knees descended and he could feel the slightly cooled liquid pooled underneath his pants. Dynadin slid across the floor, his torso lain back as to make himself a smaller target. The black rectangle approached on one side and his gun rose on his other, ready to shoot across his body. The gleam of two pairs of eyes betrayed their owners in what appeared to be a dark hallway and the sliding man released another pair of shots, each one hitting their target's pupils.

A small regurgitation of blood seemed to leap from the hallway's jowls as Dynadin slowed his maneuver and stood up, making his way to the frame of the hall.

The pool of burgundy was being diluted by the water on deck as he stepped into the mixture, slowly making his way down the eerily dark and lengthy hallway.

Although he had taken out a considerable number of men thus far, he knew there had to be more. *More importantly, where is Mr. Mustache?* By now he was certain the man was in some type of safe room. That is, if he were smart. If he were an arrogant man, he'd most likely be waiting for his assassin in some hole of the house, eager to take a cheap shot.

Eventually the hallway came to an end, and there was certainly an odd silence that had taken over the nearby rooms. Where once there had been orders being barked, feet shuffling to barricades, and weapons being loaded and reloaded, there was now the sound of nothing but white noise. The symphony had died down to something resembling several measures of rest and it was not what the conductor had intended.

The hall opened up into a well-lit and decorated foyer, one that seemed to stem from the main entrance's foyer and would connect to several other areas of the house. Directly across, he could see a massive kitchen, decked out with chrome appliances and countertops of even more rare stone. A grand staircase semi-spiraled upwards toward the back of the tall room, featuring a grey and black floral pattern of carpet that draped over its center. It had to be at least thirty steps to the second floor, but the very top of the staircase didn't even reach half the height of this room, with its walls painted a soft ashen grey. It all reminded him of the winter outside: cold, dreary, dark, but gorgeous nonetheless.

There were several other doors on the curved edges of the room, and Dynadin truly had no idea where to look first. His plan had been to follow a string of men back to their hiding spot, not unlike a child would follow a line of ants back to their hill. With everyone seemingly gone (or dead), it was now up to him to find Mr. Mustache. Given that the stairs were right next to him, he began to jog up them. It was clear that the top floor of the house was only *slightly* smaller than the bottom and a lot of natural light dispersed into several hallways. He noticed that as the dimness of the artificial light transitioned into reflected sunlight, the hues of grey on the walls morphed into very subtle, light blues. Why he was focusing on the paint color of the home's walls he did not know, but the phenomenon was mesmerizing and he begged to know what colors were created during different times of the day and different seasons.

Something snapped him out of this unusual daze.

A line of white light had just appeared, then disappeared from the cracks in the one of the doors.

There was someone there. *Who* or *how many* were answers that he did not know.

Pay attention, Dynadin. Be the conductor.

Ready to strike, he approached the slit of light. Another shadow passed on its other side and the door slammed shut, seemingly out of fear. He bolted to the door's handle and shoved it open, revealing a room that he hadn't anticipated on seeing: a child's bedroom; a boy's by the look of it. For a brief moment he thought he saw the child, or at least his hair, just above the bed. Dynadin started into the room, hoping to comfort the child and instruct him to stay hidden, but a noise to his right stole his attention as a massive shoulder rammed into him, propelling him into the nearby wall.

It wasn't the most painful thing he had ever experienced, but there was shock and discomfort as he attempted to get a grasp on what happened. He straightened out, standing against the wall he had just crashed into.

A fist the size of a grapefruit was headed for his nose, but this assault would not connect.

Dynadin brought his forearm up, swatting the trunk of an arm away and stood face to face with one of the largest men he had ever seen in his life.

Veins ran thick on the man's neck and forearms, and the muscles underneath his black, long-sleeved shirt were begging to escape from the confines of the fabric. The use of steroids was obvious, and it was evident that this man was "the muscle" of the complex's security detail.

Dynadin transitioned the grip on his knife, pointing it downward and punched the man several times in the face. Had his eyes been closed, he might have believed that he was punching one of the columns of marble back down at the pool. On the fifth punch the man pushed Dynadin at the shoulder, tossing him into the wall of the hallway.

A leg came up, surprisingly high, and connected with the small of Dynadin's back, ricocheting him once more into the wall.

Becoming increasingly dazed, Dynadin turned and held up the gun, aiming at the man's head.

A shot fired off but the man had anticipated it…somewhat.

The bullet ripped a gargantuan middle finger from the grapefruit-paw but the man's hand kept coming, grabbing the silenced barrel of the pistol toward him, and punching Dynadin in the face with the other hand.

Blood trickled down the weapon and dripped onto the floor; he had let go of the gun, but he still had his blade. His thick assailant tossed the weapon like a toothpick behind him but took his eye off Dynadin for too long.

The dark assassin's foot slashed in between the man's groin, but the larger man accepted the blow and gripped the kick with his thighs, trapping him. Dynadin tried escaping by thrashing his foot, deeper and more forcefully into the pelvic region, but it didn't seem to help. The large man picked him up, foot still locked, and threw him to the ground with a dull thud, finally releasing his foot.

"Ugh!" Dynadin coughed as the wind left his lungs and he could feel that he'd bitten his tongue. Thick blood collected in his bottom lip, but he kept it there.

As the man bent down to lay his next attack, Dynadin spit the liquid in the man's eyes, stood up, and brought his elbow down on the back of the man's neck.

The giant stumbled from the critical blow, but did not fall. As he came back up, wiping the blood away from his brow and cheeks, Dynadin leapt to straddle the hallway, and as he came back down, he wrapped his legs around the man's neck and fell back toward the staircase whence he'd come.

Laws of physics catapulted the man near to the railing that overlooked the snowy-grey foyer and Dynadin rolled with the fall, grunting as he pushed every necessary muscle fiber into getting his attacker far away from him.

The two men landed very differently from one another, with the large man shaking the floor beneath him and squeaking as he slid across the stone surface. Much to Dynadin's disappointment the man was back on his feet in seconds, charging towards the smaller assassin. *Be the conductor.*

Dynadin rolled once more, this time to the side of the charging beast, and held the curved blade stationary with two hands.

The tip of it caught in the Russian's forearm and travelled up the length of his appendage as he continued running past, eventually exiting near the man's shoulder.

Dynadin turned to look and could see that the man was shocked, less out of pain, and more so from the amount of blood he was losing. The knife's sharp curve had started as a shallow cut but eventually turned into a deep wound, nearly flaying the man from bicep to deltoid. Even Dynadin was taken aback by the outcome of what he had just done. Suffering was not the way he dealt out death, and no matter his size, this man was clearly feeling a large amount of pain right now.

Still though, he kept coming. The whooshing punches were slower, but with all his might the man continued to try and win, to protect his employer. It was rather admirable, though Dynadin held no sympathy for him given what Mr. Mustache was responsible for. He knew it was time to end this and as he continued to dodge the onslaught of punches, which were losing their forcefulness considerably, he came to where his gun had been thrown and reached down for it.

The man, realizing what was happening, garnered one last rage-induced furor and charged.

Dynadin stepped sideways, gripped the man's face, brought his knife across his neck, and put two bullets in the top of his spine.

He would suffer no more.

Knowing that time was steadily wasting at this point (he ignored the annoying thought that Mr. Mustache could have escaped the complex probably five times over by now), he ran back to the boy's room, hoping to offer some solace and keep him out of harm's way. The door had remained open during the skirmish but the hair he had seen behind the bed was now gone. Not wanting to waste time playing hide and seek, he cried out in a Russian whisper.

"BOY!" The hushed search was met with silence. "BOY! Come out. I'm not here to harm you." His Russian was a bit rusty, but these were simple words. There was further silence. "I only wish to make sure you aren't hurt and that you stay out of the way." There was silence still, but the bottom of the cover that hung over the bed flipped up and a boy's face appeared underneath. *Of course he was hiding under the bed* Dynadin smiled. Gently, he knelt down and looked the boy straight in the eye. "It is ok, child. Are you hurt at all?" The boy shook his head, but maintained eye contact. "Good. Just stay hidden here until this is all over. This is a very good hiding spot, no?" He smiled at the boy and it was returned in kind. The assassin reached up and grabbed the bed cover, placed a finger over his lips signaling the boy to remain quiet, and dropped the fabric back to the ground. *Tough boy. He will never forget this day.*

There was a slam that came from downstairs. It sounded like the tall front door closing.

Which means it had been open.

Dynadin rushed out of the room, bloodied knife and half loaded weapon still in hand. As he rounded toward the balcony he saw from where, or rather from whom, the noise had come. Two armed men stood beside Mr. Mustache, who was taller than both of them, and strangely unarmed. Traces of panic were strewn about his face; he seemed to be looking for somebody.

"There isn't much time!" He yelled. "Find my son!" Dynadin, always in motion, leapt over the railing arms first, falling gracefully towards the center where they stood. Moments might have passed where the men looked up with surprise to see an assassin charging toward them like Superman, but alas, that surprise was only reserved for the man with the mustache.

Blood spattered the pristine floor behind the other two men as Dynadin added two more headshots to his count for the day.

Needing to absorb the impact, he tucked his chin and rolled, landing close behind the man he had been waiting three days to kill. Instantly on his feet, the knife lashed out like a viper, slicing the back of the Russian's knees with a shallow but penetrating cut.

"Argh! Son of a bitch!" A thud resonated in the floor as the large man fell forward to his knees, then forward even more, stopping himself with his hands. Dynadin circled around front as Mr. Mustache pushed himself back up to a prayer kneel. "You bastard." He was breathing shallow, fast breaths. "Who are you? What are you here for?" He was met only with Dynadin's dark scowl and brown and white eyes. "Why would you prevent a man from trying to save his son?" An angry arm thrust to the sky in frustration.

"I don't wish to harm your son. He isn't the one who deserves to die." A sudden and disheartening thought entered his mind as he remembered that this pervert had dealings and fetishes for child pornography. *What a sick,*

sick man. Dynadin just hoped the boy had never been involved in any of it.

"I'm not talking about you, you…you…" he interrupted the man's search for a curse.

"What are you talking about? Who else wants to harm your son?"

"The missile headed straight for this complex courtesy of the Aqarab Mayta's provost." Dynadin was a bit surprised that this man had revealed his interaction with the group so easily. "Yeah. I'm one of them. So fuck you. Somehow they knew you were here and now they're wiping out loose ends." He was breathing deep now, trying to manage the pain from the injury to the back of his legs. Dynadin tried to comprehend how they knew he was here and to what doom he had just sentenced them all.

Interrupting the silence, Mr. Mustache's phone rang. Almost reluctantly he removed it from his front jacket pocket. A stroke of paleness sucked the color from his face as he brought the phone to his ear. Seconds later he was holding the phone out towards Dynadin. He grabbed it with his knife hand and put a bullet through Mr. Mustache's brain with the other, not noticing his body crumple. The voice on the phone was clear as day.

"I presume you just killed my associate?" A brief pause. "No matter. That's what I wanted anyway. Tell me, Dynadin…oh yes, I know your name…but tell me, how fast can you run?" Dynadin refused to answer. "Stubborn jackass you are. Do you know who this is? Ah, shit. You won't answer anyway. This is David Harper. I'm the man who will kill you. I *know* it's been you and your posse taking out my men. Truth be told, you've been

doing me a lot of favors in that regard, but you've out-
lived your usefulness." The hard voice turned into a
growl of distaste. "Enjoy the missile."

Those words had hardly digitized through the speaker
before he dropped the phone and ran full sprint up the
stairs. *Must get the boy.* The thought was visible in his
mind as a pulsing, bright white light while all other
thoughts had gone black.

Remnants of the fight with the massive man were
scattered over the scuffed floor and walls.

Dynadin tore sharply into the boy's room.

"Boy!" It came out as a yelp. He couldn't have more
than a handful of seconds left. "Boy! We must go now,
please!" Panic was overtaking him. He could not leave
the boy to die at the hands of such cruelty, but he didn't
want to lose his own life in the process. The boy remained hidden as Dynadin's pounding heart grew louder.
A part of him believed he could hear the screaming missile ripping through the air above, but it could have also
been in his head.

It was time to go.
The boy would have to die.
Dynadin had to save himself.

There was a glass window in the boy's room and he
knew there was no time to run back downstairs and exit
out the front door. He hoped there was something worth
landing on across the void of the window.

A pair of fingers poked out from beneath the bed, and
soon a whole hand.

Damn child, there is no time for games right now!

Dynadin, realizing he might permanently regret this decision, grasped the child's hand and yanked hard. With a scream the child emerged from under the bed as Dynadin started for the window, gathering the child in his arms as he went. Glass shattered as the side of his body drove into it and gravity took the man and boy toward the ground. A shallow snowbank helped to break their fall, of which Dynadin took the brunt, and the boy was still screaming, trying to escape from this snatcher's clutches.

Ignoring the boy, he scooped him up once more, snow falling off his face and clothes like soft blankets, and ran – ran as far away from the house as he could.

Heat singed the back of his neck and he could feel the skin being burned. A sound followed that was so loud it nearly caused him to pass out. These were coupled with a shockwave as the missile obliterated the house as if it were toothpicks, blasting the pair farther from the house into the forest where Dynadin had been lying in wait only a short time ago.

For a while there was nothing. His thoughts were void and his mind empty. His body was attempting to cope and repair itself from the close proximity of the missile's wrath.

Finally, he did wake. Nausea took over almost instantly and Dynadin threw up in the snow before he even had a chance to get his bearings. Sunlight was fading now, being replaced with the massive wreckage of a mansion on fire. It looked like hell had found its way to the surface. Flames licked the air and spiraled upward while the decaying structure moaned audibly, as if in pain. Bits of debris had flown far into the forest, even farther than

Dynadin, and several trees were slowly burning, hot drips of fire and ash falling off their branches and sizzling to death in the snow.

Suddenly, a memory. *The boy!*

Dynadin began glancing around frantically for the child, sitting up and feeling another strong wave of nausea. The vomit stayed down this time, his brain forcing his body to cooperate with the task at hand: finding the boy. After a few seconds of searching, he saw him, lying near the base of a tree not too far off. He made his way over to him, slowly, and was relieved to find him breathing.

"Thank God." It came out as a sigh. On the boy's brow there was a small gash, slowly oozing reddish blood, but it didn't seem life threatening. *Poor thing.* Assuming this boy had escaped his father's more detestable sins, he was now most likely an orphan with no home and no possessions other than the clothes on his back, ones that were singed black.

But at least he's alive.

Fear crept down Dynadin's spine. The missile strike had come way too close to becoming his demise and it was clear that Harper had a complete disregard for life. Yet, it was also clear that his intel was boundless and that he was the true conductor. How much Harper really knew about Dynadin and who he was working for was now a complete mystery and it was these uncertain shadows of guessing that left him feeling defeated despite the fact that Mr. Moustache was now dead.

Smoke rose from the heaping pile of wood, concrete, and stone. Off in the distance, sirens called, indicating that they were racing to a place of emergency. Dynadin glanced once more at the boy, knowing that he would be found by the authorities once they got here. There was nothing more he could do for him now and he needed to vacate the scene, quickly. This young boy's life, though now marked by tragedy, was completely in front of him. Dynadin just hoped that he did something good with it.

"Live well." He prayed for the boy.

As the sirens drew nearer, he made his way farther into the woods, back the way he had come. There would eventually be a mountain road that he would follow to a safe house where he could gather his things, change his clothes, and exit the country. Snow had stopped falling, but the temperature had dropped considerably, especially now that he was away from the wreckage. He'd been walking for less than a minute when he heard a shrill, young scream, void of any language at first but then a word.

"FATHER!" The cry in Russian cut through the silent forest with the sense of desperation that only a child's plea can bring. Dynadin hung his head, sad once more for the child to even have to see the destruction, but continued onward. Whether the boy had known how evil his father was or not was inconsequential at the moment; it was still a young life now drastically altered.

Dusk solidified itself as the assassin kept trekking through the annoying snow, a new fire having been released in his gut. He knew now who the enemy was; he had spoken to him directly on the phone.

And he had tried to kill him, nearly succeeding.

Dynadin wouldn't let that mistake happen again.

This is my symphony...

I'm the fucking conductor!

CHAPTER VI

FAMILY TIES

SATURDAY | SEPT 15TH | 2018

"Who in the hell is your assassin?"

It was an aggressive question that bit the air surrounding it. Rachel's tone was one of exasperation. She would have her answer, and she would have it right now.

Thick sunlight drenched the Costa Rican hideout that they'd been in for many months now and the homey smell of their breakfast was being replaced with the smells of the ocean just a few miles away. Still the question hung without answer, two of the parties in the room, Rachel and Ian, wondering when Someone would talk.

Someone had not revealed he had an assassin moments ago simply for dramatic effect.

No.

It was time. Time that he brought everyone up to speed. On everything. They had earned his trust over the past year. Should one of them betray him…well, at this point they were so close to the end that abandoned trust seemed to be of little consequence. *They've earned the right to know.*

This decision was one that had long been gestating within him. An assassin that he had jet-setting across the world on covert missions was actually the least of his secrets and if he wanted utter and complete devotion from these people…*employees? Friends?* Whatever he wanted to call them, he would need to know they were fully on board. It was the only way they could hope to prevent David from inflicting any further global damage. Someone took a deep breath, and exhaled.

He was ready.

"His name is Dynadin, and I met him long ago when I was working for N.E.T.S. Out of all the men I've met in my life, he is, without a doubt, one of the most just."

Rachel bit back right away. "What do you mean, 'just'? Who is he? Where has he been this whole time?"

Ian remained seated, arms crossed, as his gaze swapped between the conversing pair.

"I guess by 'just' I mean that he is a good man. He had a hard upbringing but still lives by a certain code of ethics and morals. I trust him absolutely.

"Who he is doesn't really matter. I'm sure you'll meet him soon enough. I've instructed him to return here following the mission that he is presently a part of. As to where he has been this whole time? Think about it Rachel." Someone wanted her to think critically and he prepared the statement as such. Not speaking down to her, but rather encouraging her intelligence. Like a child who received a question as an answer to their question, Rachel leveled her glowering eyes at Someone, but was actively contemplating. After a short while she had arrived at her answer.

"He's been killing the people that *we've*," She pointed to Ian then herself, "been I.D'ing this past year. Right?"

Ian interjected. "We tag 'em, he bags 'em?"

"Something like that, yes." Ian swore he saw the old man's eye's roll, but let it go. To him, these so called "secrets" that Someone was beginning to spill were all fairly obvious and, at the end of the day, they didn't affect him. The only reason he was here was because he figured this was the best path to seek retribution on David for trying to have him killed. *And the girl*…Frustrated by the subconscious thought, Ian gave his head a brief nod and focused on the conversation.

"And you have been organizing all of this behind our backs?" Some of Rachel's more fierce mannerisms were beginning to rear their formidable heads. "Who have we been marking for death? How are *you* sure they should even be killed?"

"Rachel, do I really need to answer that for you?"

"Yes! This is our conscience," She glanced at Ian who gave visual cue that he wanted no part in this. "Ok. This is *my* conscience you're fucking with!"

"I get that, but – "

"Do you? Whose blood do I have on my hands, Someone?" An exasperated laugh escaped. "And for God's sake, what is your real name?"

Ian could see this was becoming unproductive and reached out to quiet her.

"Rachel, just – "

"No. Thank you, Ian, but I can handle this." Someone interrupted politely as he trained his focus back on Rachel. "Rachel, I'm coming to you, ready to give answers to these simple questions you are asking as well as answers to questions you don't even know you have yet. So please, sit down, and shut the hell up. It's my turn to talk."

With the shocked look of a scolded child, Rachel sat back down, and pretended to look like she was ready to listen. Inside she was boiling.

How do I know I can even trust him? Even after this whole year?

What if N.E.T.S. are still the "good guys"?

Someone continued, now accompanied by welcomed silence.

"Dynadin has been acting on my behalf for many years now. I'm still fairly effective in the field, but not like him. He's like nothing I've ever seen before. The way he moves and shoots and operates…it's quite poetic actually.

"Since the fallout of The Will, around the same time that you two joined this, this, resistance, if you will, I knew it was time to begin playing the end game. Dynadin agreed. You see, the thing about end games is, they're usually violent and more than a little messy.

"As you both gathered intel from the field, I combined it with all of the tracking and spying I've been doing on David. I'll admit, without Zane inside the organization my reach has been diminished, but I've still got some access. Anyway, with intel comes names. Players. Contacts that David has covertly attributed to this organization in some fashion. We've been taking them out as they come up." Someone could see the disapproval in Rachel's scowl, but she remained silent. It was time for some tough love.

"Look. We all've seen what the Dead Scorpions are capable of. The Will was the single greatest terrorist attack in human history and by a margin so wide that it dwarfs the competition. Not a single individual has answered for that crime in the international scope of justice. The *earth's* morale is crumbling. These people are bad and they're doing bad things. This isn't an example of 'bad by association' with the Aqarab Mayta. They're helping an invisible organization run by a man who, at the moment, will never be caught. He is continuing onward, unperturbed by anyone other than us; the gnats buzzing around his head.

"We have NO time for someone to play judge, jury, and *then* executioner. Sometimes, in the face of an evil this omnipotent, one must act without hesitation, knowing they will suffer whatever consequences follow those choices. It's a burden I've been shouldering for many, many years now."

"And one that you've now *forced* onto us!" Rachel exclaimed.

"I understand that and it's just another addition to a long, long list of sins, Rachel. If it makes you feel better, I've been calling the shots here; you're acting on *my* orders. And to be fair, you've questioned them more than a handful of times. If you're worried about your purity, I'd say you're still fairly clean given the line of work you're in." There was a brief combination of rage and jealousy with that last statement, and despite an open-mouthed attempt, Rachel had no rebuttal. Someone made eye contact with Ian, but he too had nothing to say. *At least not yet.*

"Does that make sense to you two?" It was a question that stayed unanswered. "It's us versus them and we've been doing a hell of a job. Dozens of players in David's back pocket are now dead because of *us*! Our progress counts for something and despite its lack of legality, I view it as a wholly positive thing." Ian finally spoke up.

"Fine. We've been killing for you and they've been bad people. Where exactly is this conversation going? You claimed you were going to reveal truths but so far the only bombshell you've dropped is that you have an assassin in the shadows. I guessed as much several months ago. Otherwise our actions would have been useless. We get that you're feeling righteous, killing all these contacts, but just remember that I *was* one of those contacts at one point. Doesn't change the fact you're avoiding taking aim at David, and that we're avoiding whatever the real point of this discussion is."

"You simply lost your way, Ian. You were never one in the same with the people that we've been killing." Someone's tone was somber and the statement's brief hint at a greater history made the moment awkward.

"Get on with it, Someone."

The oldest man in the room nodded his head in agreement. It was time. He took a deep breath, rubbed the top of his head for no reason other than to seek the reassurance that he existed, and began.

"I think the best way to move this discussion forward is for me to tell you about David and my falling out. It came to a head on a night that has haunted my memories for all my life…"

Many, many years ago, David and I used to be colleagues, friends even. N.E.T.S. had been established for a couple of decades but was really just starting to come into its own as an agency. It was a tumultuous time around the world during the Cold War and we were constantly busy. N.E.T.S. didn't have a "head" at the time, per say; we were beginning to establish a hierarchy structure that could act independently of the very few government officials who actually knew about us. They were the ones that had been issuing our orders, but they sought even more plausible deniability and we were seeking more freedom from their red tape.

At some point during all of this I met a new female agent, Leah Lancaster, at N.E.T.S., and we fell in love and got married. She was the single most incredible person I've ever met and was truly one of the agency's best field operatives. She was lethal, seductive, and smart as hell; she always seemed to be twenty steps ahead of everyone else. Our relationship saw a bit of contention within the organization, but once the powers that be saw how well we worked together, it became a moot point. N.E.T.S. was full of professionals, who eventually accepted our relationship and, like David, seemed genuinely happy for us.

There were good years. Ones where Leah and I were the agency's go-to field runners, along with David, and we were jet-setting around the world. Dangerous missions – important missions – but in this line of work there are still many things to enjoy. It was glamorous in between the violent times, and we both trusted each other deeply. It still amazes me to this day how frequently and how close the world has come to being in a very bad predicament. I know we saw more than our fair share of very close calls.

Anyway, I started noticing changes in David early on. He had always been very patriotic and had a bit of a temper, but this was different. He was becoming very discouraged with the future of the country. I mostly ignored his huffing and puffing, something I now regret, but I do remember that when he really started getting into it, there was a subtle darkness behind his eyes. One that suggested that what he was bitching about was something on which he planned to take action. These thoughts and feelings never really outright consumed him, though I would surmise they did so internally, but Leah and I could both

*tell that the David who had been our friend was morph-
ing into someone we didn't really care for.*

*A time passed and Leah became pregnant. We were
beyond excited, slightly surprised, and happy to start
thinking about the potential of starting our lives outside
of N.E.T.S. It was always something Leah and I had discussed, though I do admit the biggest push to get serious
about the topic came at the discovery of the pregnancy.
Our fellow agents were excited for us, including David.
Looking back I think it might have been feigned joy on his
part, but I digress. Obviously the pregnancy complicated
things a bit at the agency. Leah was removed from the
field but still played a vital role in communications for
most missions. I remained out in operations, though the
missions I was selected for became increasingly less dangerous. It was odd being out there alone. I had done solo
ops before, but the weight of becoming a father added the
burden of extra caution at almost every turn.*

*The pregnancy went smoothly, all things considered,
and when it came time to find out the sex, we discovered
that Leah was carrying fraternal twin boys. Again we
were delighted, a bit scared now, but still very excited to
meet our two new additions. We prepared during the remaining months of her pregnancy and then around the 9
month mark she gave birth to two very healthy, handsome
boys. To say life was good would be an understatement.*

*Throughout all of this, N.E.T.S. was still trying to fig-
ure out their separation from the U.S. government, as
well as their hierarchy. It turns out that, right about the
time the boys were born, a position was being created. It
was designed to oversee the entire organization, so naturally it came with a lot of power, but also a lot of risk. It
was decided by the Secretary of Defense that should*

N.E.T.S. ever be discovered, the blame would fall solely on the head of the organization. Or at least that's what the government would try to set it up as. Despite our talks to leave N.E.T.S., Leah and I had some discussions around me pursuing this role, the head of N.E.T.S., some of which were a bit heated. But in the end, we both knew the job would pay well enough so that she would really be able to focus on becoming a mother, and as the leader, I would be out of the field. Not to mention, with her husband at the head of the organization it would be easy for her to get back in at some non-ops-related capacity should she get bored. Our minds were made up; I would pursue the head position of N.E.T.S.

Obviously I wasn't going to be the only person gunning for that position, though I'd argue that I was the most qualified. Several other candidates began the vetting process with me, including David Harper. By this point, Leah and I had consciously established a distance between us and David. Not drastic by any means, but I think he noticed. Either way, when it came to this role, he was easily the most aggressive of the candidates. He wanted it, and he wanted it bad. Sometimes those who seek out power the most should be the last ones to have it...

Months down the road, with Leah and me still enjoying home life with the children, the final candidates for the role were very clearly me and David. Nothing moves quickly with the federal government and this was no different, despite how eager we may have been to have the agency avoid typical, bureaucratic red tape. But it was when the pool narrowed down that things started getting bad. With neither of us really being a front runner in the process, David took his chance and ran with it. Having no fear of consequences he began to harass me and Leah, mildly at first, but then more intensely. On a few instances I got in his face and promised that I would end him should he continue to be unethical about pursuing the role. He'd back off for a time, but then come right back at it. Telling us that we were never talented in the field, that officials had been bad mouthing us in interviews, mocking us for marrying, even going so far as to deride us for having children. It was all highly unprofessional and very odd. It was like he had forgotten that we had been friends for a time, not to mention that we were fucking fellow operations agents in one of the most hidden organizations in the world. The saying goes, "sticks and stones..." I believe? It was more like bullets and fists in our world, so it was surprising that he would think we'd really take any great offense to his obnoxious heckling.

Regardless, the process was moving forward and near the end of it rumors were flying that the head role would be going to me. I certainly didn't want to count my chickens before they hatched, but I was getting the indication that said rumor would end up being true. Once this came out however, David became reclusive. He was still in the running, and still number two, but the rumblings of defeat seemed to force him to play his final hand: the attempted murder of me and my family.

My guess is that David's passion...his need to have that position of power was what finally drove him over the edge. As a N.E.T.S. agent, he was very nearly successful too.

Leah and I had just finished dinner one night, and the boys were sleeping in the living room in their cribs while

we watched TV. It's odd. How normal our lives were af-
ter the children. With Leah at home and me working a
more covert version of a 9 to 5, our lives were shock-
ingly, pleasantly mundane. That normalcy made us too
comfortable I fear.

David broke into our house – I'm still not entirely
sure how – and caught both of us off guard.

I heard the silenced shot over the TV but by the time I
was able to react in the slightest, Leah slumped forward
on the couch and slid onto the floor, blood leaking down
the back of her neck.

Despite the horror, my training and instincts kicked
in, but David was equally as trained and not nearly as
rusty. The butt of his pistol came down on me before I
could react, not knocking me out, but easily giving him
the upper hand. I turned around to face him on my knees,
with his gun trained at my forehead.

How a man who had once been our friend could do
this, I'll never know. He was dressed in all black, but left
his face exposed. I'm sure he got some sort of sick delight
in revealing himself to me but I might have guessed even
with a mask. His face was eerily relaxed and his eyes
dead; he looked like a man who both did and did not
want to carry out these actions.

I tried to remain calm, but being a father changes
you. All I wanted was for him to spare my children. As
Leah's body pooled blood onto the floor next to me, I im-
agined a similar fate for myself, one that I had accepted.
But I would not envision my children like that. David be-
gan speaking, of what I don't really remember. He
seemed to be going on and on about why he had *to be the*

Head of N.E.T.S.; something about how it was his destiny. I remember that I had begun talking, interrupting him, asking him to spare my sons.

We were two men babbling, not even listening to the other, both so deeply concentrated on what we wanted to say that we ignored the other. In hindsight, I should have used this time to strike, but at the time the thought left me even more fearful for the boys. They say hindsight is 20/20. I say that hindsight is a blind bitch.

Eventually we both arrived at silence and simply stared at each other. This was not a version of David that I had ever met and I knew in that moment that the power he would gain would be dangerous. It would be used unwisely.

That was my last thought before he fired the weapon at my head.

The bullet entered the top of my skull, skimmed through a brief portion of my brain, and exited out the back of my head. I'm sure to David it looked like I was surely dead, and doctors later told me that my being alive was a "miracle of millimeters". Had the bullet dug even a couple millimeters deeper into my brain tissue, I would have been either dead or in a vegetative state. I'll never know this for sure, but part of me thinks that David, perhaps subconsciously, pulled up at the last moment before firing. I was nearly at point blank range and he skimmed the top of my head? Perhaps a wave of guilt from Leah's execution had begun to form? I'll probably never know.

Obviously I have to fast forward the story a bit seeing as how I wasn't exactly present for David's next moves. Zane knew something was up when I wasn't at work and rescued me from the hospital, for fear that any type of investigation might lead to N.E.T.S. exposure. The media had been hushed about my family's killings, but it wouldn't be long until more N.E.T.S. agents would catch on. It had been a really dumb move on David's part. To not kill me completely that is.

Word began to spread that I, Leah, and our children had indeed been killed and Zane tells me that David spun some wild story about us having to assist some terrorist organization down in Brazil through blackmail. Somewhere he got the evidence that supported this bullshit and marked my wife and me as enemies of N.E.T.S., postmortem of course. The powers that be were impressed and given that David had been their second choice anyway, they made him Head of N.E.T.S.

As all of this moved forward, Zane and I were the only ones who knew the truth. We vowed to end the man, but at that point neither of us was in a position to do so. It would have to be slow and it would have to be with minimal damage to N.E.T.S. I eventually healed, with the help of Zane as my caretaker, and we quickly brought ourselves up to speed on David's actions, and what the organization as a whole was achieving. Truth be told, the agency was great for many years. They were performing in total secrecy, had virtually no agents that were KIA or taken as POW, averted several crises, and removed some very bad people from existence. But David's secrets ran deep.

Eventually Zane and I did uncover David's hidden agenda and all of his side hobbies. The man kept very busy and after much researching, monitoring, and analyzing, it was clear that David was the head of something very powerful apart from and in addition to N.E.T.S. He was damn good at covering his tracks, whether out of habit or suspicion I don't know, but it didn't take us too long until we had full access to his second life. Shady dealings with dangerous characters, some of whom N.E.T.S. would later eliminate, orders given to unknowns which directly conflicted with what N.E.T.S. was doing, recruitment out of all the wrong and bad places in the world, and a lot of talk about scorpions; it was all right there in front of us and we just had to piece it together. It took us longer than I would have liked but we did figure out what was going on and had been waiting for an opportune moment to take action.

That action was derailed when I discovered a secret which he had buried deeper than most; one that instantly diverted my attention elsewhere.

David hadn't killed my sons that night. He had spared them and they were still alive, growing up thousands of miles apart in different orphanages, completely unaware of the fact that the other existed. They were infants on that awful night after all. Their whole lives had been void of knowledge of any family.

I was initially relieved but devastation soon followed. I could take no action to meet them. How would I explain myself? How would they even remotely believe what I had to tell them? And even if they did, what next? David's dealings and whatever future plans he had were a threat to global security. Was I going to throw my concern and responsibility for all that away because of my sons who I hadn't seen for over a decade?

Zane and I talked about eventually bringing them in "under the tent", but that wasn't a possibility for many years down the line. So, my new job became twofold. I tracked David, and I tracked my sons. Life was lonely for a very long time, especially knowing that I had two of my own out there. Zane was my only point of contact with the outside world other than a few trivial friendships and female relationships throughout my travels. Luckily, staying in shape and "the job" kept me busy, but I cannot deny that there weren't a few really depressing periods of time.

As I tracked the boys, it was clear that their life paths would not be similar, and as I tracked David it was equally clear that, while we knew a lot, we didn't know enough. It always amazed me how much information he would not include in his dealings which made connecting the dots a very tricky thing to do. Time passed, years actually, and there came a time that I was closest to reaching out to one of my boys. David had just recruited one of them for N.E.T.S. and he had accepted. Zane talked me down off the metaphorical ledge by insisting that this worked to our advantage. Once the boy, at this point a man, had established himself within N.E.T.S., Zane would recruit him and he would work with the two of us as a double agent against Harper. I followed his advice, as it was truly sound wisdom, and we continued on with our work.

Unfortunately that plan never came to fruition as the boy became very attached to David. The man had taken him in under his wing, given him a better life, shown him what he was capable of, and seemingly became his career mentor. Again I was devastated, but what could I do? Reaching out held too much risk given their close relationship and he could have easily revealed me to David.

So I watched. And I continued keeping tabs on him. It was all I could do and it was the only way I could feel close to my son. Within N.E.T.S., he rose to the top, almost astronomically so. I thought this might have been because of his connection with David, but when I would watch some of his field footage and his stats – man was he talented. And so was his wife. Soon after joining N.E.T.S., as agents, they married and began working as a team. At first I thought this was a horrible idea, bound for tragedy like my situation, and I was frankly surprised that David let it happen. But I'll be damned. They were phenomenal together both in the real world and out on ops. Their connection was rather jarring and I was so proud of my son, and soon very proud of my daughter-in-law.

A little more than a year ago is when everything be-gan to fall apart when she was captured in Rome, and then died in Australia. It was soon after that when the President was assassinated and the world changed for-ever. As we all know The Will occurred shortly after and this is the day that my son died, giving up his life to save countless ones on the ground.

His name was Bryson Cooper and I'm his father, Ed-ward Dahlquist. But most of my friends call me Dahl.

With the story of the past finished, the room settled into an uncomfortable silence, disrupted only by the oc-casional sounds of sniffling coming from Rachel. Dahl had to admit: the confession felt good to get off his chest. For a year now he'd been lying to them, trying to gauge if he could trust them with his most personal and important secrets. There was a euphoric sense of relief cascading through him. The last half hour had been highly therapeu-tic, but he knew there was still more to discuss.

"I'm sorry it took me so long to tell you, and perhaps I should have done so sooner, but I had to know that you could be trusted." The duo across from him in the kitchen remained silent, still processing the deep tale that Dahl had just provided them. It was a lot to take in, he knew.

Ian stared at a tile on the ground, looking far past it, but directing his thoughts to its center. Dahl's story had been true, he'd watched for the classic signs of deception, but found not one. The man had sincerely spilled out his secrets, but Ian was underwhelmed. Sure, it proved that Dahl knew what he was doing, and *why* he was doing it, as tragic as it was, but Ian didn't really care about the reasoning as long as he continued to target David. Having not known Bryson other than their split second encounter on the highway and hearing of his tales of heroism over Denver, that revelation also rung hollow. He knew Rachel would take it hard though…

Rachel felt devastated, but for whom she couldn't quite decide. She knew too much now – it wasn't fair that Bryson never knew. He never truly knew his mother before she'd been brutally murdered right next to him, nor had he ever known his father was an honorable man who cared for him deeply. The painful gouge of Bryson's death was opened anew, and she missed him more than she had in months. Him and Elena.

Without consciously trying, her thoughts would shift to Someone, or "Dahl", as he preferred to be called now, and the troubled life he had lived the past few decades. Between being shot, believing your family was dead, being alone, realizing your family was mostly alive but still not being able to see them, and your son dying when you'd never actually met him – it was all a tough card to be dealt. She regretted getting mad at him, doubting him all those times, and mostly she felt guilty.

You've been a bitch, Rachel.

She immediately defended herself against the accusation realizing that she hadn't known, but even still the guilt persisted. In a situation as sad as this one, it was hard not to feel blame for something you had done. This was a family that had been torn apart by an evil man. *For Christ's sake! Bryson had never even seen his twin brother, much less known about him.* Which begged the question:

"So," Rachel started but had to sniffle. "What happened to Bryson's brother? Whatever happened to your other son?"

It was a thick question and it made the air similarly consistent; it hung like a shade. Dahl's eyes went distant, encapsulating years of secrets and history within them and he hung his head.

Out of exhaustion.

Out of relief.

Out of fear.

"He had a much different path in life than Bryson did." He began. "The orphanage he was placed into wasn't as nurturing, but after several years the boy found himself in Europe, where he studied at Oxford for a short while before an opportunity arose.

"During this time, there was a recruitment undertaking happening all throughout the world, even in America, for an organization that would see to her downfall.

"They were small, but growing quickly and they had a driving vision that appealed to many, with rich promises of certain lifestyles to those who needed more motivation. The Aqarab Mayta snatched him up, and, much like his brother, he found great success within his role." There was a pause; Dahl was realizing something. "It's funny…but David Harper became closer with both of my sons than I ever was able to." Sorrow laced the statement and Rachel wished he would keep going. She could feel herself internally willing Dahl to continue with his story. And so he did.

"My other son, Bryson's brother and fraternal twin, joined the organization that Bryson was trying to stop. Until last year, that is, when a human missile crashed between him and his brother on a highway and led to a slew of events that now has that man, my son, sitting in this room with us right now."

Ian had known all along; he had felt the connection but not been able to put a finger on what it was. Once the story began though, he had recognized it as his own.

There's no way. How could he be my father?

But he knew so much. So much of what he said was true.

About everything.

Across the room, Rachel returned to her soft sobs, the heavy emotions of the last hour weighing heavy on all three of them. There were so many angles to this that Ian couldn't even comprehend them all. His mind struggled to stick to one factoid and raced around, not stopping for more than a few precious seconds on any one thought.

Concentrate.

His lungs filled with air as he took a calming breath and closed his eyes. *The facts. What are the facts?*

You are this man's son.

This man's name is Edward Dahlquist, or "Dahl".

Your mother was murdered when you were a baby.

You had a brother. A twin.

His name was Bryson Cooper.

He worked for N.E.T.S.

He sacrificed his life.
You never knew him.
Your father works to stop David Harper.
David Harper is the man who tried to have you killed.
David Harper will die.

When Ian's eyes opened, he realized that both Rachel and Dahl were looking at him. Rachel with concern and Dahl with guilt. The man looked different now, knowing that he was his father. Aged more perhaps, but also wiser. At this point, it was too soon for Ian to tell if he was happy or mad about the revelation, but he damn sure believed it. Dahl's eyes met his and they studied each other, as if having their own private conversation. Dahl apologizing for the years lost and his mistakes, Ian acknowledging them and asking for forgiveness of his own sins. Quietly they broke their gaze, having now had their first emotional interaction as father and son in decades.

For them it had been more valuable than any hug or handshake could have hoped to be.

Rachel, accepting but not comprehending this exchange, was relieved for the two of them and quite frankly exhausted from the roller-coaster ride of a morning this was turning out to be. They were a team now, with each other's motives clear. Not to mention, everyone now had an *actual* name. This was good, and with the doubt behind her, she knew they could do some serious damage to David and the Dead Scorpions. But she had one final question that had been nagging at her ever since Dahl had revealed David as the snake in the grass.

It was more prominent than ever and she just couldn't help blurting it out. "Why would David do *any* of this?" The gears were turning. "What's his motive? What's his endgame?" Dahl squared his shoulders and told her the truth.

"That's the one thing that I've never been able to figure out. And it's the single thing that terrifies me the most."

A MIND GONE MAD

10 YEARS AGO...

A rat – vermin – already sickened with disease, sniffed the side of the subway tracks and licked the cold grimed steel. These concrete tunnels were dark; hardly lit by the deceasing bulbs that failed daily.

Without warning the rat skittered away. To where? He did not know. But he had felt the hard metal object vibrate under his tongue so he knew that the iron monsters were coming.

Soon enough, the tracks were rattling loudly, only to be outdone by the screeching of an oncoming subway train whose own devices were clashing, metal versus metal; trying to stay on the tracks safely before the next destination. Its headlights relieved the archaic tunnel lights of their duty, even if only for a brief moment, as it hurtled past, carrying a wave of hot, sweaty, stench-filled air.

This was the New York Subway and it was an ordinary day.

"Listen my nigga!" Onboard the train a young man continued to explain his predicament to his colleague. "So I got this idea right…now, hear me out nigga. But I think this shiiiiit might work." His friend seemed disinterested in his antics but begrudgingly tried to pay attention anyway. He was too busy trying to roll a joint, but the damn train's bumps and shudders had caused him to do a sloppy job thus far.

"Yeah Mike. I'm listening." The reply was monotone.

"Ok sick. So it's like this. Neither of us like to work right? Fuck that shit. Ima live my life the way it's meant to be lived you know? Fuckin bitches, doing whatever drug I fucking damn well please, and shit like that. Ya feel me my nigga?"

"Mhmm. Shit!" His bud had just crumbled and fallen to the floor. With lightning speed he picked up as much as he could, blew on it – just to make sure all the germs were off – and started his fourth attempt at rolling his joint.

"So if neither of us likes work, cause like, who the fuck does, why don't we get the government to pay for our shit? Like dawg, I've researched this shit, pshh I Googled the fuck out of it, and I'm pretty sure we would be qualified for like foodstamps, especially if we don't work because of like our low income ya'know what I'm sayin? Then I know a dude who can take those foodstamps and, I don't know what shit he does with em`, but we basically get money for em` to use on whatever the fuck we want to! Ain't that sick nigga?"

"Mhmm."

"I think we should do it. Shit would be dope. Like if you think about it, I could have the Prez straight up payin for MY fuckin green leaf. Or even better…" He lightly slapped his friend's shoulder in jubilation. "He could be payin for my fuckin pussy. Oh shiiiit!" At this he began to laugh almost hysterically while his companion glowered at him; his slap had just knocked almost half the weed out of the nearly finished product.

"God mother fucker Mike! Why'd you gotta hit me right when I was about to finish this beautiful mother fucking joint? Ya stupid ass nigga. And tha's a fuckin stupid ass idea right there too. You think the government is just going to be all like, 'Oh here Mike. Take these food stamps and switch that shit out for cash! I hope the pussy and the green is good!' Hell no! Ain't no way that shit works. It's fuckin retarded."

"Screw you, nigga! I told you I Googled that shit. It's legit!"

David Harper sat across the aisle of the train and had been listening to these two buffoons' conversation for much longer than he would have liked. There was no alternative however because, on this crammed subway train, they seemed to have no idea that their voices were carrying, and were the only things that everyone *not* wearing headphones could hear.

There were children on board, some elderly folks too, but mostly it *was* filled with headphone-wearing citizens just going to work. Even still, some of them had taken their earpieces out just to hear what all the drama was about.

On the surface, David appeared to be a man who was hardly noticing the conversation, absorbed in his own thoughts, but on the inside his blood was boiling.

These were the people that he loathed.

One of the things he found immediately interesting was that both of these fine young gentleman were Caucasian. Granted, based on their speech, and dress they seemed to be racially confused, but given the loudness and tone of their voices, and the fact that David was a black man, their use of the "N" word was incredibly offensive. Sure, it was all "part of the culture" now, but the observation that they used it so freely, without any thought attached to its despicability, and right in front of an African American person no less, made that strike one in David's book.

Strike two began and ended with their, or rather, Mike's, "fool proof" plan to swindle the government. Not only was it entirely inaccurate, it was selfish. David knew that there were certainly people in this country who had gotten away with gaming the system in different ways to work to their advantage, and they were also part of this same problem. But there were also those who worked hard and needed that extra help, treasuring each time they were able to buy something *without* government assistance.

Aside from the fact that Mike thought a simple ten-minute Google search would solve his problems (a clear sign of the failures of his public education, among other things), his resulting conclusions were so idiotic, so cheap and lazy, that it enraged David.

Ah, but it's a rage you've felt before.

Not only did Mike *not want* to work for a living, a basic expectation and right of a modern, American man, but he'd rather steal people's money via taxes and use that newfound wealth to – *how had he put it?* - fuck bitches and smoke that green? Close enough. It was despicable, vile, appalling…whatever adjective you wanted to use. What aggravated David even more is that he saw people like this on the subway *all the time*. And he knew the problem wasn't unique to New York.

No.

All across the United States, there were lazy individuals looking for their handouts, suckling on the teat of America's loophole-filled laws and regulations. It was bad enough that they were too apathetic to fend for themselves as human beings in this world, and that they were wasting the tax dollars of the upper and middle classes, but even more troublesome was that there were actually people in their predicament *trying* to make a difference and *trying* to get ahead. People who actually needed those food stamps. For food. Not drugs or booze. Not sex. Nourishing sustenance required to feed themselves and their loved ones as they worked hard trying to make a better life.

And here Mike was, trying to steal from the rich *and* the poor so that he could live a worthless existence; offering nothing to society but gluttonous exploitation. Not only had David seen his kind before, but he had dealt with his kind before.

Dealt *permanently* with his kind before.

Inside of him there was a drive, a yearning, or maybe it could even be classified as a wish that each and every citizen of this great country *did something*. That everyone contributed, or at least tried to contribute; that much he could applaud, but the combination of laziness and neediness was unacceptable. A passion boiled deep within the canyons of his soul and it was genocidal.

America would be better off without lazy freeloaders. Without people who worked little but expected the world. Without people like Mike who thought they were above the law and everyone who upheld it. Without the superficial celebrities whose only talents included: creating scandals and lacking intelligence

America would be better off if it trimmed the fat.

The *world* would be better off if it trimmed the fat.

David was going to be the butcher.

Still doing his best to ignore the two failures talking loudly about their absurd plans, David remembered when he first began to feel this way. Ever since he could remember he would experience a particular sensation in similar situations. To him, it was hardly as if he was judging a book by its cover. No…he had seen and met enough individuals cut from this brand of shitty cloth to *know* he didn't have to read the book to realize it wasn't even worth opening. They were easy to spot, the useless ones. Often begging for attention, sometimes dressed without a care in the world, noses up, but begging hands outward. No, no, no. David had always been able to tell who these people were and he had experienced the resulting cruelty of their entitlement first hand.

Early in David's life he had lived in a small rural town. Not so small that everyone knew about everyone else, but close. He'd been eleven years old and not yet able to work legally. His parents were well off enough so that they didn't need an additional source of income from their child, but David was still eager to help and wanted to do something useful with his time.

One of his favorite places in this small town was the local gas station. There were two, granted, but this one was nearer to the end of town where David's family lived. The station had much more than just gas; it had candy, snacks, magazines, and a whole mess of other, random items, most of which David couldn't identify. The aspect he enjoyed the most however was the company. The station's owner, Doug, had taken a liking to David, his most loyal customer. Even in a time where there was pervasive discrimination against African Americans, Doug, who was white, was apathetic to the differences in color between him and the boy. They had good conversations; David made him laugh, and he kept him company at times when the job became rather dull and lonely.

Unbeknownst to David, his parents reached out to Doug, explaining that their son was seeking employment, not for much money, but for the reward. Doug could sense the pride beaming from David's mother and father, and having known the boy for several months now, also felt his own version of the emotion. Without hesitation he agreed to hire the young boy on for a couple dollars an hour, a decent amount more than his parents had suggested, for ten to fifteen hours a week. Because the boy was so young, it would all be kept under the table, with Doug tallying up how much he owed the boy weekly and giving him the cash directly.

On a sunny August afternoon, Doug surprised David with the news.

"Go grab that broom over there, Harp." It was his nickname for the boy, derived from his last name.

"Yessir, Mr. Doug." David hustled to the corner of the store where he knew the broom to be kept and returned. "Here ya go, sir."

"No, Harp. That's for you to use." A smile was plastered against Doug's aging face. "You work here now."

One would have thought that David had just received an enormous birthday present or something of the like.

His face lit up, beaming ear to ear, with adulation and excitement.

"I do?" He asked, scared that the answer might reveal this to all be a dream.

"Yep! Yer parents and I discussed it last week. I'll pay you a couple dollars an hour, in cash, and you can work here up to fifteen hours every week."

"You mean it?"

"Absolutely. Only rule is that school comes first. You're not to come here until all your studies are complete. Ya understand?"

"Yessir! Thank you sir!"

"No thank you, Harp. It's about time I hire someone on to help me clean up this place and get it back in top form."

"Don't you worry, sir! It'll look great. Each and every day!"

"I'm countin on it, Harp. And now that we work together, just call me Mr. Doug. Go ahead and go sweep the aisles then we'll get to discussin' your weekly duties over a Coke. On me." David nodded and went right to work and very well might have been one of the happiest eleven year olds in the world that day.

Seasons changed from the end of summer to fall, from fall to a mild winter, and from winter into spring. David loved working at the gas station with Doug and they had become an even stronger, yet unlikely, pair of friends than before. Doug was accepted into the Harper household, often invited over for dinner with the family, and the bond they shared through David was unique but real. David's father was a strong, wise, and hardworking man who taught him many lessons throughout life, but it was Doug's teachings that seemed to stick with David more. Sermons of accountability, forethought, budgeting, presentation, personality, and right vs. wrong were just some of the many areas that Doug and David covered during their fifteen hours per week. They were close pals, but that didn't mean that Doug let up easy on David just because he could.

At dusk on one of the few winter days where it had snowed, David had left the glass door to the gas station open in order to brush the dirt out of the store. Something distracted him as he was completing the chore and during his side-tracked activity a huge gale of wind gusted through the store bringing snow and dirt and gravel in through the open door. Doug had scolded David and instructed him to clean up the mess of everything that had blown over. David was embarrassed, never angry at Doug, and did all of this with his head down and jaw wired shut.

Doug, feeling a bit guilty for the outburst, silently helped pick up snacks in the aisle where the gust had caused the most catastrophe.

"Harp, I'm sorry for yellin at you."

"No sir, Mr. Doug. I deserved it. I wasn't paying attention."

"That's right, Harp, but I'm still sorry. There is a silver lining though and that's that you learned the importance of *focus*." David kept his head down and continued cleaning the watery, cold floor. "Focus is one of the most important things in the world, Harp. It separates purpose and intention from failure. Ya' can't ever truly complete a task, a goal, a dream without *focus*. Focus, Harp, is the key ingredient for those who are successful in seeking a vision. If ya' have a vision, even one as simple as sweeping the floor of this here gas station, focusing on it will never do you wrong."

To Doug, it may have seemed like those imparted words of wisdom might have gone in one ear and out the other, but they were words that David not only heard, but cherished and began to live his life by. Their relationship grew during times such as this one and it was clear that, even at the young age of eleven, David's job at the gas station was beginning to transform him into the man he would become.

Unfortunately, another event – tragedy – would play an even larger role.

Spring was in full swing with the last remainders of cold temperatures evaporating away, lush greenery decorating lawns, roads, and parks, and the return of the good old-fashioned afternoon rainstorm.

David and Doug were working during one of these storms when both of their worlds would change forever.

The raindrops echoed, *thumthumthum*, off the roof and glass windows. David liked the thunderstorms because he enjoyed the music they made. Thunder clapped, brief and loud, miles away but David had missed the lightning that preceded it; he had been too busy realigning the products on the shelves.

Inside and out, the gas station was empty of any patrons. It was during these times that David and Doug accomplished the most. Doug was deep cleaning the main counter while David continued his chore, and they both remained working in complete silence, letting the rhythm of the rain and the shouting storm accompany them.

DING!

David heard the door's welcome bell ring, right after a belch of thunder, but kept on with his task. Several moments passed and an intuition clicked inside David. Despite the three occupants, the store was eerily quiet. He placed the last pack of Oreos at its designated spot on the shelf and peered around the corner of the aisle toward the counter. The scene didn't look abnormal at first glance, but then his eyes registered it.

A gun.

Doug's eyes were frozen on the man, staring him down face to face. Whoever this stranger was, he was soaked from the storm, water dripping from their long coat and pooling onto the floor. David whipped back around the aisle's corner, terrified and unsure of what to do.

His chest began heaving up and down.

His breaths fast and shallow.

With a tight squeeze he gripped his fingers underneath the metal shelving and closed his eyes, focusing on trying to get his breathing under control. To him, each breath sounded like a shout. As his grip relaxed, he gathered himself, still acutely afraid, but now farther from the shores of panicking than he had been. The two men who were once silent finally began to speak. Doug went first.

"What can I help you with?" It was straight. To the point. No courtesies granted.

"I…I…Give me all the money in the register!" It seemed the assailant was more nervous than Doug.

"Why would I do that? That's my hard earned money, um…I'm sorry I didn't get your name?"

"Are you…you fucking serious man? My name is Shutthefuckup. Now start packin." At this point the man was swaying, the gun's chamber bobbing slightly up and down.

"You on drugs there Mr. Shutthefuckup? I know it's raining outside but you don't look so hot."

"I swear – you, you, you will start packing this bag right now or I will shoot you and come get it myself."

"Ok. How about this? I'll give you every last cent in this register if you tell me what you're going to buy with it. Are you going to help put food on the table for your family? Donate it to charity? Rent yourself a place to stay? You tell me that and I'll even go so far as to *not* report this to the police."

David wondered why Doug was messing around with this guy. If he just gave him the money now it would be all over and they could go report it with their lives. Years after that day David would think back to it and realize why Doug had done what he did: he was a man of principles. He watched through the small gaps in the shelving as the scene continued to unfold.

These questions from Doug had rendered the man speechless. An awkward amount of time passed and David could hear sniffling. The man was crying.

"Fuck you man." He sniffled again, his voice quietly weeping between slobbering gasps. "All I wanted to do was come in here." A deep breath. "And get that money."

"I understand that." Doug replied. "That's usually how armed robberies go, but I ask: *what* do you need this money for? If I should give it to you, are you going to use it toward the betterment of society?"

There was a flash of rage from the stranger as the gun shook in the air.

"FUCK YOU! I'm using it for drugs, ok? That ok with you? I'm going to use it to buy whatever shit I want, put it into my body, and have a hell of a good time. And there ain't SHIT you can do about it. This is my FUCKing money now so pack it in the bag!" The response was full of anger and shame, the man still blubbering through a flood of tears.

"Son." Doug's response was very quiet. "I'm afraid I can't do that then." The answer hung in the air for a moment. "And frankly, I don't think you want to do this either. I can see it in your eyes."

Gun still pointed at Doug, the guest hung his rainsoaked head. The shaking had stopped and he was now rigid, breathing normally, and quiet. David waited eagerly, hoping that Doug's message had gotten through to the man and that he'd just leave.

Then came his reply, cold as ice.

"You have no idea what I want."

Two shots rang out against the storm, both men spraying blood and flying backward. Doug slammed against the wall behind the counter while the other man was lifted off his feet, catapulted backwards.

"DOUG!" David screamed out, hoping for a response from his mentor. All he heard was the rain and gurgling of hot blood in the back of throats. He ran behind the counter to Doug and knew that his friend was dead. The stranger's gun had been at neck and head level when it had gone off so there was little hope.

Smoke was seeping from underneath the cash register; it smelled like gunpowder. Keeping his distance from the grisly image of Doug, David leaned in and saw that there was a mounted shotgun within the counter. He had never known it was there. Doug must not have wanted him to, but it didn't surprise him that his friend had prepared for this type of scenario.

David rounded the cashier counter and saw that there was an exit hole for the firearm that had been conveniently covered up by a cigarette poster. Having an out-of-body experience, he followed the weapon's line of exit, judging that it had hit the man probably right below the neck. The second body was several feet away, but judging by the amount of blood David guessed he was correct.

It was once he had confirmed both men were dead that emotions overtook him. There, in the front of the store, he collapsed in a whirlwind of sorrow. He wasn't sure what had just happened – none of it made sense to him – and he didn't even really believe this was real. The possibility of dreaming came up repeatedly but no matter how hard he tried, sitting there, rocking, he couldn't wake up.

Before long and once the rain had let up some, a new patron came to the front doors, immediately seeing the distraught youngster. He walked into a nightmare of a scene, but comforted the boy all the same.

Eventually, the police were called, David was reunited with his parents, and the day ended. When the sun arose in the east the next morning, it dawned on a young boy whose outlook on life was forever changed and who would someday become the most powerful man on the planet.

A soft lurch forward brought David back from the painful memories of the past – just one of many – as the train arrived at its next stop (or had there been several?). Still across from him were the two lowlifes, whom he hated even more now having recalled the similar stranger who'd murdered Doug. After the squealing of the brakes ceased, the doors shuttled open and they stood up. Apparently this was their stop.

It wasn't David's but he exited behind them anyway, hungry for some misplaced revenge.

The duo was still talking loudly, though they were harder to hear now in the atrium of the subway station. By the looks of it, they had finally been able to roll a successful blunt and a gray line of smoke and a raunchy smell told David they were actively partaking in it. NYPD certainly had better things to be doing than busting two losers for a single blunt, but David knew you could never count *on* or *against* chance. He would need to make this quick.

Natural light alienated itself from the fluorescent, pouring in from the city stairwell leading up to the streets. David followed the pair, maintaining a fifteen to twenty foot distance, dependent on the crowd volume. Horns and engines and voices were waiting as David emerged from the tunnels and into the city. This wasn't too far from his intended destination. *Good, that should save me some time.*

Clouds hung low in the overcast skies of New York City, creating a dreary palette and a collectively somber mood. This seemed to go completely unnoticed by the two fools he was tailing, for it now seemed as if they were rapping, loudly, to one another. David enjoyed the rap genre, but their attempts were laughable and overly laden with curses. It was becoming abundantly clear to David that he would be doing the world a favor here in the next ten minutes. Confident in his anonymity, David reduced his tail to five feet or less. Just for the entertainment.

"I said, YO!"

"YO!"

"I gots me a HO! I get it in fo' free and she always wants MO!"

"Then I said, YO!"

"YO!"

"I gots me some GREEN. They say it a gateway drug, but fuck, I think it's all I NEED."

"My nigga here be trippin, most def-in-ite-LY, cause this fool done all them drugs from A to Z!"

"Now Mike here be real, Mike be tellin it TRUE, but once we get those foodstamps, we won't have to pay for…POO!"

The rap abruptly ended.

"Poo? What the fuck man, you in the first grade?"

"Fuck you, Mike. I was gonna say 'shit', but 'shit' doesn't rhyme with 'true', now does it?"

"Naw it doesn't but that's part of like the…the…artistry or rapping. You gotta think on ya toes and ya thoughts gotta be ahead of your words. So you don't go rhyming fucking 'true' with 'poo'."

David couldn't take much more of these two and increased his tail to the previous fifteen feet. The streets weren't as busy as they usually were, but they were still populous enough to cover him should the need arise. *My guess is that they will have no idea until the very end…*

Not much to David's surprise, the pair seemed to be either lost or wandering as, in the span of the last fifteen minutes, they had already circled back around. He wondered: was this what they did day in and day out? Just ride the subway, walk around, and that be it? Already he knew what kind of people they were, that much was clear, but still. It shocked him that it seemed like some people had nothing to contribute – not even a little bit of ambition. Three more minutes passed and David received his opportunity: the two idiots had bumbled into an alley.

"Yo bitch! Hold up! I gotta take a piss."

"Shit dawg. Me too I guess. Hittin up the alley?"

"You see any otha' fuckin bathroom around here?"

"True."

David stopped before the alley's corner and waited until they were deep within its darkened recesses. *Fitting that the last thing they'll ever do is take a piss.* There were smells destroying the alley's air – trash, sewage, gasoline, sweat, steam, food – it was enough to turn David's stomach, but he'd lived in New York long enough by now that he was "used" to it. Water drained down the alley's mildly sloped center, dark and dirty. Now there were two thin trails of urine draining David's way, casually mixing with the water, adding a cloudy golden hue. He stopped, only ten feet away, as they completed relieving themselves.

"Did you hear that that nigga Shawn got caught pissin in an alley one time?"

"So? What the fuck's that matter?" They both were zipping up their pants.

"The Blue caught him, gave him a ticket and shit. Told him if he didn't pay the fine he was a sex offender! Like all registered and shit."

"Man shut the fuck up. That's a load of bull – who the hell are you my nigga?" Both fools had turned, facing David.

"What the hell, fag! Were you watching us pee?" That was enough of the name calling.

"Did you two morons *really* just call *me* a fag and a nigger in the span of two seconds? Do you realize how unnecessary and inappropriate that is? Especially coming from two sickly white-boy wannabes such as your-selves?"

"We ain't no wannabes ya bitch. We hard as fuck. You tryin to step?" A frustrated David shook his head and gently pinched the bridge of his nose. If there was a scientific theory linking proximity to stupidity, this was surely evidence.

"You're hard as fuck huh? You're asking me if I'm," he mimicked the one's voice. "'Tryin to step'? I should be asking you: do you have any remote idea of who the fuck *you're* dealing with right now?"

"Some pussy ass bitch by the looks of it." Mike re-plied, a trail of false bravado and fear on his tongue. Da-vid could feel himself glowering, half remembering some phrase about *"if looks could kill"* and half planning the next thirty seconds.

"What's the matter ya little *bitch*?" The unnamed one took three strong steps toward David, hand behind his waistline. "We piss you off, old man? You ain't gon do shit." David kept an eye on him.

"I wouldn't be doing anything if you would have shut the hell up on the subway. Instead, you two pieces of shit think you are the only ones in the world. Thinking of ways to abuse the system for your gain, wasting your pa-thetic little lives away on drugs and whores rather than trying to achieve something, talking in a manner unbefit-ting of true *men* – no…no. Had you punks actually tried to make something of yourselves, if you were actually *worth* something to the people around you, well, then I wouldn't have to do this."

"The fuck you talking about old man? Whatcha think you gon do with a fucking bullet in yo brain?" It was the slowest draw of a weapon David had ever seen, but he imagined that the idiot believed it to be fast. A dilapidated and worn 9mm was facing him, stock out to the side. David stifled a jolt of laughter at the whole scene. It was absurd.

An arm came from nowhere and took the gun.

Its barrel came slamming down on the hand that had once held it, breaking four of its five fingers.

There was no scream from the lowlife who David did not know. David had stepped around, grabbing the man's neck, and snapping it clean within a second of the pistol whip. A quiet "POP" ended the scuffle.

Mike watched, partly in horror, partly in bafflement, as his friend fell limp to the ground and this executioner set his sights on him.

David was mildly surprised when Mike charged, but not remotely unprepared. The fool was too bent over, barely even looking up as the tackle came closer. His shoes scraped off the pavement with white washes of noise. There was no grip there.

A knee came up into Mike's face as a fist came down at the back of his neck. The death was fast and painless, leaving Mike's body to crumple and slide right through the small trickle of water down the alley's center.

Without wasting any time, David gathered the two bodies and positioned them seated against the alley walls. It would be a while before anyone would find these two. This hadn't been the first time he had done something like this but the sensation remained the same. It felt as if

David had been cleansed, or like he had done society some great favor. In his mind, he truly had. He had trimmed the fat. There was no need for ritual or some moment of silence. David left the alley, having already forgotten what he just did, and was sitting at his desk in N.E.T.S. HQ within a half hour, going about his day unperturbed and sipping a delicious full mug of black coffee.

PRESENT DAY…
WEDNESDAY | SEPT. 19TH | 2018

David sat at that very desk now, curious as to the journey of memories his mind had just taken him on. *Why those two?* He had done something similar several times since but the question still hung. Perhaps he had despised those two the most – they had been the epitome of what he hated.

No matter. He had appeased his partners within the Aqarab Mayta by carrying out The Will. It was a shame that many of his cohorts had such narrow minded views of violence, death, and its purpose. Many had only agreed to be on board with David if America would suffer a catastrophic attack. Forced to concur, David kept his end game in mind and knew that in order to achieve it, he would need help.

The Will was a sad day. Hell, David had even liked the President. There was no *purpose* behind these two attacks other than to show force and appease the bloodlust that came with hating America. Many good, hard-working, and beneficial American people had died on July 5th of 2017 and for that, David was truly remorseful.

On the way to a cleansing of this planet's people, sacrifices, no matter how tough of a pill they were to swallow, had to be made.

David was just glad that from here on out, this was *his* game. And it featured *his* designed ending.

A light flashed on his glass desk coupled with a small vibration. David pressed it right away.

"Go."

"Sir, this is Agent Cobble. I've found them. They're in Costa Rica. I'm there now."

"You know what you need to do."

"Sir."

The call ended.

So it begins.

CHAPTER VIII

DEATH OR DOUBLE

WEDNESDAY | SEPT. 19TH | 2018

Something had died within Agent Henry Cobble over a year ago. He'd shot that woman.

Shot her out of spite.

Out of anger.

Out of loss.

*She was a terrorist…*he always reasoned, as if his brain was an opposing lawyer arguing back. *Sure, but you didn't just shoot her. You* executed *her.*

Most often seen as the "green" agent around N.E.T.S in the past, Cobble was now Harper's right hand man having completed several high profile missions. This path had been cleared by the death of Elena and Bryson, and of the betrayal of Rachel. All the people whom Henry had looked up to were either dead or not who he thought they were. All but David.

Some of the footage Henry had seen was unbelievable. Rachel, working side by side with the man previously known as Target Zero – a known Dead Scorpion asset. She was talented; Henry had never known her field skills were so extensive. In most of the snippets David had shared she was killing someone. Efficiently.

Rachel, this man, and their associates had been making life very hard for Henry in the last year. They were a small team, but they had intelligence, from where still remained a mystery, but it was becoming increasingly annoying and detrimental to N.E.T.S. operations. They'd been able to corrupt some key N.E.T.S data and killed several people whom David reasoned were more critical to N.E.T.S. alive.

Henry admired the man. David had truly taken him under his wing in the last several months, waived any punishment for his murder of the female terrorist, and given him an ample amount of work to do both on and off the field. Henry was grateful for this, not only because it progressed his career, but because it had allowed him to take his mind off of all the *shit* that had wrenched his world on its side. How David had managed to stay sane was beyond Cobble's comprehension. There had been instances where he seemed to be hanging on by a single hinge, but given the immense pressure of dealing with the fallout of The Will and continuing to combat the Aqarab Mayta, Harper had been a pillar of consistent leadership.

Something that Harper had once told Henry had had a profound impact on him:

"As an intelligence agency, we have to be accurate 100% of the time. The one time that we aren't, people die. Terrorists, and especially the Dead Scorpions, are like blind people playing darts. They're misguided and often ill-equipped for the task at hand, but they're resilient. They keep throwing. When one of those darts lands, people die. Their hit rate only has to be 30%, 20%, hell even 1%, and they've successfully lived up to their purpose: to instill fear in everyday citizens. The President's assassination, the highway massacre and bombing, and The Will were all darts that hit. We're playing against an opponent who's only wearing an eye patch."

The smarmy, sticky air created pockets of perspiration on Henry's cloth shirt. It was annoying and brought his attention crashing back to the task at hand. For months he'd been tracking Rachel's whereabouts. It was a personal mission, but a necessary one; she had to be brought in for questioning. *Or killed if she puts up too much resistance.* The intrigue of *why* she'd gone rogue was too much for Henry to consider.

Months of research had led him to Costa Rica, away from its capital, and close to the beach. His small task force was behind him: new recruits to N.E.T.S. to whom he had no personal attachment. They had volunteered and they knew the stakes. Typical new recruits they were too. Fit guys, short hair, aviators, thinking they were about to get in the "shit". Well, they were. But Henry knew it wouldn't be as glamorous as they'd imagined. This would be a fast and hard-hitting mission. He wanted to be wheels up within the next 120 minutes. Sun rays were bearing down on the tarmac and the warping aesthetic of heat waves could be seen in the distance. It was time to update David. The phone rang.

"Go."

"Sir, this is Agent Cobble. I've found them. They're in Costa Rica. I'm there now."

"You know what you need to do." It wasn't a cold reply, just a factual one.

"Sir." Cobble didn't even hear the phone click as he'd already put it away, knowing that was the end of the discussion. "Alright." He started, turning around to his small team of three. "This isn't a fucking vacation. These are high priority targets. The *highest* priority. They're most likely armed, but even if they aren't they'll kick your ass. Don't underestimate them, you hear me?"

Three curt nods followed.

"Objective is capture alive, but our rules of engagement change if we get resistance. Injure if need be, and kill only if absolutely necessary. There're four of us and we're getting three heat signatures from their building.

"I'm hot as hell right now and sweating in uncomfortable places. I want to be back in an air conditioned plane within two hours. Got that?"

Three more nods. One man wiped the beading sweat off his brow.

"Silence your weapons and let's move out. SUVs are waiting." Henry pointed behind him through the rippling currents of heat toward a pair of silver vehicles. "I'll be in the lead, you three follow behind me."

Without confirmation he turned and started walking. He'd gone on his fair share of missions lately but he really wasn't looking forward to this one. *Maybe that's why I'm overheating so much?* His stomach was in knots as the worst case scenario of having to possibly kill Rachel loomed over him. *But she's a traitor.*

Still.

There was a part of him, one that seemed far in the past, which had known Rachel. Not incredibly well, but enough to realize that her desertion was out of character. What worried him even more was that every time these doubts crept in were Bryson and Elena. Both had been close friends with Rachel. Could they both have misjudged her character that poorly?

Within moments he was pulling out of the airport, not even considering whether or not the others were following. They knew what to do and he was deep in thought. What had begun as an honorable task of bringing in a rogue agent and known terrorist was crumbling beneath the weight of doubt. Doubt that had been on Henry's mind from the time of Bryson's death, and suppressed ever since. Suppressed by David. By the pressure to perform. By the pressure to save American lives. Now that he was so close however…*Shit, Rachel. What* are *you doing?*

These roads were rough and a pothole rocked the SUV. It startled Henry who refocused on driving. He checked his rear view out of nervous habit; the other silver vehicle was four cars behind him. Solid tail distance. All around there was lush greenery, sweating with the humidity off the ocean. Henry tried to remember what it felt like to be on a vacation. That memory didn't come to him and he laughed. Just moments ago he had started his spiel with "*This isn't a fucking vacation*" and here he was wondering what it would feel like to let wet sand press through his toes. *Much of a hypocrite, Cobble?*

Behind him, the second vehicle had fallen behind a couple more car lengths. Secretly, Henry wished he could have come on this operation alone. Thinking through how everything would shake down, he didn't see any path in which these three would be apprehended quietly, most likely resulting in the deaths or injuries of the least experienced people in the room: the three new recruits. More worrisome than the bodily harm were the potential secrets. Henry wanted to know them and he needed a conversation with Rachel, off the record. He was guessing that most of what she would tell him would be a lie, but a lie well above the recruits' paygrade. And they certainly couldn't converse once back at N.E.T.S., at least not without a half dozen different ears and eyes on them.

Another decently sized pothole swallowed up a front tire and spat it out again, shaking the vehicle as it turned onto a descending dirt path. This would lead to the identified housing structure. Henry made a mental note that it took about seventeen minutes to get here from the airport – valuable information for the impending exfiltration.

There were fields on both sides of the road, of what he wasn't sure. The tall, leafy plants swayed rhythmically in the breeze toward the direction of the home, inviting Henry with a wave. He slowed the car's progress and placed it in neutral to coast the rest of the way. They weren't expecting visitors and engine noise would be a dead giveaway. Eventually the car came to a stop on its own, a few hundred feet from the structure itself. The road curved up ahead with tall flora hiding them from view. Reluctantly, Henry placed the vehicle in park, turned it off, and exited into the dreadful heat once more. Sweat almost immediately began to produce under his arms and on his forehead. No matter how experienced of an operative you were, humidity always sucked.

Before approaching the building, Henry went to the trunk and opened it, pulling out and loading his SIG 516 assault rifle. Part of him wished that he wouldn't even need it, but walking in unarmed was like flipping a coin on suicide. The second vehicle was coasting toward him now, coming to a stop within a few feet of his rear bumper. As he predicted, the recruits inside still looked "pumped" and he was sure they wouldn't like what he was about to tell them.

He walked toward them and made a rotating finger motion to roll down the window.

"Here's how this is going to go down. You three are going to stay here, enjoying the air conditioning. I'm going in alone first to scope out the place –"

"Sir, we've already reviewed the home's layout half a dozen times. Do you really need to go in alone?"

"I'll pretend you didn't just question my authority with the promise that you keep your mouth shut the entirety of the remainder of this trip." The recruit nodded silently.

"There are a lot of angles to what we're about to do. I just want to ensure that everyone comes out of it alive." He glanced around nervously, feeling as if the men could see through his lie. "You three will come in on two occasions and two occasions only. If you hear gunfire, breach the compound. You'll most likely be collecting my body while you capture them. Second, I'll make a static pattern in our comms." Henry touched his earpiece twice in rapid succession, paused, then once more. "TapTap…Tap. That's the pattern. You get that from me, you have the go ahead to enter. Got it?" As he'd been talking, he'd placed sunglasses over his eyes and observed the quiet recruits from behind them.

"Affirmative."

With a gentle tap on the car door, Henry nodded, and walked away toward the three people he hoped to get answers from. Once he passed his own vehicle, the gun came up to the ready position and he entered, crouched, into the tall forest on the left side of the road. The density of the plants was thicker than he predicted and he found himself having to forcibly push through certain croppings of large leaves. Luckily, the ground was bare; it was nothing but moistened dirt, making his footsteps inaudible.

Even though he was mostly covered in shade from the plants surrounding him, Henry could have sworn that the temperature increased by at least ten degrees once he entered the forest. Either that or he was beginning to get more and more nervous. As he used his forearm to wipe the moisture from above his eyes, he remembered. *It wasn't much more than a year ago when I was a fairly new recruit.* Henry looked back on those days…he knew that many hadn't thought much of him. They'd thought he was "green". In truth, he very much had been up until the night he got shot in the stomach. Now he was heading a mission to apprehend or kill three terrorists, one of which was likely the man who nearly killed him. *Amazing how much difference a year and a near-death experience makes…*

Not much of the space in front of him could be seen through the thick foliage, but he was starting to make out the home in question…a rather luxurious place to be holed up. Granted, he imagined that real estate in Costa Rica was differently priced, but across the large driveway was a step-above-modest home. It seemed to be ranch style, but he guessed it had at least a porch on the other side facing the ocean. Not bad digs at all.

An older, blue, and slightly rusty car sat in the driveway much unlike the well-kept home behind it. From what Henry could tell, as he neared through the heavy leaves, no windows or doors were open. They were probably trying to keep the heat out as much as possible on a day like this.

The edge of the plant line was a stride or two ahead and the ground sloped downward several feet after, merging with the concrete driveway. Henry paused, looking through the scope on his rifle. Sweat from his hair dripped onto the top of the optics, gravity rolling it off to the side and onto Henry's clammy trigger hand. There was no evidence of anyone inside the house through the three windows that he had visible access to.

"November squad, this is Cobblepot," *I hate that nickname.* "I'm at the forest perimeter and holding. Physical surveillance of the house reveals no targets. Confirm that targets are still active inside."

"Cobblepot this is November squad. Hold please."

Three seconds passed.

"Cobblepot, confirmed. There are three heat signatures in that building. They'll be on the opposite side of the building from your location. Grouping is two tangos in living space, one tango in what's likely the restroom."

"Affirmative. Cobblepot out. Listen for the signal."

Taking one final wipe of his glistening brow, Henry moved out of the verdant flora and into the open. He always hated being exposed like this so he worked quickly to get against the siding of the home. Sunrays beat off the aluminum paneling and brick, making it even hotter than it was within the leaves. *Dear God, I need to get inside.* The pit of Henry's stomach was grumbling with anticipation. Answers were coming, one way or another.

Either Rachel is doing something undercover...or I'm not getting the whole picture back at N.E.T.S., which is doubtful...or she's a rogue agent-turned-terrorist and I'm shot on sight.

Lovely.

Along the siding Agent Cobble walked, keeping low and silent. Moving to the nearest window, he removed a length of wire that was the same size around as a piece of mechanical pencil lead. It unfurled from a small coil around his left pinky finger. Once he had enough length he pressed the end of the glove on his pinky, sending a small electric current through the wire, rigidifying it in the process. Henry held his hand above him slowly while focusing on the left lens of his sunglasses. Here, a video feed image had appeared once he charged the wire. The footage was coming from the tip of the wire itself where there was a microscopic camera transmitting the images of what was inside the home through the window above.

With a few cursory glances and swipes left and right, it appeared to be a bedroom of some sort, though remarkably clean. It was almost as if it was unused. The bed was made neatly, no clothes were strewn about, no lights were on, and the door was closed completely. Henry slowly began to make a fist and the image zoomed in at a similar clip. The dresser top in the room was barren, except for a fine layer of dust. *Extra room = my entrance.*

With a quick tap of his pinky's tip once more, the current through the wire ceased, turning off the footage in his glasses, and recoiling the limp wire around his finger to be used another time. Pressed tightly against the wall, Henry turned and extended his legs slowly so that he could reach the window, testing to see if it was locked. *Of course it is* he told himself as the window wouldn't budge.

From a small chest pocket on his tactical vest he removed another gadget that looked exactly like a pen. It was, in fact, a laser light, but not one of civilian grade. It produced an actual, cutting laser that could make its way through glass, wood, and some softer metals – though it often took some time. *My little lightsaber* the *Star Wars* fan inside of Henry mused. With the pen aimed at the ground, Henry pressed the side button to check that it was working. A bright, concentrated beam of neon purple appeared, connecting the pen to the dirt. Henry stopped and a thin trail of white smoke rose from the contact point in the dirt. *I wonder why it's purple?* Henry decided he would ask the techs back at N.E.T.S. as he brought the pen up to the window.

The lock was in the classic spot for many windows: dead center and on the bottom. Henry placed his fist against the glass, eyeballing its diameter, then turned the laser on. For every quarter length of the circle he was creating it took several seconds, but the laser was powerful enough that he didn't ever have to hold it in place. The violet light scattered throughout the rest of the glass as it moved through it, creating a gorgeous effect that shone even through the harsh sunlight. Once Henry was finished, the cut circle's edges were almost invisible to the naked eye, but he knew where the center was and gently pressed forward. Slowly, the glass circle removed itself from the rest of the window, and he was able to creep two fingers through the hole and lay the piece on the inside windowsill. He flipped the bottom latch, removed his hand, and slid the window up, climbing inside as quietly as possible. Making sure to leave no evidence, he closed the window again, latching it, and placing the glass segment back in its allotted shape.

He was in.

Luckily, they had the air conditioning on full blast and, despite his adrenaline, Henry's sweat glands began to calm down. While he'd been scoping and entering the room, his gun had been slung over his back. Now he brought it to his front, walking crouched across the sunlight-scattered room. As he distanced himself from the window, the light became dimmer and pale shadows carpeted the floors and walls, only betrayed by the light coming in from underneath the doorway. Henry neared the door.

The light underneath was interrupted by moving shadows.

Someone was on the other side. Or at least they had been.

Erring on the side of caution, Henry pushed his gun to his back and uncoiled his pinky cam once more, sending the charge through the wire after it achieved just over one foot in length. Its tip entered the shadows and fed him an image from a room away.

Typical hallway transition into a living room.

Two chairs.

One couch.

Back door to a patio.

All quite spacious.

His pinky panned from right to left and so too did the image. No one was there. Had they entered another room? Henry paused his breathing and listened. Not a thing, not even the hum of an air conditioner. Something was off and Henry ridiculed himself for not noticing it sooner. Up until now this had been too quick, too easy – completely unperturbed. Without a thought he felt his core tighten in unexplained anticipation. *Had they not had time to establish a security system yet?*

A blur filled the screen in his vision and a soft jerk was followed by a hard yank of his left arm. The assailant opened the bedroom door from the other side, slamming it into Henry's head as he fell forward, still trapped by the stiff wire under the frame.

The thud was dense and brief, tossing Henry back into the room closer to the window from which he entered. Unable to stabilize himself, his back landed awkwardly on the assault rifle slung around him.

Without so much as a scuffle, he knew he was beaten by whomever was coming through that door. As if they heard him, the indisputable readying of a handgun rang from the ajar door's shadows: *chi-CHIQ!*

Rachel made a grand entrance without even trying to as the door slammed against the beige interior wall and she stormed in, purpose filling her steps and her gaze. The barrel of the gun pressed against the side of Henry's head as he tried to ready his own weapon. Slowly, he faced the woman he had come here to meet, startled that she was the one who had bested him.

Her eyes contorted with a look of confusion followed by her own guilt.

"Henry?"

Both of them were stuck in speechlessness. Rachel had no idea that the intruder would be the most untested agent at N.E.T.S. and Henry was taken aback by just how *powerful* Rachel was.

Her stance.

Her shoulders.

Her demeanor.

It was drenching the room with confidence. This wasn't the same Rachel.

"Rachel." She took a step back, looking at the man still on his ass. She sensed that Agent Cobble was no longer the same one she'd last seen. Physically he was unchanged, but there was something in his eyes.

A sadness.

Loss.

Frustration.

The burden of leadership.

She remembered the first time she'd killed someone and knew that Henry had passed this threshold in the last year. Most likely several times. The gun lowered and went in her back pant line. With a heaving sigh, Henry got to his feet.

"What are you doing here?" was the most obvious question she could think of. Henry paused a moment and turned off his comms, removing his earpiece and leaving it dangling against his chest.

"I could ask you the same thing, Rachel. What the fuck happened?"

"You first, Cobble."

"Officially or unofficially?"

"Both."

"*Officially,*" He began, "I'm here to apprehend you and your two accomplices, bring you back to N.E.T.S., and not ask any questions. Should you decide to put up a fight, our ROEs allow us to shoot to kill if absolutely necessary." Rachel's sight narrowed and Henry noticed her tense. If it came to it, he knew she'd be a faster draw than he. Especially this version of her. He continued.

"Unofficially, I'm here to get some answers. Things have changed a lot since…well…you know, The Will. You've basically been labeled a terrorist, I've become David's personal agent, and we seem to be doing a lot of good.

"I'm not necessarily convinced. David's a good man and together we make a good team. Not anything near what Bryson and he were, but I'm trying. But there's something off. With him. With the whole situation. The Dead Scorpions. I've not been sleeping, I'm angry all the time. Some of it's the loss, but the rest of it is because I can't figure anything out. I feel like a fucking pawn on a chessboard and the worst part about it is that I *know* I'm the pawn. I just don't know who's playing me."

Arms folded across her chest, Rachel studied him. Silence loaded the space between them. She knew he was lying in some capacity, but there had been truth – sincerity – in his plea.

Rachel replied. "So what? I'm supposed to just give you the answers you want and then you're supposed to bring me in? You and your little task force you left in your SUVs?" Overwhelmed, she brought the back of her wrist to her forehead, trying to think and reason through a situation that was becoming increasingly more complicated the longer she pondered it. "Shit, Henry. Why the hell did you come here? Do you realize what you've done now?"

"What do you mean? What are you talking about?"

"I'm not going with you. Neither are the other two. I can't let you go now that you've been here. Not now that you know where we are."

Henry's reply was a stupid stare.

"You've condemned one of us to die, Henry! Don't you get that? You've condemned those three out there to death! And you just come in here looking for answers? Answers that I can't give you. Answers I shouldn't give you. How can I trust you? If you're truly David's agent." She paused, now fully grasping the gravity of the situation. "What the fuck were you thinking?"

That stupid stare was still there. *I should just shoot him now, get it over with. Put him down like a dog. He* CAN'T *be here.*

"Rachel, just start with the truth. Then we'll go from there."

"Henry…" She sighed, torn between doing what was right and doing what was safe. "How do I know you're not wearing a recording device? Why should I trust you? Give me the reason."

Henry removed his sunglasses, tossing them gently to the floor. There was a specific pain in his eyes, eyes that now stared directly into Rachel's. It was the pain of feeling lost.

"Bryson and Elena were the two people I looked up to the most, not just at work, but in life. They were *good* people. They fought for what was just. And they cared about those around them, about helping them grow. I don't have very much family outside of N.E.T.S. and I can't remember the last time I had a friend. Except for you.

"Both of those good people died. And they died evil deaths at the hands of something that I don't fully understand. They should still be here now! Not us!" There was a shake in his tone. "So…if I have the opportunity to know what happened I want to take it. I can take the consequences. This is my choice, but I *need* to know. And I'm asking my friend to tell me, because clearly she knows a whole hell of a lot more than I do."

She knew he was done speaking and felt that pang of guilt once more. Cobble was moldable, and David had taken advantage of that since her departure. Sure, she knew the truth, but she had left good people at N.E.T.S., at the hands of a bastard. Her gaze with Henry ended; he stared at the floor, downtrodden.

Shit.

"Fine." Rachel replied, unable to pretend like she'd withhold the information any longer. "There are some people you should meet and all of this will make a lot more sense." Her tone fluctuated to harshness. "Your men outside going to stay out there?" Henry nodded.

"They're not to move until my order. You don't need to worry about them."

"Fine. Come with me." Rachel turned and exited the room with Henry close in tail. They went down a narrow, but short staircase to a lowered portion of the building with a larger living room complete with a coffee table, chairs, and a sofa. Ian and Dahl were standing, discussing and semi-arguing while pointing fervently at a computer screen. They noticed Rachel entering the room, but their glance turned to wide-eyed panic, each of them drawing their weapons in less than a second, ready to shoot the man behind her.

Rachel casually raised her hands while Henry started to ready his own weapon, significantly slower than the other two.

"Boys. Put the guns down. He's with me." They all relaxed their firearms, but fingers were still on triggers. "Henry, this is Ian and Dahl." She pointed each one out. "Guys, this is Agent Henry Cobble of N.E.T.S."

Cautious glances were exchanged before Dahl spoke up.

"What's the point of this Rachel? Why did you bring him here?"

"I didn't. He was infiltrating upstairs, I caught his signature on our video feed, and confronted him. He's got three others waiting less than a quarter mile out. I know Henry from my time at N.E.T.S. For now," Her glance toward him came across like a warning. "I trust him."

"So I'll change the direction of my question." Dahl corrected, placing his gaze upon Cobble. "What are you doing here?" Rachel could see that Henry was wondering where to start first so she answered for him.

"He's here to capture us or kill us, depending on how much resistance he encounters. Either way, we're supposed to be headed back to N.E.T.S. in restraints or bags. My friend Henry here has a conscience, and has his own alternative objective: to find out what the hell is going on."

Dahl raised his chin and peered down the length of his face, gauging Henry's sincerity from afar. Ian remained constricted – tight – ready to shoot Henry if called for.

"I know who you are." Henry surprisingly spoke up, pointing at Ian. "You're Target Zero. The one who escaped our facility." His eyes moved to Dahl. "Which means you must be the one who helped him escape in that ambulance." Dahl knew what was coming next. The calculations were in Henry's eyes. "You're the one who shot me. I nearly died." There was no remorse in the statement, no anger either. He had stated it very matter-of-factly, as if it was a trivial tidbit. Truth was, it had made Agent Henry Cobble much stronger, but that was hindsight now.

Dahl appeared slightly remorseful, glanced briefly at Rachel, and apologized.

"Yes. Sorry about that, but you really left me no other choice."

"I understand." Henry replied as if Dahl had done something as simple as not held an elevator door for him. Rachel sensed something was wrong in the boy…the man. There were differences from the Cobble that she knew; she had sensed it while talking in the other room too.

Ian interrupted. "Glad you two could exchange pleasantries but can we really trust him to be in on this?"

"I think that's exactly why we *should* trust him." Dahl countered. "Ever since we lost Zane, we've been playing this game from the outside. Agent Cobble here is on the inside. Are you close to David, boy?"

Henry nodded. "I am, but why does that matter?"

Dahl returned his attention to Ian. "He could be our double agent. It's a sound tactic and all three of us know that we're going to need a deeper level of intel before the end."

Rachel gave a smile in agreement while Ian winced, reluctantly agreeing that it would be a sagacious strategic move on their part.

"Ok, but that still begs the question: how do we know we can trust him? What if we send him back to N.E.T.S. and he turns on us? We'd never recover and this whole operation would be over." Ian pressed.

"After what we're about to prove to him, how on earth would he turn on *us*?" Dahl retorted with a sense of finality, blanketing the room in silence.

"So what do you have to tell me?" Henry questioned after a moment, curious more than ever to know what this earth-shattering truth was.

"Sit down, Henry. This could take a while." Rachel instructed, offering up a nearby chair.

A soft bump woke Dynadin from his slumber as the small propeller plane landed gracefully on the hot Costa Rican runway. The next half hour saw him going through the motions, almost like a businessmen returning from a corporate trip.

Grab his small carry on from the bin space.
De-plane the small passenger jet.
Hail a cab.
Sit in mild traffic.
Turn onto the long dirt driveway.
Notice new pairs of heavy tire tracks on said driveway.

"Cabbie, stop here. I'll walk the rest of the way." Dynadin instructed.

"You sure man? My GPS shows another half mile to go."

"It's a nice day. I'd prefer to walk."

Despite the scorching heat the cab driver shrugged his shoulders, collected the total payment, and U-turned back out the way he came. Dynadin had already begun the trip back, having traded cold Russian snow for the Costa Rican heat within the span of a couple days. Once he was sure the cab was gone, he went to the tall foliage on the left side of the road, set his bags down, and removed his firearm. Security in the airports had been loose, but even still his bag was outfitted with technology to shade the gun from modern X-ray systems.

Pushing his way through the overgrowth, he ascertained that there were two SUVs that had just recently pulled in here, probably within the last hour. Against his better judgment he was hoping that it was a family of lost tourists and he'd eventually see tracks indicating they had realized their mistake and turned around.

But he knew better.

Someone was here. Someone had found them out.

After fifteen minutes of navigating through the tall, swaying forest, he paused, eyes on the two SUVs in question. The one in front was empty and the one behind had three men standing in an arc behind its trunk, talking. Each of them was lightly outfitted with simple Kevlar vests, a sidearm, sunglasses, comms, and assault rifles slung around their back. If he chose to, Dynadin could cut through them in less than seven seconds. *Is this all of them*? Now that there were potential threats around, Dynadin crept closer, but watched his noise level and where his footfalls landed.

"It's been half an hour." One man complained. "I'm hot as balls and we still have no signal. Can we sit in the car with some goddam air conditioning?"

"Shut the fuck up, Barton. We're going to stay at the ready until Cobble gives us the go ahead or we hear gun-fire."

"What's he doing anyway?" The third man asked. "It's been a while. You'd think he would have updated us by now…"

"Look, would you two quit being such pussies. He called not that long ago to check for Tangos. Cobblepot knows what he's doing. Just give him some time."

Dynadin continued to listen as the men squabbled further, hurtling insults at each other like snowballs and clearly experiencing the side effects of a "hurry-up-and-wait" command. One finally put his foot down and concluded,

"If we haven't heard anything in ten minutes, I'm advancing." The rational one began to protest. "Ah, ah, ah. Just up to the edge of the field, man. Calm the hell down. That way we'll be able to see if anything is going down and we'll be closer if he needs us to intervene." There was silence. "Come on. You can't argue with that logic."

"Fuck it. Fine. If we haven't heard anything in ten, we move in, as stealthily as humanly possible to scope things out. I'd rather do that than feel the wrath if we break radio silence."

With that, Dynadin took several paces backward, out of earshot of the men and placed a call. These men had their orders.

He was about to get his.

"So you're telling me that David Harper, the head of N.E.T.S., is also the leader of the Dead Scorpions?" Henry asked sarcastically, trying to get his point across that this was absolutely ludicrous. "And that he's attacking America, just so he can gain power from the seat he's in at N.E.T.S.?" A somewhat embarrassed silence blanketed the room. Rachel still had a hard time believing the whole situation and the summary they were receiving from their guest made it sound all the more ridiculous.

"Henry," She started. "I know it sounds impossible; I didn't believe it at first either. But Dahl has substantial evidence, some of which we've shown you. There are too many lies that David has covered up to explain it any other way." A scoff was thrown her way, eager to dismiss the plea. "He wanted both Bryson and me dead, Henry. I saw the communications." Their eyes met, exchanging the same sadness.

"Shit, Rachel. This is so messed up." Cobble looked at the other two and returned to her.

"Look, I know it's not the optimal situation but –"

"Optimal situation? You're working with a ghost and a goddamn ex-terrorist against the most secretive government organization in the world and your story, your *purpose*, sounds like nothing more than a wild conspiracy theory." His pause made it seem like a reprimand from a father. "I thought you had something substantial. I thought this was realistic." Rachel began her reply but Ian interjected.

"Look, *guy*. We don't give two shits if you believe this or not. Dahl has provided substantial proof that this is what's going down. And we're doing just fine without you. What you need to start thinking about is how you're going to come to grips with helping us. Because, in case you hadn't noticed, you're either leaving here on our side, or dead."

Rachel's jaw dropped for a moment, but she knew Ian wasn't wrong. Dahl's head hung. Now that the threat was out there, the situation that he could see forming was completely bare. They needed Henry to be their double agent or they needed him dead. There was no middle ground.

Agent Cobble released a slight gasp, as if offended. His face went pale. He understood the situation, but the realization of it in the moment was far different than hypothesizing it.

No one spoke. Then a phone rang. Dahl removed the device from his pocket, turning from the group to answer it.

"Go." No time to waste. The group watched him and Rachel wondered who he was talking to. "Yeah there's one here." – "Mhmm" – "Talking to him now." – "Possibly. Stand down for now." – "Understood. Give us five minutes. Stay on the line." Dahl turned back to the group and addressed Henry.

"It's now or never, kid. One of my men has his sights on yours. Apparently they're thinking of moving in on this location in ten minutes. That's just not going to work for us. No one here can vouch for their loyalty or credibility and we can't be telling all our secrets to the entirety of N.E.T.S. I still don't even feel good about telling *you*." A grimace followed the statement, as if thinking about revealing secrets made him sick to his stomach. "My man will kill your men as soon as they begin to press forward. It's as simple as that. You may be thinking that they'll be fine in a one-versus-three scenario, but you'd be mistaken. They'll be dead before they even realized they're being attacked. Understand?"

Henry nodded, face slowly contorting into a glower. He was being backed up against a wall.

"Good. That means you have five minutes to decide. You accept our offer to be our mole, you walk free from here, and we all work together to bring Harper and the Aqarab Mayta down. You decide to decline, I imagine there will be a bit of a bloodbath as you don't seem to be the type to lie down and die. But make no mistake, you will die. We've told you too much to let you walk without some assurance. This is bigger than you, or I, or any of us. I just felt like I should lay the cards out for you before you make your decision." Dahl checked his watch. "Four minutes."

Henry was breathing heavy, his eyes darting from person to person. Ian tightened his grip, ready to shoot if necessary. The air was hot and thick with tension and apprehension; the ultimatum on the table was a critical one. Rachel couldn't tell what Henry's move was going to be and it was killing her. She wasn't going to let someone else she knew die.

"Henry." She said gently, getting his attention.

"Three minutes." Dahl reminded.

"Enough, Dahl" Her look could have turned him to stone. "Henry…" Finally he looked at her. "We need your help. We can share the additional evidence we've mounted over the next few weeks, but you've got to say yes. I know we're asking a lot of you – probably too much – but it's the only way. Trust me." She wasn't pleading with him, but rather telling him, as a mother would a child in a time of desperation.

The room hung in suspension on Henry's next words, but they were not coming. Cold steel grew warmer against Ian's hands as he realized his grip was tightening. Dahl continued to stare intently at Agent Cobble, prepared to utter either "Stand down" or "Take them out" at a moment's notice. Across the room the only noise that could be heard was white; it was the gentle humming of the central air conditioning unit.

The eyes of a man deep in thought remained on Rachel, but their focus was through her. Henry had a thousand-mile stare, contemplating his options, of which there were very few.

Could I take them all out?
    The ex-terrorist already has his gun out.
    You'd be dead.
    Not to mention your team outside.
Is the man watching them really that deadly?
    You sure you want to test that?
Is there even a man on them?
    You sure you want to test that?

Maybe it's best if I die…
   Well that's dark.
I don't want to die…
Why would David do this?
   Don't you want to find out?
How could he get away with something like this?
   Don't you want to find out?
What if they're right? What's his endgame?
   Don't you want to find out?

"Ok." Henry vomited out, pulling back into the moment as fast as he'd left it.

"Ok, what?" Dahl clarified. Henry cleared his throat, facing the man.

"Ok. I'll do it. I'll be your double agent."

"Stand down." Dahl spoke into the phone, hanging up immediately after and putting it back in his pocket.

"But there are some things we need to discuss first, and quickly." Henry knew he now had the upper hand in the conversation.

"Ok. Shoot." Dahl replied, Rachel and Ian looking on and listening.

"What am I supposed to tell my men? We came here to apprehend you and now I'm just supposed to stroll out empty handed? And don't answer with 'We have to kill them'. That's not happening."

"Don't be crass, Cobble. I wouldn't suggest a thing like that."

"Ok then, so what's your suggestion?"

"You're a double agent now. Lying is your new favorite hobby. You'll think of something."

Rachel swore she saw Dahl's lips curl into a smirk at Henry. He was testing him. The colors of Henry's eyes darted back and forth, glancing downward and trying to innovate an excuse. Within seconds his earpiece was back in and he placed a finger against his ear.

"November squad this is Cobblepot." Rachel snorted with laughter, quickly stifling the outburst accompanied by a harsh glare from Henry.

"Cobblepot you're a go for November."

"Pack up."

"Sir?"

"Our intel was shit. I've infiltrated the residence and this isn't it."

"But sir, we were reading heat signatures…"

"Yeah, heat signatures of a family of three. I nearly caused an international incident sneaking in here, but it's not them."

"But all of our intel points – "

"You wanna come in here and double check? I checked their network and the ones we are chasing were just using this as a ping point; a common thread in their digital bouncing around to throw off their trail. This family barely has working Wi-Fi, much less the means for a small resistance force. We've been duped."

"Copy, Cobblepot. That's unfortunate. I was really hoping to get these bastards. Packing up now."

"Me too, November. Rendezvous in ten. Cobblepot out."

Most of the room was stunned, both Rachel and Ian were staring at Henry in soft surprise, but not Dahl. He had issued the test knowing that Agent Cobble would pass. He thought on his toes and was successful. Feeling more confident, Henry continued on.

"I also want some assurances. You guys are to keep me informed at all times. I don't want to be the new guy in the dark. If I'm sticking my neck out, I'm kept in the loop."

"Absolutely." Dahl affirmed.

"And if shit starts to hit the fan and I'm in danger, I want out. To come here with you. Away from David if he's getting suspicious."

"Can't confirm whether we'll be here or not, but we'll do our best to keep you safe and pull you out if the heat gets too high."

"So how do we set this up? Do you have a burner phone or something?"

"Hah! No…nothing that archaic. We'll work on setting up a remote operation on your laptop at N.E.T.S. You'll know once we set it up."

"On my *work* computer? I'll get caught within hours. They've got specialists tracking every keystroke…"

"You'll be fine. How'd you think Zane and I communicated for so many years?"

"Fine." Henry let it go. "Anything else? Any advice?"

"Stay vigilant. You know what David is now; you can see the monster in the daylight. Keep your ears open for oddities. Notice his mannerisms. *Observe*. We'll give you specific tasks as we move along but the most important aspect of all of this is the qualitative data you can gather. It's time to be a good, old-fashioned spy."

Henry nodded, either liking the sound of that or wearing a façade because he was too nervous to think of anything to say.

"You better get going, son."

"Ok. You're right. I'll…uh…be in touch then. Anything else?"

Dahl walked over to the anxious man and placed a hand on his shoulder with his other extended outward. A cold, clammy hand met Dahl's and shook it.

"Welcome to the team, Agent Cobble."

TRUTH IN FIRE

THURSDAY | OCT 4TH | 2018

Soft and smooth bare feet pattered across the chilly tile as Rachel made her way back to her bedroom, half sneaking through the dark house. The salty sea breeze rubbed across her naked body and the moonlight offered a faint white luminosity, guiding the way back to her room from Ian's, the clothes she had shed in tow under her arm.

They'd made love – *no, it was just sex* she corrected herself – a few hours previous and she'd snuck out, as she always did, once she'd woken in the middle of the night. Part of her believed that she was falling for him, but common sense told her it was the lust talking.

She closed her door silently behind her, tossed her clothes on the floor, and climbed into bed. Exhaustion was at her doorstep, even with a few hours of sleep already, but the drowsiness she was fighting now was more akin to mental fatigue. The past few weeks had really taken their toll, even without any active missions.

Henry was maintaining a decent amount of contact, now back at N.E.T.S. headquarters with David, while Dahl, Ian, Dynadin, and she were spending most of their days pouring over data that they'd acquired in previous missions or that Henry was feeding them. It was dull work at times, but it'd turned out to be surprisingly productive. It wasn't like any of them were itching to get out in the field again. After Dynadin's near death experience at the hands of Harper, Dahl was taking no risks whatsoever. "I can't afford to lose a single one of you at this point. We're all here through the end now." Or at least that's what he'd told them after Dynadin had debriefed them following Henry's departure.

The story was nothing short of incredible and miraculous because he was still alive. During their time together, there were other stories he had shared; some within the last year, others of which were from long ago. They were always entertaining in some sense, but Rachel didn't want to believe half of what she heard he had done, even if she knew it to be 100% true. The man was incredibly violent but she'd learned that wasn't necessarily an inherently bad thing. There was a deep, steadied calm within him – as if he regretted the things he'd done – and there was a mercy to his methods. He was talented, athletic to a degree which she'd never seen before, and frighteningly lethal. But in the previous weeks she'd learned he was also quiet, introverted, kind, very smart, and humble.

Once, on a warm, somewhat dull day like this one had been, Rachel had made her way down into the sparring and weight room. She liked to get a good workout in, especially during their idle periods, and Dahl had recommended refraining from outdoor training for a while. As she entered the weight room, she heard the quiet but distinct sounds of another body moving and saw that Dynadin was on a mat, moving effortlessly in his own space.

Whether or not he'd sensed her enter the large training area, she couldn't say, but he continued on as if she wasn't there. There were headphones in his ears. She wondered what type of music he listened to. For some reason she immediately guessed classical, but couldn't be sure. Dynadin, dressed in a gray athletic top and black nylon shorts, moved fluidly through the air with a gun in one hand and a knife in the other. As if practicing from a memorized set of combat moves, he quickly assaulted, defended, and evaded non-existent enemies.

She was amazed by his posture. It echoed power and confidence, but also a calculated amount of caution and risk for enemy rebuttal. The balls of his feet glided across the mats and his chest was forward, but his lower back curved, ready to strike forward or back like a coiled cobra. There was a noticeable bend in his knees and she could see all the raw power of his lower body emanating through his calves, glutes, quads, and hamstrings.

What he was doing with his arms, however, was the truly fantastic, but frightening piece. Bursts of daylight erupted from the reflection of the blade and then were gone again as the silver metal sliced through the air to its next position. Rachel noticed it was of formidable length and slightly curved. She'd never really been a fan of blades. To her they seemed like a violent step above a gun and required a much more personal encounter. She also wasn't a fan of their byproduct: blood. But to each their own, she reasoned.

Dynadin's other hand held a gun which he'd point in several directions between moves. There was no shake in his extension and no waver in his aim, at least not from where she stood. After several moves and what would have amounted to somewhere between eight and twelve shots, Dynadin made a very swift movement that Rachel's eyesight didn't fully comprehend right away.

There had been a small "clack" of noise as his hands had come together briefly, then back apart into the next motion.

Intrigued, and more than slightly entranced by this assassin's artistry, Rachel postponed her own workout and sat on the step, continuing to watch Dynadin. Once again, after around ten faux shots from the gun, another lightning fast motion, a small "click" and right back to it. This repeated itself several times, with Rachel still not coming to a solid conclusion as to what was happening. *Is he tapping the metal of the gun and knife? Is that some type of ritual?*

After another fifteen minutes, the moves became more intense, practically blurred, and Dynadin was rattling off shots and knife slits at a rapid clip. She guessed this might be his finale and the increased pace in addition to the more technically complicated moves created a crescendo of athleticism and determination. Then she saw it.

As if it was a parting move, he fired two blanks, one forward, and one behind him. With simple flicks of his wrists he lobbed the gun and knife into the air, but there was a third object – a magazine – soaring behind the gun and away from the knife. A soft thud rang from the mat as Rachel noticed the mag already in the gun had fallen to the floor. Dynadin caught the weapons in opposite hands, and with another minute wrist movement, the new magazine slid into the gun's grip.

For the first time in nearly 20 minutes, he remained still, visibly sweating with a slightly shorter breath. Slowly he stood straight, placed the gun and knife at his feet and went to rehydrate from his nearby water bottle. There was no way he hadn't noticed Rachel by this point – he seemed to be simply ignoring her. Or…*Is he shy?*

His gaze was downward and she could tell he was deliberately trying to not make a fuss about what he was doing. Shocked that this man, this beast, was timid, Rachel decided to approach him. After what she'd just witnessed, she wanted to learn from someone who was clearly the best.

"Hey!" She waved, almost a little too enthusiastically. Dynadin returned the sentiment silently and made eye contact with her. She saw a lot of well-managed pain in his brown eyes, but also a glimmer of someone who loved life and was thankful to be alive. "I was just watching you from over there…" She motioned.

"Ah, yes. I saw you. Sorry if I intruded on your workout or if I'm using any of the equipm – "

"No, no, no." She cut him off with a wave of her hand. "I was just about to get started actually. You're…um…pretty incredible. Where did you learn all of that?"

Proudly Dynadin answered. "It's self-taught. I base it on a combination of many martial arts, mainly Krav Maga, and I worked in the addition of a gun and knife."

"It's gorgeous."

Dynadin laughed at her reply. "Why thank you. It's very effective too you know?" He smiled at Rachel.

"Oh…I can only imagine. What is it that you were doing when your hands would come together? And what was that at the end?"

There was an impressed look on Dynadin's face.

"You caught that, hmm? They're one in the same, the movement at the end is just a bit fancier…and harder to pull off." He paused, adding a moment of silent suspense to his answer. "I'm reloading."

"Wait, really? *That* fast? How on…how're you?"

"It's all in the knife." He pointed back to it, still lying on the mat. "And the wrists too I suppose." Smiling, he took a swig of water, placed the bottle down, retrieved the knife and handed it to Rachel. She held it as if it was fragile, or was going to bite her. Dynadin held a magazine in his other hand and waved it over the knife's hilt. Nothing was happening and Rachel didn't quite understand what he was getting at.

"See that button there?" He asked. Rachel nodded. "Press it." She did, but nothing seemed to happen. Dynadin began to wave the mag over the hilt again, only this time the magnet inside absorbed the black metal and its bullets to its side. Rachel was slightly startled but more amazed.

"Woah." She stared down at the knife. "That is so cool."

Dynadin let out a surprisingly jolly laugh.

"Yes. I suppose it is!"

Rachel smiled and there was a brief moment of silence as she lost herself in thought looking at the weapon in her hands. Finally she spoke.

"Would you train me?"

Dynadin was taken aback by the question, though not shocked by any means. Before he could answer she spoke once more.

"I don't think I could ever do this whole knife-and-gun-quick-reload thing you created, but I'd be really appreciative if you'd work with me to stay on top of my hand-to-hand and shooting?"

That doesn't seem so bad Dynadin reasoned. Initially he was fearful that she wanted to be exactly like him. He didn't want her to become an expert dealer of death like he was, even though he knew she could do it. There was a drive in her, he sensed it, but it was a heavy cross to bear, being so good at killing.

"Sure, Rachel. I can give you some pointers and work with you. Might as well while we're stuck here!"

They both laughed in their newfound friendship and Rachel went on to have one of the toughest workouts of her life.

Sleep took her into its grasp as the recent memory of that day faded into dreams.

There was nothing but darkness for what felt like the longest time. Only the sensation of being present in the darkness, of sitting there, of standing there, of lying in it…her subconscious was aloof. Either that or busy working on what would amount to one hell of a dream. With little warning, the darkness became blotted with small particles of light.

Are those stars?

At first there was just one. Then ten. Then one hundred. Then thousands. Soon there was nearly more starlight than darkness and Rachel could see the outline of her body. Her hands were in front of her face, hair floating aimlessly around her in the zero gravity. Strangely, she had a premonition that she *should* be cold, nay freezing, up here in space.

But she wasn't.

The effortlessness of floating soothed her and there was a euphoric sensation deep in her gut and her mind about it all. Somewhere, back in the recesses of her mind, she knew there was turmoil and stress in her life. Even death. But for the life of her she couldn't recall any of those problems right now. Rachel was weightless in both

body and mind. For what could have been days, as it very
nearly felt like it, she reveled in the freedom and relaxed
in the peaceful nature of it all.

Gradually there emerged a bluish hue in the distance;
it was round in nature and growing in diameter. The complete feeling of buoyancy was mostly gone now as a pro-
pulsion, some force, pressed on Rachel's back and tugged
forward on her frame. Something was moving her toward
the blue circle of light – some formidable phantom. It
was subtle, but within moments *(or hours?)* her speed
had doubled, tripled, and now she was hurtling toward
the solid blue sphere.

It was Earth.

Even from a far, far distance she could tell what it
was and as her speed continued to exponentially increase,
the outline of the familiar blueberry in the galaxy became
strikingly crystal clear.

Her sense of peace was exchanged for worry and anxiousness because of the newly introduced sense of speed.
Although Earth wasn't approaching quickly, she knew if
her speed kept its trend she'd be there shortly. *Do I want
to be there? What is all of this?*

A cold numbness traced itself on the inner pads of her
fingers. She was holding something she hadn't been a
second ago. The other hand felt it too; it was also gripping something new and foreign. Before she took a
glance at them, she knew what they were. The weight, the
heft, the balance…they were familiar objects. Even
against the darkness of space, she could see the silenced
weapons, or at least their outlines. Their shape was normal, though the silencers looked much longer to her,
maybe twice the length. A random fact popped into her

mind about the lack of sound in space and her logic became stuck on a thought. *Why would I even need silencers in space? Why are they so long?*

The gun fired itself. Or at least she didn't remember pulling the trigger. An eruption of thunderous echoes rang from the tip of the silencer. These were not quiet at all and the discharge of a bullet had rushed Earth even closer to Rachel. She'd not shifted from her current rate of acceleration but rather the planet had raced forward slightly *toward her* and then paused. Incredulous and confused, Rachel closed her eyes, wanting this all to just go away.

It didn't.

Even without looking, the feeling of forward thrust was overwhelming and now that she was focused on it, it felt very much like something in particular: falling. An image of falling through space terrified her and the sense of impending doom, of *Earth* being that impending doom, began to overtake her. Not wanting to see anymore, she squeezed her eyelids tighter.

Another bombastic clap of violence and a shivering vibration up her arm ripped her eyes open. These guns were firing on their own as she knew for a fact she hadn't pulled the trigger that time. In a further effort to end this ordeal she released her grasp of the weapons, but to no avail. Fingers were still wrapped tightly around the grips and Rachel realized she had little muscle control in the entirety of her arms.

Panic entered the equation and her breathing became shallow.

Frantically, Rachel began looking around her, thinking she would find something. Something to get her out of here. Something to slow her down. Something to make her drop the guns. But she was in space and there was nothing.

Sounds from one of the guns' chamber roared through the vacuum of the galaxy again, but she hadn't felt the weapon glued to her arm vibrate. It had come from somewhere and someone else. There in the distance, where she'd previously been looking for reprieve from this nightmare, were nearly two dozen bodies, all falling in the same direction as she.

Earth was much closer now, and within this reality it began to look significantly different close up. Even from this great distance she could see several blocks of skyscrapers rising up from its surface; the clusters scattered only across the United States. There were what appeared to be white lines south of each city's buildings that looked as if they could spell something, but she didn't know for sure.

All around her the bodies closed in and they started to fire their weapons in attempts to kill her. *Are they trying to prevent me from reaching the world?* Hot bullets rained around her, not making any contact. The noise was intolerable and all their discharges at once caused it to play like a dull and endless bass tone.

Rachel's arms were moving now, still not tied to her control. The guns fired off round after round, aiming smoothly between each falling body. These bodies were faceless, at least from what she could see, and they didn't bleed. Her bullets would tear through them, simply creating a large hole through which she could see the stars and darkness on the other side. Luckily, it seemed that they were dying, or at least giving up, after each strike.

There was something poetic about it all; almost like her arms had done this before. They crossed her chest and fired opposite of one another, ripping a hole in one body's head and another's hip. It went on like this for a while, almost to the point where she had reached some semblance of calm. She looked down, Earth now filling most of her field of view, and she could tell that the white lines she'd perceived were in fact writing. Each city sky-line had its name written in normal white font under-neath. *What the hell*? It was odd to see *San Francisco* scribed out on the California shore, and *Chicago* on the central plains. Most of the largest cities in the country were there, almost as if the heavens had needed to scrawl some reminders.

Something before her caught her eye but there wasn't enough time to react. A body, seemingly falling *upward* was feet away from crashing into her. In a last minute ef-fort, Rachel tried to bring the handguns to her front, but they were stuck, out at her sides. The creepy, faceless hu-manoid pointed his gun at Rachel, then turned it at his own chest, firing right as he reached her. Smokeless fire exploded from where he used to be and she fell into it. It was painless...*or is it?*...but there was some odd sensa-tion of heat there. The impossible yellow and orange and blue flames swallowed her whole and followed her as she fell. The brightness was extreme and she could barely watch as the flames curled and danced with the gravity down toward Earth.

She tried to scream but nothing came out. So it was true what they say: "in space, no one can hear you scream." But they could sure as hell hear your guns fire and chest bombs explode.

Out of the flames on either side of her, two more bod-ies appeared, closing in on her flanks. There was a pres-ence to these though and each had details to their faces.

They stopped just short of crashing into her and her gut registered a wave of emotion.

On her left was Elena.

On her right was Bryson.

She tried to speak, but just as with the scream, nothing came out. Tears filled her eyes but didn't last long in the flames. Both of her dead friends stared at her, unphased that they all seemed to be plummeting to their deaths encased in the walls of a fireball. Bryson spoke,

"Rachel, why'd you leave?" It was innocent enough. Then he shouted with rage. "You're a traitor! You left me to die!"

Trying to speak, Rachel could do nothing but shed more tears and shake her head. Elena replied.

"You did what was best. You're *doing* what *is* best. David must be stopped."

"I gave my life for N.E.T.S.!" Bryson screamed. "And you turn your back on it?"

"You didn't know yet. It's not your fault. None of this is." Elena calmly mentioned.

"David is a good man!" More shouting by Bryson. "You think you'll kill him? He's the only one standing between the Dead Scorpions and all of you!"

"You've seen the proof." More reasoning by Elena. "He *is* the Dead Scorpions. You need to cut off the head, Rachel."

Bryson was strikingly calm again now. "What if you're wrong? What if they're all wrong?"

"And what if you're right?" Elena countered. "What if all of it is exactly as it sounds?"

Rachel just wanted it all to stop. Not just the dream. But everything else. All the spy bullshit. All the fear. All the lies. The sex. The violence. That wish had no sooner passed across her mind when Bryson read it.

"You like it." It was stated as fact and Rachel turned to him in pain, an accusatory look shifting to a shameful one.

The fire began to pull back and with it, Bryson and Elena. Their ghosts jerked away as if being pulled by a parachute and the flames followed, a few final tendrils embracing Rachel's arms and abdomen before leaving her once more in the darkness.

Earth was larger than ever now as she seemed to be falling through the atmosphere. More cities' names appeared on the land beneath her and the visual uprising of the ground made it very apparent that she was plummeting at an unrealistic speed.

A scream finally escaped her, though her arms were still bound by some unknown chains. Layers of thin clouds passed by and there was a chill to the air. One that she most certainly felt, be it dream or reality. Her heart beat so hard that it was nearly loud enough to hear and she feared that she might pass out from its force alone.

These cities were clearly not real, as many of the skyscrapers leaping off the land looked to be many miles high. She was only a short fall away from reaching their heights and it was now obvious that her trajectory was aimed at Denver, by no choice of her own. White clouds traded themselves for blue skies. It was odd that the only visible objects on the land were these cities. No lakes, no rivers – not even the Rocky Mountains which she should have been able to see by now.

Soon the skyscrapers swallowed her up in their towering masses, creaking in the wind and air that she brought along with her speed. Reflective blues, blacks, silvers, and browns filled her vision, though she still could not see the ground. It felt as if the air pressure had gotten thicker, pushing on her rib cage and appendages. It wasn't painful, but a sudden notion of claustrophobia overtook her, adding more adrenaline and panic to her frazzled state. At this point she couldn't tell if she was speeding up, slowing down, or if her speed was constant, but it didn't matter as she was still falling well past the threshold of physical possibility.

Without warning, her arms began moving again, extending outward and aimed at the skyscrapers framing the sides of her descent. A shot fired from each, puncturing the glass windows of the buildings and sending their shattered remains into free fall around and beneath Rachel. Each shot had been loud, but the predominant sound effect this time had been the chime-like explosion of the glass and it continued to fall with a similar musical quality.

Impossibly, as these were not fully automatic weapons, the guns began to fire a string of bullets all down the sides of the buildings to her front, sides, back, and everything in between. The chiming of broken glass became like a bout of tinnitus and Rachel's world became a drab collection of chunks, shards, and fragments.

Without pain, the sharp edges were cutting into her arms, then her face, and finally across her whole body. Wanting to wake up from this nightmare, she screamed once more but it was inaudible over the symphony of chaos around her. The end was near and she could sense it. Unable to see beneath her now, she knew the ground was rushing up…she could *feel* it about to obliterate her. Just as she expected either the dream to end or herself to die, all the glass surrounding her – every last piece –

gained extra momentum and raced to beat her to the ground. There the pieces gathered, one by one, forming one massive reflective mirror on the ground.

As the final pieces came together, Rachel knew this was the end.

You have to wake up.

A few lasting remnants fitted themselves into the mirror's puzzle.

You're going to die.

Something was not quite right about her reflection.

This is real.

Was that even her reflection?

Wake up!

The face was not hers.

Rachel!

David Harper. It was milliseconds before she smashed into the ground, surely to her pulverizing death, and the reflection staring back at her from the ground had been that of the enemy.

David. Worn. Greyed hair. Tired. Smiling.

There was no noise when she hit the ground but instead a physical and violent lurching upward. Rachel opened her eyes to discover that she was sitting in her bed, sunlight pouring into her Costa Rican bedroom.

"Holy fucking shit." It came out breathless as she put a hand to her chest, feeling her heart fluttering beneath. She moved it up to her forehead and wiped as much of the profuse sweat from her brow as she could manage. She was burning up.

Frustrated and still overwhelmed with the dream's images, not to mention any deeper meanings it might

have held, she tossed the covers off, hoping for some relief. The ceiling fan was spinning, gladly obliging by
throwing colder air downward.

What was that? Her heart rate began to slow. *I've
never had a dream like that.* Just a dream. It was all over.
"You like it". Why did he say that? It had all been so
vivid. It was not a dream Rachel would soon forget.

Breathing a little more normally now, she lowered
herself back onto her pillow, feeling the dampened sheets
beneath her. She lay on her back, staring at the fan turning round and round and round. Tranquility found her and
within moments she had stopped sweating, was breathing
fine, and was comforted to discover that her heart was no
longer trying to escape through her ribcage. But her mind
continued to race.

After several moments of lying there in open-eyed
meditation, her bedroom door swung open. Remembering
she was still completely naked without any sheets, she
began to curl up in embarrassment.

"Ummmm." Ian began but didn't know how to continue, realizing he should have knocked first. Seeing it
was him, Rachel cast modesty aside and looked at him
impatiently.

"What? It's not like you haven't seen all of this before." Ian agreed but remained awkwardly silent. "What
is it, Ian? What's going on?" He made sure to keep his
eyes locked with hers.

"Henry just sent us something this morning; we're
looking deeper into it now. It could be something big, potentially a live field op." There was a pause, the only
sound coming from the rapidly rotating fan above.
"You're going to want to see this, Rachel."

CHAPTER X

DOUBLE OR NOTHING

WEDNESDAY | OCT 3RD | 2018

This was real fear.

Henry sat at his expansive, black, glass desk at N.E.T.S. headquarters in New York City. Only a couple of weeks had passed since Costa Rica, when he'd discovered Rachel and her team and they had "convinced" him to become a double agent.

Backed against a wall, Henry had no other choice as death was the only alternative. A man named Dahl had spun some tale of David being a monster – the leader of both N.E.T.S. and the Aqarab Mayta. His agreement had seemed genuine, but in truth it had been a cautious one. Their proof was only hearsay and the lives of his men were on the line too.

Returning to N.E.T.S., he'd contemplated telling David everything. His team had bought the lie about a missed location easily enough, and quickly forgotten about it by the time they were back stateside, but David would be harder to convince, especially since he'd seen a lot of the data surrounding the Costa Rican hideout already.

But Henry didn't tell David. He'd gotten damn close, but there'd been something holding his tongue. Perhaps it was the fact that he knew it would mean eventual death for Rachel? Or maybe another part of him was worried he'd be reprimanded – or worse? He tried to reason that these were acceptable explanations but really he knew the truth: doubts lived within him. *What if they were right about David? How do I know they're not? What would happen if I'm wrong?* The potential answers to these rhetorical questions were too extreme not to send shivers down Henry's spine and thus he'd gone on with the double agent agenda.

For now.

There had been fear throughout the last few weeks and he was feeling it now again. This fear was gnawing, burning slowly at his psyche. At any minute Henry half expected someone to come and apprehend him or for David to stroll in and put a bullet in his brain himself. This was anxiety. Self-doubt. Insecurity. Constant questioning.

Henry spent a significant portion of each day mentally reviewing his interactions with other agents and David. Had he given anything away? *Did I stutter? Were my palms a little too sweaty? Was I too quick to answer that?* Every little detail was scrutinized, eating away at him until finally he'd do his best to take a deep breath and move on. He'd hoped that it would have gotten easier with each day but the truth was it was only getting more and more difficult. Remembering *who* he had spoken to, *what* he had said, and *details* he had provided…being a double agent was an ever growing psychological puzzle.

So now, after yet another interaction with David, he found himself at his desk, trying to breathe deeply and walk through the interaction that had just occurred mere minutes ago.

Recently, Henry had been researching, deceptively of course, where the IP pings had been originating from that had caused Costa Rica to look like *the* hideout for Rachel and her Rogues (as they were now being called around the office). Through the false cloud network that Dahl had worked on setting up with him, they'd been able to patchwork some details together to support the claim with believable evidence. Henry ran it past their best technology agents, who evidently were *not* better than Dahl, and they agreed with the takeaways that Henry drew from the details.

His interaction with David from moments ago had been a presentation of this data where the key conclusion Henry made was: "We do not at this time have enough proof to solidify the location of Rachel, Target Zero, and any other potential accomplices." As soon as Henry had entered David's office, there was the recognition that his superior was in a bad mood and the unsatisfying results from a few weeks research hadn't done much to propel his mood in the opposite direction.

"Why the fuck are you telling me this?" David had asked harshly.

"Sir, I wanted to explain to you why Costa Rica didn't pan out, as well as give you an update on the current intelligence of their whereabouts."

"You could have saved us both ten minutes and just told me that you and your team shit the bed in Costa Rica. You were on point for that operation and it seems to me like boots should have never touched Costa Rican soil given how wrong we were about the IP address."

"Agreed, sir." Henry shifted uncomfortably after the reprimand and continued. "Either way, we will find them. And the good news is that they've been awfully quiet in recent weeks." It was true as both Rachel's group and

N.E.T.S. had taken next to no field work in the last fort-
night.

"Would you say *awfully* quiet or *eerily* so?" David
questioned. "Not hearing anything from them makes me
worried we spooked them. Like they knew about our
Costa Rica mistake and they're just playing us or relocat-
ing." David looked at Henry, letting his eyes do the blam-
ing for what his mouth wasn't saying.

"I'm sorry, sir. We were wrong. *I* was wrong. It won't
happen again." Henry began to pack up his tablet and
notepad; clearly David wasn't in the mood and this
presentation was completed. As he turned for the door,
David cleared his throat.

"Perhaps they've been so quiet…" There was a pause
as he decided what he wanted to say. "So quiet because…they've got someone on the inside now?" Henry
froze visibly, but quickly regained his composure. *Had he
seen that*? "They did it before with Zane." David continued. "Who's to say they aren't playing the same card
again and have somehow flipped another idiot to feed
them information?"

Henry faced David and went to sit at the chair beside
his desk. Blood was rushing through his system as the
muscle in his chest pumped harder and harder and harder.
Visibly though, he appeared remarkably calm and spoke
even more so.

"Ok." He started. "Let's entertain that idea…it's a
valuable exercise especially after the Zane incident." David raised an eyebrow and squared his shoulders with
Henry, impressed by the young man's maturity in trying
to analyze his peers. "The first obvious question becomes: who do we think it is? Follow up question immediately becomes, 'why'? What proof do we have?" David

nodded, agreeing with Henry's process. Truth be told, he couldn't think of a single potential candidate as he'd been increasingly disconnected from N.E.T.S. agents since The Will. Most likely, there was no mole, but he wanted to see if Henry held a different sentiment.

If only Agent Cobble could have known for sure what was going through David's mind in that moment. As much as he tried, he couldn't calm his body's natural re-action to the discussion of the topic at hand. Beads of sweat gathered under his arms, on his forehead, and between his legs. Despite his even speech, his breath was short and staggered and he couldn't stop lightly tapping his feet. Luckily, David spoke next.

"Valid things to ask. It's a hard road to go down when you're talking about potentially accusing someone of being a double. You risk offending someone who may not be and if you take too much time, you also risk spooking the actual mole. There are some telltale signs however." The powerful man swiveled in his chair to face the city out his window as he thought and spoke. Henry stole a quick wipe of the sweat under his hairline as David continued. "Moles tend to either disconnect from those around them, or make greater efforts to get closer. There is no middle ground because they always overcompensate depending on which way they decide to go." *Noted* Henry mentally flagged. David had paused, thinking of other potential elements of mole behavior, but eventually continued. Henry was quickly overheating. *Is there no damn AC in this office?*

"Then there are the obvious physical signs. Nervous ticks, basically any facial trip up that comes with lying: lack of eye contact, weight gain or loss, newfound alcohol or drug addiction, and stuttered speech among a few others." A pause. David's face was contorted deep in thought. Henry believed that he was almost certainly speaking about him right now, but there was a hint of sincerity. Maybe he didn't know? Maybe he actually still trusted Henry?

"But we train all N.E.T.S. agents specifically on how to subvert those physical reactions. I imagine that if there was a double agent here, our agents are so highly trained that they may not even exude those characteristics. Now, if this were the F.B.I. or C.I.A., maybe, but we're at a different level." Henry felt as if he had to reply reinforce the guise of innocence.

"True, David, but then wouldn't there be potential overcompensation for those physical effects too? You listed nervous ticks or stuttered speech…those suggest consistent anxiousness. Is it possible our agents are so well trained that they may become overly calm?"

David laughed. "You're always pretty calm, Henry. Are you my mole?"

Fuck. Don't change your face.

A gut punch erupted in his stomach almost to the point of bowel movement.

Adrenaline blossomed swiftly throughout his blood stream and the sweating began to return.

Agent Cobble was certain he was made. His heart spoke out in rhythms to the entire room, pounding so loudly Henry's hearing glossed over.

David began laughing out the window and turned around.

"Oh boy…" Continued laughter. "That's a good one." A sigh released as the laugh ceased. "I haven't laughed that hard in a while…Agent Henry Cobble. The mole of

N.E.T.S. and double agent to the small resistance group that has been a thorn in my side."

Lost in confusion, Henry couldn't tell if he was still having a conversation with a sane man who'd just made a joke, or a psychopath who was playing with puppets and their strings.

This was real fear.

And it would kill him.

"You don't look so hot, Henry." David mentioned, potentially feigning sympathy. It was all Henry could do right now to not vomit on the man's desk. "You okay?" Henry coughed, and answered.

"It was a funny joke, sir." He started. "Truthfully, I had some sushi last night that has not been agreeing with me and I think it's coming to a head." A gentle rub on his stomach sold the story more. "Sorry if that's too much information but I'd love to keep having this conversation. I think it's one we *need* to have – potentially vet out every agent in here. Would you mind if I schedule some time with you tomorrow? We can talk through this when I'm hopefully not about to be sick?"

David looked taken aback: half disgusted, half surprised.

"Of course, of course. Get on out of here." He motioned him toward the door. "Go see medical and they can pump some fluids through you. We'll talk tomorrow."

"Thank you, sir." Henry got up immediately, still clutching his stomach. The shivers came as his core temperature dropped post-adrenaline and he really did feel absolutely sick now. As he was about to reach the door David spoke.

"Agent Cobble?"

"Yes, sir?"

"Feel. Better." There might have been a smirk on David's face as he said it and Henry was sure he'd stress and replay it over and over again in his head. For now, he simply nodded and exited the room.

Fuck.

Fuck.

Fuck.

Vomit escaped his mouth. Henry had barely made it to the [thankfully] empty restroom to make sure it landed in a toilet bowl, not remembering a single step from David's office door to this moment.

That real fear surged through him again and the toilet filled with more, empty vomit. The lurch had come all the way from his toes, ripping through his glutes, abdomen, rib cage, and neck. It was painful and his nostrils stung with the stomach acid. *Get control of yourself, Cobble. You're a double agent now whether you like it or not.*

He took a few deep breaths, slobber and mucus blowing in and out from his lips until he finally wiped it clean with a few sheets of toilet paper. His shoulders were shaking but he knew he was done throwing up. His heart rate was steadily coming down, the sweating had stopped, leaving a cold glaze on his face and arms, and his breathing had finally returned to somewhere near the realm of normal.

Agent Henry Cobble knew he wasn't the *best* agent in N.E.T.S., but the physical reactions he'd just experienced were completely foreign to him. Within this moment of clarity following the chaos Henry realized that was the closest he had ever come to death. David's power…his gaze…the inflection of his voice…that laugh – Henry's head was spinning with doubts and accusations. He knew.

He didn't know. He knew. He didn't know. It was like a grade school girl playing he-loves-me-not.

Pressing off the cold tile, Henry stood up, achy and shaking, flushed the toilet, and went to wash his hands. The fluorescent lights in the bathroom were annoying and giving him a headache. Across from him, the mirror reflected someone who was hideously guilty of hiding something. *Or is that just my perception?* Pale face. Clamminess. Tussled, recently sweaty hair. Weak stance. Darkening puffs under his eyes. *I look like shit. At least that sells the food poisoning angle well…*

After splashing some incredibly refreshing cold water on his face, Henry left to return to his office, hopefully avoiding David for the rest of the day. For he wasn't sure he could go through another bout of that.

Luckily he only had to feign a couple of "Hi!"s on the way back. He immediately shut the door and turned the glass walls to their full opaqueness, turning the lights off too. David's teaching echoed, *"Moles tend to either disconnect from those around them, or make greater efforts to get closer. There is no middle ground because they always overcompensate depending on which way they decide to go".*

Henry released a heavy sigh, "Fuck me." Reluctantly, and not unlike a lazy teenager, he opened his door a smidge and made his walls slightly more translucent. "How's that for overcompensating?" He had no idea who he was talking to, but he supposed it was himself. *Whatever.*

He knew he needed a distraction from all of this and that work would be his best bet. Things may have been slow on the N.E.T.S. side, but Dahl was always eager for more information and Henry had ample access to a lot of

it. Curious that he would start working on the very thing
that was causing him so much anxiety, but each interaction with David made Henry more and more suspicious.
Something was going on; his gut wasn't wrong.

Before he started he reached into his desk and took
out a few peppermint candies to settle his stomach and
give his mouth something to do while also grabbing his
chilled water bottle from the mini fridge at his side. It
was cool and had some surface condensation so he
rubbed it across his forehead, reveling in the small relief
it provided. Lastly, he grabbed his over-ear headphones
from another drawer in his desk and cycled his phone to
his workout playlist which was filled with hard, thumping
rap and bass-dropping electronic music.

He was already beginning to feel much better.

Let's get to work.

The computer screen blazed against the darkened
room and became more dramatic as the hours passed and
the day became dusk. No one had come to bother Henry
thankfully and he was in a groove. As he hunted for information – anything that he could pass along – he'd had
a minor, but obvious revelation. The quicker he could
find something of substance, some evidence that was
damning to David's entire operation, the quicker he could
get out of here and avoid terrifying encounters like the
one he'd had earlier. This new thought fueled him, along
with several cups of coffee and countless peppermints, to
pour over everything.

If there was one area within his training that Henry
Cobble was beyond proficient, it was computers and literally everything that related to them. He'd worked on his
physicality and athleticism in recent years to much im-
provement, but he came into N.E.T.S. as one of their

most promising technology prodigies in the last decade. Hacking, network access, decrypting – you name it and Henry could likely do it. Being in front of a keyboard was a home of sorts for him.

He scanned David's computer for any potential back-door IP addresses. Maybe he had a hidden cloud network access as well?

All of David's financial transactions were reviewed and scrutinized. Had he been anywhere out of the norm recently?

Phone calls from his office and cell were reviewed, but Henry quickly found that many calls traced back to false roots.

Next, Cobble reviewed David's emails. The man was insanely busy, making the task daunting, and there was a concern that all of these emails were of N.E.T.S. nature. *Would he really be digitally communicating with the Dead Scorpions on our servers?* Still though, Henry reviewed them, thousands of them. Some received quick glances – all junk mail and spam was filtered out – and others were completely read through. About halfway through this arduous task, his stomach called out for a break; the peppermints were not enough and he'd also thrown up its contents earlier. With a sigh and a rub of his eyes, he removed his headphones and paused his music.

A large, meat-filled burrito sounded delicious right about now so Henry exited the building and within a few moments he was at his favorite fast casual burrito chain, foil wrapped goodness in hand. Having had an empty stomach for most of the day, and with his physical stress now long subsided, the burrito was tastier than normal. It was all he could do to not scarf it down in a handful of bites, but he knew that would cause even more stomach issues down the line.

The restaurant was nearly empty save for a few single parties scrolling through their phones as they ate. Henry hadn't realized how late it was until he'd gotten outside, but he'd obviously been working for many hours as it was now dark. Inside it was a bit cold; they had the AC cranked too high and Henry wished he'd brought a jacket. He'd had the chills enough for one day.

After dripping some Tabasco sauce on his last large bite, he crumpled the foil, placed it in the plastic tray, and walked over to the trash receptacle, still mashing and gnawing on the delicious final morsel. Above the wooden surface with a hole to place your trash was an employee-made sign drawn with Sharpie on computer paper, "Throw Your Junk HERE ↓".

Henry thought nothing of it as he tossed the foil and empty water cup in the opening, but he glanced back at the sign, smeared marker, frayed edges and all…obsessed with one word: *junk*.

Junk.

Junk.

JUNK.

A moment occurred wherein it seemed like someone had both removed a dense fog from the room and also pulled him backward sharply by the collar of his shirt.

The JUNK mail.

Agent Cobble's head was spinning as he tried to logically approach this epiphany.

Why would an organization as secret as N.E.T.S. receive junk mail?

There was no immediate answer.

We're on some of the most secure servers on the planet. How would junk mail, of all things, get through our blocks and filters?

Again, silence from the metaphorical audience in his brain.

And why would David, the most important person at N.E.T.S., put up with any junk mail hitting his inbox? He would have seen that as a security threat the absolute first time it happened.

Henry snapped out of it momentarily and realized that he was standing awkwardly by the trashcan, frozen and blocking it from anyone potentially looking to leave. Within only a few minutes he had left the chilly restaurant, ridden the elevator to the hidden N.E.T.S. floor, and returned to his desk, peppermint in his cheek and music over his ears once more. There was a certain excitement now; he knew he was right about this. *Now I just have to prove it.*

Eager eyes poured over the emails that were labeled as junk mail and they were convincingly typical in nature. Advertisements for useless products, pictures and colors here and there. Even some text was bolded or italicized for dramatic effect – as if the email itself were an over exaggerating cheesy salesman.

But still…

They were…*normal.* Convinced that he had been onto something great here, Henry's faith was now starting to waver a tad. These truly did look like any standard junk emails. As corny as he thought it was, he couldn't help but muse: *That's what they want you to think.*

More digging revealed a message that rang awkwardly as Henry read it and he thought it might potentially have some hidden meaning. It read:

"Want love present with no **time** *or* **inter-est**? Every second newly entranced women *yearn* and remember days unlike initial vows. Take **important**, **ironclad**, **initial** action! Find others!

Visit **hookmeup.com** now!"

The grammar and cadence of the wording felt odd and off, even more so once Henry read it aloud to himself. After repeating it several times he also noticed it didn't particularly make any sense and he was also curious about much of the sentence structure and phrasing. Sure, spam email authors weren't the most competent, but there was something here. He could feel it.

It had to be a code of some sort, but if that were true then discovering and cracking it would be no simple task. He wondered if he should enlist the help of Dahl and the others, but figured against it, not wanting to waste their time if he was wrong. And also wanting to avoid embarrassment of sending them junk mail thinking there could be highly sensitive information hidden within.

So he got to work. First, Henry wrote down the mail's language on a piece of paper; working this with physical paper and pen would make it much easier. Second, he wrote out each grouping of letters based on the quantity that were present, just to get a sense for what words might potentially be formed. He counted the "A"s as such: a a a a a a a a a a a. There were eleven "A"s in total, none of which were capitalized, in case that mattered. He did this for each letter of the alphabet and after a few minutes was ready to begin really running through the possibilities of communications within this email.

Damn. Going to be a long night…

Luckily, an "all-nighter" wasn't unheard of these days at N.E.T.S. The office was generally mostly empty in the early morning hours, but several analysts would stay behind trying their hardest to unravel the mysteries of the Dead Scorpions – much like Henry was right now. Some of them did it for the thrill. Others did it because they didn't have much else going on in their lives. And a couple were solely there to impress leadership and move up. Cobble had the added benefit of already being directly under David and with that privilege came a giant, metaphorical "Do Not Disturb" sign on his door.

That long night stretched into an early morning as Henry found he'd had no success trying to figure this damn email out. So many different codes and methods had been tried, none amounting to more than just a garbled tossed salad of letters. Perhaps this was just a normal, poorly written spam email? But every time that question pleaded with Henry to stop, he remembered the evidence against it and became increasingly determined.

There was one potential last idea, and it was somewhat a variation of what he'd already done several hours before, but at this point his only reasoning to try something was: *Why the hell not?*. He took a new sheet of paper, what must have been his fortieth or fiftieth of the night and listed the first letter of each word that was contained in the main body paragraph of the mail:

W l p w n t a i E s n e w y a r d u i v T i i i a F o

Something about the three "I"s in a row was calling to him. "Important", "ironclad", and "initial" were all very deliberate choices, but Henry's brain was fried. He could think of no obvious way that the three "I"s immediately presented any clues, other than being obviously mysterious.

Sighing and throwing his pen down deliberately hard on his desk, he brought his palms to his eyes, rubbing them for moisture. The music coming through his headphones had been moved to little more than background noise the last several hours and now the device hung heavy on his ears and face. He pulled them down and hung the arch around his neck, still staring incessantly at the letters on the sheet. Eyes swimming over the page, his gaze focused on both the beginning and end of the string of letters, but his mind was darting back and forth between wondering if he should go shower, get coffee, or keep working. Subconsciously however, his brain was beginning the formations of the solution as a specific word leapt of the page:

WolF.

From the string, he'd taken the first letter…then the last…then the second…then the second from last…and received the most concrete and obvious word since he'd started many hours ago. Using this pattern he continued.

WolFpawinitiaTivEisunderway.

Henry's heart was racing; he could see the words laid out in front of him and clearly the capitalizations hadn't been important. He went through and placed spaces where appropriate:

Wolfpaw Initiative is underway.

Wolfpaw Initiative? Synapses were firing left and right in his brain as he racked his memory for any recollection of the name, be it significant or minute. Nothing came to him and the fear began to return.

Was this a codename for The Will from last year? He checked the date of the email and saw that it was sent *after* the horrendous attacks by several months.

And the fear built more.

This was *something*. There was no longer a doubt in his mind. The code was cracked by what amounted to dumb luck, but solved nonetheless. Henry couldn't help feeling he'd just unraveled the first clues of a nightmare however.

Was this a small scale operation?

Was it a recruiting tool?

Was it an assassination?

Was it a blackmail?

Was it a sign of biological warfare?

The four words were practically floating off the page in his eyes; dancing and taunting him, begging him to keep asking questions and dive down the rabbit hole of useless worrying and guessing. Recognizing what was happening, Henry took a deep breath and prevented himself from going down this potentially inefficient and fruitless path.

There were more junk emails. There had to be more code. More code meant more information. More information meant fewer questions and more answers. Answers hopefully meant putting an end to all of this, or at least getting ahead of it for the time being.

He saved his findings by placing them on the desk's wraparound to his right and turned back to the computer, opening another junk email from a date a few weeks after the one he'd just cracked. Again, Henry wrote the text on paper to make it easier, the black ink racing across the white canvas as fast as he could will it:

> "Will acid open inside ducts? ***Behold***! Introducing a unique, new *nitrous peroxide* engine.
>
> Visit hotassmotorhead.net using the link below!"

As with the first, he ignored the bolded, italicized words as well as the final sentence with the site name. It was that bulk paragraph, shorter than the first "clue" that he was focused on. The first letters created the string:

w a o i d b i a u n n p e

And using the same technique he received a new string:

weaponindubai

Adding in spaces resulted to:

Weapon in Dubai

Ho. Lee. Shit. The cold fear struck again as his forehead began to perspire. *So it* is *a weapon then...*He had to continue. At this pace, he figured he could complete five to ten per hour, depending on the length, and pass along the code and emails once he had a sufficient story to tell.

Thirty minutes passed and there was definitely a story to be told. He'd gotten pretty fast at decoding and already had five more done, some lengthier than others.

Wolfpaw Initiative is underway

Weapon in Dubai

Science for WPI checks out

Transport date soon

East Coast ground zero

Tests conclusive

Tests successful

Fear had turned to terror as Henry realized their resistance might be too late for whatever came next. The date of the most recent one, "Transport date soon", was already a few weeks old. Whatever this could be, the name certainly didn't divulge any clues; "Wolfpaw Initiative" left a lot to the imagination.

But the decrypted emails didn't.

Science, conclusive tests, *successful* tests – this was definitely some biological weapon, potentially of massive destruction. The way the emails spoke about it potentially indicated that the organization was working on this far before The Will, but all the dates of the emails were after the fact. *Maybe that's when they decided on the stupid name.*

It was now that Henry questioned whether he should put another half hour into it or get in touch with Dahl and crew to reveal these findings. Given his oncoming exhaustion, his current hygiene (or lack thereof), and the simple fact that sooner was probably significantly better than later in this situation, he began the process of reaching out to Dahl through their secure channel. As he established that, he worked on saving the small junk email files to a folder to send over along with an explanation of how to decode them. Henry was about five minutes into creating an email to send over to Dahl when there was a rap at his ajar door.

Reacting more than he should have, a small ream of papers slipped to the floor in a quiet crash and the door opened several more inches, pouring a little extra light into the shady room. Text and codes and solutions were scribbled all sorts of ways on the blank white sheets Henry realized, and he made quick actions to pick them up before he greeted his guest. A guest whom he technically had not invited in yet, but who seemed to be ignoring that detail.

"What're you working on?" David's voice carried with inquisitive authority and Henry froze ever so briefly, careful not to seem on edge. He replied as he continued to pick up the papers.

"Ugh…just something…that I've been…looking at for a whi – OH! Ouch!" Papers plopped down on the desk, face down, and Henry brought his index finger to his mouth, sucking on it. "Fucking paper cut!"

David laughed, sincerely, for a few moments. "I guess even secret agents aren't impervious to paper cuts."

He stated as the laughter trailed off. "Everyone bleeds eventually."

The statement sent a familiar shiver down Henry's back with the calculated aggressiveness with which it was delivered. David had to be taunting him at this point. And ruthlessly so. *Act normal, dammit.*

"Still hurts like a bitch though." Henry retorted. David ignored it.

"So really, what are you working on?" His hand motioned to all the papers Cobble had picked up. "You seem to be pretty holed up in here. Are you feeling better than you were yesterday?"

Henry figured the truth would be the best avenue for as much of the story as possible, so that's what he began with.

"Much better yeah. I had to have eaten something that didn't agree with me – I left your office and immediately went to the bathroom to throw up. Quite a few times too. After that, I was feeling better, *much* better actually. Even ate a pretty hefty burrito last night."

"Interesting. Wonder where you ate…if you figure it out remind me to *not* go there."

Henry gave a mostly feigned chuckle. "Will do, sir. As to what I'm working on, I took our conversation very seriously. I've been going through each agent here at HQ and trying to think critically and qualitatively about their performance and mannerisms. You cited a lot of good points about how a mole may or may not act, as well as some of the warning signs." There was a pause; he was looking for some type of gratification but received none yet. "All of this," Henry motioned to the papers. "Is the consequence of me really having to put pen to paper sometimes. I found that my opinions and notions about each person were flowing a little easier when I was writing them down. Given our discussion, I figured I was the only one that could take this on…we don't know who we can trust right now." David's nod of approval finally came.

"Old school. I like it. And thanks for taking the initiative on this, as frustrating and uncomfortable as it may be." The gratitude hung in the air for a moment. "Any findings yet?"

Henry, who was quite proud (not to mention surprised) of himself for the handling of this situation, continued the lie. Why he was actually so calm was a mystery to him, but he thanked God that his anxiety had not yet kicked in.

"I'd love to give you a concrete answer, sir, but I have none right now. A couple people here and there that I want to look into a little deeper, but I've yet to have that gut reaction to anyone. Sorry."

"Oh don't be. That's about what I expected, but I like that you're using your gut. Our intuition is a more powerful tool than we often recognize." Henry nodded and the room fell silent. "Well, I'll let you get back to it." David turned to go. "Let me know when you want to finish what we were talking about yesterday or if you find anything here."

"Will do, sir. Just need to get a Band-Aid around this paper cut before I continue!"

David laughed and replied as he left the room. "You'll live."

That spine chill returned and the door closed, leaving the room quiet and darkened. Henry could feel the panic coming back, but something was different this time. Finding all of these codes and communications finally justified that he was doing the right thing. *You bastard. You walk in here smug as a statesman, but I know your secrets.* The thought pushed tranquility into his mindset, but also confidence. He couldn't stop thinking: *You bastard.*

Back on his computer screen, which had fallen asleep by now thankfully, the file compiling was complete and the communication was ready to send to Dahl and his team. After Henry finished typing his final explanations about the decoding process, he hit send as fast as he possibly could. He was eager to see what the other emails would reveal. Inexplicably, he had a strong sensation that this finding was a concrete mark of the beginning of the end to all this chaos, mayhem, and espionage. And David had no idea that he'd been caught.

You bastard.

CHAPTER XI

RUSH JOB

THURSDAY | OCT 4TH | 2018

Fabric caught on damp skin as Rachel threw on the garments, barely getting both legs in her pants before opening the door and leaving the room.

There had been a sense of urgency in Ian's voice just moments ago, and he didn't tend to react to news dramatically. Clearly Henry had sent something substantial and after a few weeks of disappointing results, Rachel was eager to see what it was.

As she hustled barefoot down the hallway, her stomach growled obnoxiously. *Breakfast will wait today.* Instead she headed downstairs where Dynadin, Ian, and Dahl were hard at work, each in front of a computer screen. Dynadin seemed to be counting something intensely as his index finger lightly grazed across the screen, from side to side. Confused, Rachel turned to Dahl for answers, but he was completely engrossed with writing something down, shooting cursory glances back and forth between paper and screen. His glasses rested on the tip of his nose, teetering on the verge of falling off. With a small growl of frustration, he pushed them back up, not unlike a nerdy child in middle school.

Stifling her laughter, Rachel took her gaze to Ian who'd already sat down and seemed to be completing a similar task, concentration, writing, some sort of count-ing…it was all very puzzling. And not a single one of them had noticed her enter the room.

"Guys…" No response, as if they had no capacity to hear anything. "GUYYYSS!" All three popped their heads up in a way that reminded her of prairie dogs peek-ing outside of their holes. Impossible to hide her laugh at that imagery, Rachel chuckled and inquired, "What the hell is going on? What are you all so concentrated on?" Dahl ignored her questions.

"Good, you're up. You can help. Grab a pen and a piece of paper. Check your email…instructions are in there." He returned to task, head down, and the other two followed.

"Umm. Ok?" Their behavior was bordering on obses-sive and it made Rachel feel a bit uncomfortable. *What the hell did they find?* She walked over to her desk and computer, in between Dynadin and Ian, and sat.

Dahl, head still down, took enough time to state, "I sent you all the emails we'll need decoded. We're work-ing on the other ones. Get to work."

Decoded? This was exciting, but Rachel was still nervous. Everyone being on edge had created a sense of anticipatory dread in the air. Something big was happen-ing for sure.

Her computer finished booting up and the screen ig-nited with light, automatically opening her email on their private server. She scrolled to the forwarded email from Dahl that had originally been from Henry and began reading.

It didn't take long before she likely had the same pit in her stomach as the three others in the room and by the time she'd finished reading the email, she understood and adopted the urgency.

A hidden code?

A weapon?

Dubai?

Are we too late?

The instant need for answers drove her to quickly open Dahl's other email and its attachment: her assigned junk emails for decoding. With overzealous movements, she grabbed as many bits of paper as she could find around her desk – letters, sticky notes, blank sheets – and a pen. On her screen she'd already opened the first email and began the process that Henry had outlined. As she began, a drop of blood soaked into the white paper, slowly expanding with absorption. *What the hell?* Rachel looked around the hand it had come from and saw that she'd gotten a mildly grotesque papercut on the outer edge of her writing hand. *Fuck that.* She jammed the hand's side into her mouth. Ambidextrous to a certain extent, she'd do this with her other hand; there was no time to waste and the wound could wait.

The team of four worked in complete silence, save for the rustling of a paper or two and some sparse mouse clicks. Even in their haste, the air was still cool from the light air conditioning, though Rachel could feel herself perspiring under the arms every time a new solution got close. Several hours passed like this, all Maslownian needs taking a back seat to a single objective: solving the riddle. *What were the Aqarab Mayta going to do next and just how big was it going to be?*

Dynadin was the first done as he quietly announced it to the group. Ian stated he wasn't far behind and Rachel saw that, despite her cranking, she still had several more emails. Dahl instructed everyone to write out their messages in chronological order, citing the date on the same line of paper, and cut them into strips. The unperturbed silence of hours of hard work was broken by the "shick-shick" of scissors and tearing paper. It was high stakes arts and crafts.

If Dahl had split up the emails to decode evenly, they should have each had about twenty, though Rachel guessed she might have been given less since she slept in. Either way, just from her strips of paper alone, there was a wealth of knowledge to be had – their biggest issue now was time. It was already past midday and against her stomach's loudening wishes, they needed to press on until they had a plan.

"Rachel, what's your status?" Dahl checked in.

"I'm writing them all on strips right now, only two left after that."

"Mmmk. Come over here when you're done." Behind her, they'd partitioned off the white board and began taping up the strips in a vertical timeline. She grabbed her bundle of strips and turned to them.

"Here, take mine too. We should be able to fit these last ones in as we go along." Ian walked over and grabbed them, immediately turning back to the board. He was focused like Rachel had never seen him before and she knew his reasoning was different from her own. For her, this whole resistance was an act of patriotism and protection. More people in her country would die if David had his way and she had to take whatever measures were required of her to stop it. Ian, on the other hand, was an ex-terrorist. She didn't know why he did it – though she guessed it was for the adrenaline rush – but he wanted David dead out of revenge. Plain and simple.

There was no care for civilian casualties, long term consequences, or the collective American psyche. Just as long as David paid for trying to have Ian blown up by a human missile.

"You done yet, Rachel?" The stern voice asked, as if it had noticed her concentration had wandered off. "We're almost done putting all these up."

"Sorry, just one more. Give me three minutes."

Her hands cascaded across the paper furiously, intent on finishing this code as fast as possible to get over to the timeline and see what story these snippets wove. But as she began to realize what the code was spelling out, her hands started trembling. As she ordered the final three letters of the string, it was official. They practically didn't need the timeline anymore.

"Holy shit." It was an exasperated exclamation, dripping with fear. A loud noise from her chair scooting back against the floor let everyone know she was done as she rushed to the white board, ruthlessly ripped off a piece of tape, and slapped on her final decoded fragment away from the list they had going. It read:

"Transport from Dubai. Five days. Midnight."

On the strip she'd also written the email's send date:
    Tuesday October 2nd, 2018.
Two. Days. Ago.

Rachel had expected more of a reaction from the others; there was none. They stood in silence, Ian bent over the back of a chair, Dynadin with hands clasped behind back, and Dahl, arms crossed against his chest...all just staring at the piece of paper. Slowly, they were beginning to realize that whatever actions needed to be taken against this plan, it was going to have to be a rush job. Finally, the quiet was interrupted, surprisingly by Dynadin.

"Ok. Let's get to work."

Dahl nodded. "I'll email Henry and tell him to lay low and wait for further info." Ian removed his laptop from the desk and returned to the whiteboard.

"I'll take notes as we go along. Can you two begin reading these off to me?"

There was a tinge of apprehension as she approached the board. She was almost worried what exactly they would find. Dynadin nodded in her direction with encouragement. Rachel smiled and began reading off the laundry list of code fragments.

"Research is complete…" She moved to the next strip of paper. "Theoretically possible…" And on and on she went.

"Wolfpaw Initiative is name."

"Ground Zero identified."

"Highly effective zone."

"Weapon design complete."

"Need more time."

"WPI working now."

Rachel stopped there, noticing the dates on the strip she'd just read and the next one. Most of the dates between strips had been only a few days, maybe a week or so, but these dates were removed from each other by several months. She turned from the board to face the group.

"That's weird."

"What is?" Ian asked, looking up from his computer.

"The dates between these two fragments is far longer than any of the other ones. It's almost three months long." There was no response as the group individually contemplated an explanation. "Are we missing any emails?" She turned to Dahl.

"I'm not sure. There could be a few reasons why they went dark…or it could be that there just weren't any updates. I'll check with Henry though. Keep going."

Rachel turned back to the wall, unable to shake the gut feeling that something wasn't right. *You have an important weapon…why would you cut communication for that long?* Time was short and the mystery would have to wait. She continued reading aloud.

"Weapon ready."

"In holding position."

"Awaiting orders."

"Moved WPI."

"Location the Dubai Majesty." She paused at that, turning to the group again.

"On it. Looking it up now." Dynadin replied. After a few swift keystrokes he began to read off Google's main description. "The building was completed a little over a year ago – it looks like it was before The Will – but residents and companies moving in have been slow. The building is currently at half capacity…says here that the reason why is because of the explosion of real estate across Dubai and it's not competitively priced to the buildings around it."

"Ok. So why would they hide a weapon this important there?" Rachel wondered and was answered by Dahl.

"Likely just a momentary holding place until they move it to the States. Given the building's current situation I'm guessing they ask very few questions about space rental as long as you're paying the price. Not that bad of a hiding spot all things considered."

"The tower is only two blocks removed from the Burj Dubai," Dynadin continued. "Though it does still live in its shadow. The Burj stands at 2,722 feet and the Dubai Majesty stands at 2,017 feet."

"What does it look like?" Ian interjected.

"One second…" Dynadin navigated to Google Images and brought up several high-definition pictures of the immaculate tower.

"Wow." Rachel commented from afar as she approached the monitor. "Dubai certainly knows how to make a pretty skyscraper."

One of the more comprehensive pictures of the Majesty was maximized, fully displaying its impressive architecture. The building shone silver and bright in the gleaming sun, looking almost as if it were on fire. The base was wide and as the building went upward, it became narrower overall, undulating every few hundred feet like ocean waves. Perhaps most impressive was its texture, appearing to be one solid sheet of glass from top to bottom.

Dynadin cycled to a picture that featured the beauty at night, where the silver brilliance was exchanged for a faint blueish hue that covered the entirety of its surface. Both at day and at night, there was no denying the tower's simple, yet jaw-dropping design.

"How'd they get it to do that?" Rachel pondered aloud, echoing what most of the group was collectively thinking. Dynadin clicked an attached link.

"The Dubai Majesty's structure is achieved by a unique dual layer technology where the building and its wavelike appearance are attached to the core atrium underneath the seemingly singular sheet of glass. The glass on the outside isn't a single entity at all in fact, though it appears that way because the separate panes were laser etched together. The laser etching creates such a thin line of separation that often in pictures – and even relatively up close – the building appears as one fluid pour of glass to the naked eye." Dynadin looked up to the group who still seemed interested so he continued. "The glass itself is special too, consisting of millions of unique particles that both reflect and absorb light. During the day, the tower has a bright silver sheen as it reflects the sun's rays. In actuality, it is absorbing more of them, using this energy to power nearly the entirety of the building. At night, the skyscraper glows blue. This is a direct result of the particles that were once reflecting the sun's light during the day, now chemically reacting to its absence at night by emitting this soft, gorgeous hue. While it may appear bright to the general public on the outside of the building, it is, in fact, only shining outward, thus leaving the residents who stay there at night in complete peace to enjoy the darkness."

The last part was read almost with an unintentional sense of foreboding, but at that, Dynadin was done explaining the weapon's potential location.

"Ok, so what now?" Ian asked. Dahl looked at him and replied to the whole group.

"We steal that weapon right out from under them. It's still there. Not for long, but it's still there. We need to figure out how we're going to get in. How we're going to take it. And how we're going to get out." Each requirement had been represented by a singular finger in the air before he concluded. "And we need to figure this all out by *yesterday*." As it had several times already that day, silence blanketed the room as the group acknowledged their fast-approaching deadline. "So, any ideas?"

The quiet lingered. Whether the others were trying to figure out a solution or sulking over the impossibility of the task, Rachel didn't care. She walked directly to the whiteboard and began drawing.

First came the outline of the Burj Dubai. For now she wasn't worrying about scale, they'd do the math for that later. She just wanted to get her idea down on a tangible surface. Once she'd finished her crude rendition of the Burj, she drew the Majesty, approximating the distance between them horizontally as well as their vertical deltas. The last thing she drew on the board was a diagonal line between them, starting high on the Burj and ending near the middle of the Majesty. Ian immediately reacted.

"No." A violent finger pointed toward the whiteboard and Rachel. "No way. That's insane."

Rachel confirmed what he'd already assumed. "A zipline, from the Burj to the Majesty." She paused to let the idea settle before continuing on. "With it being a newer, mostly vacant building, you can bet the Scorpions beefed up security considerably. Going in through the front would be a firefight and the top is too narrow to land any sort of aircraft for an infil/exfil. If we want the element of surprise, we need to attack the middle, hopefully right where they're hiding the weapon. The only building tall enough in the vicinity that gives us that ability is the Burj Dubai."

"Yes," Ian began to protest. "But with a zipline that long and that steep, we'll be going too fast to stop on the other end. Instead of a blue hue at night, we'll give the building a red one. And just how do you plan to set up the line anyway?"

"The line doesn't have to be any larger around than a human finger. The technology exists that we could use a cannon to shoot the wire over, attach itself to the glass, and zipline down it using a controlled system." Dahl's eyebrows raised, impressed by Rachel's innovation and now taking her idea seriously. "The zipline itself is fairly standard – just some high tensile strength material. Put a suction cup attachment on one end and you've got yourself a rigid anchor."

"I'm sorry, a *suction cup*?" Ian still wasn't buying it.

"You act like you're new to this spy life." Rachel replied, a tad irritated. "Obviously it's not a standard bathtub suction cup or anything of the sort, it's a completely sealed device and I guarantee we could find one that's rated greater than a thousand pounds. Only way it comes off the glass is if we want it to or the building collapses."

Ian scoffed. "Ok. So here's your plan so far. We go to the world's tallest building. Set up a zipline to this other really tall building. Travel over without splatting on the glass or falling to our deaths, steal the weapon with little to no resistance, and then…I only see our infiltration option. We still need to get out of there."

"Simple." She smirked. "We zip back up to the Burj."

"I think it's a solid plan." Dahl spoke up. "The equipment isn't the issue, but I think we need to a have a contingency plan if something goes awry. In the event the zipline breaks or what have you, we'll need some cautionary parachutes. They'll be super lightweight and not slow us down. I can't guarantee they'll provide a soft landing, especially since we won't be much higher than a thousand feet in the air, but they'll at least ensure that we live."

"Fair." Rachel agreed. "With the mechanism that's in the zipline's attachments, we should be able to reel up at a variable speed, meaning we could potentially even zipline *up* faster than we came down. It's all up to the user. It can be a quick getaway if we need it to be."

"Excellent."

"So I guess it's decided then." Ian succumbed to the group's wishes. "Gotta admit, it's not a bad plan – just sounds unnecessarily *extreme*."

"If you have any other ideas, we're all ears, Ian." Dahl commented genuinely. There was no need for belittling each other and they seriously needed to consider all options for an operation this critical.

"I got nothing, at least not right now. So let's start figuring this one out."

Rachel smiled and Dahl approached the whiteboard with a marker, prepared to begin taking notes.

"Ok, so…" he began. "The first question is: who's participating?" He wrote all four names on the board. "Dynadin, I'm leaning toward having you as backup and evacuation. You'll be on a nearby street with our getaway vehicle and if shit hits the fan, you're about the only one of us who could take them by surprise and succeed completely." Dynadin nodded and didn't argue.

"Good. Next up is Rachel. Zipline is your idea, I say you're one of us who goes across."

"Yep. Sounds good."

"That leaves Ian and myself then. Ian, I say you go across with Rachel and I'll stay in the Burj Dubai and keep an eye on you guys from there."

"Afraid to zipline, old man?" Ian smiled as he taunted his father.

"Something like that." Dahl chuckled while interpreting the jeer as acceptance of Ian's designated duty. "So, we've got everyone's roles set – the biggest issue that's still lingering is a tough one. We have no idea what the Wolfpaw Initiative is or what it looks like. I think we've all made some educated guesses but truth is, we're going in blind. Is it a syringe? A petri dish?" The answers from the group were silence. "What if it's a bigger container? Can we still transport that across?" More silence as all parties thought hard. "We need to plan for the unexpected. Rachel, can you make sure that we've got several options with that zipline?"

"Yeah, I'll get right on it."

"Good. Ian and I will do as much digging as we can between now and then to see if we can narrow down exactly what we're dealing with." Dahl turned to his son and was awarded a nod. "And Dynadin, I want you to research the Majesty up and down. I want to know every turn we'll have to make, point of entry, and any and all escape routes should we have to use Plan B."

"What's Plan B?" Ian questioned.

"To be determined." Dahl didn't like the answer any more than the rest of them, but it was the truth. No one said anything; it was obvious to all of them that this was going to be cutting it close. Rachel changed the subject.

"What do we tell Henry?"

Dahl thought he had the answer right away but bit his tongue. There was a possibility that this was all a setup. Slight as it may be, he had to treat it as a potential certainty.

"Good question. I think we can all agree that Henry just provided us a lot of information. If it's all *true* then I think it's safe to say he's on our side…this is some pretty damning stuff."

"But…?"

"But…how do we know he hasn't been compromised? Or that he was ever on our side?" The situation was complicated and Dahl wasn't positive on how to handle it. With Zane, he'd always been loyal and there'd been no question when it came to sharing info. This needed to be a group decision.

"Henry has been helping us quite a bit these past few weeks, there's no doubt about that." Dahl began reasoning aloud. "But we need to be objective about how we're looking at this. He's still very much an unknown entity and while it may *appear* like his intel is valid on our end, there's really no way to tell. Half of what he's feeding us could be lies, and outside of double checking a few facts, we'd be none the wiser. We've got no knowledge as to whether or not he's joined us or believes our proof, nor do we have any knowledge that he's already revealed everything to David. *This*…" he paused and waved his hand the length of the whiteboard. "Is important enough that we have to act. No question about that. Part of me even believes that Henry genuinely cracked this code and found this legitimate intelligence. But that's me being an optimist and we don't have the luxury of wearing rose-colored glasses these days.

"The way I see it, we've got two options. First, we tell Henry what we've found and that we're going to Dubai to stop it. This is a high risk option if Henry is still with David. We'd almost certainly be ambushed.

"Option two is that we reply back to him stating that the emails contained fake info, thank him for the effort, and then lie about what we're doing. We could tell him we need to go dark for a few days as we follow up a different lead from Dynadin's Russian mission or something of that sort." The group was listening intently, knowing that this was a real predicament which was becoming increasingly more harrowing since Rachel had first introduced it.

"I don't feel comfortable making this decision on my own." Dahl stated. "This has got to be a group decision and we all have to be on board. So let's put it to a vote. Option One, we tell Henry. Option Two, we lie and go dark for a few days. Take a moment to think about it."

Around the room, the logic he'd just presented was being mulled over. Dahl had already chosen Option Two; there was just too much risk otherwise and he didn't know Henry well enough to justify Option One. Ian and Dynadin seemed to have their minds made up too, Dahl guessed they had come to the same conclusions as him. It was Rachel, the one who knew Henry the most, who was having a hard time deciding. Surprisingly, it didn't take her more than a couple minutes.

"I guess I'll start." Dahl began. "I vote for Option Two. I think we need to keep him in the dark on this one. Any questions?" Silence. "Ian?"

"Option Two." Confident.

"Dynadin?"

"Option Two as well." Confident.

"Rachel?"

"I really don't like that we're lying here even though that seems to be part of the job." She explained. "But there's just too much that's unaccounted for with Option One. I'm fully on board leaving Henry in the dark as we do this, even if I don't like it." Confident and well-reasoned. Dahl smiled and gave a loud clap in conclusion.

"Well that settles it. I'll shoot something over to Henry letting him know that his intel was no good and that we'll be offline a few days. Everyone else, you know what to do – get it done. We're wheels up in two hours"

Deep in the night, Dahl finished putting his email for Henry together and read the draft a final time before sending:

> *"Henry,*
>
> *Potential code was a diversion. We've stumbled onto bigger fish – no Dubai. Going dark for a few days. Lay low and stay safe. Thanks for intel."*

To him it seemed straightforward and would hopefully not elicit questions. There was a swarming in the pit of his stomach…*Is this the right thing to do?* It was inconsequential as the group had agreed the safest option was leaving Agent Cobble in the dark. That was that and Dahl clicked "Send" and shut down his laptop.

What's done is done.

Across thousands of miles, David's phone pinged loudly, waking the man from his nap and momentarily brightening his dark apartment bedroom with its screen. The email was from an indirect server that had diverted the communication to a mirror server he'd been tracking for several weeks now. With a tap of the screen the email opened, revealing the secretive text contained within:

> *"Henry,*
>
> *Potential code was a diversion. We've stumbled onto bigger fish – no Dubai. Going dark for a few days. Lay low and stay safe. Thanks for intel."*

David knew his opponent well enough to see that this was a smokescreen. He was headed to Dubai first thing in the morning.

And Henry was coming with him.

CHAPTER XII

A TALL DESCENT
SATURDAY | OCT 6ᵀᴴ | 2018

Coming over had been uneventful. Other than being a longer trip than she'd expected, Rachel was at ease with what they were planning to do. Any chatter they'd been monitoring proceeded as usual, Dahl indicated that Henry had taken their false story well, and all seemed rather…*normal*…in Dubai. Hot as hell, but completely normal.

Let's hope it stays that way.

Sand seemed to be everywhere as their Range Rover cruised across the desert highway toward the glimmering city. Against the sea of golds and yellows, the black pavement looked like an actual map line drawn in the sand. Heat waves played with their vision as they rolled above the surface, giving a visible presence to the temperature against which the SUV's air conditioning could not combat.

"There it is." Dynadin pointed toward the tallest building on the horizon. The Burj Dubai. At first, it looked almost fake – like a thin needle of light against the sky, significantly taller than the other ones. Soon though, they could see its shining blues and silvers as the building's separate stations and levels began to form.

"Where's the Dubai Majesty?" Rachel asked, craning her neck to try and see the building they'd be infiltrating soon.

"We can't quite see it from here." Dahl explained. "It's behind a few other buildings and it's not nearly tall enough to stand above them from this far out."

Winds gusted every few minutes carrying a hurl of silt and grains of desert across the road with it. The group sat in silence as the city crept closer into their view. Like many of the places she'd visited in this line of work, Rachel wished that she had the luxury to spend extra time here. It was a shame that everywhere she went was covert in nature and that she wasn't experiencing the extravagant locales the way they were meant to be explored. Soon she found herself somewhat jealous of an average woman her age, fresh out of college, potentially single with a decent-paying job…oh the things she would do with a life of normalcy. *But that's not me and I'd never actually want that.* This led her to smirk at the idea of her joining a sorority. It just didn't add up.

"All right, so here's the plan." Dahl turned from the passenger seat to look at the group. "It's about midday right now. We'll drive into the city, pass *both* buildings, note anything that may catch our eye, let Dynadin plan a couple escape routes, and then circle back to the Burj. We'll be staying there, in separate rooms on separate floors. My particular room will be the vantage point from which we launch the zipline to the Majesty.

"Once we get to the Burj, rest up for a few hours. Lord knows we could all use it. We'll commence the mission at 0300. Best case scenario, we're leaving the Burj at 0400, weapon in hand, headed home, and no one the wiser. Worst case scenario isn't an option so we won't entertain the idea of it. Any questions?" Ian half raised his hand and spoke.

"Off chance we get split up…where should we meet?"

"No meeting back up. You get removed from the group, you find your own way back to home base. The weapon is the priority here. If things go south, we may indeed have to split up and act as diversions for one another. You're all well trained and you can all get yourselves back across the world. Agreed?" There were several nods toward him and he turned back around.

Dynadin steered the vehicle into the city as the first group of skyscrapers swallowed them whole in their shadows. Dubai was a truly spectacular place with tower after tower seemingly competing for attention; each one unique and gorgeous, but mildly out of place in the barren desert landscape. Cranes were everywhere as the skeletons of incomplete buildings lined roadways, some further along than others. Thinking to the future, Rachel wondered what Dubai would look like in twenty years and was nearly as entertained by her faux mental image as with the reality right outside the car window. This city was something else entirely. Half New York City and half science fiction or fantasy, it seemed to be obstinate on defining its own personality, and it was doing a very good job at it.

For several minutes the car meandered through the streets, turning here, following the curvatures of the road there, before it came to a somewhat open space where all other buildings were dwarfed by a single, powerful structure. The Burj Dubai rose so high that Rachel couldn't even see the top of it with the window rolled up. She brought it all the way down and stuck her head out, feeling a wall of hot air blow on her face. Even with her head outside of the car, she had to crane her neck to see what appeared to be the top of the never-ending building. In the car she could hear Dahl and Dynadin talking about the best roads for various situations, but she and Ian, both in the back seat, were mesmerized by the monumental stack of metal and glass. She just could not believe that there was something *this* tall and that man had built it.

Dahl and Dynadin's conversation had slowed and ceased as they completed their trajectory around the Burj and Dynadin pointed out a building once more.

"There's the Majesty."

Rachel was required to crane her head downward, but only slightly. For the only way in which the Majesty was upstaged by its nearby, gargantuan cousin was in height. All other buildings seemed a little less bright as the skyscraper in front of them radiated silver sunlight at such an intensity that Rachel could feel herself squinting behind her sunglasses. Practical for a building to blind the general public? Not in the slightest. But impressive? Rachel had no doubts that this was an iconic building and would remain so for a very long time to come. Given what they knew about the vacancy rate in the premises, the prices for leasing space must have been astronomical.

Once one's eyes adjusted to the power of the reflection, they noticed a breathtaking structure hiding underneath. The single sheet of glass – or at least it appeared that way – looked like a pie section of a cascading and fading ripple going up, up, upward into the scorching desert sky. It was not dissimilar to what Rachel imagined a powerful tower in a popular sci-fi or fantasy movie would look like, except in real life it was more breathtaking than it ever could be on the silver screen.

"Wow." It came out as a half moan and the rest of the group answered her with similar sentiments.

"God, my eyes hurt from looking at it. That thing seems like a liability." Ian gave his opinion.

"Dubai likes to push the envelope when it comes to skyscrapers. I imagine that sales of sunglasses have gone up in the surrounding blocks." Dahl retorted and they all had a chuckle at his logic.

Rachel had hardly noticed the car was no longer moving; Dynadin had pulled over into a parking spot on the side of the street across from the Majesty and left the car idling. She could see him scanning the building intently and then he spoke.

"This single sheet of glass gimmick is going to hurt us."

"How so?"

"We're going to have to be *extra* precise with where we launch and hook the zipline. We won't have window rows and columns to count so we're going to need to go to Dahl's room and do some good old fashioned math. Even then, the actual shot across is going to be a leap of faith – we won't know that we're hooked up to the right place until we get all the way over there."

"Hmm." Rachel acknowledged.

"If we're off by a couple feet, fine. But if those couple feet become a couple floors, our escape route could be seriously difficult to get to."

"Noted." Dahl inputted. "Dynadin, let's do that before we all get some shut eye, so come to my room once we get back to the Burj and you drop off your things."

"Sounds good." Ian and Rachel leaned back into their seats and rolled their windows up, each having the false hope that doing so would make the interior cooler. "Everyone ready? Let's head to the Burj."

There were no objections so Dynadin pulled out into traffic and headed back toward the world's tallest tower. Rather than doing valet parking, he found a spot on his own and the group staggered their entrances by seven, ten, and three minutes. Rachel went in first, followed by Dahl, then Ian, and finally Dynadin, who turned off the engine once it was his turn.

Getting out of the car held an eerie sentiment for Dynadin. As he retrieved his bag, closed the trunk, and heard the horn declare itself twice quickly that the vehicle was locked, he couldn't help but feel something.

What he felt was that this was going to go all wrong.

Lavish didn't even begin to describe the inside of the Burj Dubai. Hallways were decorated with exacting precision and detail, the main entrance was grand and clean and modern, while even the elevators held some luxurious surprises of their own. Walking in from the sweltering heat the valet line had been packed with exotic cars that declared the wealth of their owners. Bugattis. Lamborghinis. Ferraris. And some that were so rare, their make and model wasn't readily apparent. Rachel was impressed, but also remembered that it was the Middle East, and that a solid handful of the wealth she was observing could've been the result of some bratty twenty-something living off mommy and daddy's oil money.

Bitter much, Rachel?

Against her better judgment, she spent some time perusing the lobby and all of its excessive embellishments, not really wanting to go to her room. Sleep would come easy, she knew. At this point she was running on fumes and the flight time and car drive over had been killer, but walking around, alone, helped her to clear her head a bit. Even if it was on autopilot.

Eventually though, she made her way to one of the many elevators and went to her room on the 97th floor. Already a bit nauseated from the time change and travel, the speedy elevator made her eyes gloss over and she grabbed the rail beside her. The feeling passed after a few moments, but it'd certainly been her calling sign to get some damn sleep.

The hallway was impressive too, but she wasn't really noticing at this point, just wanting to get to her room, draw the shades, and plummet onto a pillow. Letting her subconscious guide her, she found her room and waved her key over the sensor.

"Hey." The greeting startled her out of her trance and she turned to see Ian, going into a room several doors down. Her immediate thought was that this interaction was risky, but she could see that there were no other patrons in the hallway.

"Hi." She replied, becoming more exhausted by the minute. There was a shared moment of awkward silence between them and it became obvious what his next question was going to be.

"Do you want to uh…come over and…" He faked a cough and the question hung suspended off the walls of the hallway.

Come over and fuck? Rachel knew that's what he was getting at, but not even that would keep her awake.

"No. I'm tired as all hell and I desperately need sleep before tonight. You should get some too." It came across almost as if she was a teacher scolding a student.

"Yeah you're probably right. See you in a few then."

"Yep. See you in a bit." Any extra energy she'd had was spent on that awkward interaction and she was crashing hard. Her door opened easily enough and she kept the lights off while she stripped down to her undergarments, closed the blinds, set her alarm, double checked her alarm (habit), and did something fairly close to a dive-bomb onto the bed and pillows.

I haven't eaten anything in hours was her final thought as she was embraced by a deep slumber.

Her sleep was hollow: coma-esque. What felt like mere minutes after lying her head down on the plush, rather inviting pillows, she was awake again. Panic set in as she believed she may have slept through her alarm. Hunger subsided to make room for the more important issue, but it still grumbled like an old man from her stomach. Rachel rolled over with what one may argue was *too* much force to look at her phone.

23:15

Sometimes that was the best feeling in the world – thinking that it was time to get up, but knowing you had several more hours to sleep according to Father Time. Rachel was relieved, and thankful. She'd actually gotten several hours of sleep thus far and had a few more left before her alarm went off at 0200. *Peace out world.*

Falling Redwoods in the forest don't crash as hard as Rachel's head did on the pillow.

This time her sleep wasn't empty, but instead filled with the partial nightmare that she'd had before.

Falling.

Speed.

Stars.

Guns.

Bodies.

Bryson and Elena.

Flames and fire.

Cities listed on a global map.

Only this time it wasn't Denver she was falling toward, but Dubai.

Beep.

The Burj appeared as an elevator to the heavens as it extended upward out of the Saudi peninsula on the map and soon Rachel was once again swallowed by the skyscrapers, plummeting toward her certain demise.

Beep.

Windows exploded around her once more, glass raining upon her and beside her. Some of the larger pieces reflected back the pain and defeat in her eyes.

Beep.

Something was pulling at her consciousness, slowing down her fall. She knew that this dream ended with David's face, but the glass kept falling past her.

BEEP!

The alarm ripped Rachel from her slumber as the dream released her, knowing that its host had returned to reality. Frustrated, Rachel rolled over to turn it off and placed a weary hand on her forehead. That was twice she'd had that nightmare now. It was likely just an emotional response or some form of mild PTSD, but she doubted it was a prediction. More likely it was trying to teach her a lesson. *And either it's a shitty teacher or I'm a shitty student.*

Given the hour and the room-darkening blinds, Rachel's room was pitch black. Once more she rolled over, feeling as if she could have slept several more hours, and turned on the elegant bedside lamp. It did the job for now, lighting the room with a soft glow, but if she really wanted to wake up, she'd need all the lights on and a nice hot shower. She planned to be at Dahl's room by 0240, giving her about forty minutes.

Twenty minutes later, as she exited the shower, Rachel was sufficiently awake. The shower had been pleasant and the hot water had slowly jostled her from that foggy state. Normally a thinker in the shower, she'd mainly stood there, reviewing mission details over and over again.

Given that this was a fairly straightforward heist, she was inexplicably nervous. As she dressed, she wondered why that was. Could it be that it was maybe the end of all this craziness? Or at the very least, the beginning of the end? Or was it because it felt too easy?

That notion stuck with her as she recalled how smart David had played this game thus far – *And for decades* she reminded herself. She secured a knife to its holster on her calf and loaded her handgun, concealing it moments later. This wouldn't be her full outfit as she still had to walk in public to Dahl's room, but the rest of her gear was with him.

It was 0230 and she was ready to go, despite her long shower. She'd head down a few minutes early, but for now, the feeling that something wasn't right on this operation had taken hold of her.

And it wasn't about to let go.

"I'm at the door. Code Yankee Zulu November Niner." There was no one in the luxurious hallway, but she whispered regardless. Caution. From inside, she could hear rustling feet – thuds getting deeper and deeper – a lock turning, another lock turning, and finally the click of the door handle. No one opened the door, only unlatched it from the frame, so Rachel pushed on through, closed and locked it behind her and joined the group.

Despite her early arrival, she was the last of the group to show up and Dahl and Dynadin were sitting near the window while Ian put together the zipline and launcher.

"Good." Dahl stated as if he were a professor beginning class. "Everyone's here a bit early, so let's get this show on the road." There was a sheet of paper on the coffee table and he picked it up as he walked to the window. "Rachel, come over here." Dahl held the paper up against the window and as Rachel approached she could see several lines of re-worked math scribbled on the page. Beyond that however, was an outline of the Majesty that, when Dahl held it up against the glass, outlined the tower perfectly. There was a red circle near the bottom of the page which amounted to about half the height of the Majesty.

"That where we're going in?" She asked.

"Mhmm. That should be the floor we're looking for, just beyond the glass surface of the building. We've got a small issue though." Rachel's eyebrows rose.

"Do tell…"

"My extra precaution? The parachutes? They'll be borderline useless from this height." He pointed once more to the circle on the paper Majesty. "Maybe they'll

keep you alive, but most likely with a pair of broken ankles."

"Well let's hope we won't have to use them then."
Rachel smiled and turned back to the others.

"Agreed." Dahl returned the gesture and followed
her.

Rachel didn't like the fact that that one potential escape plan was already off the table and the mission
wasn't even live yet. *There's always got to be at least one
snag* she justified to herself.

Although she'd been in the room for a few minutes,
she hadn't really noticed its beauty and layout until now.
It was larger than hers....much larger in fact…and it
seemed to be a "corner" unit, if that was even possible on
the Burj Dubai. Windows covered an entire side of the
room in a U-shape, with elegant tapestries of cloth acting
as the blinds. The window from which they'd be exiting
was on one leg of the U, with similar windows on the opposite side. It was an interesting setup and made the room
feel much grander, almost royal, than she believed necessary.

"Like the room?" Dahl asked, noticing Rachel studying it.

"It's a bit much isn't it?"

"Oh it's far more than a 'bit much'. *But* it had the best
window for us to use for the zipline's angle." Dahl nodded over toward Ian.

"Ian's setting it up now, but I'll explain it to the both
of you while he works. The Burj Dubai is 2,722 feet tall,
as I'm sure you remember. We're currently at about
1,947 feet right now, slightly lower than the top of the
Dubai Majesty that stands at 2,017 feet. We'll be aiming
for a floor that's right at the 1,000 foot mark, meaning

that your vertical delta during travel will be about 947 feet. Let's just call it 950 so it's an even number.

"I won't bore you with the mathematical details, but that's a lot of cable from here to there, and you're going to still be *very* high up and gathering a lot of speed if you don't control your descent."

"Isn't that what the handheld motors are for?" Rachel countered.

"Yes. Yes." Dahl waved his hands as if shaking off the point. This amused Rachel as this response to logic generally came from elderly folk. "I know you have the motors and brakes and everything. But it's still going to be a lot different in practice than it is in theory. Just be cautious is all." Ian turned from what he was doing on the floor.

"Aww. Does the old man have some feelings for us?" Even Dynadin cracked a smile at this as Rachel approached Dahl and laid a palm on his chest.

"We'll be fine."

"I know."

"It will probably even be fun!" Rachel tried to change his mood until Ian chimed in.

"Ehhh. I don't know about *fun*. More like really damn high."

The conversation reached a natural end as Ian finalized the launcher. Dynadin began laser cutting the curved rectangular window after he'd placed two large suction handles near the middle. They worked in concentrated silence. Rachel leaned in toward Dahl.

"Heard anything from Henry since you let him know?" Dahl shook his head.

"No. My guess is that when I said we were going dark that he did too. It's not exactly a bad idea, though I do find it a little strange I didn't get any sort of confirmation from him."

Rachel hoped he would be ok. She knew Henry had been stressed the past couple weeks, but, given the knowledge he'd just disseminated to them, she figured he had to be even more on edge right now. Probably frustrated that he thought things hadn't panned out, but also frightened if those emails had been bait on a hook. *If only you knew how wrong you are, Henry.*

There was a ripping sound as Dynadin pulled the suction cup handles into the room. A large rectangle of glass spanning the floor to Dyanadin's height came back with him and the air pressure in the room changed noticeably. Their shared silence was broken as windfalls and air gathered outside the hole and entered the room with a cool touch.

Rachel noticed Ian tense his shoulders briefly, then return to the cannon setup which seemed to be almost done. Grunting, Dynadin waddled with the weight of the glass over to a solid wall, leaning it gently against it.

"Ian, what's the ETA on the zipline?" Dahl barked. The potential of death through an open window at nearly 2,000 feet had cast a seriousness over the group.

"Five minutes."

"Make it three…Rachel, suit up. Dynadin, head on down to the car. We're on channel seven everyone. Stay in communication."

With that, everyone got to work. Ian seemed to double time his coiling of the zipline cable, Rachel put on the remainder of her outfit that included safety pads, goggles, and a thermal, Dynadin left the room, and Dahl opened a long suitcase and began to piece together the rifle he'd use to cover them in the other building.

"O…K. Done." Ian stood, holding the grey cannon in both arms. "Who's firing this thing?"

"You okay with doing it yourself?" Dahl answered as he threaded the barrel of the rifle onto its body.

"Yeah. I'll figure it out." He approached the open spot in the window, wind still blowing furiously outside, and acting as a warning to stay indoors. Even for someone with very few fears, this height was penetrating his thoughts and the juxtaposition between solid ground and nothingness was more and more unnerving as he approached the opening. He lifted the cannon and placed it on top of his right shoulder, bearing its weight with ease, and situating it so that the digital eyepiece was pressed to his face.

Through it he could see the Majesty, but there was a neon green grid that mapped itself against the horizon. Dynadin had already sent the target specifics to the cannon's computer so as Ian aimed, a red circle appeared in his vision against the blue tint of the building.

"Hold on to that thing before you fire it." Dahl instructed. "It's got to use a lot of horsepower to carry all that cable and it's going to want to pull you over the edge with it." Ian turned back, perturbed.

"Comforting. Thanks for that." With the slightest of pulls, Ian inched the trigger closer toward its firing position. The pressure on the trigger caused a bright blue outline to appear on the grid, several centimeters away from the red one. Carefully, Ian lined up the outlines of both circles, eventually resulting in a purple circle. *Here goes nothing…*

Spewing out a loud but brief bark, the cable leapt from the cannon out into the dark Dubai ether. By this time, Rachel and Dahl had turned to watch the process, observing as the cable kept uncoiling and uncoiling and uncoiling from its spindle within the launcher. Frighteningly thin now that it was visible, the wire held a penetrating shine to it – almost as if it were producing moonlight.

Finally the sound of a giant bee that had filled the room ended and the line appeared taut. Ian brought his face back up to the optical display to double check his work. The other end of the zipline hadn't landed in dead center of the target as he had hoped, but it was damn close. It would do.

"We're good."

"Excellent. Ian, very carefully walk backwards into the room. We're going to wrap our end around this marble pillar here." A slightly smaller buzzing noise returned as the coil unfurled more while Ian backed toward the elegant stone support, made his way around it, and greeted the cable again on the other side. "That should definitely hold. Clasp it down and let's get going." Ian nodded and brought the under-barrel of the launcher close to the wire. There was a hook that absorbed the wire, securing it to the contraption itself. The mouth of the launcher was set against the floor and, with the press of a button, three metallic legs sprung from its sides and leapt into the floor. Ian walked away from it with the launcher resting at a peaceful 45 degree angle. He gently kicked the anchor as a test and it didn't budge an inch.

"Anchor in place." Rachel was finished getting into her extra gear and it appeared that Ian had been working in his this entire time. Over by the cargo trunk that had transported the zipline cannon were the two motor pulleys. Rachel picked up and handed one off to Ian. Maybe it was her nerves or maybe it was a real weather shift, but the room got noticeably cooler as a swell of wind echoed from outside. Even the cable shook, nay *vibrated*, but it held in place all the same.

"Weapons?" Dahl inquired. Ian responded with a cocking of his gun. Rachel replied audibly.

"Check."

"Comms?"

"Check. Checking. Come in." Rachel tested. Dynadin, now down on the street replied.

"Read you loud and clear."

"Chhhheccckk." Ian tested his.

"Ditto. You're good to go."

"Ok. This is it then. Just a reminder: you two will zipline over. The floor we've researched should be the one that contains the weapon…it's the only floor that they've leased out. I'll cover you from over here the best I can. Dynadin will be down on the ground for extract if we need him or as a third gun in a worst case scenario. Objective is simple: find the weapon, secure it, and get back here. Any complications? Use the comms. Got it?"

Both Rachel and Ian remained silent but offered nods. That was all Dahl needed.

"Let's get this done and figure out what that bastard's been hiding." A second nod from both of them indicated they were ready. They were in the zone. Dahl backed away from the ledge, allowing them room to get situated on the thin, tight link.

Determined, Rachel hooked her motor onto the metallic wire and approached the ledge. Behind her, Ian did the same and they both clipped into their motor via a carabiner link on their suits. Both of their weights caused the wire to moan lightly as it became accustomed to its new burden. Outside was a vision: one of shades of grand towers against the night, each with random pockets of light scattered like stars across their surface. It was eerily calming but as a strong gale of wind poured over the side of the Burj Dubai, Rachel suddenly remembered how high she was and how thin of a wire she'd be supported by once those two legs left that floor. *Don't think, just go, Rachel. This was your idea.*

There wasn't a second thought after that. Inside the gloves, her hands were slightly clammy, but they wound tightly around the motor's handles. Her legs were woozy, unaware of what was really going on, but they leapt from the open window all the same. Wind splayed against her face, quiet at first but then louder, louder, as the night enveloped her. She had not fallen to her death as was evidenced by the high-pitched squeal coming from the motor attachment interacting with that thin, dangerous line above her. Within, her heart raced and her mind played – she was enjoying this.

Out in front, the blueish monstrosity grew larger and the wire emerging from it reflected that hue like a laser. The vertical descent of the trip was intense and her stomach rose to her ribcage, eager to be under the influence of gravity once more. Without a moment's panic, Rachel began to apply the brakes on the contraption that was preserving her life and the high-pitched squeal of metal against metal morphed into a yawn of straining forces opposing one another.

Above her, the line bowed briefly and regained its rigidity which she could only assume was Ian jumping out behind her. Cautious to not break too hard and be hit from behind, she released her tight grasp of the mechanism slightly and once more picked up speed. The plummet was shocking – even after understanding the math behind it, the steepness of their approach was far more radical in practice. Now Rachel was about three quarters of the way across, body dangling thousands of feet above the street and she applied the brake once more. Even with that grace however, the Majesty rushed to meet her a bit faster than expected and she stuck out her heels. They struck the glass with a dull thump. Without thinking, Rachel let go of the handles of the motor and swiveled to face backward, dangling safely from her carabiner.

Ian was still a ways back – he'd been more liberal with his braking than she had – but she anticipated catching him all the same. Eventually he made it to her while she steadied him on the line behind her and turned back around to the glass of the structure. Despite hanging by a hook of metal hundreds of feet off the ground, it was actually a peaceful night. Darkness cascaded over much of the city but you could still make out faint starlight. The weather was pleasantly cool without being cold and only a small, reoccurring breeze could be felt.

Rachel spoke to Ian.

"That wasn't so bad huh?"

"No…quite thrilling as long as you don't look down."

Rachel laughed. "I suppose so! Line is secure," She grabbed it near the base of the suction cup and gave it a shake. "So I'm going to cut into the glass." The communication was less for Ian and more for their other two compatriots who weren't currently hanging from the side of a building. Reaching into one of the many pockets on her person, she removed a small instrument, only a third the size of a Hot Wheels toy, and held its wheels up against the glass. "Take it away, Dynadin!"

"Copy. Give me sixty seconds." Removing her hand from the toy-like object, it remained stuck to the glass and began spinning and turning its wheels. Once it was at a starting point, the laser underneath began, emanating a tiny, but bright red light from below. It drove up the glass and turned right, drove another, shorter distance, and turned downward. Dynadin's soon-to-be door was coming into formation as the vehicle paused. It removed a small piece of grey metal from its top and placed it on the glass directly over the spot it had just cut. Three more of these would act as the door's hinges – a gateway into the structure's blue heart.

Watching the spy toy was both mesmerizing and entertaining, even if Dynadin was moving along like a professional. In less than a minute the door was complete and Dynadin treated the crew to a quick 360 spin on the glass to signal he was done.

"Thanks, Dynadin."

"My pleasure."

Switching hands, Rachel placed the tool back in her pocket and retrieved a second, slightly larger item: a door handle. Much like their zip anchor that resided to the left of the new doorway, this handle was equipped with high-strength suction cups. Within seconds Rachel had glass pulling away from the skyscraper's exterior, held in place by four hinges no larger than paperclips. Ian seemed to read her mind.

"Crazy times we live in…"

"Yeah." She agreed. "Seriously."

Within the glass door was an interesting creature. There was little light in front of them in the concrete void between the stylish exterior and purposeful concrete atrium. A building that had once appeared lavish and exquisite seemed dead inside, hollowed and spit back out as grey rejection. Rachel looked up farther into the atrium and could see that certain floors had windows that were shared with the glass they'd cut through. The waves of the design of the building allowed for there to be places where atrium and glass met to provide a view of the outside world. *Very interesting…*Rachel mused. *Not how I would design a building, but hey, this* is *Dubai.*

Within the atrium and almost directly in front of them was a ladder up to a small landing with a door built into the concrete. Rachel guessed it was some sort of service access point for them to perform maintenance on the glass exterior if need be. Given that the door was less than three feet away from them, she was even more impressed with Dynadin's calculations and Ian's aim of the launcher. They'd gotten it just about as close as one could hope.

Behind her, Ian removed a small square platform no larger than a laptop from a compartment on his back.

"Here." He turned the black device over to Rachel. A squeeze of a hidden lever on the bottom caused the square to elongate into a rectangle. Longer and longer it stretched, not losing any of its width, and once it reached slightly more than Rachel's estimate of three feet, she placed it down between the glass's cut edge and the platform within the atrium. *Perfect.*

Cautious as ever, she unhooked herself from the zipline: an act so small, yet one that could go so wrong, that her mind ran away with momentary worst-case-scenarios. With a brisk couple of paces, she trotted across their "bridge" and turned back to watch Ian and check in with everyone else.

"This is Seven-Seven. We're inside the building's atrium, about to infiltrate through a service door. Alpha Nine is disconnecting from line now."

"Copy that Seven-Seven. Scottish, what's your status?" Dahl asked Dynadin over the comms.

"All good here, Grandpap. Haven't seen any action in or out of the building thus far." Rachel and Ian tried to stifle their laughter but some of it made it through the communication channel.

"Grandpap, huh? So that's my codename now?"

"Sorry, sir. They told me I should change it last minute." Rachel could practically hear Dynadin smiling.

"Clever little shits aren't you?" Dahl joked with a small laugh. "Fine. Grandpap it is for this mission and this mission only." Ian and Rachel replied in unison.

"Thanks, Grandpap!" And then giggled softly.

Ian was over on the platform by now and working on breaking into the service door. It took only a few seconds before the latch gave and it swung open. The time for jokes had clearly passed as Rachel replied to the progress by removing her weapon and clearing the other side of the door, Ian right behind her.

Back to back they made their way through the dark hallway, lights from the under-barrels of their weapons guiding them. Something felt off. This wasn't a lab or even a residence. This floor was unfinished – vacant – and Rachel suddenly realized it was completely facing away from Dahl's sniper cover. The windows in front of them were on the backside of the building, away from the Burj.

"Shit!" Rachel whispered, lowering her gun and speaking to the larger group. Ian turned to watch her, feeling the same pit in his stomach. "Guys, this is Seven-Seven."

"What is it Seven-Seven? Have you already found it?"

"No. We fucked up." She started. "This side of the building is protected from your sniper fire should we need it – the windows are on the far side facing away from the Burj." There was momentary silence. "Are we sure this is the right floor?"

Dynadin responded, "Positive. The messages indicated it and my calculations should be correct."

"Seven-Seven, proceed as normal. With any luck, you won't need my cover. Shit happens. Ian and you are very capable."

"Copy, Grandpap. Something still feels off here, but Alpha Nine and I will keep going. We'll check in once we've found the Wolfpaw."

It was still dark as all hell as they made their way from one side of the building to the other across the barren floor of ghosts.

"This is creepy." Rachel told Ian.

"Mhmm." Was his only reply. She could tell he was beginning to worry as well. *What if the emails had been fake?* Just the thought sent her head spinning. *That's an insane amount of work to just throw someone off a trail.*

Or...

   Or...

      Or...trap them.

"Fuck!" It may have come out as a whisper but Ian whipped around to face her nonetheless.

"What is it?"

"This doesn't feel right. Like really, really off. Am I just being paranoid?"

"No. I feel it too. This isn't a place where you hide a world-ending weapon. Unless we're on the wrong floor. Or they moved it before we got here?"

"Fuck this." Rachel switched her comms to address the larger group. "This is Seven-Seven. We've searched this place top-to-bottom. There's nothing here. We're doing one more sweep and then leaving."

She'd no sooner finished the syllable and the floor became flooded with lights; they'd all turned on at the same time. A brief scratching screech could be heard on their communication channel followed by a voice that was not one of their own. Rachel went rigid. A gut-punch of fear rocked her core.

"None of you…" The voice sounded agitated, angry. "Are going anywhere."

Instantly recognizable. The voice was David Harper's.

CHAPTER XIII

AS THE PENDULUM SWINGS...
SUNDAY | OCT 7ᵀᴴ | 2018

"Where's that coming from?!" Dahl was loudly whispering into their ears. Over in the nearly-barren floor of the Majesty, Rachel and Ian's eyes were still adjusting to the flood of light, but from what they could tell they were still alone. David was toying with them.

"Dahl, I can hear you." Replied the ominous voice. "By the way, how've you been all these years? Lots of headaches I presume?" Dahl remained silent, yet steaming. He knew they should have seen this coming. "I'll tell you how you've been all these years: fucking annoying. Like a goddam thorn in my side. When I first learned you were alive, I thought, 'Well good for him. He'll have a second chance now.' Yet somehow, you made your way back into the fray.

Your transgressions started out small. I didn't give a damn. But lately…*lately* you've really been pissing me off." The voice took a break, clearly getting emotional, but trying to reign it in. Rachel looked at Ian and knew they were both thinking the same thing: *Should we get out of here*? Harper's voice returned, calmer and more terrifying than before.

"Don't you see what I'm trying to do here, Dahl? How am I supposed to keep our country safe from the Dead Scorpions if I have you and your team constantly undermining my every move? What you four have been doing the past year or more has been just as detrimental, *if not more*, to the safety of our nation. What exactly do you have to say for yourself?" A father scolding his children.

"You killed over twenty thousand people, Harper. Don't hide behind your wall of lies now. It's too late." Dahl chided back, dark undertones lacing his language.

"And what proof do you have? Hmmm? This game you've been playing for months is based on nothing more than mistaken intuition and paranoia. What? You think I run *both* the Aqarab Mayta *and* N.E.T.S.? At the same time?" His questions made Dahl seem crazy. "Forget how exhausting that would be, but what on earth would I stand to gain from doing that?"

Rachel could almost feel the shame seeping through Dahl on the comm line. David was discrediting him and she wouldn't have any of it. She'd seen the proof, she knew it was there.

"You killed Bryson and Elena, David. You had both of them murdered to get them out of the way." While Rachel spoke, Dahl came to his senses and conducted a text to the group, hoping their phones weren't tapped as well.

> "Scottish, be ready. May need quick getaway. 77 and A9, don't do anything brash. Still unconfirmed if Harper is on site."

"Rachel...sweet, stupid Rachel. You think I put the bullet in Elena's back in Australia? Do you think I somehow fell from the sky with Bryson? Be realistic now. I had nothing to do with their deaths and the suggestion that I did is offensive."

"Oh shove it, David." Rachel interjected. "We've got more than enough proof connecting you to all of this. Hell, how'd we even end up in Dubai if not for the fact that you're with the Scorpions?"

"Because I long-conned you." The reply was even and calm. "I began to realize that we were often one step off from one another and I needed to end this ludicrousness once and for all. So I jumped twenty steps ahead of you, and here we are today. Personally, I'd like to get back to the task at hand of stopping and eliminating the Aqarab Mayta."

"Pfft. Fuck you." Rachel rebutted, getting increasingly angry that she was the only one saying anything. "You can hide behind that silver tongue of yours, but you're not fooling anyone here."

"Enough!" Dahl interrupted. "We're leaving, David. I'm not sure what this little escapade was for other than to prove your power but either way, fuck off. 77 and Alpha Nine, let's go."

"Terrible nicknames, but I must inform you: no one is going anywhere." Farther in the distance of the Majesty's floor, Rachel and Ian could hear the slams of doors opening. Dahl could hear it mildly over the comms. *Shit.* Ian and Rachel stood back to back, firearms at the ready. Several men, looking like soldiers, were decked out in nearly full riot gear and faced the two of them. Taking in her surroundings, Rachel realized she was only a few paces from the hallway that would lead them back to the service door and zipline. *Assuming that's still there.* Behind the group of men David Harper strolled in, wearing slacks and a white button up shirt, several top buttons remaining open. Behind him, Henry timidly approached, knowing that he was in probably the worst position out of everyone in the room. Refraining from risking any semblance of recognition, Rachel turned away.

"Told you so." David said with open arms. He reached into his ear canal and removed the comm device, tossing it aside.

Without a word, the entire team that had planned to infiltrate this building, steal a weapon, and evacuate knew that things had gone about as south as they could. They'd been played and didn't have a contingency for this. Rachel's only thought was to keep talking until someone made a move.

"So who're your friends?"

"Oh these fellows? Just some armed associates I like to keep with me while in dangerous company. And this," he turned to Henry. "This is my top agent at N.E.T.S.: Agent Henry Cobble. You remember him, don't you Rachel? From when you used to be on the *right* side of this whole mess?"

"Sure. So he's in on this whole thing too now?"

"If by 'in on it' you mean that he's well aware of the *bullshit* you all have pulled," Harper pointed to Ian and Rachel. "Then yes, he's very well aware."

"Does he know who you *really* are? Do any of these men?" David's face drew a thin line.

"They've heard your theories, and I'd appreciate it if my name stopped getting dragged through the mud. You and your little band of crusaders have concocted quite an elaborate tale of conspiracy and lies." He paused, wondering why he had to ask it again. "You *truly* believe that I'm the one in charge of the Aqarab Mayta as well?" He was breathless, trying to prove a point. "How on earth?" His hands went to his hips, thinking how he could prove himself. A hand reached out to Henry. "Give me your weapon."

There was a slightly bewildered look on Henry's face, surprised that he was even being spoken to. He did as he was told and handed over his handgun to David.

"Now come up here." A hand motion led Henry to the front of the group and David took his hand, placing the dark steel grip of the pistol in it. "If you truly think I'm the provost of the Dead Scorpions and that I'm responsible for The Will and *all* of their other transgressions, then shoot me right now." Still holding Henry's hands, he raised them so that the gun's barrel was mere centimeters from his forehead.

Across the divide, Dahl held his breath. As much as he wanted David dead, he had a bad feeling about this and was positive that this was not the way it needed to be done. *Come on, Henry. Be smart. Don't do this.*

Meanwhile, Rachel and Ian were still standing in the room, hearts similarly skipping a beat as Henry puffed his chest and looked deep into Harper's eyes. There was no tremble in his hand and Rachel was almost confident that he was going to kill David. Not a waiver. Not a flinch. It was confidence that painfully reminded her of Bryson. *Unless…what if this whole email setup was Henry? What if he and Harper orchestrated all of this together?*

It may have been just a thought, but as only a single thought often can, it had immediately shifted her opinion of Henry. Here, in this moment, there was no way to truly know whose side he was on. The realization put a growling pit in her stomach that was soon followed by another as Henry calmly lowered his weapon and turned back to face her. David let out a wretched smile, knowing that this was soon to be over. It had been a while since the feeling had captured her, but Rachel had rarely felt so alone. This lifestyle was never a constant and trust was a fickle bitch.

Ian could feel the heat coming off Rachel and felt a minor shift in her posture. The room had changed and this was no longer a safe mission. Death would become someone…it hung in the air with syrupy tension. It was moments like these that Ian hated. This lifestyle was barely his by choice. *That's a lie.* He loved the action of it all, but all the politics, double crossing, and backstabbing bullshit wore on him. Give him a distraction and he'd have a fair shake at killing everyone in this room, but among the "allies" and "foes" picking sides he didn't care. David was going to die. That's what he was here for now and that's what he'd accomplish.

Anger and suspicion shot wordlessly between the eyes of the two groups. Dahl knew David was in control. He had the firepower and they sadly had no cards up their sleeves unless they wanted to risk Dynadin. *But we still may need a quick getaway.*

"Ok kids." The silence collapsed around David's rude interruption. "Let's get this over with." Boldly, Rachel raised her weapon and pointed it towards the aging man. "Rachel," He chastised. "You're smarter than that. Put the fucking gun down." It remained.

"Henry…" David glanced over to the agent who had held his life in his hands. "Shoot the man. Target Zero I believe?"

Rachel heard Dahl yelling in her ear.

"Stand down, Rachel!"

Ian took a deep breath. Mad. Disrespect. The words danced around in his head and he could feel his neck and head getting warm.

"You know who I am." He growled. "I did EVERY-THING for you. And you tried to have me killed! Like a pawn!"

"That's what you are." David replied.

Ian's gun rose.

Henry's fired.

Blood leapt hot onto the side of Rachel's face.

Ian tumbled to the floor, body lifeless and missing part of a face.

Instant shock racked Rachel, mouth agape, and gun now too heavy to hold up.

Henry had just taken Ian's life and Dahl knew he'd had no other choice. Being alone in the Burj, he'd broken down the different scenarios and knew it was likely going to end with Henry being tested. Tested for trust. For loyalty. But either way he had to pass.

Killing Ian had been the passing grade.

Somehow the gunshot still rang through the room for Rachel. *Was that real? Is that sound real?* She was lost in a space between emotion and retribution. Ian had been a terrorist at one point, but she'd changed him. They'd loved, no matter what either of them wanted to call it. Now he was dead. Unceremoniously dead. She couldn't swallow and her limbs shook gently.

What...

The...

Fuc –

"Good, Henry." David smiled and the used-to-be-na-ïve-agent turned to his new mentor. "I'd say I'm sorry. But I'm not." The motion was fluid but soon a thin trail of smoke filled the room that had been preceded by a loud bang and a blur around David's waist.

Henry fell to the floor, clutching his stomach with blood almost immediately rising to his mouth and coating his lips.

"Argh!" He was in tremendous pain. "What the fuck?"

David took a single step closer, the gun he'd taken from his waist aimed at his protégé.

"You little shit. You don't think I know you were the mole?" Blood spurt from Henry's mouth onto the hard floor. His final moments would be spent in disbelief. Weakly, he attempted to raise his own weapon. It was a slow, useless effort but David toyed with him and eventually fired another round.

The gun flew out of Henry's hand in a reaction of sparks and blood, removing a finger in the process. Defeated, he coughed up more blood and lay flat on the floor.

Inexplicably, Rachel felt sorry for the boy. Moments ago she'd hated him for being a traitor against them. *But maybe he never betrayed us?* His was a position which she did not envy, nor would she ever know or understand. But he was dying and it didn't matter anymore. Recognizing that her shock had been momentarily lifted, she pieced together the scene. She would not be a casualty tonight.

Hope.

Even with the blood of her partner fresh on her cheek and a miniscule chance of not getting pegged by a bullet, it kept her in the game. A new energy overtook her and the clarity was there. *I need a diversion.* David was clearly distracted by Henry's useless attempt to cling to life. The hall back to the zipline was only feet away.

"So sad, Henry. For a split second I had true faith in you. I thought you'd see things my way. You betrayed N.E.T.S. and I'm well within my rights of the organization to do this."

Absolutely nothing could have stopped Rachel in that moment. She turned on her heels and was off, possibly the fastest she'd ever run, down the hallway of the glass side of the building. There had been a gunshot right as she'd ran, but it had been for Henry's head rather than hers. After a slight delay, bullets spat through the wall. The hallway was a mess of drywall and glass and dust, but they'd not anticipated how fast she was. Everything was behind her. Everything but the zipline and an escape.

It was a deafening noise…not the rattles and explosions of gunfire. No, that was background noise now. The sound of *escape* was deafening. It was a tangible thing as she ran closer to the service door. Part of her wondered if her mind had subconsciously shut down her hearing to channel the energy for that resource elsewhere. There wasn't even the sound of a heartbeat or an exacerbated breath.

With a crash, the service door to the atrium swung open and there was all their zipline gear, still hanging from the thin, precarious wire. Rachel didn't hesitate for a moment, knowing that there was no time to safely buckle into the equipment. With an Olympic leap from the service door platform, she reached out and grabbed the motor's handles that Ian had used on the way down. *I hope these things are as fast as designed…*Unwisely, she briefly looked down and was greeted with the haunting, concrete cavern of the atrium. A split-second thought terrified her: *I'm only going to be going higher*, before her body told her mind to shut the hell up and she cranked the small throttle on the motor.

This was fast becoming the most exhilarating and disturbing moment in her life as the motor went to work immediately, catapulting Rachel out into the Dubai night, zooming upward. Its acceleration had been so quick that Rachel had almost dislocated her shoulder, not to mention let go altogether, and was now hanging on for dear life. There was absolutely no doubt now that these devices could haul ass.

Across the distance, she could just start to see the cracks of dawn on the sandy horizon – a thin line of golden light against the black and blue of this terrible night. Her hair billowed in the darkness, almost like a superhero's cape. She didn't dare look down again, but Rachel knew that if she let go, her fall would be too short for the parachute to be effective.

Through the ripping chilly air of the night, a sneaking sound and a flash passed her, mere inches from her head. Then a second…a third…a fourth. As much as she could, she glanced back to see David's men shooting at her, bullets tracing across the darkness like lasers. They continued to pass her, many of them slamming into random windows and rooms of the Burj. *David has lost his mind.*

Dahl looked down at the situation and could hardly believe his eyes. Still reeling from what had just transpired in the other building, Rachel was now fighting for her life. Or rather, fleeing for her life. He could see her form getting closer, but she still had a way to go and bullets were all around her, some just narrowly missing their mark. She needed his help. Now.

He dropped to a knee.

Sniper extended over the open precipice.

Stock pressed firmly into his shoulder.

Eye gently against the scope.

Night vision turned on.

Inhale.

Relax.

Exhale.

Against his body, he could feel the sniper pounce. Its bullet leapt joyously across the gap between the two buildings and smashed into the neck of one of the men. Dahl repeated most of the motions and a second bullet found its mark, taking another victim with it. Quickly, he glanced away from the scope to see where Rachel was. *A little more than halfway. Come on...you can make it.*

Rachel noticed the shooting from behind her had slowed its pace momentarily. It was a slight, but welcomed reprieve. Struggling against the pain in her forearms, she clenched her grip around the handles once more, pressing her thumbs against the outside of her own fingers. *I'll be damned if I die of fatigue.* It was only a little bit farther…

Dahl went back to the scope just as a new horror began to unfold. And he was too late to stop it.

One of David's men was shooting out the glass surrounding the suction anchor of the zipline. Part of the glass that the line was attached to broke away and it was hanging by a thin, crystal thread now. Dahl put the man down, the bullet entering just under his collarbone and catapulting him against the service door. His eyes and mind were set on the piece of glass holding the zipline taut, trying to will it to hold just a little bit longer.

"Stay…*stay*…don't you break you piece of shit." Whispers weren't going to help the situation and Dahl saw in terror as the glass shook violently and plummeted down, dropping the other end of the zipline with it.

Rachel felt an odd vibration in the cable above her that was immediately followed by the sensation of her stomach in her throat.

She was falling to her death.

How…what…why…I'm still holding on! The realization didn't compute for a second and the nausea that hit made her arms feel like jelly. But then it came to her.

They cut the cord.

She wasn't right, but it didn't matter now…Rachel knew she had to figure out how to survive this. If she'd thought she'd been going fast before, she was now at the mercy of gravity on what amounted to a very large pendulum. The motor was whirring above her, not able to grasp onto anything substantial as they fell and she let up on the throttle. Luckily the mechanism had an anti-slip functionality built in so she wasn't sliding down the cable. All she had to do was hold on, but she soon grasped that would be easier said than done.

All around her, the other buildings and stars and night sky were slowly transforming. What had once been questionably real was now etched into the reflection of glass fast approaching her. If this was a pendulum then she was a weighted bob, swinging directly into the side of the Burj Dubai, over a thousand feet above the ground. As she approached the clean glass, she glimpsed a reflection of herself incoming. Her eyes locked onto the image and reveled in the madness of it. She saw a fierce, determined, drained, saddened, and strong woman coming toward her. It was an image that she knew would be burned into her memory forever…she just hoped forever would end up being a little bit longer than the next few seconds.

The moment was fast approaching and Rachel had planned out about the only course of action that was afforded to her. Rather than hitting the glass head on, she knew she needed to take the impact another way and with her last few seconds of free-fall swinging, she threw her back toward the building, bracing the muscles as much as she could.

The impact came sooner than she'd expected and rattled her body.

Her only focus was to hang onto the handles, but even with that solitary thought, one of her arms slipped and let go.

There was a substantial spider-web of cracks in the glass where her body had made contact and it was an observable metaphor for how her body felt. There were likely no broken bones, but she knew that the bruising would be substantial. Now dangling by one hand, she groaned as she reached to get two hands back on the device. Even that hurt and she could feel tears welling up from the effort. Once she had a grip on both handles, she took a moment, knowing she didn't really have one to spare.

"Fuck."... *That hurt so much.* But she was alive and that's what mattered. After a couple deep and slightly painful breaths, she pressed the throttle. For a few seconds, the engine whirred uselessly as it had before, but then, much to her delight, it caught the wire and started transporting her up.

Bullets had stopped flying in her direction and she guessed that the men were either dead by Dahl's hand or fully aware of the potential for collateral damage they'd assume by continuing to shoot at her now. Sliding against the glass and metal of the building was becoming painful so Rachel maneuvered herself to walk up. She'd just have to monitor how hard she cranked the throttle. The biggest question to ponder now was: *How will Dahl and I escape the Burj?* Followed by: *Did Dynadin make it?*

Unable to see an outcome where Dynadin did *not* make it, she assumed he was still in play but the preceding question continued to haunt her. David could easily monitor the Burj and slowly weed them out. In fact, he and his men, not to mention some additional backups, were probably headed there now, a couple thousand feet below her. Rachel dared not look down as seeing them moving would be near impossible and all it would do is rattle her nerves. Instead, she kept moving onward and upward.

In her ear came a scratching that eventually morphed into a voice. Dahl had remained silent this whole time, probably for the better.

"Rachel? Rachel, are you still there?" She could detect a sense of panic.

"I'm here, Dahl. Barely. Making my way up the side of the Burj now. Should be to you in less than five." No response followed, but she figured that's all he'd been hoping to hear. She on the other hand, had more questions. "Dahl?"

"Yes, Rachel?"

"What the hell happened? I…I mean…we were blind-sided."

"That's precisely what happened. We were tremendously set up by a man who's proven time and time again that he's several steps ahead of us." There was anger in his words. "And it's not over yet."

"Is Dynadin…"

"He's alive. Once everything started happening I made the decision to hold him back for a getaway. I sent you all a text but…" Rachel realized she hadn't even noticed. The whir of the motor interacting with the wire was the only sound around her for a moment.

"And Ian? Henry?"

"They're both gone, Rachel. David was tying up loose ends. He learned his lesson well enough with me that you don't take half measures."

With a harsh bite, the moment settled and the two of them contemplated the fact that their numbers in this war had just dwindled significantly. *What hope do we have now?* Rachel's thought tormented her the rest of the way up the line. Above her, Dahl looked down as she finished the final hundred feet or so, reaching for her hand as she got closer. Still in pain, Rachel reached out for Dahl and, with little effort on her part, was pulled back into the Burj.

The strenuous act…the last ten minutes…the daunting future…had drained them and they lie side by side on the floor of the glorious hotel room, one of Dahl's feet hanging over the edge. They could not afford to waste time like this, they both knew, but they also both needed a respite. Tiles on the floor cooled Rachel down as she let her mind truly process what was going on. Rarely a selfish person, the first thought she latched on to was a tragic one: *Dahl has now lost both of his sons. He has nobody left.*

It came out as a croak. "Dahl…I…"

"I know, Rachel. I'll be ok. I just…need time."

And time was what she gave him. They remained there, in their own thoughts and sorrow and emotions for several minutes, knowing that David and his men were likely making their way over to the Burj and up to their floor. Panic was one emotion that Rachel did not feel and she wondered if that was because she'd given up. *Is this over? Did we lose?* An abrupt scratch interrupted the night breeze.

"Rachel. Dahl. What's your status? This is Scottish." Surprisingly, even after all that had transpired, there was a lack of worry in his voice. Ever the professional. Dahl tapped his finger to his ear, but remained lying on the ground.

"We're fine, Scottish. Alpha Nine and Henry are down. David and his men are likely headed our way."

"What are you doing?"

Dahl smirked. "Taking a breather."

"Well you better get a move on. They're already at the Burj."

"Copy that Scottish. Stay hidden. We're going to need an evac. Let us think for a second."

Still lying next to him, Rachel wasn't really thinking about how to escape. She hadn't given up, just rather knew that Dahl could figure this out on his own. Next to her she could feel Dahl sit up and look about the room, almost akin to the way a prairie dog observes his surroundings outside of his hole. He got up completely and walked over to the glass behind them, on the opposite side of the U-shaped room. There was pacing back and forth and Rachel decided to rest her eyes. Either they'd be leaving the building in a few moments, or dead, so she wanted some peace and quiet.

PCHEWW!

PCHEWW!

PCHEWW!

Three rounds from Dahl's rifle were followed by the sprinkle of glass shattering. Rachel jolted up from her shortened breather, immediately experiencing the sudden movement as a distinct pain emanated from her ribcage.

"Son of a bitch. Ow…oww." She grit her teeth and got control of it. "What on earth are you doing?"

"Getting us out of here."

"Through the *other* window?" It sounded accusatory. "If you'll excuse me, I've had enough of the outdoors from two thousand feet today."

"You have any better ideas?"

"Stairs or elevator would be a start…"

Dahl shook his head. "David will likely have tapped into the building's security. That means any conventional way we take down will make us ripe for an ambush. Not to mention, both of those methods are slow."

"So what, we're just going to jump and grow wings?"

"The parachutes, Rachel." He started. "This side of the building will make it easier to aim for the exfil point below."

It all began to connect with her. Somehow in the midst of all the craziness she'd forgotten that they had tagged along some emergency chutes, but now she was glad they did. Dahl was right, *this* was how they'd have to get down.

Dahl walked over to the large gear pack in the room and took out a parachute from it as Rachel finally got up, double checking to make sure that hers was secure. It was so light and thin that it was no wonder she forgot about it.

"Scottish, this is Grandpap. We've got an exit strategy. Be ready on the southeast side of the building."

"Copy. How will I know what exit to be at?"

"You'll look up." Dahl stated commandingly and closed the comm line. "Ready?"

"After this," Rachel began. "I'm never doing anything with heights again." Dahl smiled and she let out a small laugh.

"Just remember, this is still a fairly low jump. Clear the building as much as possible and then pull your chute ASAP." He pointed to the shattered window where hundreds of glass bits had pooled on the floor. "Ladies first?"

"Fine. Fine. Just backup so I can get a running start." Rachel crossed the room opposite the newly broken window. They were sure going to be leaving this room in shambles. Somehow she believed that the Burj could afford it, even if it was an inconvenience. Her heart was beating excessively and she felt…*nervous*.

Pull it together. You have to get out of here. Despite her shitty pep talk, there was still the desensitizing blur of fear cascading over her. A pop in her ears made the world go mute around her while her vision tunneled to only that of which was directly in front of her. It was nauseating and she wasn't quite sure what was going on but she didn't have time to figure it out.

Run. And jump. That's it.

Well, and pull your chute. Don't forget that.

Just a few strides in, Rachel could begin to feel the pain in her core and bones; it was a deep ache. But as she put her foot on the edge of the building's threshold into night, all her senses came rushing back, courtesy of adrenaline. She'd taken quite an effective leap and was able to clear a considerable distance away from the building. Very much in the moment, she eagerly yanked the chute cord from the thin pack on her back. The excited "whirrrrrr" of the chute unraveling could be heard and after a few moments of will-it/wont-it worrying, the fabric yanked hard against the air on which it fell. *Thank God.* She wasn't sure she could have dealt appropriately with one more thing going wrong.

Falling, or rather gliding, offered her some brief relaxation. She could tell that once this was all done, she was going to be exhausted, but it certainly wasn't going to be what got her killed. Unfortunately, she was still headed toward the ground at a speed that would lead to yet another rough landing. Below her, looking like a frantic ant, she could see the Range Rover's headlights and the faint outline of the vehicle pacing the streets, trying to anticipate their approach. Scoping her surroundings, Rachel spotted a wide intersection of streets that she'd aim for, hopefully making it easy for herself and Dynadin to meet.

With her landing pad chosen, she took the final few moments to enjoy the scenery. Behind her, towering massively above, was the lit up, majestic outline of the world's tallest building. Below was an equally as impressive elliptical array of greenery and roads, with extensive water features on one side. Against the calm night, the mini lake looked eerily like glass: reflecting its immense benefactor horizontally across its plane. It was all quite magnificent and added to a long list of places Rachel would have liked to visit on vacation rather than on a mission. *And a deadly mission at that.*

As she took in the details of the ground, it became obvious that her speed was still too fast. She'd live, sure, but with her bruised and battered frame, it would hurt like a bitch. And most likely do more damage. The Range Rover had come to a halt less than a hundred feet below her and Dynadin could be seen through the windshield. Rachel winced in pain, expecting the hit far before it would come.

There was a sharp yank at her back and a harsh ripping sound. She opened her eyes and glanced back seeing that her chute had caught on a billboard or street light or something of the sort. Now it was ripping away from the pack. Kicking frantically and not wanting to be stuck, Rachel was able to keep the ripping momentum down the chute and much to her delight, was slowly lowered onto the concrete. Her toes skimmed the surface as she swayed in the night so she undid her pack, landing lightly, and more importantly, unharmed, on the ground.

Dynadin reached over and pushed the passenger door open for Rachel. She sprinted, as fast as one who was beset with pain could, over to the vehicle. A thud from behind her must have been Dahl and he no sooner stood up before he yelled.

"Rachel!" He took a breath, likely trying to catch it as his landing had been much rougher than hers. "You're in the back seat. You're in rough shape and we're going to need a gunman up front."

She began to protest, and any other day she would have, but she knew he was right. Truthfully, she felt better about this decision so she slid to the back without a rebuttal. Dahl hopped in the car.

"Where we going?" Dynadin asked.

"Just get us the fuck out of here first." Dynadin peeled away without question as Dahl kept speaking. "We're going to head to safe house Echo. It's a little farther away, but I think if we can make it there with no tail, we just might still have a fighting chance." No sound was heard other than the dull roar of the engine's cylinders. "Once we lose them, we'll trade cars in case they're somehow tracking this one."

Silence once more. The air spoke all that needed to be said; the group was coming to terms with the fact that they were leaving here with one less seat filled. A boisterous thud startled Rachel.

"FUCK!" Dahl had taken his fist to the dashboard of the Rover. Again and again. "FUCK! FUCK! FUCK!" Saliva had produced on his lips. Hairs hung in front of his eyes and he swept them aside with a shaky hand. It was what they were all feeling, in some form or another, and the cabin remained quiet afterward.

Night enveloped them in its final hour of embrace as the soft lights from the towering structures lit their cautious path. It felt strange that they were the only vehicle on the road – a ghost town of luxury. But why weren't they being followed? David undoubtedly had more men at his disposal (likely N.E.T.S. agents), but where were they?

"Something's not right." Rachel's statement held both fear and confidence. Dynadin remained silent as he continued maneuvering the vehicle through the city. Dahl replied.

"She's right…where are they?" Dynadin glanced in the rear view mirror, squinted, and returned his eyes to the road.

"Buckle up. They're coming." Dahl and Rachel both twisted around to get a glimpse and indeed, there were headlights in the distance behind them, at least four SUVs.

"You think Harper is along for the ride?" Rachel asked although she already knew the answer.

"Doubtful. He doesn't like to get his hands *that* dirty."

"So how are we going to deal with these guys? They're N.E.T.S. agents, not terrorists. They don't need to die."

"You think they're saying the same thing about us?"

"It doesn't matter." She replied. "They're acting on orders from a man they trust."

"Fine. We'll try to escape with minimal casualties, but the second they start firing at us, we're fighting back. I won't lose anyone else here." Rachel knew that was the best she would get and let it go. She hoped Dynadin was as talented behind the wheel as he was on foot.

Dynadin turned and pointed below the back seat. Underneath Rachel pulled out a silenced M4, painted blue with digital camouflage and a small scope. Dahl's response was a raised eyebrow at Dynadin, who was currently being visually scolded by Rachel.

"For when they fire at us." Then it was back to driving as he punched the gas and they tore away.

CHAPTER XIV

SAND, SPIKES, & SPEED

SUNDAY | OCT 7ᵀᴴ | 2018

If Dynadin was frantic, Rachel couldn't tell. He wove throughout the city as if he'd run this route a hundred times and it was keeping their pursuers at bay. Luckily no police had witnessed the chase thus far. *That's just what we'd need.* There was a chance that they could make it out of here in one piece and without any further casualties.

Lying in the back seat, trying to find some form of comfort and rest her eyes, even briefly, Rachel refused to let her mind wander. Gripped tightly in her hands and across her chest was the M4 and she focused on physical contact with that. Too much had just transpired and trying to absorb it all now would be detrimental. She imagined that everyone else in the car was trying to do the same after Dahl's outburst.

Dynadin was busy driving.

Dahl was keeping an eye on the tails and instructing Dynadin when needed.

And I'm in the back seat clutching a gun that I'm trying not *to use while I'm trying* not *to think about what David just did. Fuck me, right?*

"We're almost out of the main city." The dark man's eyes remained on the road as he spoke, calmly enough to settle everyone else's nerves. *Does he ever get scared?*

Nervous? Angry? "After that, we'll be on the highways where it's pretty much just us and desert. It'll be hard to lose them there without a fight, especially if they're packing bigger engines under the hood. So get ready."

Dahl, view still intensely focused on the passenger side rear view mirror, primed his weapon with a bullet in the chamber and Rachel sat up, somewhat reluctantly. She also readied the weapon and laid out several additional mags should they be needed.

"That asshole…" Dahl sighed. Rachel turned to him then back to see what he was looking at.

"What is it-oh c'mon." Even Dynadin glanced back and let out a quiet curse.

"*Shit.*"

"That's probably why they were holding back." Dahl reasoned. "They were waiting for reinforcements. A fucking helicopter." Behind them was a fast approaching single rotor copter. It looked like it belonged more to a news room than a secret agency (and indeed it might have) but Rachel knew there would be guns and men inside. No matter which way she rolled the dice, this was going to be a fight. And likely not a pretty one.

Even with the helicopter closing in, Dynadin pressed onward. The towers were getting smaller now as they were definitely on the city's outskirts – smart for the chopper pilot to wait until there were no obstacles. Rachel rolled down the passenger back window. Blue and red lights flashed as she did this and for a brief moment she was frightened they were getting pulled over. A hidden police vehicle, likely not doing much in the wee hours of the morning, had seen them. They wouldn't be pulling over any time soon, and the other SUVs quickly passed him. Unsure of what he'd gotten himself into, there would likely be backup on the way.

"Hopefully they serve as more of a distraction than an actual threat…" Dahl spoke what was on everyone's mind. Rachel wasn't so sure. It was starting to feel like them against the world.

Frighteningly, that wasn't far from the truth.

As the blue and red lights faded in the background – for now – the dim white glow of the angry, pursuing headlights was getting closer and closer. Also becoming ominously present was the dull thud of the rotating chopper blades. Eventually that overtook the engine of the rover; the copter was low and darted overhead crossing from right to left. Its guttural lion's roar had made itself known and all three heads in the car followed it as it flew parallel to their left side. It was a small, unarmored thing, but inside there were at least four agents ready to fire.

But they weren't…

Each of their necks whipped back to front in unison. Dynadin got control of the wheel before they began to spin, and Dahl turned to see the SUV that had just rammed them from behind. The Rover leapt into top gear once more as they attempted to pull away, but the car behind them was getting ready to act again.

The hulking black mass of a vehicle took a wide right in preparation to fishtail them. Out of the corner of his eye, Dynadin was timing a counter move to the wildly obvious play. They were definitely outside the city now as the highway was opening up and leading them into a dark ocean of sand and dust. Behind them, the other vehicle leaned hard left but it had made its intentions too obvious. Dynadin hit the brakes hard, now behind the opposition that crossed in front of them, fully exposing its left rear. As fast as he'd pumped the brakes, Dynadin gunned it, slammed hard and fast into their side, pushing them into a spin. There was no hope for them then and Rachel watched as he continued rotating off to the wide road's shoulder.

A Dubai police officer, new to the evening's show, collided hard with the spun out vehicle. He'd tried to dodge, but still managed to clip it, sending him airborne and the vibrant blue-red lights crunching to the pavement.

Dahl looked at Dynadin; they were all a bit more comfortable being in the hands of such a talented driver.

"Nice one."

Dynadin acknowledged with a nod and kept his steely gaze on the road and speedometer. They *would* make it out of this. A pitter-pattering of bullets lurched into the side and roof of their vehicle, making several obvious dents within the interior. None punctured through the covertly armored sides, but it was only a matter of time. The metal projectiles were coming from the men inside the chopper. Given how open the landscape was, there was little room for them to dodge or weave out of the way.

"Rachel, a little help here?" Dahl looked back and nodded at the M4. Temporarily forgetting that she had a weapon in her lap, she snapped into action and rolled the window down far enough to stick the barrel of the weapon out. Using short bursts, she fired at the aircraft, peppering it with sparks from bullet contact. One man took a hit in the upper chest and tumbled from the compartment, sailing downward – hand in hand with gravity – and slamming hard into a sand dune. Rachel saw the upper plume of tan sand in the emerging morning light. Acknowledging its recent loss, the helicopter dropped back for the time being.

"Thought you were trying to avoid casualties?" Dahl reminded. Rachel felt guilty about the man, but it was clear that retaliatory violence was the only thing that would keep them alive.

"He shot first." She reasoned, and left it at that. Internally she knew none of them would survive this without dealing out some death. There would be plenty to mourn over later, but that time was not now.

There was little reprieve however as Dynadin swerved abruptly to avoid a batch of incoming police officers. Once passed, they all attempted to pull U-turns. Most were sloppy and one officer again collided with a member of the pursuing party. Dynadin witnessed the accident in his rear view.

"They're proving to be a better distraction than we'd hoped. Practically doing our job for us."

"Seems the Dubai police aren't exactly well trained in pursuits." Dahl stated.

Rachel countered. "I bet *that* one is." Coming up fast behind them was a lean, sleek, exotic police cruiser, designed for high speed pursuits. Cars like this weren't foreign to the population of Dubai, so it made sense that their police force had invested in something that could catch the higher end criminals if need be. It was black with stripes of white and blue and the top lights were a sleek LED strip across the upper windshield, rather than a gaudy bracket of mounted lights. Incredibly, it looked an awful lot like a military jet, sans wings. Even pushing their Rover to the limits of its speed, this new pursuer passed them as if they were driving in sludge. Dynadin named the vehicle as it pulled in front.

"Lamborghini Centenario." He whistled, approving of the choice. "0-60 in 2.8 seconds and a top speed of 217 miles per hour, though I'm sure they have it outfitted to do a little bit better than that."

"Damn, that's a gorgeous car." Dahl admired.

"Yes boys; it's very sexy. But it's also directly in front of us likely about to pull some very quick maneuver." Sound had no sooner left Rachel's lips as there was a flash from the Centenario's backside and a slamming thud that seemed to come from the bottom of their undercarriage. Rachel thought she'd seen something skidding on the ground in front of them directly after the flash, but couldn't be sure.

"What the…" There was no damage to the car it seemed and several seconds had passed by. "If that was an explosive, I think it must have been a dud." Dynadin seemed confident. Moments later the vehicle's center console screen went black and was replaced by the facial image of another driver. The person was wearing a helmet and several seatbelts across their body. A British male spoke.

"This is the Dubai Police High Speed Officer. Pull over now! You are resisting arrest."

"Must be the guy in the Lamborghini." Dahl mumbled. Almost instantly there was a reply.

"Yes, I am the driver of the Lamborghini. I love this car very much, so please don't make me take you down with it."

Dahl fired back. "This is a matter of national and possibly global security. You're out of your element here and don't know who you're dealing with, including the three of us inside this car. Why're you only pursuing *us* anyway? In case you didn't notice, there're a handful of idiots behind us!" He was yelling at the screen by now.

"I don't have orders to pursue them. My orders are for you and you alone." He replied with a wicked smile formed under his helmet.

Shit. David's gotten to the Dubai Police Dahl realized. By the look on Dynadin's face, he'd connected the dots too. "Fallback if you know what's good for you."

"No thanks! I'm already out here so why don't we all just pull over and talk about it? I think it's **you** underestimating who **you're** dealing with."

"Cheeky little shit aren't you?" Dahl cocked his head at the screen. "No dice. Do your worst."

"So be it." There was a noticeable shift in the weight of the vehicle. It was slowing down.

"Whatever he fired back must've been some type of remote hack." Dynadin turned the wheel. Nothing. Turned it the other way. Again nothing. He pressed the radio button on the console. Not even that was working. "Shit. He's got complete control of the car."

Behind them, all of their pursuers were gaining ground, those that were left anyway. Before long they'd be completely stopped in the middle of the road.

"We're down to 80 and dropping. He's not using the brakes – just letting the lack of acceleration slow us." Dahl jumped in.

"Rachel, check underneath the vehicle. See if you can locate the device. We need it off this car ASAP. I'll cover you against anyone that catches up." She nodded and handed him the M4. She tried the back left door, but it was locked.

"He's locked the car too."

"The car's locks may be controlled electronically by the computer, but they're inherently mechanical devices. Try forcing the lock up on the door on your own and then –" There was a loud triplet of gunshots and a cracking sound as Rachel peeled away the interior casing of the door, revealing the lock beneath and setting her handgun aside. "Ok. Guess you got it."

Even with her bulked physique from the last year, opening the door proved to be a challenge. Wind, along with a blast of heat seared into the vehicle, whistling and humming. After a good push and a loud grunt, the door was open with Rachel pressing her weight against it. Hidden within the wind's howling, she could hear the car's engine dwindling. In the cabin, Rachel wrapped a seatbelt around her leg and cinched it off before leaning out upside down on the driver side. Below her was the dark pavement with painted lines racing by and blurring together. Her hair, in a ponytail, danced and bounced as it came in contact with the road; the tickle of it reminding her of how solid the ground could be.

Dust covered the undercarriage of the Rover, encrusting the metal frame and mechanics. She wasn't entirely sure what she was looking for, but Rachel guessed that it would be less sandy than everything else. If she had seen the Lamborghini's projectile correctly, it was likely a small, black, magnetic disk. There was a yell from the cabin.

"We're down to 65. Whatever you're going to do down there, Rachel, do it now!"

"I'm working on it!" She bit back. But still there was nothing she could see. A spray of bullets rattled the rear bumper close enough to her that she could hear the twang of the projectiles bouncing off the hull.

"What the fuck, Dahl?! A little cover fire please!"

She kept scanning the vehicle as she heard the M4's *clapclapclap* deliver bursts of fire from the passenger window. The Rover had an annoyingly large undercarriage surface area and she had no inkling how big the disk was. "Where are you…" The whisper died quickly, barely audible above the roaring road beneath. Rachel adjusted within the cabin to lean farther down while her eyes continued to quickly scan under the vehicle. It was a precarious position, but she still felt secure with the seatbelt. The added weight of the car door from the wind resistance was becoming substantial though. She wasn't sure how much longer she could hold it…

"Shit. Shitshitshit." Rachel's eyes darted back and forth along the bottom, still not detecting the resting location of the hacking device. Emerging sunlight was rising against the horizon and it gently painted a portion of the bottom's metal parts.

A reflection caught her eye – a piece of metal undusted by desert sand – and there it was. Rachel saw the disk, with a small turquoise light pulsing and about the size of a beer can's circumference; much smaller than she expected. Her eyes had been scanning too quickly it seemed as the device, luckily, was on her side of the vehicle, directly under the driver. She reached for it but was just barely short.

Inside the cabin she kicked her foot, loosening the seatbelt's hold on it, lowering herself farther toward the pavement while stabilizing with her other leg against the cabin floor. Hard pavement was only a few inches beneath her now and she didn't want to think about what would happen if she fell.

"Rachel…" Dahl longed with worry. "How's it coming down there?" He fired another burst of bullets from the assault rifle, trying desperately to keep their gaining pursuers at bay.

She screamed back. "I'm working on it, Dahl!" With her new stance she sought after the circular bastard once more, this time obtaining a firm grip on it. "I got it!" She tugged on the device but it didn't budge; the magnet within was too strong.

"You've…"

Another pull.

"Got to…"

Harder this time.

"Be fucking."

Her grip was weakening.

"Kidding me!"

"Rachel!" Dahl had fear in his voice. Rachel could feel the car's deceleration

"Fuck it." With a rising motion she sat up, still pressing the door open and reached into the cabin. On the back seat was her gun and with a nonchalant grab, she fell back toward the road, new tool in hand.

"We've got the helicopter trying to come back around…" Dynadin informed. Rachel didn't hear him, already jamming the butt of the firearm into the device. It was an awkward angle, with little room for momentum in any of her swings, but she was still making forceful contact.

Ahead of them, the Centenario was readying its next move, seemingly toying with them now. Dynadin squinted against the dawn's light to try and make it out, as did Dahl. Before either of them truly saw the device, their minds put two and two together, recognizing the logical next chess play.

"Is that what I think it is?" Dahl asked, staring at the metallic tool that was now hanging from the back of the Lamborghini. Dynadin didn't answer right away as he watched the metal flatten out into a strip that extended the width of the car, and then kept going, almost doubling its length within a few moments.

"Spike strip!" Dahl screamed, hoping that Rachel would hear him. With vigor, he took shots at every pursuer, including the helicopter in the distance, frantic to keep them back and away from Rachel.

Below the cabin, Rachel's rage kicked in. "Fuck this." She quickly turned the weapon around and curled her fingers around its grip. It leapt in her hand and there was a loud blast of gunfire. Or two. Or three. Rachel didn't really know, she was just trying to get the damn thing off. On the third shot she made contact, observing as the annoying but omnipotent power over their vehicle fell to the pavement and behind them.

She yelled inside. "It's off!"

Mere meters in front of them now, the Centenario released the spike strip. It dropped to the ground, creating small flowers of sparks as it slid with momentum along the pavement, quickly coming to rest.

"Hold on!" Dynadin shouted as he swerved the vehicle right. Rachel gasped as she watched underneath the door she was hanging out of. Feet away lay the spike strip, shining in the morning brilliance of the sun. From her center, she could feel that she was falling out of the car and reached for the closest thing inside: the seatbelt around her leg. The fabric gave way slightly before it locked, hovering Rachel inches above the speeding road.

Her breath caught. *This is it. They'll go on without me.* Instinctively, she crunched her abdomen.

Spikes rose to her left.

Her eyes were locked on the front tire, still turning.

It missed the edge of the spike strip by the width of a pencil.

She wouldn't be so lucky.

As much as she could, she rose up.

A spike tore into her shoulder, ripping the tissue and leaving it behind. But she was still traveling with the vehicle. Flesh wrapped around her hand and pulled her in – Dahl offering some assistance. She tossed the gun onto the other side of the backseat and clutched her shoulder, turning so that she was facing forward. Weakly, she closed the door, blood pouring out between her fingers from the gash.

Dahl immediately took action, M4 still in hand. He was standing through the sunroof that he'd just opened, and fired on the Lamborghini. The tactic forced the lethal speed-demon to zoom off, at least for the time being. He removed his shirt, revealing an aged, but still chiseled physique beneath, peppered with gray hairs.

"Take my shirt, wrap it around your shoulder. We need to stop the bleeding." Rachel did as she was told and went to tie it off. "Come here, let me do it. It needs to be tight." Gently, she leaned forward and Dahl yanked on both ends of the shirt.

"Nice work down there." Dynadin complimented. Rachel appreciated it, even though it didn't help her shoulder feel any less pain. She nodded, realizing they weren't out of this yet. Behind them there were at least half a dozen police vehicles and four additional SUVs. The helicopter still hung somewhere in the distance. And that

God forsaken Centenario was still in front of them. It was clear to her now, amplified through the pain and the need to survive.

"We need to take the offensive. Or else we're never going to make it out of here."

"Agreed." Dahl replied, reloading the M4. He jammed the new mag in. "But you need to catch your breath. Sit back and call them out." Rachel, now wracked with pain once more, cautiously turned in her seat. Up through the sunroof went Dahl, again listening intently for her directions.

"Your eleven o' clock!" There was one of the pursuing N.E.T.S. vehicles, probably the deadliest predators after them at the moment. *Though I bet the Centenario feels differently*... Two three-round bursts came from up top and she saw an explosion as the hood of the vehicle leapt up, obstructing the driver's view. They were out of commission.

"Rachel!" Dynadin urged. She turned to him and saw the Lamborghini had decided to come back to play.

"Six o' clock!" Dahl pivoted in less than a second and fired another succession of three-round bursts at their good old friend. Once more, the Lambo sped ahead, nearly out of sight, knowing he'd have to change his strategy.

"Two o' clock!" Another call-out, more shots fired, and this time a cop car swerved into the concrete median with a destroyed front tire.

"Twelve o' clock!" Only a few shots came before an audible *click*.

"New mag!" Dahl yelled, dropping the old one into the Rover and holding out his palm. Rachel slammed a new one into his grasp and within moments, several more shots rang out. A N.E.T.S. SUV had lost its windshield and front tire and now rolled down the highway, quickly losing speed and ground on them.

Ahead of them by several miles, the Lamborghini Centenario exited the highway out of their sight. Left of the exit, the road went under the highway as it bridged above. It was here he would wait – wait for the storm to pass and to strike again from behind.

"Ten o' clock!" Slowly they were narrowing down their pursuers to a manageable quantity. Rachel was beginning to believe that they might actually make it out of this alive or at least not behind bars. As another police vehicle took a tumble behind them, she handed Dahl a new mag as he reached for it. Behind the pursuers, there across the brightening, golden sky, was the helicopter, deciding if it should make its next move.

"Dynadin?" Rachel asked toward the front, Dahl still scanning, weapon at the ready up top. "Where are we going? When does this chase end?" He sighed.

"I'm not really sure. I've been keeping my eye out for anywhere we *could* lose them, but it's just desert mostly." Rachel came to her own conclusions from that but he finished his thought anyway. "We're going to have to get rid of all of them I fear." Dahl fired several more rounds and Rachel watched as one of the final police vehicles flew off a raised cut of the road and into a sand bank, sending a plume of hard brown grit feet into the air.

"One more police…" Rachel reported to Dahl. "The Lambo…" *Wherever that guy is now…*Counting the remaining SUVs. "Two more N.E.T.S…" She was forgetting something. "And the helicopter!" *Five more vehicles. That's all we need to get out of here.* "Dynadin, slow down a tad. Let them catch up…we're going to end this here."

Within moments, one of the hulking SUVs was close enough to receive Dahl's bullets. And he made sure they did. Its front windshield shattered with a spray and smoke rose from its engine. Unceremoniously, it dropped out of the race, slowing and eventually stopping – down for the count. The final police vehicle sped past it, boldly taking its place. Dahl yelled down, not really directing his thought toward anyone in particular.

"Did this guy not see what I've done to the last, what, six? Six guys!" Almost spastically, he ducked back into the cabin. "What the…!" A slow succession of bullets rattled the car and sailed overhead. Muttering under his breath, Rachel couldn't help but smile and laugh softly.

"What's the matter, Grandpap? Angry when they fight back?" Dynadin snorted a laugh and Dahl quit muttering, realizing she was right. Instead, he smiled, appreciating the brief moment of lightheartedness during the chaos. A few more hollow thuds came against their vehicle and Dahl grit his teeth, rose through the sunroof, took aim, and fired. One of the front wheels of the pursuer came completely off and it leapt into the air, landing and sliding on its side for a moment before finally resting on its roof. Rachel patted Dahl's leg from the cabin as an "atta boy".

Their minor victory was cut short. From somewhere, the Centenario had appeared back on the highway, a sun beam gleaming off one of its sharp, jagged angles. It sped forward, bringing the sun glare with it, it's low, almost flat visual footprint getting steadily larger on the horizon.

"Our friend is back. Punch it Dynadin." Their Rover lurched forward but even still, they couldn't compete with 200 miles per hour. He was on them soon enough, the whiny, but powerful engine out-blasting their own. Dahl remained standing but did not fire; he'd become distracted by a third party that had decided to rejoin the chase as well: the helicopter. Quickly, it caught up to the pack, flying low and fast, sand swirling all around. Knowing there were armed men inside, Dahl ducked back in the cabin.

Eager and violent, the helicopter swooped low, almost scraping their car roof and the men aboard fired into it. The armor held, but small dents could be seen from inside the cabin. Meanwhile the Centenario battered against them like an angry gnat. It wasn't doing any damage, but was obviously a diversion. Dahl had closed the sunroof by now and it was clear that they weren't going to be shooting out of it anytime soon. Unless they wanted to be shred to pieces.

Sand baked by the hues of the sun swirled all around and in front of them, making driving difficult for Dynadin and making the Lamborghini invisible at times.

"Mother fucker!" Dahl yelled, angry at everything that had happened on this Godforsaken mission. He felt it was his fault; he should have seen all of this coming. David was always two steps ahead and right now was no different. People were dead because of him and all three of them were facing the same fate. Captured alive with pending torture at best. "We need a damn plan!" His teeth were clenched together. No one had anything. Until…

"Wait!" Dynadin shifted in his seat, excited and trying to piece together his thoughts. "Rachel, look in the trunk. What do you see?" Leaning back she responded just as another blast of bullets rained from above. She was cut quiet and waited until they had passed.

"There's extra zipline gear back here but that's about it. A couple extra pairs of thermal gear…pants, shirts…why?" A smile plastered itself to Dynadin's face.

"The zipline! It's crazy, yeah…but it will definitely work. Look in the medium sized bag back there too." He waited. "Is there a grenade?"

"Yeah but just one." Rachel replied, confused. She looked at Dahl. He wasn't tracking either. "What're you getting at?" Dynadin spoke calmly, but quickly, as if he was a commander in war before a strike.

"Rachel, you're going to get the zipline gear. Dahl, be prepared to lay down as much cover fire as possible. This is all about timing so we'll likely only get one shot at this.

"Rachel, you're going to fire the zipline at the Lambo – the suction cup end. Aim for a broad surface without too many lines. Either way it should stick. When the helicopter comes at us again like that, you're going to have to be quick and wrap the other end of the cable around it's landing legs." Rachel could now see where this was going and a grin crept onto her face too.

"What about the grenade?" She asked.

"Did you see the front of the Centenario? It's got two very deep hood scoops – I want you to aim for those. Grenade falls in there, goes off, car gets tossed into the air and rips the helo down with it." Dahl grabbed Dynadin's shoulder and gave it a good squeeze.

"Brilliant. Rachel, let me know once you're ready. I'll lay down cover fire as best I can and for as long as I can from the sunroof." Immediately, Rachel got to it, rolling the zipline cable into the launcher and placing the grenade between her legs for the time being.

Outside, chaos, sun, and sand remained. The Lamborghini had rammed them no less than seven times, though it was backing off slightly now, and the helicopter was lining up for its fourth pass. Their roof, as armored as it was, wouldn't take many more powerful shots and eventually some bullets would make it through. It was now or never.

"Ready." Rachel stated, rolling down the window on her side of the car. Dahl nodded.

"On my mark. Wait for the chopper to get a little closer." Rachel put the grenade in her mouth, hands busy with the launcher.

"Okkkk…Let's go!" Dahl sprung from the sunroof and began firing at the chopper that was already leaning across the air toward them.

Rachel sat on the windowsill and aimed the launcher across the Rover's roof toward the Centenario. A swirl of dust impeded her vision.

"Suh-uh-a-hit" She mumbled, her curse muffled by the explosive in her mouth. Dahl kept firing in short bursts at the copter. Before long it would already be past them. For a moment the dust cleared and Rachel could see the gleaming, sleek, and *wide* panel of the driver door. Sand clouded her vision again but that was all she needed and the launcher fired with a thud. It kicked once

it had made contact and without even testing if the suction cup had stuck, Rachel unclipped the tail end of the
cable, tossing the launcher onto the road like a discarded
child's plaything.

Behind her, the helicopter was coming low once more
– probably its lowest yet. Three more bullets left Dahl's
weapon and tagged the side of the bird. Rachel barely had
any time to wrap the cable around the landing legs, duck-
ing as it came at her, reaching, and clamping the wire just
as it left arm's reach.

But it worked.

They were attached.

And completely unaware of it, at least until the dust
cleared.

Rachel dropped the grenade into her right hand, holding onto the frame of the Rover with her left. Pain
coursed through the extremity, echoing from the torn
shoulder. She yanked the pin with her teeth, spitting it
out, but not flipping the safety lever quite yet. Slowly, the
sand was clearing from the air. Closer to them than she
was expecting was the Centenario, silver cable proudly
beaming the sun's rays, stretching, stretching up toward
the helicopter.

With her only throw, Rachel chucked the grenade,
sans safety lever, at the front of the pursuing vehicle. It
disappeared from her sight once it made contact, and nes-
tled into the left hood vent. Above her there was a motor
roar and she watched as the helicopter noticed the tether,
and tried to pull away from the Lamborghini. But all was
for naught as within seconds there was a thunderous
boom that launched the exotic police cruiser into the air,
tearing off a section of its front.

In a show of black smoke, gold sand, flames, and charred metal, the hulk flipped a few times before being yanked by the zipline and crashing back down to earth. For a moment the helicopter seemed to gain control, but the weight of an entire car, light as that particular model might be, was too much. The blades of the rotor tilted, more and more, until they were rotating against the pavement, sparks and disintegrating metal filling the air. Eventually the hull slammed into the ground and tumbled over and over again, crunching more each time.

By this time Dynadin had come to a stop, mostly to see if his grandiose plan had worked.

It had.

Spectacularly.

Behind all the carnage, there was still one more trailing SUV however and Dynadin began to pull away, ready to begin the final pursuit. One versus one were odds he could deal with.

"Wait!" Rachel instructed, still sitting out of her window. Dynadin was confused.

"What? There's one last car. Let's go!"

"Just…wait! And watch."

Then Dynadin saw it himself. Among all the wreckage that had just taken place, were the two vehicles, land and air, on separate sides of the highway, creating an avenue toward them. Across that avenue, something glinted in the new morning sun, subtle, but still there. Another grin came as he realized his plan was about to work better than he'd originally intended.

<hr style="width:80%" />

Knowing it was the last chance, the final SUV sped forward, aiming to bring these bastards down once and for all. The driver wasn't quite sure how the Lamborghini and chopper had been taken out so fast – and so close together. They'd been too far back and the sand had been thick in the air for a time.

"All right boys. These traitors are terrorists and Harper wants them dead. We're the last ones left." He paused, gunning it even more. "Weapons hot. Shoot to kill."

Two separate, destroyed, vehicles were coming up on them on either side of the road. There may be survivors in the chopper, but they'd have to wait. He couldn't care less if the cop had survived, though he was sad to see the car go.

Something flashed in his eye, bright and nearly painful; had it had been some sort of reflection from the sun? He assumed it was a piece of bright shrapnel from the road –

"SIR, LOOK O–"

Zipline cable that had been splayed tightly across the road crunched through the bottom of the front grill and into their wheel wells, exploding the rubber underneath. The car lurched downward at first, with the backend rising above it, black and hulking against a sea of sand. The sound had been shockingly quick – a brief but violent clatter and squeal as metal and plastic separated – but then it was over as the vehicle was airborne. It completed a full rotation and landed, hard, on its roof, with more sounds of metal compressing and glass raining against pavement. It hardly slid after that and the momentum with which it had crashed down could only mean death for those inside.

It was over.

"Oh…ohh. Jesus." Rachel couldn't look away from the spectacle, impressed but not quite able to even believe what she'd seen.

"How did we get through that?" Dahl asked both pensively and seriously. No one replied. It wasn't a time for celebration, but it **was** a time for a bit of relief. Too many people had just died, some very violently, and some had been their friends. Or…at least as close to friends as you could become in this world. They each needed there to be an emotional fallout from the last couple of hours, but fear won out.

Somehow David had known, like he'd been toying with them all along. He had set out to obliterate their group tonight and nearly succeeded. Not to mention, they managed to stop absolutely nothing, *nada*, when it came to the Wolfpaw Initiative.

If there even was such a thing.

Their thoughts were all one and the same as the beat-to-shit Rover continued through the desert. But it was Dahl who spoke first, and with his voice came the finality of something. *The beginning of the end* Rachel mused.

"We need to get off the grid. Just the three of us. We regroup, heal, and plan. That son of a bitch has been ahead of us every step of the way…it's time we make moves to return the favor."

CHAPTER XV

PAIN IN DEFEAT

MONDAY | OCT 8TH | 2018

Rachel stirred from her incredibly deep slumber, the sleep clawing at her to just put her weary head back down on the luscious pillow.

The pillow wasn't really all that luscious, nor was the bed she lay in all that comfortable, but she had been near comatose; she needed the sleep to repair her, to make sense of all this, to remove her from this world she now felt hopeless in. Her mind though – her mind wanted her back in reality.

It was still dark in the room and she was unsure of how long she'd been sleeping. Not really wanting to move, Rachel remained in bed piecing together what had transpired, half hoping that it had all been just a dream.

The mission to Dubai had been a failure. A catastrophic one.

David had been there.

Ian and Henry were both dead.

These covers are so comfy. Maybe I'll just rest my eyes some more.

She escaped, barely.

God, my body hurts. My ribs feel bruised.

Dahl, Dynadin, and she had fled the city.

They were chased by local authorities and N.E.T.S. agents.

They had all hardly escaped.

Why does my shoulder feel like it's on fire?

Spike strip. Helicopter. Grenade. The details started aligning in her mind.

Dynadin had driven them to a smaller city nearby.

They exchanged vehicles.

Another drive to their current safe house. If one could call it that.

More like a safe shack.

Sleep. Sleeeeeeeep. Wonderful sleep.

Rachel shook her head trying to rid her spirit of the understandable, but annoying desire to go back to sleep. She had no idea what their next moves would be, but she knew they needed to reconvene. Hopefully the others had gotten some rest as well.

There was a creak and groan from the bed as she sat up, imitating something old and decrepit, which was exactly how she felt. Throughout her core she felt as if she had been punched by one large fist. *Yeah, it's called slamming into the Burj Dubai.* On her shoulder there was the odd sensation of extra weight. She brought her hand up to examine what was a sizeable bandage, slightly wet in the center with blood. With her attention now on the wound, she could feel its intense sting and briefly flashed back to it being torn open by a spikestrip while hanging out of a car. Rachel smiled, almost proud to have the battle scar. It would be a badge of sorts. *That* is *a really badass story.*

She was wearing an old T-shirt with no pants, completely unsure of when she'd changed, though she guessed the exhaustion had come on quickly once they arrived here.

Not quite remembering where *here* was, she tried to gather her bearings. From what she could tell, this seemed to be a wood and stone hut or home of some sort. It was actually almost cold here and dark enough that her eyes were still trying to adjust. A brief memory of pulling up to the edge of a small town all but confirmed that this place was essentially in the middle of nowhere.

The room she was in seemed to be only hers; neither Dahl nor Dynadin were anywhere to be found. In a corner, half on a chair and half on the floor, were the clothes she'd been wearing. Beside her on a bedside table was a full glass of water she must not have had time to drink before plummeting into oblivion. Realizing that she was parched, she grabbed it, glass still cool to the touch, and chugged. Water dribbled around the edge of her glass and down her chin, plopping quietly on the bed.

Once it was drained, she observed her surroundings some more, trying to divert her attention away from the painful bruises and deep cuts that were actively hurting now that she was awake. She scanned the very old and rudimentary home, if one could call it a home, and concluded that Dahl and Dynadin must have been sleeping as well. There was no light shining underneath the door and the only reason she could see at all was the soft moonlight making its way through a grimy window.

Even more worrisome was the complete lack of sound. Within the house, there was no noise and it creeped her out. Stifling her anxiety, Rachel realized that she could probably use all the sleep she could get.

As soon as the thought had crossed her mind, her entire body agreed and forced her to lay back down where she began to drift off to sleep once more. A final thought about a Wolfpaw made her mind want to put up one last fight, but by the time her head made it to the pillow, all the disastrous memories fled, leaving her with nothing.

She did not dream. She barely moved. It was a fully engrossing kind of sleep. It was her mind's gift to her body; it needed healing before what was to come.

But…it was all too fleeting. The darkness had felt like forever, but in a contrary fashion it had felt like she'd only slept mere seconds. Given the new warmth of the room and the abundance of light, it became frustrating that the former seemed truer. Outside her door she could hear very light rustling; likely Dynadin and Dahl were already up and she wondered for how long. For the past year or so there had been a bit of a running joke about Rachel always sleeping in, but given the circumstances she figured no one would be throwing barbs this morning. *Or was it afternoon?*

Reluctantly, she moved her covers aside and got out of bed, put her pants on, and tossed her hair a bit to straighten some of the messy curls. The hesitation to get moving this morning was not rooted in its normal, less significant, laziness but rather a dread of facing reality. It was a dramatically different morning than the last time she'd awoken, and certainly not for the better. People were dead. Their last year had seemingly been for naught. And she was more confused about David and his motives than ever before. Not to mention, much further away from fulfilling her promise of killing him.

This wasn't typical morning laziness, no.

It was defeat.

As she exited her room, the door moaned on its hinges, announcing to the men that she was awake. Dynadin sat at a table, typing and scrolling through something on a laptop. His gaze didn't move but Dahl's had, noticing Rachel briefly as he paced around the small room, which was the main one of this structure. Both of them looked like shit and Rachel wondered if they had gotten any sleep at all. Dahl's gray hair was disheveled and seemed wiry. Meanwhile Dynadin had bags under his eyes and looked like some unfortunate combination of hungry, angry, beaten, and tired as all hell.

Quietly, Rachel made her way to their gear and rummaged through one of the backpacks. There was a protein bar and a jar of nuts, both of which she grabbed. While the table's other chair would have been the logical place to take a seat, she felt more like sitting on the floor, back upright against the wall with legs outstretched. The wall she laid the back of her head onto was rough but she just sat in silence save for the munching of nuts every few minutes.

The group was *defeated*. They were ashamed to talk to one another and were each keeping busy with their menial tasks.

Dynadin researching something.

Dahl pondering and pacing.

Rachel eating and sitting.

After the long period of silence, Dahl spoke, unconvincingly, and with a waver in his voice.

"Despite what I may have said in the car, I think we need to consider our options with David. Emotions and adrenaline were high."

"What do you mean?" Rachel broke her silence.

"I think we need to let this go." Dahl replied. Dynadin remained silent, still working. Rachel half expected herself to have an outburst in protest. It never came. Instead, she sat there, exhausted, racked with pain, and finishing her lunch, or dinner (or God knows what meal) as she stared at the ceiling. *I want to be done with this so badly...*

Dahl continued. "We need to recognize the signs right in front of us. Our resources were weak in comparison to begin with. Now we're a man down without a mole back at N.E.T.S." He paused, out of respect for the fallen, and to gather his thoughts. "David has always been ahead of the curve – this is his game and we're in it. It nearly cost Dynadin his life earlier, and almost all of us our lives yesterday. It only seems like a matter of time before we don't get so lucky."

"I don't feel very lucky." Rachel winced as the pain in her shoulder flared and dissipated.

"My point exactly. We very nearly lost you, Rachel." There was a soft chitter-clatter of keys as Dynadin typed, but otherwise nothing. "We also have to ask ourselves: *what has David done?*"

The question infuriated Rachel. *What has he done? Are you fucking serious?* But again, she was too defeated to protest.

"Yes, he killed both of my sons." Dahl stated bitterly. "He organized The Will and killed thousands upon thousands of civilians. Not to mention a handful of atrocities we probably don't know about. But...now that the Wolfpaw Initiative is fake – just a piece of fiction to get us out in the open – we need to critically think if David may be done." At this, Dynadin turned.

"So you're assuming that the Wolfpaw Initiative is fake?"

"Not assuming. Call it an educated guess. It was a brilliant move by David, but The Will is over, does he really need another big game plan?"

"I'm sorry, Dahl. I'm not with you on this one. David's motives are more refined than just killing a bunch of Americans. There's something else going on."

"Fine. Rachel, what's your opinion?" Dahl looked over to her while Dynadin went back to his computer, still listening.

"Honestly? Between the torn shoulder, the bruised ribs, and seeing a friend's head blown open, I'm having a hard time giving a shit." Anger lingered on her voice and on her lips, and her brain was firing on all cylinders. "But…I think on the surface that this whole excursion to Dubai was a plan to kill us."

"Thank you." Dahl affirmed.

"I'm not finished." Rachel grabbed the conversation back. "Since when has David been a surface-level guy? There have always been layers with him…more than meets the eye. He's smart. I hate him, but he's smart as hell." She rested her voice a moment, listening to her body. Dahl's attention remained on her and even Dynadin had turned to actively listen now. "Every part of me wants to be done with this, but my gut and even my head to a certain degree are telling me that David's not done. That The Will wasn't his magnum opus. That the Wolfpaw Initiative, or at least something of the sort, is real."

Dahl looked surprised to hear this, almost a tad disappointed. His hand came to his chin as he scratched the gray stubble that had started growing there.

"Do you *really* think David's done with his power?" Rachel asked, mostly rhetorically, letting the question simmer and linger in the air. Dahl's scratching became more aggressive until he finally threw his hands down to his side, briefly startling Rachel. Back and forth his feet paced in short strides, and when his face would turn in Rachel's direction it looked almost tormented. A pungent mix of anger and deep sadness.

Without warning he picked up the wooden chair next to Dynadin by its back and lifted it above his head, bringing it crashing to the floor. It splintered and shattered with a colossal boom that was louder than anything Rachel had heard in the last 48 hours. Dynadin stopped what he was doing, turning to face his friend.

Tears were now freely flowing from his glistening eyes. The anger had relieved itself; now it was time for the sadness. His hands came to his face to shamefully cover his sobbing and his knees buckled, sending him to the floor. Dynadin was too quick however, and caught him as he fell, gently lowering to the floor with him.

Rachel, snapping out of her post-mission angst, immediately felt empathy toward the man, their unequivocal leader, now breaking down in front of them. It almost made her feel a little better inside knowing he was emotional and she rose from the floor, going to where he sat in Dynadin's arms.

"He killed…" [a sob] "…killed both" [sob] "of my sons!" Rachel placed a gentle hand on his leg, letting him know it was ok. Dahl had gone through too much – it was time for him to be a real human being now. There were some incomprehensible words amongst the tears but he'd eventually string some sentences along, as if he had to explain his anguish.

"I…I…I never" [sobbing] "never even really knew them!" It was true. Despite his short time with one of his sons these past few months, Dahl really hadn't been able to understand, nurture, or bond with either of his sons in a meaningful way. It was this knowledge that was perhaps the most painful.

As Dahl came to terms with his loss, something he'd been bottling up for over a year, they sat there. Their presence was all he silently asked for. Eventually the crying slowed, his breathing returned to normal, and the tasks at hand became priority once more. As he and Dynadin slowly got up off the floor, Rachel following suit, Dahl spoke without tears.

"To answer your question, Rachel: no. I don't think David is done with his power. I think The Will was just the opening act." Dynadin returned to his computer which slightly perturbed Rachel. *What on earth could be so important over there?* After a sideways glance, she turned back to Dahl.

"So what're we going to do then?"

"I have absolutely no idea." Even though the reply was delivered evenly, it sent a wave of discomfort from Rachel's heels to her head. Dahl, unaware of what to do next, was frightening in his indecisiveness and she felt immediately vulnerable.

"How often has that happened since you've started this?" It came out meekly.

"Not very." Dahl began to rub his forehead, frustrated at this impasse with the future. "I want so badly to take action against him but he has the upper hand in every scenario I can think of." He explained. "A direct attack just for the sake of killing him would get us all killed. Continuing our work of the past year to take out his network would lead us nowhere. He knows who we are and will likely just set more traps. Trying to lock down another mole would probably end up worse – my guess is that another N.E.T.S. agent would die."

All Rachel could do was nod. Dahl was right and she couldn't think of anything innovative or useful either. Dynadin was still frustratingly typing furiously away, paying almost no attention to the task at hand. *Is he booking a flight to escape or something?*

"Dynadin, care to fill us in on whatever it is you're working on over there?" It came out with more bite than she had intended and Rachel immediately felt embarrassed. They were all a team here. Now was not the time for petty frustration. Despite the delivery, Dynadin stopped what he was doing and gently turned to answer, seeming unaware of the attitude-laced inquiry.

"I have an idea, and it may be a longshot, but if it works then this thing is basically over."

"Care to elaborate?"

"Sure." He turned the chair to get more comfortable. "When I was on the several day stakeout mission in Russia –"

"The one to kill Mr. Mustache?" Rachel interjected.

"Yes. When I was there, I recorded and stored all the audio that I could using a highly sensitive directional microphone located in the scope of my sniper.

"It's several days of data, and it could honestly lead us to nothing. I don't want either of you to get your hopes up, but I realized two things in the last twelve hours or so." He held two fingers up and grabbed one with his other hand. "First, I never reviewed the data or recordings. We rarely do this anyway because it's a lot of white noise and after things went south there, I don't think any of us thought it was necessary. Which leads me to my second point.

"I noticed that during my stakeout waiting to get a shot, there was a particular room of the house that the Russian would go to by himself. It was used exclusively for private phone calls and whenever I'd track him into there, it would distort what the microphone could pick up. It had to have been equipped with some type of specific material that blocks sound waves, potentially even something digital was achieving this. At first I thought it was absolutely blocking my ability to hear anything, but I have a new hypothesis: the room scrambled everything that was said. And my second hypothesis is: whatever that man was talking about in that room had to have been important. At that time, he had no idea I was listening in, so the protection the room provided was from his own men's ears." The story paused. "If David was on the other end of that line, it could have been something game-changing."

Rachel and Dahl's faces were doubtful, but thankful. Dynadin could see they thought it was a long shot at best. Hell, he even thought it was a Hail Mary. But it was *something*. Dahl agreed as much.

"Dynadin, I appreciate you looking into that. Have we gotten anywhere with it?"

"Not yet. I'm still trying to unscramble the audio from the few conversations that took place in there. It's…a slow process."

"Understood. Well, at least it's something. That's more than either Rachel or I have right now." She nodded in agreement at the call out. "What do you need from us?"

"Just time. I should know within the next few hours if this is a fruitless endeavor or something worthwhile."

"We can do that. In the meantime, Rachel, let's you and I work on an extraction plan. Costa Rica is likely a bust and we need a new place to lie low." An audible stomach growl could be heard across the room. "And I'm hungry as hell. Let's go into town and see if we can't pick something up."

"Be careful out there." Dynadin warned. "You never know who may be watching." Dahl nodded as he took a scarf from near their packs and also handed one to Rachel. They wrapped their heads so only their eyes were uncovered, stepping silently out into the day and leaving Dynadin to finish his work.

Wind threw sand into the air that swirled around them, then fell to the ground, and would pick back up again. As they walked away from the small building they each put sunglasses on to shield their eyes, and Rachel was able to see their hideout and getaway car for the first time. The building itself was no more than a square structure, somewhat crumbling from the outside and unsurprising from what she'd seen inside. The getaway car was more dramatically dated: a worn down, somewhat rusted burgundy car of which she didn't even recognize the make or model. Sand was caked to the corners of its windows and there was a general sheen of golden grit smeared over the deep red. It was a wonder they made it away at all. She turned to Dahl as they began walking the few blocks into the town.

"So what were your plans for extraction?"

"We're not going to talk extraction." Dahl replied, purposefully walking toward food. "We won't be extracting from here until we know our next move, whether we decide to make one or not."

"Okay…so why're we outside?"

"Food. I'm actually very hungry and I need to get out of that room." Rachel met that with silence. "I wanted to talk to you about Dynadin. What do you think of his plan?" It came across like a loaded question, but Rachel knew Dahl well enough that she could tell he genuinely wanted to know. So she was honest.

"I think it's farfetched. I recognize the logic – at the time Mr. Mustache was pretty high up in the Dead Scorpions, at least according to our intel. There's a good chance they could have had some type of incriminating conversation." She paused. "But I just don't see it. To me it feels like we're grasping at straws." Saying that felt bad, almost insulting to Dynadin, but it was true. "What about you?"

"I'm on the same page as you. I just wanted to hear you explain it first." She could sense him smiling under his scarf. "Something that you should know about Dynadin – if you haven't picked it up already – is that he will never give up. It's not in his circuitry. With all that life has thrown at him, to see where and what he is today, it's really no wonder." Rachel didn't understand.

"So are you saying we should give up? What about back there?"

"I'm not saying that. Nor am I saying that we should go charging in or waste years of our lives doing petty side missions with the hopes we get close to him. What I'm saying is that we need a very tactical approach to what comes next." Rachel backed down with a nod that was mostly unnoticeable beneath the layers of scarf. "What I'm getting at is that I may need your help 'calming him down', for lack of a better phrase. We're still reeling from what happened back at Dubai, whether we want to admit it or not. I won't have that happen again."

Wind howled between them and kicked up more grains of earth. It brought a moving wall in front of them and the sun punctured through the dust, enveloping all they could see in a golden haze. Rachel knew Dahl had more to elaborate on, but let him in his own time. It didn't take long.

"The next time we see David, I want it to be the absolute last. Do you understand me?" In other circumstances, Rachel would have perceived it as fatherly scolding, but here she knew it wasn't of that nature.

"I do. And I agree."

"Good to hear."

For a time they made their way along the town's dusty main road toward the small market near its center. The wind continued and it made their journey slower than either of them would have liked.

After a while they arrived in the town square, if you could really call it that. It was simply an opening among the aged houses and shacks, not unlike their own, where vendors had set up. Casually they made their way through the different stalls, but each of them was also cautiously eyeing each and every resident and person they came in contact with.

Unfortunately, the stand with meats was rather picked over and the remaining supply of what was left didn't exactly look…fresh. Rachel and Dahl moved on quickly to a fruit cart and shop where they picked through several items, purchasing enough for a day or two and taking

Dynadin's portions into consideration. Near the end of the market was a bread and grain seller. Rachel could smell the goodness from far off and it sent her stomach in a twirl. Given how much Dahl purchased, she sensed that he was as hungry as she was. *I wonder if he's even eaten since we escaped?* Rice, loaves of bread, and even some beans came with them as they walked away, leaving a particular vendor happy with his day's work.

By now the dust storm from the wind had almost completely died down and they both sauntered back to the hideout, slowly munching on some bread as they did.

"So how's your shoulder?" Dahl asked between bites. "And your ribs for that matter?" Rachel had nearly forgotten about both but now the reminder opened up the dull pains in each place once more.

"I'm in rough shape. I think my core will be fine. It's bruised but I may have escaped without cracking any ribs. Decently yellow and purple everywhere though." She paused to eat a piece of bread, just as delicious as it smelled. "The shoulder hurts the most and the cut is pretty deep. I figure I'll need to keep it bandaged for at least a couple more weeks and it'll probably take half that long for the skin to fuse back instead of being a gross flap. Monitoring it for infection will be key but I think as long as that doesn't happen it'll be fine. I still have full range of motion and it didn't do too much damage to the muscle, just skin mostly."

"Good to hear. Let's check the bandages when we get back and replace them if we need to. We're void of any antibiotics out here so infection is definitely a concern."

With that, their conversation was mutually over and they continued the quicker walk back "home", still munching on their bread. Rachel briefly wondered why she didn't feel more apprehensive – they were on the run after all – but some part of her, maybe woman's intuition, decided that David wouldn't have had his men come out this far. Not to mention, they were three highly trained spies. *Not exactly the easiest people to track.*

The shack was unchanged from how they'd left it save for some sand shifting around its edges and entrance. Once inside, they both began to remove their scarves and sunglasses.

No sooner had Rachel gotten one loop of the scarf around her neck and Dynadin had busted out of his chair, sending it falling behind him, and rushing over to them. Panic struck in her belly, worried that something had happened or there was someone in here with them. Dynadin didn't hesitate to speak.

"I'm glad you're back. I found something." His eyes were huge, not excited, but almost horrified with his discovery. Dahl gave Rachel a sidelong glance as he too continued to undo his scarf.

"Dynadin, what did you find?" Dahl's tone was cautious, almost worried.

"You're going to want to sit down. This is it."

"What do you mean, 'this is it'?" Rachel prodded.

"I found out why David is doing all of this. I found it *all.*"

Chapter XVI

The Solution
Monday | Oct 8TH | 2018

Rachel and Dahl sat around the small, wooden table after placing their market purchases by their bags along the wall. Dynadin seemed equally excited and terrified as he too took a seat and orchestrated some button clicks on his computer.

"The first part starts out a little fuzzy. I can't quite recover what's there, but I'm fairly confident that, other than pleasantries, I've captured everything."

"Ok." Dahl said, adjusting and leaning forward in his seat. Rachel shifted too, prepared to get comfortable. An odd buzz had taken over their space. She sensed its palpable nature. Something was about to change.

Dynadin clicked the mouse one time.

"Here we go."

A fair amount of static played through the speakers. Voices could be heard in the background and there was a rustling as if someone were shifting a microphone while accidentally making contact with it.

"-erythi-…is well." More static and shuffling. Another voice.

"-ood to h-…how-…ur boy?" It was nearly impossible to piece together effectively. The voices dropped momentarily and then came back, fresh and clear. One was speaking in a mild Russian accent, Mr. Moustache.

"He's very good. I think he likes it out here in the wilderness. Lots of space for adventures. Amazing thing the mind of a child. So full of imagination."

"Yes, quite." The responding voice was unmistakably David's. A tinge of disgust could be heard in the reply, likely based in the knowledge of the Russian man's less than favorable dealings with children. There was a moment of awkward, strained silence before David spoke. "So what did you want to talk about? What was so urgent?"

"Ahhh yes. Thank you sir for taking the time." The Russian seemed shy and intimidated and took a moment to compose his confidence. "I'd like to know what's going on."

"Elaborate."

"Specifically, I'd like to know what we're working toward. The Will was over a year ago. Through my channel of wealth, I've helped you considerably for the last few decades. Over the past five years I've given or spent more on your endeavor than the previous years combined. What for?" Any trace of fright in the man's tone was gone and he'd shifted to assertiveness. The tension could be felt through the recording.

"You have done well for me. I'll admit that. Because of you we were able to capture recruits we may never have even known of, not to mention your scientific contributions to the organization."

"Yes! And that is what I'm wondering. The Will was some bombs and wingsuits. What is all this scientific research we've been funding?"

"Did you just interrupt me?" David's question was cold as ice, almost as if he was threatening to hang up then and there.

"I'm sorry sir. I got ahead of myself. Please continue." The tininess had crept back in as David continued.

"Apologies. I haven't gotten much sleep and I've a hell of a headache. Like I was saying, you've done well for the Aqarab Mayta. We certainly wouldn't be as far along as we are today without you. I imagine you'd like to know where your money and resources have been pooling – much as I would in your position. Before we continue, is this line secure?"

"Yes. The line is a private and encrypted one which only I can call out from. I'm in a soundproofed room and have ordered my men to leave me alone. We'll have no disturbances or unwanted guests."

"Good. Good. I think the first thing I should explain is that I never desired for The Will to happen." David waited for a reaction on this but the Russian gave no audible one. "We're both thinking men. Whether you're a man of religion or not, I think you can agree that, in general, today's terrorists are moronic and disturbingly narrow-minded. As I built the Dead Scorpions from the ground up, I knew I'd eventually have to sacrifice *something* in order to not only gain trust, but gain *absolute* trust. I needed to obtain the attention of powerful, smart men such as yourself and in order to do that I had to pick up some sheep along the way. Example here would be the radical Islamic population." There was a pause, as if David was giving the man time to speak. Nothing came so he continued.

"As misguided as they are, I suppose I can say that they're quite tenacious. I put some of my best people in charge of their upper ranks and, somewhat to my surprise, we began to cater to a slightly different audience. People from various backgrounds, gender, and nationality were recruited, though realistically in this day and age that's not wholly surprising. There are dumbasses all over the world. My only guiding principle was absolute discretion. For the Aqarab Mayta to be successful, secrecy until the perfect moment was of the utmost importance. I'd say we pulled that off fairly well, but it was shockingly easier than I presumed when you have other groups like Al Qaeda and ISIS parading around like a bunch of peacocks.

"I digress. A long story somewhat shorter is that radical Islam loves to target America. Really Western culture in general, but they're so blinded by their rage for America that it often clouds their vision. Everyone wants to be part of the next "9/11". It's nauseating actually. A lot of good, decent people died that day.

"As I worked on the endgame, The Will grew bigger and bigger. The final result was something that made me sick to my stomach. Too many people lost their lives, many of whom shouldn't have. I struggled for weeks afterward to cope with what I had essentially carried through with an invisible hand. Reminding myself that it was all for the greater good was even difficult at times. You see..." A moment's pause. "I'm a patriot. I love this country, even if it has become something I don't look at with pride anymore. What I did to it will forever be in the darkest pages of its history and I'll have to take that with me to my grave, hypocritical as it may sound. But it had to be done. Promises were made to a lot of powerful, wealthy, and discreet people. In the meantime, I gained all the manpower and resources that I would ever need to apply to something much more grand, effective, and humane than a nation-wide thunderstorm of suicide bombers." David stopped, thinking of his next words.

"I had no idea, sir." The Russian sympathized. The notion of two men bonding over one's perceived "forced" choice to kill over 27,000 people was surreal and disgusting.

"You're one of the very few who does. Truth be told it actually feels kind of nice to get it off my chest. It's a heavy burden to bear."

"So what is the ultimate purpose? If The Will wasn't the Dead Scorpion's main attack, what is?" There was a sensation through the recording that David was almost irritated at Mr. Mustache for asking questions. It was indescribable, but based on the way he'd been telling the tale, one could surmise that he wanted to do it his way and on his time. Somewhat ignoring the man's question, David continued.

"The world is currently plagued. This will all sound genocidal, and maybe it is to a certain extent I suppose, but there are significant issues underneath the surface. There are a lot of attractive and hip topics that the sheep of the world like to think are the actual drivers of all their problems. Things like global warming, the gap between rich and poor, corporate greed…the list goes on.

"The truth of the matter is that all of those things, and many more, are driven by several underlying factors. They're opportunities that only exist when you remove your head from your own ass' bubble and see the human race as just that: a *race*. We are a species. We are the *best* species, at least in our current earth-bound existence, yet we're a species that is beginning to actually degrade.

"This degradation is happening for a plethora of reasons, but I'll mention the two biggest: the lack of a recent catastrophic event or plague *and* uncontrolled population growth. The former is a long overdue ticket from Mother Nature but results in an unforgiving and violent outcome. She doesn't target specific individuals; her choices are sobering. Meanwhile, we've got a world population of over 7.5 billion people that continues to grow. There's of course speculation among the scientific community that the *rate* of growth is slowing, but that's really neither here nor there because the fact remains: *it's still growing.*

"At some instance our globe, our planet, has a 'tipping point' in which human life will no longer be sustainable because there are too many of us. The human race is just as much prey as they are predator. The only issue is that our predator hasn't successfully hunted us for a while. We keep diffusing the bomb that is Mother Nature. Cures for diseases, effective quarantines, and trillions of dollars towards medical research. It's all '*good*' in the sense that it's only delaying the inevitable."

The Russian could be heard shifting in his seat, likely uncomfortably. He remained silent, realizing that The Will was a very, very far memory now. If David's plans were as grandiose as his gathering explanation…God help them all.

"As much as this conversation thus far would suggest otherwise, I'm not a barbarian." David continued. "I have no pointless discriminatory agenda. What I do have is *science* and a vision. Let me ask you something." He cleared his throat briefly. "Who are the worst kind of people in the world?"

The Russian man thought for a while, unsure of how to reply. His response was what he thought David wanted to hear.

"Black people, sir?"

"Really?" David mocked, a trail of anger on his tongue. "Black people? So…what about all the African Americans that have moved society forward? Martin Luther King Jr. is the obvious example, but what about Jackie Robinson, Katherine Johnson, Condoleezza Rice, Barack Obama, Oprah Winfrey…the list goes on and on."

Immediately the Russian knew it had been the wrong answer.

"Did you know that I'm black?" David inquired. If you listened closely enough you could hear Mr. Moustache's stomach drop.

"Sir…I didn't…I." He paused to take a breath. "I am very sorry. I did not know what you wanted me to say. And I did not know that you were African American."

Surprisingly, David let out a chuckle.

"How could you have? Hell, you don't even know if I'm telling the truth right now." Another laugh. "I didn't need you to answer the question correctly, I just wanted to prove a point. People think that cleansing our world is all about race or gender or something of the like. It's not about any of those things.

"You want to know who the worst people in the world are? The unfailingly lazy. They are the ones who don't contribute to society in any way. They don't *add value* to the people or environment around them. In fact, they detract from them, making life harder for those who are contributing. They're the tit-suckers of government funds that expect assistance like it's their birth right. They're the drugged out whack-jobs who rob a family man to get their next high, not wanting to be cured of their addiction. They're the spoiled brats who count on mommy and daddy and their inheritance to see them through life as they piss it away. In simpler terms: they are the ones who do not *try*. *Those* are the worst people in the world and they come in all colors, sizes, creeds, and ages." There was a deep, meaningful pause. "Wouldn't you agree?"

"I…I…do sir. That actually makes a lot of sense."

"It's something I realized as a young man and has stayed with me my entire life. I've seen far too many good men and powerful women taken from this earth while all the freaks you see on the subways or fools you see wandering the streets continue on with their pathetic lives. The humans who do *try* are also an inclusive variety. I've met a mentally disabled man who took the utmost pride in his job of bagging groceries. A small task with a small impact, but he was a *contributor to society*. Similarly, I've known stories of poor men and women, as unlucky as they may be, who put forth the effort to make something of themselves. Whether it be going to college, starting a small deli, or even just working 'for the man'. They're *trying*.

"I tell these anecdotes to reiterate that humans are not divided by their race or their religion. It has nothing to do with their nationality or their gender. And it certainly isn't about their size or financial status. No…no, no, no. It's a split between those who have the right attitude and those who don't. Those who put forth the effort and those who hope, or demand, that effort be put forth by someone else on their behalf.

"Once it became apparent that the world was creating its own population problem, I knew that N.E.T.S. alone would not be able to stop it. Even N.E.T.S. is a narrow-minded entity half the time, usually just focused on the very next task or mission and not taking the distant future into consideration. Far after we are both gone, there will be no turning back. No matter how many humans actually 'try', the problem will be unsolvable. That is, of course, unless we solve it right here, right now."

Mr. Moustache could be heard clearing his throat on the other end and once more readjusting in his seat. There was a sound similar to someone taking a drink and the clink of a setting glass after. The Russian, curious now, spoke.

"Is that what all the white coats and money for research was for? To figure out how to solve this problem?"

"In essence, yes. But the first piece of the puzzle was how to connect the two problems. How does one even begin to define 'human laziness' or one's capacity to put forth effort? How do we effectively quantify that?"

"I've no idea, sir."

"Nor did I at the time. It was a frustrating dilemma, and one I wasn't wholly positive would have an absolute answer. And that is precisely what all of your funding went toward, along with large sums of money from other assets. For over a decade there was an extensive search to find the answer. Simple ones like 'nature vs. nurture' arose or mathematical models that guessed a person's worth based on location, gender, race, etc. All the things we talked about that *don't* define a person. Luckily though there was an eventual breakthrough. A concrete definition of the worst trait in humanity existed and it was better than I had ever hoped for." David milked the dramatic tension with a pause. "There was a biological connection."

"A *biological* connection?" It was clear the Russian wasn't fully tracking.

"How familiar are you with human genetics? DNA?" David inquired.

"Not very much at all sir. Apologies."

"Nonsense. I'll give you a brief overview." David could be heard taking a breath and likely sitting up straighter in his chair. "A biological connection is really best defined as a genetic one. Our genes define almost all of what we are – they are related to our DNA and effectively *code* who we are. Like a computer. Have blue eyes? This is determined by a gene. Brown hair? White skin? Each of those are represented by a specific combination of genes; a unique code.

"Genes determine more than just our physical traits however. While, at least in the collegiate scientific community, most of this science is 'unconfirmed', we've been able to confirm several layers deeper than they have, thanks in part to research funds you helped provide. Sexuality, temperament…hell even political leanings have some tie to it all. Of course there's still the proven belief that we're all 'products of our environment' and that does continue to drive a lot of who each of us is as a person, but suffice it to say that we've had several monumental scientific breakthroughs. This is science that won't be confirmed for another few decades.

"I digress from the topic though. The hypothesis for our genetic research was this: there is a specific combination of genes that dictates several undesirable traits in a human: lack of motivation, lethargy, entitlement, cheating, unwilling to change, free-loading, addiction, and several others. These are known as the Errors. These are human traits that, quite frankly, are holding back the race as a whole. Humans who experience these traits are predominately relying so heavily on their brethren that they're draining resources. Time, money, effort – all are net losses from our race for helping these people. These people who don't want help, don't want change, don't want to be a productive members of society. These people who don't want to contribute to the future, but want to suck from the present. Do you know people like this?"

David had been revealing the details for so long and so methodically that the question took Mr. Moustache off guard. His answer took some time.

"I…I do sir. I know exactly who you're talking about."

"We all know them. It sounds awful, I know, but they're all defects in the human code. We like to think of ourselves as these complex, biological, amazing creatures. We are, to a certain extent, but we're also just an elaborate layout of ones and zeroes. We're still made of molecules just like everything else. I say this not to diminish the human race, I say this to diminish the severity of what I've been implying. That the Errors have to go."

The Russian, intensely intrigued now, interrupted.

"Wouldn't that eliminate a lot of people, sir? You mentioned things like laziness and cheating…addiction. I think it's safe to say that *most* humans have experienced some form of that in their lifetime."

"Ahhh but that's the brilliant piece." David replied, brushing off the interruption and excited about the discourse. "We thought that too. How on earth does one condemn an entire race to the subjugation of a trait or two? Isn't that nearly as bad as discrimination by race or religion? Over the past several years a challenging part of determining the solution has been mathematically discovering what combination of these traits equates to the type of people that we've been discussing. The premise of eugenics started out with good intentions, but it was easily perverted throughout history. This is similar, but *far* more calculated.

"Many think that all humans are created equal. That's simply not true for many reasons, but we've now set out to prove it. For countless years we've been testing hypothesis after hypothesis of exactly which composite of genes gets us the most significant mapping of the Errors. As you alluded to, someone could have genes that indicate they may be prone to cheating – hell, maybe they're actively cheating – but that doesn't mean they're a worthless human being. Not at all.

We found that there's a very specific mixture of genes that creates the targets we're looking for. It's actually several groups of combinations, but I won't delve into the math of it all because it even makes MY head spin. I trust it though. Modern test cases of people who fall under one of the Error listings have been observed in real life and they're exactly who you might've been envisioning during this conversation. These are the people *not* created equal; they're dragging down the race as a whole for a multitude of reasons I've explained."

"Ok, that makes sense, but then how does this affect the other side of the equation? How does the population concern relate to this?"

Excitement rested in David's voice. "What percentage of the human population do you think we classified

as an Error? Which percentage is part of the specific al-
gorithms we came up with?"

The Russian thought for a second, doing some mental
math. "Half a percent." He stated confidently.

"Ok so around 37 to 38 million people?" The number
sounded staggering even through the phone. The Russian
immediately began to alter his answer.

"Ahh that sounds high. Maybe something like a tenth
of a percent?"

"7.5 million people?" David asked almost mockingly.

"Lower?" the Russian said beseechingly.

"Let me frame the question this way. It may sound
humorous, but take your time to think about it. What percentage of *people you've met or know* would fall under
this umbrella?"

Again the man with the Moustache took time to ponder. "8 percent." There was even *less* confidence in his
voice.

"You're getting closer."

"Higher?" There was shock in the question. "That's
already…" A moment of mental math. "That's 600 million people!"

"10.37%." David stated, almost proud of it. The Russian gasped.

"No…"

"777.75 million people and some change. That's how
large the problem has grown. Obviously, as with any sta-
tistic, there's room for error. Probably a plus or minus
two percent given how much time we've spent narrowing
down the results."

"Jesus. That's…that's…"

"Substantial? I know it is. So, to answer your previous question, this relates to the population problem because it effectively *solves* it. Taking emotions out of it and looking at the way, way, *way* bigger picture, this trims the fat. It helps us to be more prudent and ensure that the humans on earth are the ones that move the species forward.

"I mentioned earlier that the rate of the world's population growth *is* slowing, but that it is, in fact, still growing. This doesn't outright reverse that but it does give us more time and it does solve the issue permanently."

There was a deep, foreboding silence. Ominous in nature, but begging for a question to be asked.

"So how do they die?" The Russian quietly asked.

David shot back. "What do you mean?"

"I'm guessing it's biological or viral given the sheer scale. I can't imagine anything else being as effective unless it's World War III you're starting."

"I'm no savage!" David retorted. "Though I do realize now that I've left out an important detail and I can understand your confusion. There is more of this story to tell." He waited for the Russian to urge him onward, but it didn't come. "Anyway, when the number became that high I quickly realized this had to be a humane endeavor. If I'm being honest, it was a guiding principle as we went through the research. Obviously, you want these people gone as fast as possible, but outright killing nearly 800 million people has insane consequences on the psyche of the world, its economy, its stability, the environment…I mean, there are just so many factors that go into something like that.

"You are right then, about the 'cure', so to speak, being biological. But how do you solve the issue without killing them?" An answer did not come. "You *prevent* them. From having children. We decided the most humane, effective, and least observable way to accomplish this was a silent, airborne contagion, specifically engineered for the gene sets we discussed, that neuters the host. Permanently. It's barely traceable and there's really no history of anything else like this. Doctors don't know what to think of it and a cure will likely never be developed, if the strain is ever even identified. It will live within the human race for a very long time, radically altering our future landscape into an incredibly positive and exciting one. No one's lives are in danger; they're just not allowed to create a life."

A quiet humming resonated through the phone. The biblical scale of David's grand plan was laid bare and the Russian was speechless. This lasted for a prolonged moment and David let it. Finally a reply.

"Part of me wants to hate it." The Russian started. "Part of me doesn't want to admit that I contain the evil in which any aspect of this becomes okay." His speech was calculated, methodical. "When I take my emotions out of it though, I keep coming around to the same conclusion."

"And that is?"

"It's brilliant. Absolutely brilliant. The whole thing really. From gathering resources, having to sacrifice American citizens in The Will, the connection of two very substantial world issues, to the non-violent ending of it all…you, sir…if you don't mind me saying this…you're going to shape the history of the world – of mankind – without anyone ever knowing!"

David could be heard chuckling over the excitement. "Thank you, thank you. I'd like to take credit, but it's really a blend of a lot of money, time, and effort from a lot of very smart minds pointed at a concrete solution. And I should correct you." He spoke slightly louder. "It's not *going* to change the world. It already is."

"It…it's...what, sir?"

"The Wolfpaw Initiative has already begun to change the world, my friend. Since August of last year."

CHAPTER XVII

GAME CHANGER
MONDAY | OCT 8TH | 2018

Dynadin stopped the tape. The room was silent. There was a stench, stale and annoying, hanging around them. It was the smell of utter confusion and hopelessness.

"Is that all of it?" Dahl asked, seated with his eyes at the floor. The question sounded exhausted.

"There's a bit more." Dynadin answered. "But it's mostly just gloating." He waited. "Do you want me to play it?"

Dahl waved him off.

None of them knew where to begin. There was a lot to process now that David's motives had finally been revealed. In an incredibly happenstance manner, the answers that Dahl had been searching decades for had laid themselves bare.

They were ugly.

And far grander than he had ever imagined.

Rachel stood and went over to where their food from the market rested, grabbed a piece of bread and began munching while pacing the room.

"How do we know this is true?" She finally asked. "The whole junk email thing was elaborate – how are we so sure that this isn't the same thing?"

Neither Dynadin nor Dahl had an immediate answer.

"I feel like…" Rachel stuffed more bread in her mouth, thinking aloud. "If something *this* big had happened over a year ago now…wouldn't we have heard about it?" Once more, no answers came, but the men's attention was firmly on her now. "The numbers they were talking about in that call were massive. How could a virus or some biological attack like that sneak under the surface?"

"Keep in mind it's not killing anyone though." Dahl reasoned. "It's making people infertile. That's a much less alarming condition. People who aren't trying to have kids right now likely wouldn't even know."

"We're talking nearly 800 million people here, Dahl! Even with that explanation this would have to be visible."

Dynadin began typing furiously on the laptop, navigating several webpages seemingly all at once. The group turned their attention toward him and waited for his reply. He read some lines from each page and after a few minutes turned back around.

"It may be designed to be a delayed effect, but infertility rates are on the rise worldwide. There's several articles here confirming that the percentages have nearly tripled in the last year and are continuing upward."

"So why is that not front page news?" Rachel was shocked.

"It sounds like it's about to be. In the first few months the spike was thrown away as a weird anomaly. Every trend in history has them eventually. In recent months researchers are beginning to fear the worst seeing as how the spike is just getting higher and higher. The World Health Organization is now involved and there are talks of a virus or something of the sort." He fell silent as he came to terms with a sobering thought. "They have no idea…"

"Where is the spike occurring?"

"Where?" Dynadin wasn't tracking with her question.

"Like what country or countries?"

"From what I can tell, it's all of them. Western and Eastern Europe, North and South America, Asia…Australia it seems. Even some reports of increases in Africa too."

"Fuck." Dahl cursed.

"Oh my God…" Rachel sighed, placing her hand on her forehead. The bread she'd been chewing suddenly felt heavy and overly moist with saliva. She sensed that it wanted to choke her. *Maybe it just should.*

"Rates aren't anywhere near what David mentioned on the call, at least not yet. Hence why I think it may be a delayed reaction in some people. Given the complexity of the virus, it'll likely take about half a generation to fully kick in. Let me check real quick…"

He tore a sheet of paper from a notebook and began expeditiously jotting notes down. Rachel glanced at the writing and it was clear he was doing some extensive mathematics; Dynadin never ceased to amaze her.

"Wow. I may have been way off." Dynadin looked from his work back to the computer screen then back at his work. Dahl motioned to Rachel for the bread and she tossed it to him, still watching Dynadin intently. He was scrolling through various online articles now and writing numbers without looking. Then back to his sheet once more. "Yeah it's not going to take half a generation."

"What do you mean?" Dahl inquired, mouth half full of bread.

"I was way off. At the current rate of increase, and assuming that there's a significant portion of people that don't actually *know* they're infertile yet, David's 10.37% is going to happen sometime in 2020, if not sooner."

"Holy fucking shit." Rachel knew the cursing wasn't helping but sometimes it just felt good. She glanced over at Dahl and could tell the bread was now taking a similar effect on him. His face grimaced, his chews were heavy and muscular, and he reached, placing the bread on the corner of the table. Dynadin looked a tad wounded, as if he were responsible for the horrendous news.

Silence and a creeping stale stench overtook the group once more.

In 2020 the world will be a radically different place. Rachel began to think, but then reasoned with herself. *The effects of this won't be felt for decades. 2020 will just be the start.* She began grasping for understanding.

"Why in the hell would David tell this to the Russian? He was an asset, sure, but it felt almost staged." Dahl considered this a moment before Dynadin reasoned.

"Keep in mind that he killed the Russian barely over a day later. He knew he'd be a loose end. Maybe just telling him the plan made him a liability and that's why he was killed?"

"If I had a secret that big, that *historical*, I'd want to tell someone too. That's a big weight to bear and if the man was sentenced to die then why the hell not?" Dahl questioned. "It's not like he's going to tell anyone anyway – it's unbelievable."

"Not to mention, David's likely a sociopath. Part of him is proud of this 'accomplishment'. It probably makes him feel like a god." Rachel surmised, rethinking her question.

Each of them thought to themselves, accepting the truth. David had taken a risk telling the Russian, but given the man's ultimate fate, he had eventually tied up yet another loose end. What purpose would he have lying to someone who'd be dead within a handful of hours?

"Fine. That makes sense." Rachel conceded. "For the sake of making a plan, let's assume this is all true." She shook her head, feeling as if she might burst into tears. "It's certainly looking that way. So what if the virus or whatever it *actually* is – what if it's inaccurate?"

"Meaning?" Dahl questioned.

"Meaning…what if it's targeting the wrong people? What if the margin of error is humongous? What if the unintentional effect is 45% instead of 10.37%?"

None of them had answers to those questions and Rachel knew it. She'd felt it while listening to the tape but now that they were in the weeds of this discussion she believed it.

They were defeated.

They were a team of three – battered, bruised, and beaten.

There was no coming back from this. The Wolfpaw Initiative had been released and was a widespread epidemic that would shape the world. What would they be able to do?

Why are we even still trying? It's over.

"The way I see it…" Dynadin started, "I imagine that it is a precisely designed disease. Meaning…I think that David likely spent the time, money, insane discretion, and resources to get it right. Otherwise it would have been released a decade ago, wreaking whatever havoc they could have slapped together quickly.

"Obviously, I could be wrong, but that's my gut feeling. If the science is there identifying specific genes as they relate to those traits, there's no reason to think that it won't target those individuals specifically. As with all things like this, there will likely be a margin of error making some people infertile who shouldn't have been and vice versa."

He paused, looking at his counterparts. Heads were hung, stubbornly listening to his sound reasoning. A part of him felt guilty for the logic, but now was not the time to hold back thoughts.

"This *will* alter the world as we know it, but not to the degree that I think David is hoping for. If my quick math is correct, I think that the population will continue to increase, but at a much slower rate. If a large scale, natural pandemic were to occur, we'd likely see years of steep decline. I can't speak much to the "weeding" out process that he speaks of – I'm frankly still a little shocked that certain traits like that are determined by genes. If it goes the way it was intended, I'm not entirely sure what that world will look like."

He could tell they were overwhelmed by his continued reasoning so he stopped talking.

"Dahl, you've been awfully quiet here." Rachel said, defeated. "What do you think?"

"What I think scares the absolute shit out of me." Dahl's head still hung and the response was muted because of it.

"What do you mean?" Rachel followed up.

"David has been my life. My life has been upended in so many ways by that man that it's almost too much to bare at times. He took my job, he took my career, he took my wife, and he took BOTH of my sons! The man has ruined me. He has outsmarted me more times than I'm willing to admit and I've rarely bested him." There was a rich, purposeful anger in his voice now, akin to a growl. "I hate the fuck out of him. There is no longer any justice I could serve him that would feel appropriate."

So why try?

"So imagine how scared I am that I agree with this man. This man who has taken so much from me. The man I loathe. And I'm sitting here listening to this bastard talk on a tape about how he plans to change the world, half nodding as he does it."

Now the silence had turned awkward. There was no comfort to be had between the trio, clearly all in different places of acceptance or denial surrounding their defeat. Dahl hated the silence and filled it with his thoughts.

"Is it wrong? Is what David is doing wrong? Of course it is. But it's wrong in the way that you know it will solve problems. You know it will be *effective.* He's thinking bigger than any of us ever imagined he was. We assumed he was at a 5,000 foot altitude and he's up in space. This is about the human race. Improving it. Saving it from itself. When I remove my emotions and think about it strategically and with the next millennium in mind, I can't find fault in David's methods."

"Dahl, that's…"

"I know, Rachel. Ok? I know it's fucking crazy, but I encourage you to do the same. David is a terrible human being. That much we all agree on. He'll have to answer for his sins someday. What he's doing here though? It's bigger than all of us. It's bigger than N.E.T.S., it's bigger than The Will, it's bigger than revenge, and it's bigger than his power. Both of you know that."

He pointed at each of them, almost accusatorily. Rachel replied with a wounded look. It was deep with pain from their losses, sadness for Dahl's misplaced belief in David, and a hint of shame in knowing that what he said was the truth.

"I can't believe you're saying this." Her head was shaking, more in disproval than acceptance. "He's infecting millions upon millions of people!"

"Exactly, Rachel! Infecting them with a harmless disease. No one is going to die from this!" Their voices were gradually raising.

"Maybe not, but he's removing the choice from countless couples around the world who want to have children. Is that fair?" Her eyes were trained right at him now. "Is it fair that a couple who wants a family of their own will never be able to because of a madman who *took* that from them?"

"Of course not, but – "

"There are no 'buts', Dahl!" She shouted. "This is almost as close to murder as it gets and –"

"Oh come on, Rachel."

"AND it's perhaps even worse. Removing a basic human right from an individual's existence?"

"Rachel!" Dahl took command back. "Now think about this. Your emotions and drive for human rights are interfering here. You don't think those alarms aren't going off in my head? You think I'm just conveniently forgetting that people's lives are being fucked with? All without their knowledge or say-so?" They were glaring at each other, but Dahl continued. "I'm not. I already said I was scared of my opinion toward this so I don't need your patronization or politics. I'm simply recognizing that we are undone. This group failed. We set out to stop

David and he's already achieved his end goal over 12 months ago." A deep breath, calming and slightly wavering, came from him. "All I'm saying is that, if we were going to fail to stop something catastrophic, it could have been much, much worse."

She paced a few steps in different directions and then slumped against the wall, sliding down until she reached the floor. A cursory glance at her hand caught sight of a ragged nail and she began to chew at it, distracting her from their conversation.

"I guess I don't disagree with that." She finally stated, somberly.

"I hate it too. In a way, we're really lucky I suppose." Dahl continued to reason to the utterly defeated group. "David's master plan, as grandiose and life-altering as it may be, is based in science. We don't have the resources to come up with a cure and if it were a deadly plague we'd definitely be shit out of luck. Instead it's something the World Health Organization can tackle with likely far more success than we could ever hope to achieve." Rachel waved for him to stop talking. She'd had enough of his self-serving justification.

"Dynadin." Her eyes looked to him, pleading. "What do you think?"

His eyes met hers, searching for a long time before he spoke. It wasn't that he didn't know how he felt; he was aware of Rachel's sentiments and wanted to phrase his answer sympathetically.

"I think…" He began, slowly. "That we're in a precarious spot. This is a moral dilemma far more perplexing than what a single human has ever been expected to comprehend. There are so many facets of what David has done that it makes it increasingly complex.

"You have the fact that a portion of the human population will be sterile. That will have ramifications for centuries, easily. Then you consider that this is *not* a naturally occurring biological event. It's an attack by a single individual or organization that thinks they can play God. Above all else is the moral conundrum that comes with the genocidal selection of who is affected and who is not.

"I don't take issue with the first part. The human population has been slowly spiraling out of control and it was only a matter of time before our footprint on this planet became unsustainable. I also don't take much issue with who's going to be sterile." Rachel tried to hide her shock. "Let me explain. Previous genocides or mass exterminations events were based on attributes that are completely irrelevant when determining a person's character. Things like eye or hair color, religion, gender…This is the first time that something is actually targeting the root of human failures. It is not some overzealous opinion that these things are bad; it is essentially based in fact. Can we not agree that compulsive lying or sustained languor are undesirable traits of our race?"

"That doesn't mean people should die because of them!" Rachel retorted immediately.

"But they aren't Rachel. Their option to procreate is being removed, but otherwise their lives will go on as normal. Many will likely have long, happy lives. And eventually, many decades from now, probably long after we're gone, we'll have an entire generation of purposeful, high-performing, and eager human beings that want to learn and create and solve and propel society forward. Does that sound so bad?"

His eyes were warmly begging Rachel to take a step back and think about the much, much bigger picture.

"I understand where you both are coming from. I really do." There was hesitation in her voice as if she knew where she wanted to go, but didn't quite know how to get there. "But who are we to decide that those people shouldn't have access to that right? Who are we to make such a drastic alteration to the future of the human race, even if it is an inherently positive one?"

"Let me ask you this: are *we* the ones making that decision?" Dynadin reasoned.

"We are if we choose to do nothing about it." She snapped back.

"What do you expect us to do?"

The question stung, especially coming from Dynadin. Rachel looked wounded and tight lipped. She had no answer. Dynadin's inquiry had rang true for each of them. *What* could *they do at this point?* He too thought of potential avenues, but the recent loss and overall defeat of their Dubai mission was clouding his opinion.

We are too small.

What's done is done.

It's out of our hands.

We can't make a difference.

"So you just think that David should walk free?" Rachel asked, almost meek as a mouse. Dynadin blinked at her and smiled briefly. He knew they wouldn't disagree on this point.

"Ah. I didn't finish. Where I *do* take issue with this outcome is the perpetrator. Somehow, someway in David's life he's absorbed this warped vision that it's his duty to cleanse the earth. If any one person truly believes that about themselves then they should be prepared to die as well. That level of ego and narcissism is just as much a cancer as all the things David sought to destroy." He paused, the opinion ringing true across the room. "Not to mention, the several transgressions he's had against each of us personally, some within the last 48 hours, must be answered for." Rachel was smiling, but Dahl seemed distant.

"What can we even do at this point?" He countered. "I want to kill David as much as anyone, but I keep getting the constant gut feeling that we are now, officially, shit out of luck. A team of three is no match for either N.E.T.S. or the Dead Scorpions."

What was interesting about his statement was that it was not a somber realization for the group; each of them already knew this. In that moment however, it became apparent that what they *wanted* to do and were *capable* of doing were vastly different possibilities. They needed a changing of the tide.

"I think we need to get organized in our thinking first, specifically as a group." Dynadin began to reason, taking the lead.

"What do you mean?"

"I mean that there are a lot of differing opinions in the room, but they're not really getting us anywhere. We feel stuck talking about all this when in all honesty, there's nothing we can do to change some specific outcomes. So…" He took a deep breath. "Can we all agree that there's nothing we can do about the Wolfpaw Initiative itself?"

Dahl nodded but Rachel was hesitant.

"Can't we warn the WHO or at least let them know what they're up against? It could speed up their research."

Dynadin thought for a second and agreed.

"I think that's fine as long as it comes from a place of complete anonymity. Would you mind drafting that communication? I think we should lean away from declaring it a terrorist attack so as not to incite a mass global panic."

Rachel nodded in agreement.

"But otherwise you agree there's nothing we can do?"

Reluctantly she responded. "Yes. I agree."

"Ok. So next order of business. Do we all agree that David should die?"

"Yes." Dahl and Rachel answered quickly in unison.

"And do we all agree that we're too outmanned to do it ourselves?"

"Agreed." Dahl answered.

"Yes." Rachel followed.

"What's our most powerful asset right now?" Dynadin asked, confusing the group in the process.

"Dynadin," Dahl started. "It's been a long day. What're you getting at? What are you trying to get us to see here?"

"I'm honestly not quite sure, but I think I'm starting to gather an idea."

"I know what it is." The response from Rachel was confident. Dahl and Dynadin both granted her their attention. "It's the recording."

The declaration certainly was no revelation, but each of them began piecing it together now. It was as if the air in the room grew lighter; the mood had instantly changed.

"But we can't release the recording to the public…" Dynadin reasoned, concentrating hard. "Either they won't believe a man whose identity is unknown *or* it'll cause mass hysteria. The world is a fragile enough place right now, it can't take much more bad news."

"The public will find out about it eventually. We need the additional manpower now." Dahl added.

"So we send it to N.E.T.S." Rachel's comment dropped on the group like a hammer. Exciting, but filled with potential danger. "N.E.T.S. is full of good people who don't know a thing about the *real* David. I say it's about fucking time that they do."

Dynadin was nodding in agreement. "I like this." His encouragement invigorated Rachel.

"We have a point blank recording of his admittance of guilt. I say we make a video of our own, explain who we really are, the situation at hand, and then play the damn tape. Let them decide for themselves."

"What if they believe the recording to be doctored?" Dahl challenged.

"It's unmistakably Harper on that call, but ultimately, that's their choice to make. Best case scenario is that we can convince enough people so that David no longer feels safe at N.E.T.S. If we're going to kill him we need to separate him from his resources."

"He'll still have the Aqarab Mayta."

"True." Rachel acknowledged. She hadn't quite thought through the finalities of the approach. "But who's to say we can't handle them? Especially if we've got a few people at N.E.T.S. helping us?"

"It's a good point, Dahl." Dynadin added. "If we can create enough chaos with the release of the recording, we'll have our best chance at getting David. He'll be unfocused, flustered, angry, potentially even scared. Likely on the run for at least some period of time."

"What have we got to lose?" Rachel asked.

"Each other, for starters." Dahl immediately bounced back, head hung with conflicting sentiments. It grew quiet as the sobering reality of the two they'd just lost became vivid once more.

Eventually, Rachel spoke. "At some point, this has got to end. We could walk away right now and each live happy lives, but I for one am not ready for it to be over while that bastard is alive and well. We thought we didn't have a chance before. We were right. This recording gives us that opportunity though. It's the leverage we need to turn the tide. It's the *game changer*. It's maybe the first time that we've gotten utterly lucky throughout this entire ordeal and I don't think we should waste it." Dahl wasn't responding.

"If we find it doesn't work…if we find that everyone at N.E.T.S. is fiercely loyal to him or we can't get the drop on him, we'll pull out. Be done. My gut tells me the chances of either of those happening are very low."

"I'm in." Dynadin confirmed, hoping to prod Dahl along.

I've lost so much…I'm so tired. What is David's death worth to me? Dahl thought hard on these while his companions gave him time. The same question kept echoing in his thoughts: *What have you got to lose?* A response finally came.

"I'm in, on one condition. We lay low for the next few days, maybe even a week. We can create our introduction video and explain ourselves, but you need time to heal, Rachel." He looked at her with serious, fatherly eyes. "If this works, shit could hit the fan real fast and we'll need you at a hundred percent when that time comes. You're in rough shape right now."

Rachel couldn't even argue with that, nodding her head in agreement.

"Are we safe here?" Dynadin wondered.

"I figure so. If anything, David will think we fled the country to lick our wounds as fast as possible. We separated ourselves from them by quite a distance and there aren't exactly a ton of cameras out here to aid in spotting us." Dahl reasoned to the group. "*But*, it would probably be wise to keep watches at night and use some sort of disguise when going outside. You never know who may be watching."

"So what now?" There was a hint of excitement in her voice.

"Dynadin, you work on cleaning up that recording. We need it clear as day if we want to convince people. Rachel, get working on a script for the video. People at N.E.T.S. will trust you most. Work off of that. Explain why you did what you did, what we believe David is guilty of, what evidence we have, and then get to the recording quickly. We don't want people to stop watching before they even get there. I'll see what I can do to dig up some resources. With any luck we may gain some allies with N.E.T.S. but I know some people who owe me favors too. Now's as good as time as any to cash them in."

Dahl stopped talking, confident that he'd covered everything. It would keep them busy and focused for the next several hours at least.

Like a coach, he sent them on their way. "Well what are you all waiting for? Let's get to work!"

CHAPTER XVIII

HUMP DAY

WEDNESDAY | OCT 10ᵀᴴ | 2018

Karen woke early Wednesday morning, somewhat dreading going into N.E.T.S. It was "Hump Day" and in classic Tuesday fashion, she'd drank too much wine by herself last night. *Hell, that's not just Tuesday nights…*

The hangover was small and dull, its only remnant being an irritating headache at the back of her skull (fairly typical given that she had been drinking Merlot). In her attempt to get a little more work done remotely and watch a cooking competition show, she'd polished off nearly a whole bottle of wine before heading to bed, or rather stumbling to bed, at around 10 P.M.

The wine had been delicious and expensive. As an International Analyst at N.E.T.S., Karen made great money. She supposed it was to make up for all the other things in life she missed out on, not to mention that they couldn't exactly just "let her go". She knew too much – or just enough. Either way, the pay was N.E.T.S.'s way of saying, "Let's just not go down *that* road. Here's a shit ton of money."

Given the problems facing the world currently, she couldn't help but laugh internally at her mild-mannered, self-induced head pain and lazy case of the Wednesday's. *If only people knew what was really going on.* The sentiment had no longer left her mind before she refuted it, knowing that the public was barely keeping itself together already. Between a Presidential assassination and The Will, they were still trying to cope and move on. It had been over a year, sure, but the going was still rough. Karen often recognized how lucky she was – despite how intense her position could be – that she had fantastic job security. Not many others could have said that in recent months.

Moving on from her thoughts, she rolled over and checked the clock next to her bed. It was still dark out and sure enough, "4:32 A.M." shone bright and neon blue back at her. Getting out of bed was always hard, but today was especially difficult. Keeping with the sloth-like theme of the morning thus far, Karen reluctantly rolled out of bed and sauntered in the dark to her bathroom. With a flip of a switch, the lights turned on and momentarily blinded her, making her head pulse in the process.

After she relieved herself, she washed her hands, cupped the faucet's coldest water, and splashed it onto her face. It was a fantastic trick that she'd adopted, if you could even call it a trick, and did wonders to wake her up every morning. For good measure she did it one more time, though to lesser effect. She crossed her expansive apartment in the dark to a room on the opposite end of her unit. The light came on and she was simultaneously faced with both her worst enemy and best friend: the spin bike.

Putting on the clip-in shoes only took a minute and she reached into her workout dresser, putting on a sports bra and leggings. While a part of her (the part that adored sleep) hated this aspect of the morning routine, she knew that she rarely regretted starting her day out this way. In

just a few minutes, after that initial tug of morning muscles, she'd be feeling active and slowly sweating out the
toxins from the Italian countryside wine from the night
before. Before hopping on she took a long swig from her
water bottle and reached down to touch her toes.

The bike seat felt normal under her now, though she
painfully remembered how uncomfortable the thin thing
had been at the beginning. *Good God, my ass hurt those
days*. She began peddling, waking up the electronics of
the sizable screen attached to the bike. The initial pedals
were light and loose with no resistance as she scrolled
through various options of locales she could bike
through. Yesterday had been Cairo, Egypt; both dull and
highly interesting at the same time. *Today I'll
chooooose…let's do Queenstown, New Zealand!* It was
often one of her favorite stretches and the virtual ride was
breathtaking. Just what she needed to conquer this
Wednesday.

The screen displayed a pre-recorded ride through a
gorgeous day on the south island of the country and the
bike's resistance kicked in, low at first, while Karen continued to pedal. The 45-minute course she had chosen
would take her out of the city of Queesntown and into the
nearby hills and mountains, featuring several substantial
climbs along the way. Back in the real world, it was still
considerably dark outside her well-lit, New York City
apartment. The alone time was maybe what she enjoyed
the most about this exercise, even as her muscles tensed
and resisted the very easy climb of her first hill. It was
just her, the bike, and a location. Quiet together, in a
room, doing something good for herself.

After ten minutes, the first steep climb kicked in and
she started to feel good. Sweat gathered on her brow,

chest, and arms as she pressed one leg after the other down against the bike's considerable resistance. Sweating felt freeing and she took another swig from her cold water bottle, replacing some of the fluids she was losing.

The hills and flat stretches oscillated over the next ten minutes before Karen pressed the internet app on the right side of the screen. Typically she'd catch up on the news of the day as she closed out the latter half of the course. Sleekly, she snapped the virtual course display to the left side of her monitor and the internet app, now displaying a news home page, to the right. This New Zealand course had about five minutes of flats (or very small hills) coming up, so she began scrolling through the news using dials on the inside of her handlebar. She clicked the first story and skimmed through part of it. It seemed to be an op-ed piece.

> *Despite weak gains last week, the first in over 3 months, the Dow Jones and NASDAQ fell again this week amid speculation of another attack.*
>
> *Decreased consumer confidence around the world has led to uneven markets ever since the former President's assassination and The Will over one year ago. Analysts fear the trend may continue for several more months as no resolution in the form of justice has been made following the attacks.*
>
> *Markets around the world continue to suffer and the eerie quiet from the Dead Scorpions has ignited debate that they're planning their next strike soon.*

There wasn't much more to the story that she didn't already know so she backed out of it and scrolled through some more articles. Eventually she clicked on another titled, "President Greyson to Meet Concerning The Will Family Stipend Act"

President Greyson will meet with Congress today concerning the The Will Family Stipend Act. The act aims to provide additional financial care for families affected by The Will.

After the attacks last July, the death and damage toll was so significant that most insurance companies are unable to meet coverage obligations after increased demand. Many life insurance policies are still pending for the deceased and medical insurance companies have seen significant claim submissions regarding sustained injuries.

The $10 billion act will split funds proportionately among victims and their families to help cover medical, funeral, bereavement, and child care costs, especially for the many orphans of that day.

President Greyson called it an "unprecedented act of government assistance for these unprecedented times" in his announcement last month.

With no opposition to the act so far, another unprecedented event in Washington, it is expected to be approved by unanimous vote this afternoon.

Well that's some good news Karen thought as the peddling became harder. She glanced over to the New Zealand screen and could see she was at the base of a large hill so she dug in and focused. For some reason the extra effort, or maybe it was the type of news she was reading, pushed her mind back to a time shortly after The Will. It had been such a dark, catastrophic day – one of America's bleakest. And that was saying something because it had come after a string of very dark days. Even the security that came with working at N.E.T.S. had offered her no reassurance. Karen had felt scared and vulnerable. The whole country had been played a fool and now it was decimated.

Sweat began to drip from both temples and she lifted her butt off the seat to get leverage on the harder hill, pedaling with purpose. It was truly amazing that the country was still standing at all, it occurred to her. She didn't know exactly what was *supposed* to happen after twenty-seven-thousand-plus people die, but she was sure that things could probably be worse than they were currently. People had grieved, but moved on. They'd gone back to work. Back to school. There were graduations, somber ones, but graduations all the same. After a brief hiatus, sports (both collegiate and professional), television, and movies – all had returned to offer up distractions. People were still going out, meeting friends, meeting dates, *dating*, making relationships. *Life moved on* Karen realized as she reached the crest of the hill. It didn't come so much as a revelation to her as it did a powerful reminder of the tenacity of people, especially Americans.

The pedals underneath her feet loosened considerably, spinning with almost no resistance. That had been

the largest hill on the course and now the remaining
seven or so minutes were a cool down. Karen revisited
the news stories from the day, seeing if there were anymore that piqued her interest.

Some celebrity dating gossip.

More info on the The Will Family Stipend Act.

Something about the results of some singing competition from last night.

The next article she opened and began to read, not entirely sure why it seemed so interesting to her. There was
a gut feeling compelling her to do so.

> *The World Health Organization (WHO) and
> the Center for Disease Control (CDC) are work-
> ing together to investigate a new, disturbing
> trend worldwide.*
>
> *In the last year, scientists have found that
> the infertility rate of many countries has in-
> creased, for males and females alike.*
>
> *"While spikes in infertility are documented
> throughout history," Dr. Tony Velor explained
> to us, "The concerning trend here is that it's
> happening worldwide. More often than not we
> can link these spikes back to a particular disease
> or environmental factor in the region. At this
> time, we can find no similar or definitive causa-
> tion."*
>
> *Dr. Velor is one of the chief experts on birth
> rates and infertility worldwide and he's working
> with the CDC and WHO to tackle this problem
> head on. He reiterated to us that there is nothing
> to worry about.*

The final minutes of her spin course were ticking away as Karen finished reading. The article was more than a bit disconcerting, but she agreed with the doctor. For stuff like this, she imagined that a year's worth of data was almost worthless at distinguishing any type of concrete trajectory. *Still very odd though…*

Dripping sweat, but feeling fresh and well woken, she hopped off the bike, took some final swigs of her water, and removed her workout clothes, throwing them in a hamper of ever-growing dirty sports bras and leggings. *I should probably do laundry sometime this week.*

Casually, she strode across her apartment floor to the bathroom where she turned on the shower, brushed her teeth, and then got in. The steam felt wonderful on her post-workout body and part of her wished she could indulge in a twenty minute shower, but she knew she needed to be into work relatively early this morning and it was already 5:45. If anything, she was behind schedule now.

The faucet turned off with a slight squeak and within 5 minutes she was dressed and back in front of her bathroom mirror putting on a hint of makeup here and there. Luckily she didn't need much to deem herself worthy of "looking good", something she was thankful for every morning come crunch time. Knowing that she had gained back some lost time, she calmed down, moving more slowly around the apartment as she packed her bag, grabbed her oats n` fruit medley from the fridge, and shut all the lights off.

On her phone she opened up an app, courtesy of N.E.T.S., that locked down her entire apartment, making it virtually impenetrable. Bolts on her bulletproof windows all locked and hid themselves in the window mantle, her gas, electric, and internet lines all stopped functioning, and her door dead-bolted itself no fewer than seventeen times, among a variety of other measures. By this time however, she was already down the hall and waiting for the elevator to take her to the garage.

It eventually arrived after an annoying wait. Either way she'd still be into work on time because she was technically ahead of schedule right now. *By about 3 minutes.* The elevator sped away from her floor, down to the first parking level where she immediately clicked the remote start button on her car. The newest Tesla Model S's lights shone back at her, greeting her in the dreary darkness of the garage. She pulled out of her parking space and into New York City traffic, needing only 10 minutes to reach work on time.

As she emerged into the day, she noticed for the first time that it was a rather grey and cold one. She probably hadn't noticed from her apartment because it had still been dark, but now that it was "daytime" (despite the absence of any sunlight) she could see that it was an overcast, dreary day. The windshield wipers on her Tesla acknowledged it too as they swished away the first rain droplets of the morning.

Luckily, Karen didn't have to drive in this mess. The Tesla did it for her. She knew that it was "technically" illegal – self-driving cars hadn't been fully approved yet, despite being almost always better at the task than their human counterparts. Regardless, she enjoyed sitting back, listening to some music, or drinking in the city's life as the Tesla drove the route to N.E.T.S. HQ. It had been surreal at first, letting your car drive you around, but she'd eventually gotten used to it and even *trusted* it after a history of being accident free. There were even a few instances where the car had avoided several accidents she wasn't so sure she'd have been able to, including a near miss with a pedestrian biker.

As early as it was, there was still an absurd amount of traffic. The rain wasn't helping, but it did make for some striking visuals and interesting people watching. Lights of the city blurred through small droplets on her window. All sorts of blues and whites and reds and greens, bleeding together as the water would collect and stream down the glass. It felt cold just to look at it, but Karen didn't mind. The people outside were determined, trying to get to where they needed to go. And they were going to, rain be damned, even if it meant only having a newspaper over their heads as an umbrella. It didn't seem to be raining hard, just a consistent sprinkle that wouldn't let up. Karen could barely hear the pitter-patter of it even with her music off.

Slowly, the Tesla navigated toward the office. Traffic was annoyingly stop-and-go on the main street that she used to travel, but according to the navigation system, the side roads were clearer and would get her there about one minute faster. Karen approved the change in route and the car turned right and then quickly left onto a much less busy street. No matter who or what was driving, traffic was a disaster.

On the last block, Karen grabbed the steering wheel and took over manually so that she could navigate the parking lot. She'd never let the Tesla "park" itself – it was one function she still didn't quite trust it to accomplish without incident. Despite the weather and early hour, there were a surprising number of vehicles within the cordoned-off N.E.T.S section of the parking garage. Part of Karen found this annoying as she preferred to be one of the first people in the office while she simultaneously wondered if something was going on. Clearly it wasn't something *too* big or she would have been notified about it. *But you haven't checked your email since yesterday...*

After backing her car in, she grabbed her bag and was on the elevator, one only usable by N.E.T.S. operatives. The doors "pinged" open and instantly she could feel the buzz of the floor.

Different than usual.

On her way to her desk, she glanced over at David Harper's office to see he wasn't there. *Where the fuck is he?* The sentiment stemmed more from annoyance than concern as he'd been gone for several days now. Before reaching her desk, Karen stopped by one of the few kitchens on the floor and grabbed some coffee. Much to her delight, it was delicious and because of that, it saved her trips to other coffee shops. No one else was there which she found odd. Usually people were slow to get going in the morning and could be found taking their time to get coffee or put away their food or even just stand there, looking at their phones.

This morning however, everyone seemed glued to their computers, eyes unblinking, some typing furiously. A few others were watching their peer's computers over their shoulders, sometimes in silence, sometimes pointing out something on the screen. *Ok, Karen. Time to haul ass to your desk. Something's up.*

Within moments, her coffee was down and her computer screen was on with her email up. She had about 50 unanswered emails and got started on them, figuring that all the commotion was hidden somewhere in there. As she sorted some of the more menial ones, she glanced over the frosted glass walls of her cubicle. People's faces were pale, worried, some even looked sad while a few others expressed clear anger. *Jesus, what is going on?*

Faster now she sped through yesterday's after-hours unanswered emails basically ignoring anything that didn't seem highly important within the first half sentence. Eventually she came across an email, sent at 12:01 A.M. that had no content other than two attachments. The email's subject header was simply, "The Truth" and it appeared the attachments were a lengthy video (given the file size) and some type of audio file. Was this it? Karen clicked the video, anticipation rising in her stomach like an oncoming sneeze. She could feel herself clenching and tightening, for really no good reason, and as soon as it started, she knew this was it.

It was Rachel. And she was in what looked like a desert bunker or hideout of sorts. She was speaking, but Karen was barely listening, instead trying to gather clues as to where she was. There wasn't much to go on, but Rachel looked tired – worn and beaten. She sat awkwardly and Karen wondered if she'd been injured by the events that had taken place in Dubai. Technically she wasn't even supposed to know about that, but she figured she wouldn't be a very good International Analyst for the most secret organization in the world if she didn't. From what she could tell, Rachel and her gang of…terrorists? (Karen didn't know what to call them)…had gotten in an altercation with a N.E.T.S. team over there. The news story to the public had been spun as something completely different, but putting the pieces together had been fairly simple.

Are you still in Dubai, Rachel?

Several minutes had gone by and Karen realized she wasn't actually *listening* to the video, just trying to piece together fragments of what was going on. She started it over from the beginning, intent on listening to what Rachel was saying, especially since the email had been titled, "The Truth". From the start of the video, there was a heft of emotion within Rachel's voice.

"My name is Rachel Monroe and many of you already know me. I used to be a non-field operative for the New York City branch of N.E.T.S. About a year ago, only days before The Will, I began to unravel a mystery that would lead me away from N.E.T.S. and toward the truth.

It is true that I have defected from N.E.T.S., but not from the United States. And not from human kind for that matter. What I've uncovered, with the help of my small team, will shake the foundations of history. While they wish to remain anonymous, I wanted to become a voice. One of reason, explanation, and whistleblowing on one of the most powerful men in the world.

Many months ago, we discovered that David Harper is not only the head of N.E.T.S., but also the provost of the Aqarab Mayta – better known as the Dead Scorpions. This is the group that was behind the murder of Elena Cooper, the assassination of the President, the highway bombing, and The Will which resulted in the death of Bryson Cooper. David Harper is responsible for all of it and we have the proof.

For years, David has been asserting his power in tenacious ways, running two lives simultaneously in order to get where he is today. Why he wanted this much power remained a mystery to my team and I, until recently when we, by a stroke of luck, uncovered his monstrous endgame. David wanted the control of two organizations not for the power or the glory, but instead for the resources to solve a problem. A problem with which he believes this planet is plagued."

Karen paused the video just as Rachel was shifting uncomfortably in her seat. It was likely she was suffering from an injury to her core, probably her ribs.

What on earth is going on? How can that be true?

Rachel had always been a sweet girl, bonding with nearly everyone in the office to some degree. She and Karen had maintained some semblance of a friendship, as much as you can in this line of work. A deep part of her wanted to trust Rachel. A deeper part of her already did. She'd been highly curious of Rachel's departure over a year ago. It had been sudden and complete; they'd never heard another thing from her. Eventually they were briefed that she'd "turned" and was now a betrayer and an enemy of the country. Karen hadn't known how to accept that and didn't see that possibility within Rachel. She pondered whether or not she'd been kidnapped and held against her will, if she maybe had just disappeared after the traumatic events of the attack, or maybe, just maybe, if she was on the right side of this war.

From what Rachel was revealing in this video, it seemed to be the latter.

With a deep breath, Karen pressed play on the video and it continued.

"David Harper has already created and deployed a solution to his problem and there's nothing we can do to stop it. We are all too late. Within the past year, an airborne biological weapon has spread that targets individuals who possess certain genetic traits. It has made almost all of them infertile. Nearly 800 million people who have 'unacceptable' character traits as adjudged by David will be rendered incapable of reproducing. People who contain characteristics such as inherent laziness, entitlement, excessive lying and cheating – all are being targeted by this weapon. The science behind it is ahead of its time – though it checks out – and my team and I have confirmed that it has already started to take effect. Infertility rates around the globe are on the rise and will continue to do so. Sadly, it is even likely that some of you have been affected, statistically speaking, and given the possibility for error."

Jesus. Karen's mind flashed back to the article she'd read this morning. *This is insane.* It was so much bigger than she had imagined. Rachel kept talking after a moment of silence.

"Some of you may not believe me. Some of you may even hate me and still wish to see me dead. So be it. Attached to this email you'll find an audio file of David, on record, that corroborates all of this information. For some of you, I know that won't be enough. Right now, I'm speaking to those of you who might suspect that I'm right, who have felt something off for the past year or more. This is the truth. There is no longer any mystery around the Dead Scorpions or around David. Some of you may think that they've won. They killed our President, two of our best agents, carried out The Will, and now enacted a radical change to our planet that's one degree removed from genocide. I won't argue with you. I feel beaten too. But I also want to see justice served, as trivial as that may be.

This is where I need your help.

My team and I have just suffered a great loss and are nearly out of resources. We have no idea where David is or what his next move might be. In order to end this, we need his location. I've sent this to the entirety of N.E.T.S. in the hopes that *someone* will help us. On my life, I swear this is the truth and in time a deeper explanation will come. Right now, we need David's location because we're going to kill that son of a bitch."

Karen saw her reflection in the computer monitor as the screen went black and the video ended. Her heart rate was up and she could feel herself perspiring. Rising from her cubicle, she glanced around the office. Many faces reflected hers: complete shock, a smattering of disbelief, and a hint of nausea. Some of the men looked angry. Surely *David* wasn't the head of a terrorist organization! They looked up to him.

This is going to be a shit show. Karen sat back down, breathing hard. A choice was on the table and the stakes had never been higher. The part of her that trusted Rachel had grown, *was growing*. There had been no signs of lying or manipulation in her voice or body language, just utter sincerity. She'd been speaking from the heart and mind, not reading from any notes and it hadn't seemed like she was being held by force.

Quickly, she listened to the entirety of the additional audio file. Karen's daily interaction with David was often minimal, but it was definitely him speaking. The evidence was damning.

Her mind was made up.

Karen would help Rachel, discreetly. Even in an office full of agents, Rachel was the only one she felt she could trust right now.

CHAPTER XIX

AN EARLY RETIREMENT

FRIDAY | OCT 12ᵀᴴ | 2018

David stirred from his sleep with an aching gut. It was the kind that felt like a hollow pit: something deep within the center of his stomach, wanting to escape, but also wanting to cause as much discomfort to the host as possible.

He tossed in his king-size bed and reshuffled some pillows around in an effort to get comfortable. The clock by his bedside read 2:57 A.M.

Naturally, his mind began to wander and he hoped it would find its way back to sleep. Much had happened in the last week and he was struggling to see what his next move could or should be. Dubai had been a bit of a clusterfuck, albeit a semi-successful one. Leaving part of Dahl's group alive hadn't been the plan, but they were good. *Still…2 out of 5 ain't bad.* Part of him had hoped it would be a big enough blow to them that they'd just give the hell up.

Even in sleep, David felt consistently exhausted. He wanted this over. Hell, it was pretty much already over. He couldn't stand the fact that they remained alive and if he knew anything about them it was that they wouldn't stop until they were all in the ground. Commendable. Impressive even, especially considering what they pulled off in Dubai. But very, very stupid.

Ah…maybe not so much anymore.

The thing in his stomach lurched, making him flinch in bed. It held for a couple of seconds then gave way, releasing the tension in his muscles. As hard as he tried, David couldn't forget about the new development in his life: the video that Rachel had created and thus distributed to all of N.E.T.S. It was the reason he'd been "away" from work ever since Dubai and likely the reason why his stomach was keeping him up now.

Her video, and the audio file, exposed everything. Every single aspect of what she was saying was the truth and she'd told it to everyone. Luckily, believability and loyalty were mostly on David's side – her claims sounded preposterous and too monumental to believe and David knew that he still had good standing with his agents and operatives. There were ways the audio could have been faked too. In the last year, the view of Rachel had shifted to one of a deserter in some of the milder groups and to outright terrorist in others. As anxious as he was, he continued to try and convince himself that he still had the upper hand.

How in the fuck did they figure everything out? The question had been on his mind for days. As he tried to think of the answer and it continued to elude him, the tendrils of sleep clasped him, but swiftly let go. *Fuck if I even care that they found out.* By his bed was a bottle of whiskey. *Do you really mean that?* He took a massive pull, burning his throat and nostrils. It felt great as it slid down his esophagus and began to go to war with the thing in his stomach. *I'll be fine. I always am.* Another swig, smaller this time. *Will you?*

"FUCK!" Even his thoughts were annoying him; unable to decide whether this was the end or if he'd live a long life. A third pull from the bottle made him cough, some of the liquid dribbling down his chin and landing on his sheets. Clumsily, he screwed the cap on and put the liquor back.

This time the tendrils of sleep – and alcohol – took him fully.

Rachel was disgruntled and disappointed. Not to mention, getting a bit of cabin fever. It had been over a month since she released the video to N.E.T.S. and there hadn't been a single reply as of yet.

You overestimated them, Rachel.

Angrily, she reminded herself that people needed more time to cope, to understand, and to make a decision. Immediately after this argument she'd be playing devil's advocate and reminding herself that these were N.E.T.S. agents and not "normal" people and the frustration would arise anew.

Dahl and Dynadin remained calm and reminded her that it could take time –they had a good thing going here.

"It's clear they're not actively looking for us in this town and we have more than enough food and water to lay low for a while." Dahl had explained. "We'll sit it out." He'd added.

Fuck 'sitting it out'.

Rachel contemplated making another video, another plea. Surely there was someone within N.E.T.S. who had seen that David had changed? Someone who researched

Rachel's claims to see that things with him didn't add up? Every time she mentioned another video though, Dynadin and Dahl were vehemently against it.

"Maybe at some point down the road, but we've barely given them any time. We can't risk ourselves or our location by making an ongoing series of videos. Sooner or later, someone would put the pieces together." Dynadin had reasoned with her.

She'd understood that, but that didn't stop her from being frustrated and pissed off about it.

As a way to pass the time and get a workout, she and Dynadin had been sparring regularly. Her aggravation would come through in their fights, often to her demise. Their incident in Dubai was still fresh and both her ribs and shoulder continued to ache. Each injury was healing well, but sparring certainly didn't help matters especially when she'd yelled at Dynadin to stop "going easy on her". So he hadn't. And now she was sore most of the time.

Boredom was very much becoming a thing as Dahl limited their time outdoors and in the small town. Other than the walk to the market for food, there wasn't much else they were allowed to do. To make matters worse, they weren't able to get a ping on David's location whatsoever. He'd basically been a ghost since they'd last seen him and it was evident that they were going to need N.E.T.S. help to get anywhere.

————————  ————————

FRIDAY | OCT 12TH | 2018

David Harper *had* dreamt of something that night, contrary to the void that usually engulfed his slumber. There had been a beach, one of fine, smooth sand, which extended for miles in either direction. On this beach, he sat in a low chair, feet buried up to his ankles in the cooling sand.

It was nearly the end of the day and the sun had just reached the horizon, leaving behind streaks of pink and orange and yellow in exchange for deep blues and grey. There was a beer in his hand, half finished with a lime wedge at the bottom. Only a handful of people were on the beach, most of them several hundred feet away and any noise they could have been making was masked by the rolling ocean waves.

David sat and watched as the waves would gently roll up the glossy sand hill and rush back down, pulling out just a tad farther each time. Every fifth wave or so would bring a violent crash onto the shore as the waves from two separate oscillations fought against one another.

It was peaceful.

David was at peace. Something he hadn't felt in a very long time. He hadn't the slightest clue of where he was or what he was doing there. He just sat. And he sat with the weight of a great accomplishment satisfyingly heavy on his chest. There was ease and finality about the dream and its deeper meaning couldn't have been clearer:

Time to retire.

The sentiment sat with David all morning as he did random things around his apartment. A flood of questions came as the possibility continued to entertain itself.

What would retirement look like for me?

How would I get away, completely, from both organizations?

Is my work done?

Will I always be looking over my shoulder?

What will I do? Will I be bored?

Will I be happy?

There were nascent answers swimming around in his head, but part of him couldn't believe he was even contemplating this. *But you have to now. The audio condemns you.*

One question continued to surge out at him because of his uncertainty around it: *Is my work done?*

He knew his work would truly never be done, but he had achieved the majority of what he'd set out to do. The Wolfpaw Initiative would alter the landscape of mankind for centuries and even though the path there had been extreme, the solution was proving to be effective.

Though he still worried…

What will America become without me? Fresh waves of guilt washed over him; he knew that he'd thrown this country into turmoil over the past year and a half. Its people were weak, crippled by fear and overwhelming loss and uncertainty. News of the sterility epidemic would eventually break and it would make matters worse. He knew many would see it as "the end".

If he stayed, his next move would have been to turn his back on the Aqarab Mayta and slowly dismantle the organization. They were no longer needed and the lot of them were quite evil anyway. It would have been a consistent string of wins in the eyes of the American people.

First, he would have revealed the Dead Scorpions outright, making the associates underneath him visible to the public eye. They'd have a target on their faces.

Next, he'd take out the Top 3 in rapid succession, co-ordinating with the sitting President and making their takedowns highly public.

After that it would be several months of easy clean up, taking targets out around the globe. After about a year, the Dead Scorpions would be completely elimi-nated, dismantled, or scared into hiding.

David knew the way the American people reacted to-ward news like that. They'd be overjoyed and impressed with their government. Each death of the Aqarab Mayta would bring them more hope and more resolve to carry on. After a year, when the terrorist group was wiped off the face of the earth, they'd feel unstoppable, and it would carry over into their personal lives.

America would be America again.

But that was before the video. Rachel, smart as she was, had ruined that opportunity for him and hurt the American people in the process. David had no N.E.T.S. to go back to. If people didn't outright attack him, there'd be a constant wave of doubt and mistrust from here on out.

His work *was* done then.

No, there's still one more thing you can do.

He finished it and within a few hours he was on an in-ternational flight.

THURSDAY | JAN 17TH | 2019

Two more months had passed and Rachel still had nothing to show for her message. The New Year had come and gone. *Pissed* was one word she wanted to use, but *defeated* was the one that continuously cropped up instead.

Dahl and Dynadin were doing their parts to keep her spirits up, but it wasn't helping. They didn't seem to be phased by the lack of any type of response.

Rachel knew that was bullshit. They were nervous and she could tell it in the small quirks they thought they were hiding. Each of them, in some form, believed they had made the wrong choice in releasing the video.

It bothered Rachel night and day and she was trying to get creative with next steps. The sitting around was slowly driving her mad, especially given the tight quarters of their current "home". At one point she'd proposed the idea of releasing a more extensive video to the *public*, one with more background and context. It would out N.E.T.S. for sure, but it would also out David to the world and maybe even crowdsource a sighting of him.

Dahl had immediately shot it down, and for good reason. "It would cause an absolute panic." He had started. "You'd effectively be telling everyone who watched it that their next generation of kin may have already been genocidally eliminated." Rachel had dropped it and she even agreed with Dahl's point. It had been a desperate idea with no objective other than to make her feel like she was doing something.

Needing to get some fresh air, Rachel volunteered for market duty that day. It was a characteristically hot, but pretty morning and there was a stiff breeze that kept her cool. Vigilance was still necessary when leaving their structure, but she'd become more and more relaxed as the weeks since Dubai had passed. Today, she went to parts of the market that she hadn't been to before and walked around some of the surrounding neighborhoods. For the most part, they were in a very poor region, but the people here seemed happy. Challenged in life, sure, but overall happy and content. She wondered how many of them were affected by the Wolfpaw Initiative. Part of her didn't think any of them would be, but statistically she knew that wasn't possible.

The other side of the market was much more focused on products than actual food. It was mostly all primitive things – people working with what they had – but it was charming. Necklaces and bracelets made of rocks, small gems, stone, and wire were being offered next to a stand of colored fabrics, many of which hung from a rod on the side of the shop as scarves and hijabs. One bracelet caught Rachel's eye. It was simple, with a single grey stone in the middle of two, painted, blue ones. The rest was wire. But the center grey stone was perfectly smooth in its ovular shape. Every other stone at that stand was rugged or cornered or featured some kind of blemish. All except for this one.

Rachel was unsure of why this particular, modest bracelet was drawing her in so, and she felt an urge to buy it. Essentials were the only thing she was technically supposed to be purchasing, but she knew the bracelet wouldn't break the bank and she guessed that the shop owner could use any help available.

The sun beat down on her as she turned to leave. She fastened the clasp of the bracelet around her wrist and it fit perfectly. The transaction had been pleasant and swift and Rachel had been right: the bracelet was cheap and would lose them maybe a ration of bread, if that. *It's not like we're exactly pressed for money anyway.*

As she stared at the object on her wrist and navigated through the market to where the food was, she became slightly annoyed with the two blue stones next to the grey one. They looked fake and ugly with their blue paint; jealous of the perfect natural stone between them. The only physical discomfort was stemming from them too as the jagged, cube like stones (were they even *stone*?) would press against Rachel's skin.

She took pause and knelt down on the side of the market, looking for a stone. Finding what she was look-ing for, she carefully removed the bracelet and laid it on a flat rock, separating the stones from one another. Using the other rock, she tapped a blue pebble until it cracked, broke, and fell off the wire. Then she repeated the same technique with the other blue stone, equally as successful. *There's the bracelet I want.* Feeling proud, she clasped the single, grey, smooth stone bracelet around her wrist and was on her way, perfectly comfortable with her alter-ation of the artist's work.

After another twenty minutes, she was ready to head back "home" as she'd gathered all the food they needed for now. They bought only day-to-day necessities in case they'd need to leave at any moment. Rachel realized that the bracelet and the market had calmed her; she hadn't thought about the video, or David, or Wolfpaw for at least the last half hour and that had to be some kind of record. It put her in better spirits as she walked into their main room with Dahl and Dynadin more or less right where she had left them.

Dahl turned to her, noticed her slightly odd disposi-tion, and then the bracelet on her wrist. Rachel didn't even care and acted as if it wasn't even there. Dahl followed suit and remained silent, switching his gaze back to his computer. Each of them continued their work as Rachel sorted what she had gotten, placed it down on their makeshift pantry on the ground, and returned to her computer as well.

The stone turned smoothly in her fingers and she liked touching it. It distracted her and that was exactly what she needed right now. Her computer screen lit up, awake from its slumber, and she navigated to her email. Over the past weeks, it was common for it to be bone dry. Today however, there was a message in it. Encrypted and coupled with an attachment by the looks of it. With a header titled *The help you seek...* and Rachel couldn't click on it fast enough.

"Hi Rachel,

I'm hoping this message finds you well. Apologies for what will likely be a lengthy email.

The video you created and the audio you attached with it caused quite a stir here at headquarters. People are unsure of your motives. Confused by the information you provided. Most can't help you. They're too afraid right now. That's okay. They'll come around.

I can help you though. I see the writing on the wall and David's been 'gone' for months now. He never came back to the office after your Du-

*bai encounter and everyone here is growing sus-
picious. He likely knows about the communication. I think he's hiding.*

*I'm outside of my bounds here, but I'm not sure
those exist anymore. I believed your video so
I'm hoping it was the truth. For the past few
months I've been digging (tirelessly I might add)
to try and locate David. He's a hard man to find.
Skilled. He can become a ghost. But it looks like
he made a mistake. Or rather, one of his bodyguards did.*

*They're using facial recognition jammers that
are highly effective, but they don't work with re-
flections. Someone in Shanghai took a picture in
front of an apartment complex and it caught the
image of a N.E.T.S. operative's face against a
glass panel, likely as he was passing through a
door. I ran a check and the agent in our system
is listed as 'CLASSIFIED' so I hacked our own
system and found that he's not even supposed to
be in Shanghai, but on bedrest. I'm guessing
that's just some sort of cover tactic for David's
private guards.*

*I've sent you the image I collected and the ad-
dress/image of the apartment complex. My guess
is that David went all out and bought out the top
floor or several floors. I wish I had more to go
on. An actual image of David would have been
nice. I hope this helps. I hope you end this. And I
hope I was right in helping you.*

-Karen

Rachel stopped reading, nearly breathless by now. The email and information, limited as they might be, had been an exhilarating read, if only for the fact that someone at N.E.T.S. *was* actually helping her. She began typing out a reply, but then thought better of it. She wanted so badly for this to be true and for Karen's outreach to be *genuine*. Rachel thought back on their previous, but few, interactions. Karen was a bit of a badass around N.E.T.S. and one of the top International Analysts they had. She kept to herself mostly, but Rachel couldn't think of a single negative thing anyone had ever said about her. Their exchanges had been pleasant. Reluctantly, Rachel knew she needed to involve Dynadin and Dahl, but was worried about how they'd view the situation.

"Guys, I may have something." It came out cautiously, almost mouse-like.

"What is it?" Dahl and Dynadin looked up from their work.

"Someone reaching out to help us." Still cautious, but with optimism. Dahl's eyebrows raised.

"Ok so who is it?"

"A N.E.T.S. analyst, Karen. I know her. She's good people." There was no skepticism in her voice.

"Karen? Karen…" Dahl was trying to recall.

"International Analyst."

"Ah yes! I concur. Throughout my screenings in recent years, she's one of the cleanest operatives N.E.T.S. has. Very talented too."

"Agreed." Rachel was happy to see that Dahl already thought highly of her. "Let me read you the email."

As she read, she tried to keep her excitement to a minimum even though she was already halfway to Shanghai in her mind. The room was quiet and both men let her read through the whole thing before speaking.

"Interesting…" Dynadin pondered, looking up to the ceiling.

"You already know what my first thought is going to be don't you?" Dahl asked Rachel.

"That it's a trap."

"Precisely."

"It's a necessary risk, Dahl. If he's gone dark, this could be our only chance."

"Oh I don't disagree with you, Rachel. And I'm glad it came from Karen. It seems a lot less like a trap because of her."

"But…?"

"But…*what* is David doing? Is he setting his own trap for us? Is he conducting business as usual? Making his next big moves? Or is he just done?"

"What do you mean 'done'?"

"I'm not exactly sure. Retired? Or walking away. Whatever you call it in this sort of life."

Rachel scrunched her nose, still not quite understanding or agreeing.

"Think about it." Dahl started. "I'm assuming his master plan was the Wolfpaw Initiative. I don't see how it gets much bigger than that. It's been live for over a year. He doesn't need the Aqarab Mayta anymore. He doesn't even really need N.E.T.S. anymore and after your video, I doubt he could go back there and continue to be effective. What does he have left to do?"

"Other than kill us." Dynadin chimed in.

"True, but I don't think that's such a high priority that he'd risk exposure or his life over it. Probably why he didn't pursue us himself in Dubai. We're unfortunate loose ends, sure, but if he disappears completely then he doesn't give a shit about us."

Per usual, Dahl had thought out the logic and had a damn good point. Rachel hadn't thought of it that way, but it could definitely be true. Her video had potentially forced him into retirement.

"Ok. So what do we do then?" She asked.

"Just to be clear…if we go after David, it's for the sole purpose of killing him. There's no other reason for us to risk it and we need to be clear about that right now."

Dynadin and Rachel both nodded, determination on their faces.

"Then I say we go get the bastard." Dahl said with a smile on his face.

It was the middle of the night in Shanghai and David was having a hard time sleeping. Again. Despite the luxury apartment that took up the entire top floor, an elegant bed with equally opulent sheets and pillows, and the soft buzz of white noise, being "retired" didn't come with full nights of sleep.

In these quiet moments, alone in the dark with his thoughts, he knew it was something more. It was guilt. It was uncertainty. It was caution. And it was a bit of paranoia. He'd changed the world and almost no one knew about it. *How could that be true?* These were all things he'd anticipated feeling at one point or another, but it didn't make processing them any easier.

Think of all the worthless people you've prevented from being born. From draining human resources. Think about how much humanity will benefit from a worldwide society of people that put forth effort.

But was the cost too great?

The thought often lingered with him, especially when he considered the 27,000-plus innocent American lives that had to be sacrificed to get to this point. He'd had a plan to put America back together, but now he'd not be able to carry it out. The *incompleteness* of it all left him…annoyed.

It'll just take time. He reminded himself. A long yawn came and passed. David knew he needed to get some shut eye; the last thing he wanted was to get sick.

Outside his floor-to-ceiling windows, the neon lights of the city billboards danced high in the sky. They were peaceful and his eyes felt heavy.

And as David finally fell asleep that night, an ultimate, incomplete task evaded his memory:

Getting rid of Dahl and his team.

CHAPTER XX

COFFEE NIGHTS

"We're almost finished."

Dahl's hand shook Rachel awake, though "awake" would indicate she'd been sleeping. Really, her eyes had just been closed and the nap she desperately chased eluded her.

Dynadin and Dahl had been driving around Shanghai picking up the gear they needed for surveillance and a full scale infiltration should it come to that. Their supplies were somewhat limited after the Dubai mission and it was too risky to head back to Costa Rica first, not to mention completely out of the way. Dahl had been confident that he had enough contacts within Shanghai that they'd be fine.

Rachel looked around the SUV they'd acquired and could see he hadn't been bluffing. Several weapons were piled in the back as well as scopes, tactical clothing, extra magazines, sat phones, miniature cameras, a couple of computers, and a few other odds and ends.

"How'd you get all of this? We hardly had anything with us after Dubai." She was genuinely curious, turning to look at Dahl from the passenger seat.

"I've amassed some contacts over the years. Many of them owe me favors." Dahl smiled from the back. Rachel rolled her eyes playfully.

"Where are we staying?"

Dynadin answered her question this time. "We secured an apartment in a high rise. The altitude of our level is comparable to David's new residence, but we're a ways off. We'll be able to do some surveillance from a distance with minimal chance of our cover being blown. It'll be mostly through scopes and binoculars though; we're about a mile away."

"That's good. What's the surveillance plan?"

"We're leaving that up to you." Dahl replied. Rachel didn't let them see her surprise.

"Ok. So let's monitor the apartment for 12 hours a day with 3 separate 4-hour-shifts. One in the morning, one in afternoon, one in the evening into night.

"At least once a day, two of us should do a drive-by, just to see what we're working with on apartment security. It's a rich building so they're likely to have some decent protection. I think any more than once a day may raise suspicion.

"Also, one of us should go to other points around the city to get a different angle on the building. That way we can at least do our best at analyzing the inside structure and also gain some extra surveillance time. Were we able to get the building blueprints?" All of it had come out nearly breathless. Dahl's eyebrows were raised.

"Rachel, my dear, I think you're officially a field agent now, if you weren't before." Dynadin smiled and she laughed.

"Fuck you, Dahl!"

"That sounds like a perfect plan to me." Dynadin chimed in.

"Agreed." Dahl provided through a smile. Rachel was excited.

"Good. Let's get started tonight then."

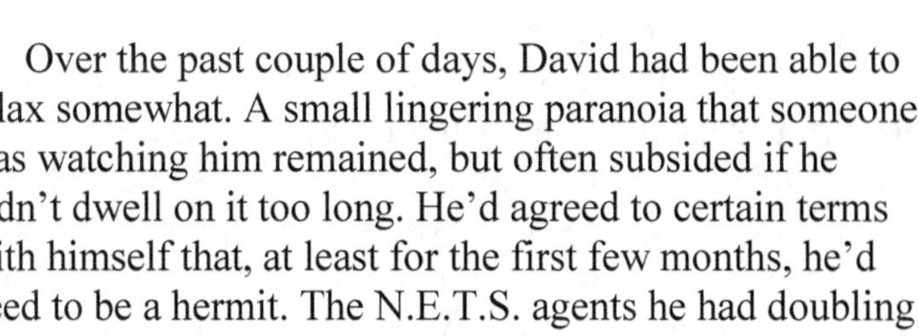

Over the past couple of days, David had been able to relax somewhat. A small lingering paranoia that someone was watching him remained, but often subsided if he didn't dwell on it too long. He'd agreed to certain terms with himself that, at least for the first few months, he'd need to be a hermit. The N.E.T.S. agents he had doubling as his personal bodyguards were loyal, in addition to being compensated handsomely. They'd do all of his minor errands for him and be with him for at least the first year of this "retirement".

In the meantime, it meant that David couldn't go anywhere. He even eliminated the time he spent out on his balcony, despite how much he enjoyed sitting there with his morning coffee. For the first time in a long time, his life felt somewhat…normal. He'd been reading a lot of books – ones that he'd always wanted to get through but hadn't had the time – and even watching some TV shows he'd always heard rave reviews about. There was a place for him to train and spar on a section of his floor, he'd been cooking his own meals, and spent some time each day keeping up with current affairs. It was all rather mundane, in the best of ways.

It feels nice to finally let my guard down.

"What've we got so far?" Dahl asked as he came into the room.

"Frustratingly, not much. It's been days and we haven't really gotten any clear answers. We haven't even seen David yet."

"Have we gotten a lay of the land? Do we know what the apartment looks like inside?"

"Yes and no. The windows are heavily tinted and the blueprints we got are likely not up-to-date. The top floor was originally a handful of larger units but some tech millionaire bought it several years back and made it into a single penthouse suite. He moved out, it was on the market for a little while, and now David owns it."

"So what part of that qualifies as 'yes' to my question?"

"We've gotten a general idea of what the exterior of the floor is like. We know where certain rooms stop and end and what they may be used for. We also know that parts of the original blueprint had to remain the same. The elevator atrium for example."

"What about the drive-by's and research we've been doing from other vantage points?"

"Dynadin's driving past the place as we speak, but even those give us minimal details about the place. David's men aren't waiting outside the complex, we're guessing they're on his floor or in the elevator lobby. And similarly from the other vantage points, we're seeing heavily tinted windows."

"Have we used any type of infrared or night vision?"

"Yes. And we've been able to assess some people within the building, but that's also difficult. There's a certain protective screen on the windows that filters out specific radiation."

"Damn." Dahl fell silent, thinking.

"I say we give it five more days." Rachel began to offer her opinion. "If, after that time, we don't see anything of note, we make a decision. I can email Karen to continue scanning for David in the meantime; maybe this place is a diversion or just an honest mistake."

"So what do we do in five days if nothing has changed?"

"If it were up to me? We'd still go in. Unfortunately we'd be blind, but I'm confident David's here in Shanghai, in that building."

"What makes you so sure?" Dahl asked.

"Because if this were a trap, they'd already have sprung it by now." There was utter confidence in the statement. Dahl thought for a moment realizing that it was the truth. The only thing they were losing by taking this slow was time and, for once, that was something they had plenty of.

A scratch of static broke their concentration. Dynadin's voice came over the radio.

"Paw Collector this is November Zulu. You copy?"

"Copy Zulu. Collector here. What's up? How'd this pass go?"

"Fine. Nothing new to report. I think I may have a tail though."

Shit. How?

"You say a tail? How?"

"Not sure. Picked him up shortly after leaving the complex. So far he's matched me turn for turn."

"Lose him." Rachel ordered. "Let us know once you do or if you need assistance."

"Copy." Dynadin ended the call.

"Paw Collector?" Dahl asked, amused. He seemed unshaken from the potential of Dynadin's tail.

"The Wolfpaw Initiative. I thought it had a ring to it." Rachel reasoned with a smirk.

"You kids and your codenames." Dahl chuckled.

"Now you really do sound like a *Grandpap*!"

Dynadin kept his cool and wove through traffic with a combination of haste and safety. If this was a tail, he wanted to shake it, but he wanted to stay within the rules of the road to avoid raising suspicion. The pursuing car was some sort of Mercedes-Benz, a newer one by the looks of it. It was keeping its distance, but Dynadin had now made no fewer than six turns and it had matched him on every one. The likelihood of it being coincidence was low.

He turned left onto a less busy street and decelerated. Sure enough, the Benz took the same turn, though it didn't seem to be slowing down. Dynadin's heart began to race, anticipating that this would be a fight soon. Still intending to drive normally, he pulled the SUV into a parallel spot on the side of the street. The Mercedes was almost on his butt now. Dynadin leaned back in his seat, putting his body behind the car door pillar, for whatever protection that was worth. He grabbed his gun from the center console and took aim through his door.

The Benz closed in, not slowing down for his vehicle at all.

Dynadin tensed, hoping this would not be a firefight.

As it passed, he got a look at the driver.

And the passenger.

And he started to laugh.

Inside the Mercedes, behind the dark glass, was an elderly Chinese couple. They were bickering away while looking at a smartphone, likely having a hard time following its driving directions.

A wave of relief washed over him and the adrenaline that had been gripping him faded away. He got on the radio, prepared to take some shit.

"Remember that tail I told you about?"

"Uh-huh…" There was anticipation in Rachel's voice.

"It was a false alarm." He hoped that would be the end of it.

"False alarm? What do you mean?"

"It was not a tail. It was…an…elderly couple. They were lost trying to navigate the city."

"Oh really?" He could hear the borderline laughter in her voice. "So you dealt with them did you?"

"To be fair, they followed me for a good ten minutes."

"Sure they did."

Dynadin could feel his face flush with embarrassment.

"Why don't you come back here? Dahl and I want to discuss next steps."

"Copy that. On my way." He put the car in drive and pulled back out onto the street.

"Oh and Dynadin?" Rachel asked.

"Yeah?"

"Be on the lookout for any rogue geriatrics. We've gotten reports that they're armed and highly dangerous." She had started laughing through the radio before it cut.

"Har, har." Dynadin smiled knowing that Rachel was having way too much fun with this.

Days had passed and spirits were on the decline. Their technique had remained the same, but no new info had been gleaned. Dynadin had continued driving by the complex with no luck and his assessments of the apartment from other vantage points didn't reveal any additional info. Rachel, thinking she'd get lucky, had searched high and low on previous real estate websites to see if the original listing of the combined penthouse suite was ever posted. Of course it hadn't been so they were back to square one.

Dahl suggested that they hack into something with a camera located within the apartment to get the lay of the land which was quickly shot down by Dynadin. David would likely have top cybersecurity and know the second an intruder, even a skilled one, was being a peeping tom.

Rachel had suggested purchasing a drone and getting it much closer to the building. Preferably at night. Both men considered it – it wasn't an awful idea – but everyone felt it was too strong of a play and could give them away immediately.

As they approached the ultimatum date that Rachel had set, it was looking more and more like they'd be taking their chances by going in blind. In the back of their minds, they knew the 5-day deadline was nothing more than a arbitrarily chosen number and, if it came to it, they'd give it five more, ten more, or however many more days they needed until they felt confident.

They had no need to be in a rush but the lack of a timeline made each of them eager.

That night, Rachel was having a hard time sleeping – why exactly, she couldn't pinpoint – but she didn't feel tired at all. She got out of bed, left her room and walked over to Dynadin who was watching David's supposed apartment.

"Anything?"

"Not a thing." He sounded almost disappointed.

"Go get some sleep." He looked back at her, curious. "I can't sleep anyway and I'm strangely not that tired."

"You sure?"

"Yep. Go for it." He handed her the binoculars, got up from his seat, and went toward his own room. Rachel looked at the chair but wanted some fresh air. *It's going to be cold out there.* Some coffee sounded marvelous so she made some as quietly as she could in their mini kitchen. Their patio was small, but the view was fairly spectacular given how high up they were. Shanghai's air was cool this evening, with no breeze. *Thankfully.*

Taking a sip of the hot liquid filled Rachel with heat. She didn't need the caffeine, but more so just wanted something to taste; something to occupy the time. The binoculars were a heavy weight in her hand, a pair of the largest she'd ever seen. When she brought them up to her face she was reminded why: they were powerful as hell.

There was a HUD overlaid on the lens. It clocked distance, time, wind speed, altitude, and even the date. Rachel was familiar with it since she'd been using it the past couple days, but was still surprised by its heft. Whereas everything else in the technological world seemed to be shrinking exponentially, apparently they hadn't figured out the best way to minimize the colossal tool she now held. *Or maybe this was the best we had available.* It was

2019, she was sure there were more compact versions out there.

The city seemed quiet tonight outside of the normal bustle below. There was a certain peace to being high up on a comfortable night; it made Rachel enjoy her coffee even more. Oddly enough, she found contentment with what she was doing. *Spying.*

David's apartment was seemingly empty right now, but it didn't matter because they still couldn't see through any of the windows. With a sigh she predicted that it would be another night of absolutely zero activity.

Twenty minutes passed as she sipped her coffee and intermittently scanned the apartment.

The night moved forward.

Dynadin and Dahl remained sleeping.

Rachel looked down into the mug and saw that she was out. There was plenty more in the pot and she went inside for a refill. It poured out hot, a thin vapor of steam rising from its surface. *Ugh. I love coffee.* Brisk air reached her as she went back out onto the patio. She took as much of a sip as the hot coffee would allow and looked through the binoculars again. They'd been on an infrared setting before she'd gone inside.

Colors exploded on the balcony of the apartment. Green. Yellow. Orange.

They were in the shape of a person.

Rachel moved the binoculars away from her eyes and looked down, jaw dropped. Was there really someone there? Did they finally have something? Realizing that she was wasting the opportunity, they came back up to her face. The colors outlining a person were still there and she pressed a button near her index finger. It took a picture and sent it to their computer inside. With the press of a different button, the infrared disappeared and showed the nighttime and all its blue and black hues. Faintly she could make someone out on the balcony, just standing there, not at all dissimilar to her.

The face was obscured by shadows and all she could tell was that it was very likely male. She snapped another picture and remained on the figure, hoping he'd move more into the angles of moonlight on his balcony.

But he didn't.

Excited, Rachel switched the binoculars to night vision. The image was a bit blurry as her eyes adjusted and the filter settled in. Across the distance, the protruding platform came into greater focus as did the character's form.

The face, still small in her view, became clear.

She snapped a picture.

It was David. It was David standing out on his balcony.

Her gut did a somersault. Her body tensed.

He was looking away, off into the distance. Even from afar, she could tell he was thinking hard about something. Rachel snapped several more photos.

David turned his head. His eyes, tiny as they were, pierced through her. The mug of coffee fell from her hand, sailing stories down to the road below. They were looking right at each other.

A thought terrified Rachel:

Fuck.

He can see me.

CHAPTER XXI

THE UPPER HAND
SATURDAY | JAN 26TH | 2019

Being outside was actually wonderful. After being cooped up for this long, even with the windows open, it felt better to get real, fresh air. David took in a deep breath of night and exhaled. The air was a little crisp, but very comfortable, and he was surprised that there wasn't even a small breeze up this high. He approached the edge of the balcony and leaned against the outer railing, taking in the sights and sounds of the foreign city.

Part of him knew he shouldn't be out here. Everything was too recent, too fresh, for him to be taking unnecessary risks. But he was sick and tired of his paranoia. There had been no fine balance about it and he had spent the last few months trying to persuade himself that he was in the clear. *No one is there. Just enjoy a few minutes in the night.*

So he did. He looked around and was amazed by the gorgeous city, filled with beautiful, flowing neon lights and stunning architecture. From his balcony he could see, to varying degrees, some iconic buildings. The Shanghai Tower was elegant and seemed to flow like glass, towering over all the other buildings. The city's World Financial Center looked like a large bottle cap opener with its stunning hole at the top. And then there was the Oriental Pearl Tower and its spheres, less an actual building and more a structure, but dazzling and unique nonetheless, especially at night.

He admired the darkness and the buildings a little longer and went back inside, somewhat at peace with his thoughts and glad he'd gone outside. That rest of the night was the best sleep David had gotten in a very long time.

Oh what the fuck.
What do I do?
Somewhere in the back of her mind Rachel knew she was freaking out. She knew it was unreasonable. She knew there was no way David had actually *seen* her, especially at night. He'd shown no signs of acknowledgement or surprise that someone was staring at him through binoculars and after a few more minutes he'd gone back inside.

He just needed fresh air.
There's no way he could have seen me from that distance. Impossible.
Fear was slowly turning to excitement as she wound herself down from "nearly" being spotted. That had sure as shit been David and she didn't need any type of computer algorithm to tell her so. He was here, in that apartment, just like Karen had reported.

Quickly, Rachel got back inside and on Dynadin's laptop, the one connected to the binocular's camera feature. She tabbed through the various pictures she'd taken in infrared, normal, and nightvision filters. David was most vividly obvious in the nightvision pictures that she'd captured. Rachel needed to get them up. Now.

After a few gentle (followed by two significantly more demanding) knocks on doors and "You-need-to-get-up-and-see-this" instructions, they were all awake and approaching the computer.

"There's coffee in the pot if you need some, but let it wait until after this."

"What exactly are we looking at, Rachel? Did something happen?"

"You could say that." Rachel didn't even bother flipping through the pictures and instead went immediately to the most distinctive one of David. "I went bird watching tonight and saw a *rare* one." Dynadin laughed at that. Dahl remained silent, deeply analyzing the picture.

"It seems to be him."

"*Seems* to be? It's definitely him." Rachel shot back.

"Yeah." Dahl couldn't help but agree. There was a moment of awkward silence. It was as if the group had been chasing something that they weren't quite sure what to do with now that they'd caught it. Dynadin asked a question.

"What was he doing?"

"Honestly? I think he was just getting fresh air." Rachel replied and continued on. "He came outside, leaned against the balcony railing, looked around – I swear we made eye contact but there's no possible way – and then he just strolled back inside." Another silence. "He seemed content? I don't know. Maybe a little lonely too."

"You a psychiatrist now?" Dahl joked.

"No, just making observations. It seems important for what we might do next."

"And what exactly *are* we doing next?" Dahl asked, eyebrows raised.

"We're going to kill him. And he doesn't even see it coming."

A hush fell on the room. They all knew that was what they were here for, but the situation had just gotten a lot more real with the confirmation of David's presence. No one disagreed with her, but there was a sense of anticipation, particularly from Dahl.

"We know he's here, we should go in and do it. And we should do it soon. There's no use prolonging this." She argued.

"There's no use rushing it either." The retort came quickly.

"You're being awfully silent." She looked to Dynadin. He blinked slowly before contributing.

"We know what we're here for, but we don't need to lose our lives in the process. There's also another aspect we're not considering."

"Which is?"

"The N.E.T.S. agents, or rather, *former* N.E.T.S. agents protecting him."

Rachel hadn't thought of that, but she didn't particularly think it was a big deal.

"If they're N.E.T.S., they've seen the video. If they still choose to follow David, that's on them."

"So we kill them?"

"Is it any different than it was in Dubai?" The logic seemed harsh. "If they're threatening our lives, we'll be forced to take theirs."

"What if we can navigate around them completely?"

"I don't think that's possible, but I'm listening." Dahl continued to think through his plan and amended his statement.

"Ok maybe not *completely*. Close though." The wheels were turning. "There's a lot of avenues to take, obviously. I want to lure him out. It gives us a better chance to see what we're working with and it automatically puts him on the defensive."

"And how will we lure him out? He's barely spent any time on his own damn balcony."

"We threaten his legacy."

"What?"

"I think our mutual friend," Dahl pointed to himself then Dynadin. "Can help us with one more favor."

David had found that his emails were scarce lately. It seemed to be a side effect of being retired and disconnecting from his previous accounts. All that was left was his personal email and he both dreaded and looked forward to the day when he'd eventually receive junk mail (if it ever made it through his several firewalls).

So he was taken aback that morning when he had an anonymous email, the title bold and loud on his screen, that morning: **THE CURE**. From an unknown sender. He began to read the message, becoming more and more furious with each line.

Mr. Harper,

"*Línghún*" went into his search bar and he slammed the Enter key down with vigor. *Fucking bullshit*. It was a nightclub, a fancy one by the looks of it, located about halfway up Shanghai Tower. Apparently it was one of the "premiere" nightclub spots in the city.

Aggravated by the thought of discussing a proposition so delicate within the bowels of a bass-thumping, disgusting nightclub, David attempted to reply to the email. The gist of the message was an elongated way of saying, "Go fuck yourself", but the message would not send. Still mad, David felt a bit silly for even trying and instead spent the next couple hours studying the layout of the nightclub, anticipating where the meeting would take place, what the exits would be at hand for him and his guards, and any available details on the owner – if that was even who he'd be meeting with.

Through their communication channel he told the eight men he had with him that they were going out to-night. And it wasn't a social call.

Why he didn't immediately suspect Dahl and his re-maining helpers escaped him. In the months since the re-lease of the video and their interactions in Dubai, David had become rusty, yes, but also distracted. Time was an enemy of memory, particularly for an older man like Da-vid. The threat in this email had been so bold, and posed such a great risk, that he failed to suspect the one group that wanted to hurt him most.

And it would cost him.

The night was young in Shanghai and the vicinity around Línghún was bustling. A crowd of Chinese mil-lennials, some already drunk, were trying to get into the trendy nightclub.

David and his men bypassed the cabs and walkers up to the base of the Shanghai Tower. Their vehicles came to a halt, doors open, and they were on their way. There would be little ceremony to this and the less time David spent outside, the better. There were bouncers in the lobby funneling people to the correct elevator and ensuring that no one went wandering off. A rather large one, likely an ex-sumo wrestler, eyed David and his other men, pointed to them, an elevator, and spoke something into his earpiece. *At least we don't have to wait in this fucking line* David was thankful for that courtesy.

The elevator was glamorous but not flashy and all nine persons fit inside. There were no buttons to push and it rocketed upward. David's ears popped with the altitude change as he remembered just how damn tall this building was. With a soft "ping", the doors opened and a world of electronic music, tangy sweat, alcohol, and far too much perfume and cologne met their senses. There was a grimace on David's face and now he wanted to finish this even faster.

"Mr. Harper." An equally large bouncer guided them out of the elevator. "Right this way please."

David wasn't happy about the man knowing his name, but he figured that was probably all he knew.

Thankfully.

Hopefully.

The music, specifically the bass, grew stronger as they wove deeper into the club. To their left was an elaborate bar, stocked full of every liquor imaginable. It was kept immaculately clean – for being as busy as it was – and the bar countertop and shelves were made of translucent blue glass with deep black flecks of shiny granite.

On their right was a large dance floor with several seating areas and VIP couches scattered around its edges. Another less impressive bar could be seen across the way. Above everyone, suspended on their own glass-bottomed platform was the DJ. A few large HD monitors were placed above the crowd to show them the DJ's face and hands, with the camera angles shifting every few seconds. David had no idea who the DJ was, but he looked just like every other DJ he'd seen. Surprisingly, he quite enjoyed electronic music, but usually only when he was working out or training. It got his blood flowing and he could see why it had grown so popular.

The crowd seemed to be loving the current song and David had to admit it wasn't half bad. He was certain he hadn't heard it before but it had moments of genuine talent scattered throughout the cliché noises and bass drops. Línghún's sound system was incredible. David could *feel* that it was loud on the dancefloor, but the noise was filtered on the edges in such a way that you could still hear the music, but also each other.

As they continued around the edge, they approached a staircase that hugged the windows of the building. It felt like there were eyes on them and David nervously glanced around. He quickly realized that no one was paying them any special attention; they were all obsessed with the drink in their hands, the person in front of them, or the social media on their phone.

The staircase was wide and elegant and the views out the windows were magnificent. The city of Shanghai had one of the most gorgeous night skylines and from this height it was nothing short of breathtaking. Lights from the city fought their way through the club's tinted glass and painted a tapestry of blues and yellows.

David could see now there was a room above the dance floor, above the suspended DJ booth even, that was sidelined by two additional bouncers. They weren't sumo-wrestling size, but still burly and capable. As they approached the doors, the men opened them for David.

He paused, looked in, and entered, his men in tow behind him.

"Welcome! Welcome!" There was a morbidly obese man sitting in an elaborate chair beckoning them in. He was of Asian descent and wore a silk-like robe of some sort, colored with various shades of deep red. The room itself was larger than David expected, easily a couple thousand square feet. To his left was a massive desk that spanned nearly the whole length of the room and behind that in the wall was an equally massive fish thank. On the ground lay a rug of fur, but of which animal David could not tell. Once all of his men were inside with him, the double doors shut behind them and the music nearly disappeared. The room had substantial soundproofing but you could still see out the floor-to-ceiling glass window that overlooked the club. Having sized the place up, David turned his attention to the man.

"Hello, Mr. Harper! Thank you for joining me this evening." There was a slight Asian accent there, but his English was otherwise very good.

"You've got about 15 minutes of my time." David's reply was cold as ice. He could feel his men on edge behind him.

"Wonderful! So plenty of time for introductory drink, no?" He snapped his fingers and the doors opened, sounds from below flooding back in. David looked out the glass to his right as a flash of one of the dancefloor's lasers caught his eye. They died against the thick glass, but the contraptions kept on spinning and projecting colors onto the dancing people below.

There were footfalls behind them now, those of a woman in heels. He turned to look and saw a cocktail waitress with a platter of neon yellow shots. She was taller than most Asian women and dressed in little other than a short skirt and a matching bra. Her hair was black and cut at her shoulders, but she kept her face down. David guessed it was a cultural thing or some type of power rule that this man had over her. Quietly she handed each of David's men one of the drinks, then David received his.

He wasn't quite sure what it was, but there was something familiar about her. Her movements. Some mannerisms. Her size and proportions. *Something* familiar, but he hadn't a clue as to what. As she turned from him to give the man in the throne chair a shot, he noticed the light reflecting off her shoulder. It was a bit too shiny to be skin and it looked off. Deep in his gut, small alarms were going off, but he knew that causing a scene wouldn't help matters. *Especially if this man actually knows everything.*

The fat man took his shot from his platter, gave a small courtesy nod to the waitress – she returned the same – and spoke to David and his men.

"To new partnerships! And changing the world!" Without hesitation, he threw back the shot into his gullet and slammed the glass down on the thick arm of his chair, wiping away some moisture from his lips with the back of his hand.

David hesitated, as did his men. They were not idiots.

"Go ahead dear! I purchase one for you too!" With a hefty swing, he smacked her rear. She took the final shot off the platter and enjoyed it, tossing it back with ease. The empty glass went back on her tray and she reached to grab the fat man's as well. No one else in the room had taken theirs yet.

"Mr. Harper, I assure you, I have no reason to poison you or your men, if that's what you're thinking. This shot is a customary greeting of parties at Línghún. It is quite delicious, I promise you."

Staring the man straight in the eyes, David warily gulped down his shot and placed the glass on the tray as the waitress walked by. His guards quickly took theirs and returned to a ready position. Something felt the slightest bit off, but David couldn't pinpoint it. Nor could he leave; this man knew too much.

"Who are you?" He asked sternly, losing patience with the pageantry.

"Ah yes. So sorry! Very rude of me." The large man chuckled. "I am Mr. Crimson." He smiled at David.

"And what do you do? Why am I here?" There was irritation in his voice.

"I do many things, Mr. Harper. Mostly things that make me money." He held up his hands saying, "look around" with them. "You are here because I believe we can make some great money together." There was a devilish smile on his face. "But first I must properly motivate you to come out of your retirement."

As David glowered at the man, the sweet taste of the shot still on his tongue, he wondered what courses of action he could take.

What would killing the man do? Likely make him another enemy, sure, but he didn't have the time or comfort for someone who knew as much as this Mr. Crimson. He'd brought plenty of backup along with him. Maybe he'd lose a couple men, but getting out of here safe didn't seem like it would be too challenging. *Getting out of here quietly on the other hand...*

What if he just walked away and said no? There was something off about this room, this man…the deal. David felt eyes on him and was unsure of how much manpower Crimson had. Not to mention if David called his bluff the whole world would know what was going on with the infertility epidemic.

Or there was the path of smarter resistance: David could agree with Crimson today, go along with his plan, and kill him at some point down the road. Perhaps *that* would be the best way to go and it would allow him time to gather more intel.

THUMP!

Behind David it sounded like a sack of potatoes had been carelessly dropped. He turned to look and found one of his men, utterly crumpled on the floor. Lifeless. Another guard reached for his companion, stumbling. His legs wobbled like a newborn giraffe's and his face held shock and confusion. His head hit the ground and he was out.

David watched as his men, one by one, fell to the floor as if they'd had one too many drinks in a frat house. A few had realized what was happening and tried wielding their guns, but their vision and lack of balance hadn't allowed them to get much further than removing them from their jacket pockets and dropping them to the ground.

Strangely, David wasn't afraid. In fact, he was almost relieved. He'd figured something had to be in the shots as it was an odd request to start off with. His worry about what had been "off" with the vibe of the room was dissipating.

Now it was just these two men and they could talk. David returned his gaze to the fat man.

"What'd you do to them?" He casually shook his head in the direction of the decommissioned colleagues behind him.

"Well I'm a man of my word, Harper! I did *not* poison them." He chuckled, deep from his belly. "But I didn't say anything about not *drugging* them!"

"Cute. Now that it's just us two, how about you cut the bullshit and tell me why I'm here."

"*Tsk, tsk, tsk.* So pushy, David." The smile disappeared and the man became almost instantaneously angry. "You should show some fucking respect when you're in another man's house." Spittle formed on the rim of his lips.

"With all due *respect*, Crimson, my patience is running low, you're the one blackmailing *me*, and you just drugged my men. I've had enough of your hospitality and now I'm starting to get pissed off."

In his throne chair the fat man blinked several times, recognizing his outburst, and let out another deep chuckle.

"Fair enough! Fair enough!" He leaned back in his chair, seeming to get comfortable. "I should reveal to you that I am not the reason you are here." Hectic sound from the pulsating club below came into the room behind David. The doors had opened and closed, taking the sound back with them. "They are."

There wasn't shock on David's face when he turned to see Rachel, Dahl, and the man he believed to be Dynadin. Rachel was standing in the same outfit as the cocktail waitress and in the process of removing a synthetic mask that had featured Asian characteristics.

The dots connected now. It was all very simple and, if anything, David was frustrated with himself that he hadn't recognized this evening's "twist" right away. A few months of retirement had apparently made him rusty.

Though…there was a subconscious part of him, one that was very proud to admit it, that had known it had been Dahl's team all along. He'd never *truly* forgotten about them. In fact, this strike was coming sooner than he'd anticipated. The day of reckoning was finally here. It was *that* part of David that *wanted* this lame attempt at a trap to be Dahl all along.

I'm going to enjoy this.

Each of the three behind him came farther into the room. David turned back around to see Crimson leaving through a side door; he'd been just a ploy. Anger and rage filled the room with negative emotion. One could feel it dripping from the ceiling and echoing from each of their steps. Especially Dahl's. Not a single one of David's drugged men were able to make the slightest attempt to help the one they were supposed to be protecting. He'd have to weather this storm on his own.

"Returned for another ass whooping?" David directed the question mainly towards Dahl.

"We've come to kill you, David." Rachel stated instead.

"Have you now?" He mocked them. "And how has that quest been going for you?"

"It doesn't matter what's happened before. This time is different." She started to explain. "You unleashed the Wolfpaw Initiative. Your mark on the world is permanent for all of history. Congratulations." The sentiment dripped with disgust and David remained silent. "We're not here to 'take you in' or attempt to extract any intel from you. We know there's nothing else we can do for the world."

David was curious as to why Dahl wasn't the one speaking. Quickly he looked to him and saw a calm rage. It was terrifying. Rachel spoke once more.

"But there is something we can do for ourselves. For Elena. For Bryson. For Zane. For Henry. For Ian."

"For Leah." Dahl growled. David had forgotten about Dahl's wife and the rage was understandable now. They were here to end his life or die trying.

"So what the fuck are you waiting for? You have me right here. There's three of you. End it."

"Oh…" Dahl started. "It won't be that easy." A certain chill filled the room as Dynadin and Rachel took steps back. They'd agreed that David's death was for Dahl to carry out.

Seeing what was happening in the room, David liked his chances a little more. He squared up with Dahl who still had that insane look of rage that proved he was right on the edge. The only question that remained was: what kind of shape was Dahl in? David was more than confident in his abilities and had been spending considerable time honing in his physical skills within the last few months. It had helped to pass a lot of time.

Dahl swung at David and the punch missed. It was a heavy punch, slow in the air and with a big windup. David leaned outside of its range easily and followed up with a backhanded chop to Dahl's neck. The hit connected, but he seemed unphased by it and the muscle tone in his body was surprising. He'd kept in shape.

With a slight juke of his body, Dahl faked a punch from his left but instead scooped down and kicked David in his knee, forcing him to buckle. In a move that would have made Dynadin proud, Dahl jumped, circled his legs around David's neck and torso and rolled him to the floor. The back of David's head was in between Dahl's legs and he began to beat the ever-living shit out of the skull.

After five fists had landed, David twisted, gained leverage with his feet and brought his head down right on Dahl's groin. Rachel winced as she watched Dahl writhe from the hit. This was going to end up being an ugly blood bath.

David staggered to get up, his eyes swimming from the blows to the back of his head. There was an attempt to hit Dahl, still keeled-over, but he'd been bluffing and instead stepped out of the way, throwing David into a group of drink cabinets along the side wall.

The metal dented as David's head and shoulders slammed into it with a thunderous smack. Glasses cracked together, shattering, and the man was slow to get up.

"Arghhhhh!" Given their purpose and intent toward each other, it might as well have been a gladiator match for the ages. Dahl simply stood, with anger and a need for justice fueling him, and waited for the man he hated so much to come for more.

David could feel something underneath him, just below his ribs. It wasn't pain like his shoulders were experiencing right now; it was more of a discomfort. As he attempted to stand, he looked underneath him. There was a gun, one dropped from his drugged men, pressing into his stomach. Inconspicuously, David reached down and grabbed the weapon and rolled to his side facing Dahl.

Dahl could see something black in David's hands and dodged in a random direction. The gunshot sounded like a clap in the room as it missed Dahl and crashed into the glass behind him. A spider-web of cracks began to form and travel across the length of the window.

Another clap from the weapon shattered the window, sending glass bits raining into the room and onto the dance floor below. The sound of music filled the new volume of space available to it and the lights and lasers from the floating booth danced in and out of the windowless room.

The second shot had not missed its mark though. At least not completely. Dahl was hit and the bullet had deeply grazed his abdomen. Rachel watched in horror as David readied to fire again. She couldn't hear it over the music, but she could see the gun jam and the confusion on David's face, right as a green laser danced around him and moved on.

Clutching his side with a small amount of blood seeping through between his fingers, Dahl ran to David and kicked him in the mouth. The gun dropped to the floor and Dahl kicked that too.

David countered, mouth bloodied and bruising, with a swift kick to the back of Dahl's legs, sending him right to the ground with him. It was clear to both of them now that the other had retained at least some of their training and almost all of their strength. Winning this brawl would not come easy.

Blood spat from his lips in a thick wad, sticking to the carpet. He could feel it between his teeth as he slammed his elbow into Dahl's stomach, aggravating the bullet wound. There was no yelp and it was almost as if Dahl didn't feel it. A wild look was behind his eyes; he was enhanced.

"I see you took something…" David punched him in the stomach again. "Old friend." Dahl rolled his back and kicked David in the mouth again, blood spraying onto his forehead.

"Adrenaline." The kick had sent David staggering and his mouth looked abysmal now. Several teeth were loose.

"I'm flattered." His reply dripped with sarcasm and it would be the last words spoken during the fight. With vigor, they both took steps toward one another. Fists, forearms, and elbows flew, feet light on the floor.

Rachel and Dynadin watched in awe as the two men fought and moved like they'd never seen them do before. The brutal fight that had been playing out was gone, and instead replaced with a skilled ballet of strikes and blocks. The speed at which they were moving, back and forth, rivaled even that of Dynadin.

Finally, David missed a block and Dahl's elbow connected with the side of his head as he twisted around. Rachel had lost count of the blows to David's cranium and it was likely that he had a concussion by now. Crimson blood ran in thin streams, matting his hair and covering his face.

Even David must have known it as he backed away from Dahl, a hint of fear beneath the blood. He stayed away, and did not charge in. On the opposite end of the room, Dahl was amped; the electricity coming from him was violent – passionate – and he was *ready*. Blood seeped through his shirt where the bullet had hit, but there was no visible acknowledgement of the pain.

With powerful steps he walked toward David who tensed. On his way across the room, Dahl grabbed a metal and plastic chair, and got a full, twisting swing before tossing it straight at David's frame.

Bass thumped loudly from the speakers below and two lasers, green and blue, danced in the room before moving on. The electronic chorus took over as a driving extension of Dahl's fire. Its catchy, powerful beat became a symphony for the fight.

The chair had collided with David, forcing him to take a few steps back, distracted. He returned by lashing out with a few unconcentrated fists, one of which brushed Dahl while the others missed. Dahl clutched David's neck, fingers pressing into the skin, and then followed with his other hand.

The fight was coming to an end.

It wasn't being lifted in the air that killed David. Dahl had brought him off the ground by his neck while David's eyes bulged. His mind screamed to aim a kick or a punch, but the life was seeping out of him.

It wasn't being thrown onto the glass table that killed David. Dahl had used the entirety of his core to turn and throw him onto the blue glass table behind them. It shattered under the force and David felt glass enter his back, some shards deeper than others. He remembered another green laser peeping into the room and playing all sorts of tricks reflecting off the glass shards and onto the ceiling like a mini Milky Way.

It wasn't being pummeled with a barrage of fists that killed David. Dahl began to lay into him as he lay in the glass catastrophe. Fists to his stomach, his ribs, his face; they sent him to a dark place. David, a fighter, realized that this was it. He could either give up now and die or dig down deep and try to find some way out of it.

His own form of adrenaline kicked in, one based in survival instinct and pride. He landed a punch into Dahl's rib cage and followed with one to the opposite side. You could have heard the crack if it weren't for the loud music. His hand quickly searched Dahl's lower abdomen, finding the slick opening on his side.

A jammed thumb in his bullet wound was the first thing that Dahl actually felt during the fight and it was intensely awful. Pinpoint, sharp pain jutted from his side, rippling to his shoulders and down his legs.

David searched the ground with his other hand, scraping and tearing it against the pools of glass. Soon he found a large shard, gripped it (causing his own hand to bleed), and jammed it into Dahl's back. Now doubled up in pain over David, Dahl felt another shard enter his side.

Again, into his shoulder.

One more, between two ribs.

Without adrenaline, Dahl would have passed out by now. Rachel gasped as she watched what was happening. Dynadin and she had strict instructions not to interfere until one of them was dead. *Like hell* had been her mental response to the command and she was about to interfere. Fuck Dahl's pride. He'd live.

It wasn't the glass blade that Dahl pulled out of his side and plunged into David's collarbone that killed David. A twitch at the last second had forced the shard to miss his throat by inches but the pain was still considerable. The wound went hot with blood escaping the opening; David took his remaining strength and pushed Dahl off him.

Both men stood up, slowly, miserably. The duel could very well take both of their lives, but neither would give up. David saw the open window behind Dahl and knew that one more effort, one last struggle, would end this.

Again, the chorus of the song below chimed in. Both men could feel the vibration of the bass in their bones and in their wounds. Their minds and hearts pulsed with a different beat: one of hatred. They were silent, but their stares and the grievances they'd just inflicted upon each other spoke volumes.

One last time, they collided, arms grabbed and at a stalemate. They turned and navigated across the room, David using every bit of energy he had to guide them to the window. Grunts and growls were heard, shoes scraping glass along the hard floor. Rachel saw what was happening.

She intervened.

No.

What killed David was the fall, specifically the bounce his head took on the suspended booth that broke his neck.

Both men had been struggling and moving toward the remnants of the window high above the dancing people below.

Rachel charged David.

Dynadin reached after her, but was too slow.

With surprising force, she pushed David toward the window.

He let go of Dahl.

And grabbed onto her.

No.

What killed David was the fall.

And Dahl was certain it had killed Rachel too.

CHAPTER XXII

THE WORLD SPINS ON

3 YEARS LATER...

It had been three years since David's death. The world never knew who he was.

Since then, humanity had learned to live with the card that he, acting as a god, had dealt them. No cure had been developed despite the best efforts of scientists from a collective of countries. The 10.37% predicted effective rate of the airborne contagion had been based in faulty calculations. Rather, the calculations were correct had the disease behaved as designed.

Instead, it morphed, and rendered 28.54% of the population sterile. Roughly around 2 billion people were affected.

Dynadin's back-of-the-envelope calculations had been correct; the full effect rate of the condition had been felt by 2020. During the rest of 2019, governments all around the world provided testing for free in order to gain an idea of how drastic the situation was. By mid-year, word was out: the pandemic would forever alter the landscape of the human race. *Why* certain people were targeted was never revealed – it would have been too detrimental to those affected. The high rate of infection forced governments and companies all across the planet to begin planning for a decreased population. It was a small blessing that they'd have years, even decades, to adjust but there was still growing concern over how the world would cope with less people overall. It would take several years for the population to actually start decreasing, and scientists predicted that it would eventually stabilize and increase again, but it would still be a challenge. Buildings would cease to remain full with either workers or tenants. Companies would struggle to fill all positions and need to adjust their revenue expectations. Local and federal governments would have to proportionally adjust the services they provided and how much money they'd pool into such things.

Some saw the pandemic as a blessing in disguise. They argued that it could have been worse and many believed that, while unfortunate, it solved several population-related problems without immediate death. Surprisingly, this was a coping mechanism shared by both those affected and persons who hadn't been.

Others saw it, along with all the events that had preceded it, as a sign of the apocalypse. They were convinced that the human race was being "phased out" by Mother Nature.

Most people carried on. They lived their lives as they had before, recognizing that there was nothing they could do against the tide. Many were saddened by news of loved ones or even themselves being declared sterile, but most found ways to compensate. Adoption rates around the world skyrocketed. Extended families could focus on the children they *currently* had and provide support. College sponsorship programs were established for couples who couldn't have their own child, but wanted to ensure the education of the next generation.

Emerging from the ugliness of the Wolfpaw Initiative came the beauty of the human heart and the spirit of the race itself.

The night of David's death, they'd left before the police had arrived and Mr. Crimson covered for them stating that David had been belligerent during their meeting and required security to intervene. Things had gone south and he'd fallen to his death. A few local authorities had required small bribes, but the whole night had soon blown over.

For some.

Rachel woke a day later, stabilized and strapped to a solid wood gurney, with no feeling in her legs. She was on a flight back to the U.S. and broke down in tears. Dynadin comforted her; none of them knew the extent of the damage to her spine yet.

Dahl was broken too and Dynadin had spent most of the night tending to his various wounds as they waited for Mr. Crimson to arrange them a private trip home. After the adrenaline had worn off, Dahl had quickly passed out, overcome by the pain inflicted by his encounter. He'd survive though. Time would heal all wounds, leaving him a collection of new scars.

Things happened quickly at N.E.T.S. News of David abandoning his post quickly spread, as did the news of his death. Dahl worked with Karen to release the slew of documents and files they had to all agents both domestic and international. The men who had declared their loyalty to David and fallen prey to Crimson's tainted shots all scattered to the wind. No one heard from them again. Within a matter of a few weeks, everyone at N.E.T.S. was fully debriefed, many ashamed for not believing it before. A tenth of their agency resigned or retired, all un-challenged by Dahl who was taking over as the "interim" head.

Rachel didn't remain in a wheel chair for long. The damage to her spine was miraculously repairable and between her fighting personality and some physical therapy she had what the doctor told her was "the fastest recovery I've ever seen from this type of injury".

In addition to her recovery efforts, she buried herself into repairing N.E.T.S. and its image. Several days after David's death, a letter had come to Rachel from beyond the grave . She almost hadn't opened it, but curiosity overcame rage and what she found had been surprising.

Hello Rachel,

I've decided to leave my old life behind and officially "retire". Please do not come searching for me as I fear it will not end well for you.

This letter is designed to be a very small token of penance. I know what I have done to the world. I know what it means. And I'd do it again if I had to.

Unfortunately, the fact of the matter is that I created an evil entity in my quest for the Wolf-paw Initiative: the Aqarab Mayta. It is ill-fated that I had to take this path, but it was the only way in which I could gather enough resources. Still, that is no excuse and I must take care of the consequences of my actions.

Within the enclosed drive you'll find intelligence on every single member within the Dead

Scorpions that has any sort of power. Do with it what you will, but I'd encourage you to disman-tle the organization. There's already enough evil in the world and America could use a win.

I guess I'd always imagined you ending up back at N.E.T.S. once this is all said and done, though I'm not sure how. If this info finds you still with Dahl, I wish you both the best of luck.

I know that you loathe me and you have every right to, but I hope that you'll be wise and put this knowledge to good use. It could accom-plish a lot to make the world a better place and I never meant to destroy America in the process.

Rebuild her again.

-David

Tucked away and taped to the inside of the envelope was a thumb drive that contained hundreds of documents, all of the nature that David had promised. Rachel wasn't above accepting help from David, but the situation frustrated her.

"It doesn't make him any less of a despicable creature." Dahl had explained once she'd shown him. "He still did what he did and an afterthought letter doesn't even get close to making up for that." Clearly he was frustrated too with the thought of David's image being anything less than appalling in his mind. "We'd be foolish *not* to use it."

Once Dahl had accepted his role as interim commander of the organization, he shared the intelligence with each agent who had high enough clearance. By the end of 2019, the Dead Scorpions had been completely eradicated; and N.E.T.S. anonymously shared the news, and credit, with the U.S. government.

It had been a small win for a country and a world begging for hope. For many it restored their faith in their governments and, coupled with the lack of any terrorist activity since The Will, provided a path to healing. The globe would eventually have less people in it, but there was now hope for a generally peaceful existence.

In secret, Dahl had been preparing his exit from N.E.T.S. and grooming a replacement. In July 2020, Rachel Monroe became the official head of N.E.T.S., only the second in its history, not including Dahl's brief stint. At first she had been reluctant, but Dahl had convinced and assured her that she was exactly what a highly covert government agency needed:

Someone with brains.

Someone with guts.

Someone with compassion.

Someone with understanding.

And someone with goodness in her heart.

Dynadin became the agency's top field operative (after some much needed vacation) and acted as an advisor to Rachel. From day one, she had his full support.

After all the chaos that had befallen the world, even after all the changes they were still yet to face, Rachel remained hopeful for mankind; a race whose existence still had pages to be written. Tough times had come and history had been rewritten unexpectedly. As it always did though, life would go on and the globe would keep spinning.

For a time she'd been furious with David. The real understanding of what the Wolfpaw Initiative meant was devastating to her, particularly as a young woman. The possibility of not being able to experience falling in love and *creating* a child with someone was both heartbreaking and angering. Couples all around the world would now have an additional decision to make depending on each parties' affected status.

Her work was what helped her cope.

She dedicated herself to not letting the positon of power corrupt her; to not becoming the monster that David had become. The world could be virtuous again and so could America. So could N.E.T.S. It could be more than an assassination machine. More than just an executioner. It could help the world with its resources while still remaining secretive and, slowly but surely, could try to rewrite some of the sins from its history.

Rachel approached every day of her deeply important responsibility with a mantra:

I will make Bryson and Elena proud. I will make Henry and Ian proud. I will continue to make Dynadin and Dahl proud. I am a good person and I will do great things.

I am a good person and I will do great things.

GRATITUDE

If you had asked me when I started writing the original *Agents & Angels* that I'd be finishing up a sequel in a fairly timely manner, I would have thought you were crazy. With the original coming out in late 2014, there was a part of me that wondered if it would be nearly half a decade or more before I'd get around to and have the proper ideation to construct a worthwhile follow-up.

What you've just finished reading is a work that I'm very proud of and have put a lot of thought and effort into making a better, world-building, yet story-concluding sequel. And there are a lot of people to thank for not only inspiring me, but assisting in improving the novel itself.

My beta readers – Pat, Jared, Gary, and Ryan – are the true heroes here and I appreciate their candor, attention to detail, and encouragement. You'd be surprised how hard it is to find a good beta reader these days so to those of you that made the time, I truly appreciate it. Remnants from each of yours feedback can be found in spades throughout this work.

I'd like to make a special call out to Pat who provided me with such detailed and thorough reactions that I feel like she gets a separate round of metaphorical applause. The book you just got done reading is in MUCH better shape because of her willingness to assist me.

Gary, I'd also like to give you a special shout-out too. It's your verbal encouragement and motivation that has really helped me to persist throughout this endeavor when I may think, "Oh, that idea is stupid" or "Is that *too*

dark?" You give me honest, but supportive feedback, and
even though we've never actually met in person, I appreciate the advice you've given me.

To my editor, Lexi. This has been our second adven-
ture together and not only have you provided me much
needed criticisms and grammatical suggestions, but hearing that you (and your husband) have thoroughly enjoyed
each of the *Agents & Angels* books has been the final
"push" of encouragement I've needed in the publishing
realm.

Molly, you're a true gem. You may not have known
me for the entire process of writing this book, but from
the very beginning you have been interested in it and
proud of me for taking on something like this. You've
been a supportive girlfriend by buying and reading the
first one, just so you could catch up on what I was working on, and then beta reading *Wolfpaw* and offering your
advice/critiques. Similarly, this came in handy in some of
the sections I was more worried about and knowing
you've got my back is a great feeling to have. Love you!

One of my last "serious" wishings of gratitude goes
again to my 6th grade writing teacher, Mrs. Littleford.
She'll likely never read one of my books (one can
dream!) but it was her tenacity with writing that caused
me to fall head over heels for the rush of it and the process of telling a story. She was a tough teacher, but taught
me that it was okay to be good at writing, and even better
to actually *like* it. Years ago when I first contemplated
writing a book – a feat that seemed very difficult – it was
her in my head who I imagined asking, "Well who on

earth is going to stop you?" The answer, as it turns out, is only me.

I'd also like to extend a thank you to the movies, TV shows, videogames, and other books that have inspired me throughout the years. I won't list them all out, but suffice it to say that this work was inspired by a conglomerate of my favorite works and represents something that I *hope* makes you think and have fun.

Lastly, YOU. Writing novels is a hobby of mine. A demanding one, sure, but a highly rewarding one. I'm glad I can share my works with others and by supporting my endeavor, you've shown me that you care. Whether you purchased just this sequel, or both of the *Agents & Angels* stories, I'm honored that you are trusting me to take you on a journey. I hope it was unforgettable. Thank you!

As to whether I ever publish another book, my answer would be: I sure as hell hope so! I could say that as life goes on it gets harder and harder, but that's just an excuse. Too many people make those in lieu of chasing their passions. I will say that I've had some ideas brewing – far different from *Agents & Angels* – that I'd love to share with an audience someday. I just don't know when that day will be at the moment!

Thanks again to all!

ABOUT THE AUTHOR

Agents & Angels II: The Wolfpaw Initiative is the second book from author J. T. Rath and the direct sequel to *Agents & Angels*. Writing is one of Rath's favorite hobbies and you can find more of his works on his website where he reviews movies and videogames: http://www.raths-reviews.com

Rath lives in downtown Denver where he enjoys experiencing the excitement of the city with friends, family, and his girlfriend.

While he plans to take a short break from writing full-length novels, J.T. Rath is always thinking of potential avenues and ideas for what his next book and/or series could be.

He loves reading fan mail, reader suggestions, and especially hearing from and assisting fellow indie writers. If you'd like to reach him, please mail: jordan.t.rath@gmail.com